I0563502

Of Platinum and Steel

Published by:

James Giglio

10 9 8 7 6 5 4 3 2 1

First Edition © 2026 by James Giglio

Softcover ISBN: 979-8-9942927-0-9

All rights reserved. No part of this publication may be reproduced, stored in a retrieval system, or transmitted in any form or by any means, electronic, mechanical, photocopying, recording, scanning, or otherwise, except as permitted under Sections 107 or 108 of the 1976 United States Copyright Act, without the prior written permission of the publisher. Requests to the publisher for permission should be addressed to kitikithakis@gmail.com.

"*Every chapter ends in whispers,*

because every legend begins in rumor."

Dedicated to

My father, my hero, my strength.

And…

Most of all, my beautiful wife,

the one who helped me grow, who made me carry on, and

who, most of all, saved my life.

♜ Author's Note ♜

These are not idle tales.

Every word, every silence, every breath carries purpose.

What you see upon the page is only the surface—life stirs beneath it.

What is said, what is left unsaid, what seems chance or fate…

As in life…everything matters.

Every word.

Read slowly, my friends. Watch closely.

The truth hides between the lines.

…puuuurrrr

♖ *Contents* ♖

PROLOGUE:
A Dispensation of Gods

Skippin stood at the edge of the marble path, his gaze fixed on the distant veil. His voice was low, almost breaking as he struggled with himself. *'She wants a child. More than she wants the sun to rise…and yet I can't set foot in that realm to gift her one.'* He felt helpless. She had captured his attention purely by accident: a sad smile, a heart too pained, far too young for her sagging shoulders. He knew. Yet his heart hurt for her.

Hearthmae came to his side, her warmth a quiet comfort, almost motherly.

'There are places even we can't go, Skippin, gray places, rules. It's the rules that keep the balance.'

He shook his head, eyes bright with frustration. But he knew. He knew it all too well.

Hearthmae looked toward the veil, her hand brushing his arm. She could almost feel the sadness in his heart.

'Everything happens for a reason.'

But those were not Hearthmae's words. Those were HER words. SHE spoke them—often. Sometimes, he was tired of hearing HER words. He wanted to be angry, but he knew she was right. His shoulders sagged almost in defeat.

He sighed. *'And, yet, that balance doesn't comfort an empty cradle.'*

'Truly…but sometimes, someone else can.'

It began to get colder. SHE was near.

From the shadows came a voice, calm and certain, like the gentle breeze through a forest.

'It is done.'

Lady Destiny stood apart, her unconcerned gaze locked into the shimmering veil of the mortal world, watching events unfold far below.

Behind her, like the faint clink of coins, a lazy, rhythmic chime. Velkhar, the Greedy One, stepped into view, rolling a single gold token over his knuckles, each flip catching the light.

'*An interesting choice, Lady,*' he said, voice smooth as oiled silk. His eyes glinted with equal parts amusement and hunger. '*What will happen next, I wonder?*'

Lady Destiny turned only slightly, offering him a sidelong glance and the barest curve of a knowing smile.

'*Yes, I wonder,*' she said.

There hung a short, silent pause. She already knew his mind. It was HER way.

'*Shall we reeve?*' She grinned inwardly.

The coin stilled between Velkhar's fingers. His grin widened, slow and certain.

'*But of course.*'

'*...shall I deal?*'

The Threads We Weave

She could not return home with an empty basket. She just couldn't. The wheat, barley and potatoes had died from the unusually long drought, and there was nothing to use for trade. The ground had cracked from no rain, and dust swirled in fields of dead grain. The family cow began to wither from lack of hay and water, and rather than let it fall to illness, they butchered it. At least there would be meat to stew with what was left of the withered vegetables. To make matters worse, the children had no milk, and there was little flour left from the stockpile to even make bread.

The other townsfolk weren't in much better shape, and all the pleas from the lords and elders to the king had gone unheard.

Her brow furrowed, deep in thought. *I'm the oldest child. I should know how to help*, she scolded herself. *Mum and Da are afraid. They work and try so hard for us. They think I can't see it, but I do. I hear Mother cry. I hear Da trying to calm her. But what else can I do?* She forced back tears.

But she had little coin to spend and even less sunlight to do her buying. She wandered aimlessly in thought, trying to figure out a better way to help them.

"OI! Watch out. Ya almost run me wife over, ya blind halfwit," a large man said, glaring at her, his wife scowling as they passed.

"I'm so sorry, Mum—truly," she said, disoriented and quickly walked off.

Once away, she stopped for a second to gather her thoughts and come up with a plan. She stared off into the sky, begging the gods for help, wanting to cry at her helplessness.

"Talith, dear."

The sound of her name startled her and caused her to look in the direction of the caller.

It was old Madam Garven who owned the farm down the road from hers. She was one of the elders in the hamlet, but she was as sweet as honeysuckle, and she loved Talith as her own. She showed a wide grin and said as she arrived, "Good ta see ya, lass. Right blistering midday ain't it?"

Talith wasn't really in the mood to speak, but she had to be courteous at least and make the time of day.

"Why, hello, madam," she said with a forced grin, feigning interest. "And aye, it is hot today. But it'll turn cool soon. Master Tashlin always says that with a hot summer comes a cold winter."

"Yes, indeed, an' he ain't hardly never wrong, now, is he?" She looked Talith up and down. "An' whatcha be doin' in town alone like this, lass?"

"Mother sent me to get dried meats and such for the table tonight." Her smile waned.

The woman's gnarled finger touched the bottom of Talith's chin. "And perhaps maybe a lad, eh?" she said with a wink. "Sad thing, a good lass like you with no man."

If it was one thing people loved about her, it was the fact she spoke her mind and was as honest as the midday sun. But this time her words cut deep. She didn't mean to, but it hurt her, nonetheless. Folks in small towns always seem to know the goings on, and for years, people had been asking her the same questions. Why don't you have a husband yet? Is there a young man in your future? Talith grew increasingly sad as she thought about it.

She wasn't a beauty to turn heads, nor was she ugly, merely plain in a world that prized sparkle. Talith did not care what people said; she only wished that one good man would see her for who she was. There had been callers, but none truly looked at her. Her parents tried to help her get a man out of desperation, it seemed, even spending their hard-earned coin to get her to town to help find one, but nothing worked. It was almost as if they wanted to sell her off, but she knew better. They may not have very much, but they always had an abundance of love. And she so desperately wanted kids of her own. She was so used to caring for her sisters that she did not know if she could do without some of her own. It broke her heart whenever anyone asked about it. They didn't mean any malice; they just wanted her to be happy.

"We'll see, madam. Perhaps this year." She gave a sad, halfhearted smile, but, deep inside, she doubted it. She did everything she could to keep from showing her desperation. Was it desperation or just a means to get people to stop asking about it? She concluded that it no longer really mattered. If the gods willed it, it would be.

"Well, don't you be afeared, lass. The gods'll bless ya when they're ready." She patted Talith on her arm with her worn, frail hand, gave another smile and winked as she walked off.

Hoping to cheer herself up, Talith turned and walked toward an apple stand a short distance away. It was a true sight. There were rarely any apples from the king's orchard available, and those who could afford them usually bought them in bushels.

Like a tormenting ghost, the words returned, *Well, don't you be afeared, lass. The gods'll bless ya when they're ready.* The words struck home, and she began to sob, quietly but freely. They wouldn't stop. *When will it be my turn? Am I that ugly?* She pulled the kerchief from her sleeve and covered her eyes so no one else could see the tears.

Just then, she felt a gentle hand on her shoulder. She looked up to see it was an older woman, dressed commonly, with a gray cowl wrapped about her to keep the sun off. Talith noticed that she had a remarkably kind face and oddly dark eyes. But her smile, sad but hopeful, somehow filled Talith with a peaceful, calm feeling.

The woman didn't say a word, but for no apparent reason, she stretched out her arms and enveloped Talith in a soft, reassuring hug that only a mother could give. Talith looked around, feeling awkward, but the woman held her for a moment longer and when she pulled away, smiled and nodded as if she knew something. Talith felt an inner warmth, as if everything were going to be fine. Almost an inner peace, then the lady walked away.

Talith stood there for a second trying to understand what had just happened, but when she turned to see the lady to ask her why, she was already gone. It was odd, to be sure. She felt a strange cool breeze brushing her face and, looking toward the midday sun, decided to leave for home, as she had a long walk ahead of her.

She turned and started down the main road toward home, picking up her pace to ensure she'd be there before dusk. Once again, the feeling that things would be all right struck her like a wave of joy. It was odd and yet reassuring, but strange and unshakable.

She felt the urge to look back toward town and saw the lady who hugged her. She had a broad grin and was waving happily. Talith waved back and grinned as well, thinking, *What a lovely lady…truly.*

She continued her journey home. It was still a fair distance to walk, but she started to feel the effects of her emotional afternoon. Her legs began to feel heavier, yet she forced herself to continue, occasionally glancing into the forest and allowing her mind to wander. One never knew what could leap out near this place. Perhaps she would see one of those Valyn like her mum talked about. Maybe then she'd find out if the tales were true or, if in fact, they were just stories to bring wonder to her eyes. She chuckled to herself but hoped for the latter. She recalled what the townsfolk used to say about them, how the Valyn would come out and torment those who were out after nightfall. *Woodfolk.* She shook her head. Most believed them to be a fairytale anyway; something mothers tell their children to make them behave. Mum used to say the stories weren't true and that the Valyn were children of Hearthmae, the motherly Goddess of the Harvest and Fertility. She said they had always been there, tending the forest and were a blessing to all farmers. Talith believed Mum, naturally. Why would such a loving goddess put something horrible or evil in the woods to harm folks?

At least they didn't live near Crimson Lake, she countered. She would have had to stay at the inn, then. Bad place after nightfall, that. The elders would make offerings every now and again to the mist or the spirit of the lake; she never really knew which. She was never quite sure why, but the elders always walked away more content when it happened. They would say, "It's better to place an appeasing offering than not to and suffer." No one knew for certain if there were bad spirits, monsters or just plain evil there, and no one wanted to ever find out.

As one tale went, at certain times of the year when the evening sun set and the dying light reflected from the glassy surface, the water would turn crimson as blood, and a mist would rise like ghostly adversaries. Both would wind down crevasses and up ravines toward each other, and, if they ever met, dreadful things would happen. Creatures of the woods would silence; dogs would bay, families would ensure their stock was indoors and then bar their homes tightly until sunup. Strange sounds and unexplainable footprints of all sorts appeared near homes and barns. But worst of all, folks would go missing. Master Atwater, the butcher, lost his son one night. Poor lad fell asleep at the lake fishing and was never seen or heard from again. All they found in the morning was a broken fishing rod and spatters of blood.

She didn't know if the tale was true, but she knew one thing: She never wanted to find out. She shivered at the thought.

She looked up from her daydream…and walked directly into the back end of a stationary horse. Startled and shocked, she lost her footing and fell hard to the dirt road.

The young rider turned to see why his horse startled just in time to see her land hard on her bottom. "Oh my, lady, are you hurt?"

He slid from the horse and went to Talith's side, reaching down to gently help her to her feet.

"Are you quite alright?"

She felt both silly and embarrassed. Still looking down, she tried to brush herself off the best she could.

"Please, lady, say something," he begged.

She raised her head and looked into his...sky-blue eyes. She wanted to be angry, but all she did was gasp, her breath catching in her throat. No words came. Her head began to swim with the sight she beheld. In her eyes, this man was the most striking she'd ever seen. She tried to look away, but just couldn't, enthralled. He was not overly handsome, but he was tall and well-muscled, which added to her delight. His short, brown hair was tussled, but it suited him well. His leather trousers, blue wool shirt and leather vest were of fine make. His kind face had the beginnings of a beard, though scraggly, and he looked to be about her own youthful age.

He looked into her eyes deeply, worried she'd been knocked witless. "M'lady? Please. I beg of you, say anything," he said again.

"I'm...I'm alright." She finally broke her gaze. "I'm sorry, lord. I wasn't myself. I was...deep in thought." She looked down, embarrassed.

"Lady, if you please, I'm no lord," he said, still carefully looking at her. "I'm the son of Lord Galgun's stablemaster, Trellin Soryn. I'm Coelric. Coelric Soryn and I live up in Tantyn Manor across from Hazelwood."

He let out a sigh of relief. "I'm so glad you aren't injured. I feared the worst." He nervously reached out his hand. "Are you alright to walk? I must be sure you are not further injured."

She took his hand and, feeling hot, began to swoon. *What is happening?*

"If you wish, we can sit until you feel up to walking," he said, motioning to a fallen tree. She nodded, and he led her to sit, unaware that he was still holding her hand. She would normally have pulled away, thinking it was another boy trying to be forward, but this time it just felt...right. She looked around, trying to think of something, anything to say. Her pause was broken by the gentle chirping of a faraway songbird, a gentle breeze kissing her cheek, a ray of moonlight catching her eye, and she looked back at him.

"May I have the honor of knowing your name?" he asked, concern still in his eyes.

She blushed and looked at her hands. "Talith. My father is Wesley the fielder." It rang as music to his ears. *Talith.*

"Why are you walking the road unaccompanied, if I might ask? It is extremely dangerous here of late, what with all the bandits and wild animals about."

He felt he should release her hand, but he enjoyed how soft her skin was and was still unsure of her steadiness.

He looked at them sheepishly, still holding hands, and finally got the courage to let go. When he did, she gave a slight look of disappointment. He felt the warmth of embarrassment across his face. A chill, gentle breeze cut through the warmth of the evening and tried to cool it, but failed.

"If I might be so bold, where might you be heading?" he asked.

She looked at him, and once more she was caught in his eyes. Those eyes—she was lost in them. It was as if sweet music filled her mind when she looked at them.

There was no reason for it, yet she felt…safe, the kind of safe that made her breath catch in her throat. Heat crept up her neck, and she forced herself to steady her voice. "I…I'm going just up the road, to Mapleton, actually." She wished the cool breeze would brush the warmth from her face.

"Well, lady, if you wish, I could accompany you as an escort for your safety."

"Please, sir, I don't wish to be a bother. I'm alright to continue alone, really."

The soft sounds of songbirds were carried on the breeze, which began to blow ever so slightly. He stood and held his hand out to her. "Please, lady, it is not a bother at all. It would be my honor to accompany you."

What are you doing, fool? She would never be interested in the stablemaster's son, especially the likes of you, he thought.

Coelric had never thought very highly of himself. He spent all of his waking hours either in animal stalls or tending to horse tack, and rarely left the manor grounds. His father had always said he was far better with animals than with people, then he would snort and say that he should stay with what he knew.

She blushed. "I…I would enjoy that. Very much," she said as she smiled sweetly.

Coelric's face lit up with pride and joy. His heart leaped. His head filled with the soft music of her voice.

He led her to the horse, which was waiting patiently. "If I may…" He placed his hands on her waist and lifted her to the saddle. He noticed how light she was, and she noticed just how strong he was. Both smiled with shy embarrassment. She centered herself sideways on the saddle, crossed her legs as a lady should and hoped she was doing it correctly.

He reached for the horse's reins and gently pulled the horse to a walk. "Easy, boy. We're escorting a lady today. Best behavior, yes?" he said as he rubbed the side of his head on the big stallion's cheek. He smiled and looked up at her beautiful face. *What do I say now? What do I ask?* he thought.

Coelric had never been in this situation before and was completely out of sorts. He felt as if he were walking on a cloud, and when he spoke, it was measured and careful, at first, but the longer they conversed, the more at ease they became. They casually walked and basked in their very presence with the music of the night singing in both of their hearts. The world seemed to melt away, and only they mattered, only that moment.

They walked for quite some time discussing their homes, their families and what they did. Talith tried not to show her embarrassment about her family being poor, but Coelric was so enamored that he never noticed. They laughed along the way and became comfortable in each other's company. Night fell, but neither noticed. The gentle, cool breeze touched their faces as they neared the outskirts of Mapleton, unknowingly. To them, it mattered not; their hearts were fluttering together with happiness and joy.

Soon, they reached her home, where she tried to hide her face in shame. It was little more than an over-glorified shack, but it was only her that he cared about.

He stepped forward, one hand on the reins, the other offered to her. *Could this be what real love feels like?* he thought. *If it is, then I pray the gods, it never ends.*

Talith took it, expecting the rough, callused grip of a stablemaster's son, but found it steady, warm. *Dear Hearthmae, please let this night be true and not just another dream*, she prayed. He guided her down with care, his hand lingering a moment longer than needed before letting go.

"Thank you," she said, brushing a stray hair from her cheek.

Coelric started to step back, then paused. His hand found hers again, just briefly, a gentle squeeze and the faintest ghost of a smile.

"Maybe I'll see you again?" The words were simple, but the tone…the tone was steady. Certain.

Talith tilted her head, a touch of surprise and a glint in her eyes. "Maybe you will," she said shyly.

They parted, but his words lingered longer than she expected. He briefly looked down and shuffled the dirt under his feet, almost disappointed that the night would end this way. He so wanted to stay, if nothing more than to just be close to her.

Noticing he was looking down, she took a chance and stepped toward him. She lightly gave him a kiss on his forehead, then looked away girlishly, heart beating madly, and scurried to her front door. She looked back at him for a moment with a smile, and he waved, also smiling.

After she closed the door, he took a deep breath and climbed up on the big horse. Just for a second, he sat and began reliving the evening.

What just happened? he asked himself joyfully. He patted his steed on the neck. "What an evening, boy. What an evening," he said softly, still enamored with the lady's beauty.

He nudged his mount forward, a wide grin of happiness on his face. *I can't believe it*, he thought, pushing his chest out like a proud conqueror. He glanced around quickly to make sure he was alone to avoid looking foolish, then he gave a short laugh and made for home.

Neither slept that night, eyes searching the stars, remembering, their hearts begging to return to that one moment, that one place, each grinning in the dark like children with sweets. *What is happening*…came silky words in the breeze that touched each one. Neither noticed. Neither cared.

'...a nice beginning'

The next day, Coelric went about his chores as always. He'd gotten up before the break of day to feed and water the horses and clean their stalls. But this morning he had a grin on his face and joy in his heart as he remembered the beautiful lady he'd met the evening before. He leaned heavily against his shovel, daydreaming. Her smile, the touch of her skin, the light in her eyes, the melodious song of her voice; it was as if she were still there near him. The world was much brighter today.

"Gods all-seeing, what are ya doin', boy?" His father was angry. As stablemaster, it was his job to make sure the stablehands, namely his son and two others, kept the stalls and horses clean and the riding equipment ready.

"You've not done a damn thing all morning. Where's your head, boy?" he demanded.

Coelric didn't realize that most of the morning had already passed, and he had done very few of the chores he was assigned. He looked at his father, ashamed. "I don't know, Da. I was thinking."

"Thinkin'? Oh, yer a scholar now, are ya? A thinkin' stableboy? Maybe a philosopher of horse shite or groomin' mage, yeah?" Angrily stepping in front of his son, he wanted to thrash him as a lesson to the other boys, but couldn't. He looked into the boy's eyes and could see they were telling a story, and he wanted to know what it was. Still angry, he asked, "Alright, boy. Spit it out. What's troubling ya?"

A grin came over Coelric's face, but he was still hesitant to speak about it. In a lower, almost menacing tone, he said, "I'll not ask again, son. What's troubling ya? And it better be good."

He looked directly into his father's eyes. "A young lady, Da." His father silently stared back.

"Get on with it." He was intrigued but maintained an outwardly angry demeanor. The boy had never really shown interest in girls his age, nor was he very comfortable around them, which took Trellin by surprise.

"I'm listenin'."

Coelric relaxed a bit, took a breath and said, "I met her on the road from town. She bumped into the horse and fell, so I jumped down to help her up. I thought she was hurt, so I made sure she was alright." He paused. Trellin's eyebrow raised. "Go on."

He looked down and shuffled his feet. "Well, when I helped her up, I looked in…into her eyes." He looked at his father's weather-worn face. "She was beautiful, Da," he said. "I couldn't stop looking at her." Trellin relaxed. He looked deeply into his son's eyes, the story now apparent. He put his elbow into his hand, tapped his lips with a raised finger and thought for a second. *Finally. Dammit, boy, finally.*

Looking past Coelric, Trellin barked his orders to another stableboy, "Oi, Jerin, ya got the groomin' duties today. Coelric's feeling poorly. Tell Haverd to help ya." He put his hand on Coelric's shoulder and motioned his head in the direction of the small room he used as an office.

"Sit."

They both sat, son facing father. Trellin just looked at him, trying to decide how to handle this. He folded his arms across his chest, took a breath and began. "Soooo, ya were ridin' back from town an' a lass bumped into the horse's bum and fell over…." He sat silently, waiting for his son to continue his story.

Coelric caught on and said, "Aye, Da. I couldn't stop lookin' at her."

"Well, go on with ya already. I don't have all day here."

He nodded. "I got her up and helped her to a log so she could get her wits about her. She fell hard." He looked upward as if he were reliving the moment. "When we sat, I touched her hand to ask if she were truly alright, and I felt…I felt…" He paused, trying to find the right words. Trellin was now becoming amused, watching his son struggle with his emotions.

"Well, it was as if a lightning bolt went up me arm to me head. I felt like I was on fire." A grin came over his face. "Do ya know what I'm tellin ya?" he sincerely asked. Trellin's demeanor softened. Now, it wasn't a stablemaster speaking to a hand. It was father to son.

"Yes, son, I know exactly what ya mean." Now it was Trellin's turn to look up in remembrance. "I felt that same thing with yer mum; gods preserve her." Several summers ago, when the fever took her, and there were no healers around, even the lord tried to find one, gods know, but with no luck.

"It was then I knew I wanted her to be with me fer the rest of me days." Looking down, he rubbed his callused hand with his thumb, remembering. She, too, had beauty he couldn't stop gazing upon. Trellin had just left military service when he met her. A blade had run straight through his side, and he could barely lift a shield,

14

but he still put himself between his lord and death. She nursed him for days, sewing the wound and refusing to leave his side. In that time, they fell in love. Even now, he winced when lifting his arm to shoulder height. In repayment, the honorable lord made him stablemaster, despite Trellin knowing little about horses.

"We were joined under the Harvest moon in this very town," he began. "Lord Galgun and a priest of Hearthmae recited the ceremony. Half the town were there, and the celebration lasted well into night." It was as if it were still happening. "I was the happiest man alive that day and the proudest, the gods can attest. She were a beauty, yer mum." He paused and was almost lost in fond memory.

Coelric had heard his mother tell it. Oddly enough, it was almost the same story, word for word, but it made him wish more and more for the same thing. He knew that one day Hearthmae would smile her blessing on him if he were worthy, or at least he prayed for it, hoping it wouldn't be ignored.

His father shook his head back to the matter at hand. "So, what do ya plan to do about it, lad?"

Coelric thought about it, remembering how poor she was. His father would never agree to this. He was the stablemaster of a lord, after all, a man of some esteem and some stature. He was embarrassed. "Father...," he hesitated, "I..."

Arms still folded over his stomach, Trellin said, "Come on now, boy, what in the eyes of the gods are ya gonna do about it?"

Coelric knew he had to tell him. He took a breath and quickly let it come out.

"She's poor, Father—poor as dirt. She lives with her family outside of Mapleton. Her father's a fieldworker and herdsman. Her mum tends four children and keeps the house...shack more or less. They're in a bad way, but," he added, "I can't seem to keep my mind off of her."

There. It's said. Now, cringing, he waited for the yelling.

Silence.

15

He felt Trellin's eyes on him, and his silence was deafening. It felt as if time had stopped.

"Huh." His father sat for a second, thinking. "So, ya think ya love her, do ya? Is that it?" he asked. Without so much as a hesitation, Coelric quickly said, "By the goddess herself, yes."

He couldn't believe he'd said it. He hadn't a clue what love was or what it even felt like, but if this was it, then, yes, he loved her or knew he could.

"And does she you?"

"I don't know, Da. I think she could. I pray she does."

"Let me think on it a bit. It's not a no, mind ya, but this could be…concerning ta certain folks."

As if the Lord would mind. He's a good man with a good heart. Trellin thought, smiling inwardly.

Talith woke to the sound of her sisters crying. Morning light crept through the cracks in the shutters, pale and thin as milk. As always, Father was already in the fields, working beside the other townsfolk, tending the cattle, turning the soil. Out back, Mother was stooped over the washbasin, wringing life back into their battered clothes, sweat dripping from her brow.

They never seemed to have enough food, milk, or even decent clothing. Talith's patched dress was the best they owned, though its color had long since faded to a weary gray. Her sisters were twelve, nine, and five, and at nearly fifteen, she was already more caretaker than child.

Her mother relied on her for everything, keeping the little ones quiet, fetching water, mending what could still be mended, and even cooking if things got too busy. It was the rhythm of her days: work, exhaustion, eat, sleep. Once every fortnight, if a few coins could be spared, she was allowed to walk into town for necessities and for a glimpse, however brief, of a world larger than their small, ragged home. She began her day kneading some bread with the little rye flour they had left; the children were hungry as always. She mixed it with water and began to smile, thinking of the boy she met the night before, his gentle touch, his smile, as if the sun rose on a new day and warmed her. She daydreamed. Could he be her prince, something she'd dreamed of since she was little? She leaned on the table dreamily, deep in thought.

"So, where'd yer journey take ya this time, young lady? The castle? A ship leaving for far-off lands?" Mom had come in and caught her daydreaming, again. It wasn't the first time, of course. She mostly dreamed about what it would be like to be far away from the hamlet, away from this life. Perhaps being in the city. All those fine people, the colors, the buildings.

She started kneading faster. "Sorry, mother." She began to berate herself. "Sakes, Talith. The kids are cryin', and you're dreamin'. What am I to do with ya?"

Annoyed, her mother wiped the dirt from her hands with her yet dirty apron and nudged Talith out of the way. "By the mother, I don't know what's gotten into ya, child," she said, shaking her head.

"Mother?" Talith began. She couldn't hold it in any longer. It just blurted out. "Coming home from town last night, I met someone on the road."

Her mom stopped. "On the road?" Kalla slowly turned to her with worry on her face.

"No, no, no. It wasn't bad, not at all," She paused. "I wasn't paying attention as I walked and I…bumped…into a young man."

Kalla frowned.

"It's alright. He didn't get angry; he was actually truly kind."

Kalla raised her eyebrow. "So. What happened when you *bumped* into this young man?"

A smile began on her face. "We sat, and he made sure I was alright."

"You sat," she said, now curious. She began kneading the dough again.

"Yes, we sat…and talked." The dreamy look returned to her face as she spoke. "But I realized what time it was and knew I had to get home, so I tried to excuse myself, but he offered to escort me."

"Is that so?" she said, a slight smile creeping across her face.

Talith nodded, almost child-like, "Yes, he actually…offered." She looked into her mother's eyes with a wide grin. "Then he helped me onto his horse, and he walked me all the way here."

"He walked you? By the lady, that's more than a league. My, he must be a strong one." She tried to stifle a smile.

Talith smiled sheepishly. "I couldn't say, but he didn't strain lifting me on the horse, to be sure."

Mom held back a grin. *Well, now,* Kalla thought, beginning to approve. "And what then?" she asked, feigning boredom.

"Well, we talked the whole way—he about himself and his family and me…about mine." She looked down when she said that, and her mother's heart nearly broke. They always tried to make a better life for the girls, but, as would always seem to happen, one thing led to another and Skippin the Piper, God of the downtrodden, would always seem to pass them by. No matter how hard they worked, they only seemed to survive.

She gulped hard to keep her emotions in check. "And who might this young man be?"

Talith looked up, and it was as if light began to glisten in her eyes as she said, "Coelric—Coelric Soryn."

Her mother stopped cold. She knew the name. Her heart began to beat faster. *Dear Mother, what have you done?* She turned to Talith. "The son of the lord's stablemaster?"

Talith nodded her head excitedly.

"No, no, no. You can't." She was almost frantic. "This can only end badly." She hated to say it, but she knew this could only end up with broken hearts…or worse.

"By the gods, Talith, he's almost royalty. We are peasants to these people. They have house servants who earn more respect than we do." She gulped hard.

Those people had been known to seek vengeance on their sort, for even the smallest of infractions, and this one wouldn't be considered small by any means.

Talith's eyes widened in shock. Did she hear this right?

"Dear, sweet girl, please don't pursue this further. I beg of you," she pleaded.

Talith stared at her mother in disbelief, eyes welling with tears. Stunned, she didn't know what to say. Her mother covered her mouth with both hands, not believing what she'd done, yet realizing it had to be said. She couldn't stop. If the lord found out about this forbidden thing, he could very well imprison the entire family.

"I know. I know, but this can't happen. I have the girls to think about."

Without another word, Talith bolted from the room and dove onto her bed, sobbing as only a broken heart could. Why had her mother denied her? He was a nice boy. She couldn't understand it. It just wasn't right.

She lay there for most of the day, head covered by her pillow, hiding the streams of tears. After some time, her mother came in and sat at the foot of her bed, placing her hand on Talith's foot. She recoiled in anger.

"Oh, Talith, I'm so sorry. I am," her mother said. "But you don't understand." How could she explain better? "I don't expect you to. This world…this world is so complicated. There are so many things you don't know."

"WHY!" Talith yelled. "TELL ME WHY!" Her face was red with fury.

Her mother fell silent for a second in thought, Talith's enflamed eyes glaring.

"My sweet child," she began in an even tone, "you know I love you more than life itself. And I want nothing but the best that we can give. But he's the stablemaster's son." She tried to get her to understand.

Talith buried her head in the pillow again. "He lives in a manor, Talith. He works for the stablemaster...of a lord...a vassal of the king himself. We are nothing more than poor people who are lower than the cattle we tend, in their eyes. I'm trying to save you from a broken..." she paused, staying silent and just listening to her daughter's shattered heart. "I know it seems that I'm the cause of it right now, doesn't it?" She sighed. "You'll understand as you get older. I'm sorry." She began to fumble with the edge of her apron.

Talith sat upright, sighed and said in a faint voice, almost a whisper, "I finally met someone who likes me...likes me for ME, for being myself, and you say we can't be. Because of what? What people will think? What they might say?" She sighed again. "I don't understand. Everyone has someone...But not me. I'm not allowed. Is that right?" She wiped a tear from her cheek. "Go away. I'm tired." She lay her head back down and closed her eyes, trying to will the world away.

Her mother tried to touch her foot again, and this time Talith let her. She gave it a squeeze of understanding and perhaps some pity, stood, and walked out. A tear fell from Kalla's eye, feeling just as broken-hearted for her daughter as she was for the boy.

The rest of the day passed in silence. Kalla went about the day's chores and wished she could explain things so Talith could better understand, but she didn't know how. She didn't know the words. The world was a complicated thing, and for people of their low stature, dreams like this were simply impossible. The best they could hope for was to survive another day and maybe, one day, find someone of like stature and settle down.

As the sun ebbed, Wesley returned home from the fields, filthy, bloody and smelly. Kalla had always been insistent that at least he wash his face and hands before supper, but this time, she required that and a full change of clothing as well. She always said it was an affront to the Harvest Mother to look upon Her gifts of food with filth and grime at the table. It was the one thing Father allowed her to oversee, and there was rarely any dissent.

The fire was crackling as if alive, and the smell of supper filled the air of the tiny, darkly lit shack. It wasn't much, yet again; a meager stew of old, wilted potatoes and carrots mixed with a two-day-old rabbit. Kalla always weaved her motherly magic and managed to make it taste like a king's banquet...or what Talith fantasized a banquet would be.

"The town lost another cow today." Wesley shook his head in disgust. "I done what I could, but th' calf was breach, an' th' ma lost too much blood." He was silent. Every animal in the hamlet was worth its weight in gold, and each loss was akin to a person dying. He was a good man, and he loved his family dearly. He took on any extra work he could to help them live a better life, but things never seemed to work out, no matter how hard he tried.

"Eat yer dinner, love. Don't think on it too much tonight. Tomorrow'll be brighter; you'll see." Mother always tried to see the good in everything, even though they all saw little hope. They didn't live; they survived, and survival was one thing at which they were practiced.

They ate in silence, like so many nights in the past. Then came the unmistakable sound of hooves echoing from outside. They could tell that they were heavy, but could not tell how many there were. Kalla's eyes got wide as Wesley nervously pointed to the back room. As he stood, he made sure his family got there quickly and quietly. Their hearts began to beat furiously. Father started for the door, the sound of a mailed fist pounding just as he reached to open it. Fearing the worst, he slowly cracked it open and peered out.

The man standing before him was a giant, almost too large to walk through the door, it seemed. He was clad in a red tunic, sword by his side and a dagger in his belt. Wesley looked up at the man's grizzled face. Fear crept into his bones, for he knew he could not defend himself or his family against this monstrosity even if he had a mind to.

Timidly, he hoped they would take pity and leave, "We have nothing to take, good sir. Please, we're too poor to bother with, m'lord." He was almost shaking now.

The man's grizzled face softened. "Fear not, my friend. I bring no harm to you or your family this day. Are you the father of a lass named…Talith?"

Now, Wesley was truly afraid. What had she done that would send a brute like this to their door?

The big man realized the fear in the pitiful man before him. "My apologies, sir," the big man said. "Where are my manners? Let me introduce myself and my companion."

Another large man presented himself. He was almost as tall as the grizzled man but far better dressed and much less intimidating. His tunic was green with fine, golden brocade and wooden toggles, and his smile could warm the heart of the dead.

Wesley opened the door fully as the grizzled man continued, "I am Trellin Soryn, Stablemaster and father of the boy, Coelric. I am in the employ of Lord Reginald Galgun." He bowed to the well-dressed man as he introduced him.

Not knowing what to do, Wesley bowed his head and fell to his knees. "M'lord."

"Stand, my good man, please." Lord Galgun motioned for Wesley to stand, which he did clumsily.

"Please, sirs, come in. Come in. My gravest apologies for the disarray of our home," he said, embarrassed.

He turned and yelled, "KALLA! Quick, woman. We've guests."
He turned back to the men. "No one ever visits here, so I'm not
sure what to do, m'lord." He was completely flummoxed.

Kalla scurried out from the back, bowing as she moved. She
rushed and began to spoon some stew into bowls for the giant men.

Wesley quickly moved two chairs to the table and brushed them
off, then motioned them to sit.

"Thank you.… I didn't get your name, sir," said Lord Galgun.

Wesley almost fainted from fear at his forgetfulness. "W-W-
Wesley, m'lord. Wesley. I tend th' village fields an' help with th'
cattle."

Trellin glanced and nodded toward his lord.

Kalla leaned in and placed the bowls of stew before them.
"Pardon, sirs." She hurried off to get some drink. Wesley smiled,
grabbed Kalla's hand and pulled her close. "And this be my wife,
Kalla," he said with a proud grin. Both men nodded and said "Lady"
in greeting. She smiled and curtsied as best she could, wringing her
hands in her dirty apron nervously.

Both men dipped their spoons and filled their mouths with the
hot stew as the pair looked on. As their taste buds identified the
food, each looked at the other, wincing at the horrible taste.
Decorum prevented them from spitting it out, so both men feigned
satisfaction as they choked it down and complimented Kalla on her
creation.

"I must apologize for not eating more, lady, but our time is
short, and we've other dealings to attend," the lord said.

Reginald nodded to Trellin, who stood and asked, "You have a
daughter named Talith, am I correct in assuming?"

Kalla looked at Wesley, clearly afraid. "Y-yes, sire, we do."

Trellin saw the fear in both of their eyes. "Please, again, I assure
you there will be no harm done here today. You have my word.
Please, be at ease." The lord gave a nod of agreement.

Wesley sighed in relief. "But I don't understand, sire. What 'as she done?"

Trellin smiled, confusing Wesley. *What is going on here?* he thought.

"Well, apparently she stands accused of kidnapping a young man's heart and will not release it," he said, with a broad smile on his face.

Kalla's eyes widened, Wesley's face turned white, and he almost fainted.

"I'd like to meet this young lady if I may. I believe we may have some serious matters to tend to."

Wesley's mouth stopped working. He lost all words, and his head began to swim. Without moving, Kalla yelled, "Talith. Come out here, girl."

Seeing Wesley in a bad way, Trellin stood and helped the man to a chair, where Kalla plied him with water. "Drink," she whispered and helped him hold the cup.

Talith shyly came from the back room and curtsied, poorly, before Reginald and Trellin. "I-I'm Talith, m'lord," she said, not looking at them. She was nervous, more than she'd ever been. Never had she been in the presence of men this powerful before, and she was genuinely afraid, remembering what her mother told her earlier.

Trellin and Reginald matched glances. "I am Trellin Soryn, young lady, Lord Galgun's stablemaster and father to Coelric, whom I believe you met last night." He sat.

She had no idea what to do. Was she in trouble? "Um, aye lord, I know Coelric."

"Please explain the events of last night if you will. Lord Galgun and I are very interested. Tell it all, tell it true."

Talith glanced at her parents quickly, saw the fear in their eyes, took a deep breath and began to recount their meeting. She nervously wrung her hands but kept her eyes planted toward the floor as she told it. Her breath caught when she described looking into his eyes; she paused, remembering. The men shared smiling glances as she continued. She even added the kiss on the forehead, which she hadn't even told her mother about. When her explanation was done, she took another deep breath, preparing for the worst. "But he was a perfect gentleman, m'lords. He really was," she said.

Trellin looked at Galgun. "That's exactly the way Coelric explained it to me as well, my lord—except he managed to omit the kiss on the forehead." He gave a sideways grin at Talith, who blushed upon seeing it.

Lord Galgun nodded, and both men stood, backs straight as if about to pass judgment. "Wesley, Lady Kalla, please sit," he requested. Both parents gasped. No one of this station had *ever* done this, to their knowledge. Puzzled, they both did as request, still holding hands with a white-knuckled grip.

Lord Galgun drew himself up regally. "Since Trellin is in my employ and his son, my charge, I am bound by honor and promise to fulfill a request issued by Trellin…or should I say, Sir Trellin." He looked at Trellin, who lowered his eyes. "My apologies, Sir Trellin. I know you disdain the title, but this is an official contract, and decorum dictates it be adhered to." Trellin bowed his head to the lord in understanding.

He continued. "By his request and wishes, you are hereby afforded the honor and privilege of being in the employ of myself and, under the supervision of Sir Trellin, at Tantyn Manor, where you will be properly housed, fed and paid in accordance with your positions in perpetuity. It is hoped, but not mandatory, that Coelric and the Lady Talith be afforded courtship rights, as well, under the supervision of myself, Sir Trellin, yourselves, and the Harvest Mother." None of the three moved, mouths open, eyes wide with disbelief and shock. None had words.

Trellin softened his disposition and spoke first. He took her hands in his and said, "Talith, you seem to be a fine young lady, as my son tells me. He is enamored with you as you probably are with

him, and as you can see, I will do anything for him. He's all I have."
He smiled. "Even he admits it was only a moonlight walk, but
you've managed to capture his heart. I know it is completely out of
the ordinary for an honor of this magnitude to be afforded
to…please excuse my wording…people such as you, but I will do
anything for my son's happiness." He looked into her eyes. "Lord
Galgun has granted me this, and I wish to pass it on to you and your
family, if you will only allow me."

Lord Galgun looked at Wesley, smiling and said, "I have need of
a husbandman and herdsman, and according to the gossip of the
town, you seem to be their best."

Talith blinked herself back to reality. She thought a second for
the right words and began carefully, "Sir, I know about your missus,
and I am deeply sorry. Coelric was crushed, as were you, by his
telling. I can't speak for my family, but it would be an honor for me
to accept your request."

When she finished, Kalla and Wesley regained themselves and
blurted, "By th' Gods, yes, we accept. Anythin', lord, anythin' ya
needs, please, command us." They began to cry with joy. Did
Skippin finally shine a blessing on them?

Wesley fell to the feet of Reginald and hugged his knees while
crying. "Thank you, lord. Thank you. We won't disappoint; ya 'ave
me word." Reginald helped the man to his feet. "Of that I have no
doubt. Now, calm yourself, please. Get sleep. My men will come
tomorrow and help you move your belongings to Tantyn Manor."

Kalla looked at Lord Galgun with shame. "Lord, if ya please, we
'ave nothin'." She held out her hands. "Our pallets be straw. Our
clothes be handmade an' the only real items we own be an old
washtub, cook pot, an' wooden bowls an' spoons that Talith made a
few years past." She pointed to the table, "Mother's mercy, this table
an' chairs was made from old barrels and's more kindlin' than table."
She tried to hide her embarrassment.

Reginald looked sternly at Trellin, who nodded back. "Nonetheless, lady, my men will be by tomorrow to help in any way they can."

The two men stepped toward the door. Lord Reginald asked, "One more thing. Are all the families in this hamlet in as poor a way as you?"

Wesley looked at the floor and said, "Yes, lord. We do what we can, but none here be doin' any better."

A look of great concern showed on the lord's face. The two men bowed to the family and made their exit. As they mounted, Lord Reginald said to Trellin, "My old friend. I think it's time to visit Elder Edgerly to discuss some things."

"I couldn't agree more, my lord," he said with a grin. "This should be enjoyable."

The two men pulled their reins right, spurred their steeds on and dashed off to see the Elder of Mapleton.

'...this should be enjoyable indeed.'

The winter was bitter this season; snow drifts formed against houses, roads became unusable, but thank The Piper, Wesley and his family barely noticed. They had plenty of food and wood to stay comfortable, and enough blankets to keep them warm. Wesley continued to work, though now in service to Lord Galgun, yet he still made the trek into the hamlet to help as many people as he could. He told Kalla that, though they had been blessed by Skippin, he didn't want to forget where they came from or who their friends were. Some still needed wood chopped or windows patched, and he felt it was the least he could do to ease his guilt for their bestowed blessing.

They came to love and respect their new lord, finding that he was more than fair, and oddly enough, cared about his people no matter who they were or what they did. He would pass by occasionally to check on the workers in the fields and the stables and would always ensure his people's homes were well-tended. They wondered why Elder Edgerly never did this in Mapleton or how Lord Galgun didn't notice the town's mismanagement.

Talith and Coelric spent quite a bit of time together as the days passed. Trellin would allow him more time away from the stables than normal to be with her, much to the other stablehand's dismay. There was no doubt that the two were deeply in love and not just adolescent love; it was as if they had already been joined. Trellin, Wesley and Kalla had never seen two people more meant for each other than these two had become. And the families had become more than stablemaster and fieldworkers. They became friends—family.

Almost a year had passed, and the decision was finally made for the two young lovers to be joined, much to their elation. Lord Reginald Galgun, Hearthmae's priest and both families were dressed in their finest attire for the rite of joining. Lord Reginald couldn't have been prouder of Wesley and Kalla. They not only raised a beautiful family, but they also became close friends to him as well, which really helped to fill a void left by the passing of his wife. It was as if they were his own family being joined, and he reveled in their happiness.

The rite of joining took place in Hearth Hall at the four corners on the early morning of the Flower Moon. It shone large and bright as the two held hands, adorned with wreaths upon their heads and a ribbon drawn across their clasped hands. The silvery light cast a gentle glow as the priest raised his arms to the goddess and asked her blessing upon the two; that their lives and love be bountiful; that they grow from two into one, and that their days be filled with eternal happiness. They sealed their betrothal with a kiss. Both fathers wrapped each in a shawl of woven flowers and wheat to prepare them for the blessings of Hearthmae, the Mother of the Harvest and Fertility.

The celebration lasted long into the warm, sunny day. The crossroads had been decorated with streamers, banners and flags of all shapes and colors by the townsfolk. The people of the four hamlets turned out to dance, drink and sing with the rich aroma of spiced lamb and beef drifting on the breeze. Children shrieked as they chased each other between the long tables, their bare feet kicking up petals and dust. Mugs clinked as toasts were shouted over the pipers' songs. As always, the elders sat shoulder to shoulder with their folk, while Lord Reginald and a few visiting nobles joined in, laughing among the peasants as if, for one day, the world had no walls or rank between them. Even the guards and soldiers were allowed to participate in the festivities on this day. Through all the merriment, no one ever noticed that Elder Edgerly of Mapleton was not present, nor would he attend ever again.

The couple's table was magnificent. The edges were adorned with wreaths of green tree branches suspended from streamers of wheat and flowers, tied together with brightly colored pieces of cloth and wool. Bowls and baskets of fruits and flowers from all over the land sat atop bright red tablecloths decorated with gold brocade; a gift from Lord Balven of The Glen. Haunches of spiced meat sat atop silver platters on each table while the mead, ale and wine flowed like water.

Coelric and his new bride proudly sat at the center of the long table, sharing smiles of love and anticipation; wreaths of flowers still set upon their heads. Sir Trellin sat to his son's right, Talith's family to her left, both crying tears of pure joy. Her sisters sat at the far end, laughing and teasing.

Lord Galgun was seated at the high table just above the happy couple, taking it all in. These were his people, his family, his children. Most lords would think this a frivolous waste spent on common people who were inconsequential and meaningless to their station. They would try to look down on him for his actions, but to him, these were the children his wife never got the chance to bless

29

him with, and he couldn't care less about what others thought. Unbeknownst to the happy crowd before him, he fought to hold back tears of both sadness and joy. *THIS, my love, this is for you. I hope you know my joy…and my melancholy.*

He stood and raised his hands. Very quickly, the merriment quieted with all eyes turning to their host.

"My good folk, we are here to celebrate love, to celebrate joy, to celebrate life." He lowered his hands in the direction of the couple. "Master Coelric, Lady Talith, as lord of this land, it is my honor to present this feast in your names on the day of your oaths of joining."

He reached out and lifted a large silver goblet, waiting for everyone to do likewise. "I drink this cup to you both and wish for your health, happiness…" he paused for just a second, and with a huge knowing grin, "and many, many children." Everyone laughed and cheered while ale and mead splashed across many of the less sober revelers.

As Lord Reginald sat, Sir Trellin stood and said, "If I may, my lord." Lord Galgun gave an approving nod.

"Good people of Tantyn. I have been in the service of our lord," he turned and bowed to Reginald with a teasing wink, "for countless years, yet unending, it seems." That brought a laugh from everyone. "But it truly has been an honor and privilege to be in the service of such a good and proper man." He moved between the couple and placed a hand on their shoulders. "Son, I am so proud of you. I only wish your mother were here to witness this day and your joy." He turned to Talith. "My…daughter," he looked to the sky, "by the gods, I never thought I'd say that. My daughter, you have made my son so very happy. Whatever you need, call on me, and please look to me as your father. I am proud to welcome you into my family." He bent down and kissed her forehead.

The crowd cheered, mugs and tankards clinked, and tears flowed.

Kalla nudged her husband and, with her eyes, motioned for him to speak. Wesley slowly stood. He bowed to Lord Galgun and Sir

Trellin. He had become more confident now that he'd been witness to courtly manners.

He looked at the crowd. "Ye all know me, know how I earn a living." He turned to Coelric and Talith. "My son," he smiled broadly, "I have nothing ta bestow upon ya," he looked down, ashamed, "except for my beautiful daughter here." He looked up to Lord Galgun. "If it wasn't for th' good lord, here, I'd still be living in my hovel outside o' town." He swallowed hard. "But I have my family, and now ya be part of it. And I'm right glad ya are." He looked at his beautiful daughter. Memories of her running through the house as a little girl made his eyes tear up. Where had the time gone?

He sighed. "My beautiful Talith, you are th' star o' my eye. When the goddess brought ya to us, we ne'er realized what a treasure ya were—so fine, so beautiful." He wiped away a tear. "An' now, ya grown to a fine, fine woman." He inhaled deeply. "I tried to be th' best father I could. I worked hard ta see ya got th' best I could give, to make sure you an' th' family was as happy as I could. Now, I see what th' fruits o' my toils come to." He moved to his daughter and hugged her tightly.

He turned to Coelric. "And now…my son." The young man faced his new father. Wesley wrapped his arms around him and squeezed tightly. Then he looked Coelric in the eyes.

"I ain't a strong or powerful man like yer da or Lord Reginald here. But I be a proud man, and I be her father."

He dropped his arms and took a step backward. He looked Coelric squarely in the eyes and placed his finger in the center of the boy's chest, poking with every sentence.

"If ya ever bring harm ta me treasure, if ya ever wrong her, if I think that there be any discord 'tween ya, have no doubt, have no question, I WILL find ya, and I WILL right that wrong."

He took another deep breath and hugged his new son again. "Have no doubt," he whispered sincerely once again.

He stepped back and turned his gaze to Trellin, who grinned while giving an approving nod and stood himself. The revelers were silent for a moment, waiting to see what would happen next.

Trellin walked to Wesley and put his hands on both his shoulders. "If he wrongs your daughter, I will right that wrong with you," he said, grabbing the man in a bear hug so tight that Wesley thought his spine would snap.

Cheering and whistling came from all throughout the four corners.

As the applause abated, a minstrel strumming a lute requested the happy couple come to the forefront and dance their first dance to honor the Hearth Mother. The pipes began the tune with lute, harp and drums following in a happy, upbeat rhythm.

As they danced, Coelric looked deeply into Talith's eyes. The love he felt at that moment erased every aspect of the world around him. She had become life itself, and he promised himself that no harm would ever befall her. Death take him if he failed.

The music played. They whirled and clapped, laughing and laughing. She could not believe what had transpired in the last year. All her life, she wanted nothing more than to be a wife, to be a mother of beautiful children, to finally be happy. Then, as if the Mother herself had listened, she was gifted the most wonderful man she had ever laid eyes on. Skippin had to be in league with Hearthmae because the bounty they had been served fulfilled every wish that could possibly be dreamed.

As they danced, she clasped her hands around his neck and looked into his beautiful eyes.

This time, she spoke the words, "What is happening?" and they kissed deeply, the cheers of the crowd going unheard.

The traditional second dance soon began. Kalla was paired with Coelric, and Trellin with Talith, as the minstrel called for a fast, joyful tune to honor The Piper God. The entire square joined in dancing, laughing, and singing songs of love in hopes the gods would smile their many blessings upon the newly joined couple.

Soon, it came time for the newly joined couple to depart, where individual well wishes, advice, prayers and blessings had all been bestowed. Just before the couple departed to solidify their nuptials, Lord Galgun gathered the family together one last time before he departed. With pride, he announced to them that he had a home just on the outskirts of Hazelwood that was theirs to keep in perpetuity and without fear of taxation. It was an honor to fulfill a life debt that he owed Sir Trellin for his service those many years past. Talith was so excited at the news that she completely forgot herself and threw herself at Lord Reginald, wrapped her arms around his neck and kissed his cheek. Realizing what she had done, she quickly pulled away and made her apologies.

Lord Reginald Galgun, the Lord of Tantyn, blushed for the first time since his wife passed. "Have no fear, lady," he said with a grin. "It does my heart good to see such lust for life again in this land." He leaned over, grabbed Talith's hand and kissed it.

Then he turned to Trellin and reached for his arm as he lightly stumbled. "Are you alright, my lord?" he asked. Just for a second, there was concern in his eyes.

"Yes, yes," Reginald said, regaining his composure. "I had forgotten how stout the drink was in this village," he said with a halfhearted laugh. Trellin wasn't so sure.

"Sir Trellin, I must speak to you later, if you will," he announced.

"As you wish, my lord. Shall we go?" he asked.

"No, no. Be with your family. It's a joyful day. Enjoy them, please." He gave a slight bow to the families and made his exit.

The rest of the night, all the newly joined couple could see was each other, sneaking loving glances, holding hands and shyly smiling. The world had stopped for them that night; they simply reveled in each other.

Reginald ordered his guards to escort the couple to their new home. They were shuttled off to a waiting carriage adorned with flowers, wreaths and a multitude of colored banners and streamers hanging from the rear. It was the first time she had ever been in a carriage, which made her feel like a true princess. After a short ride, the sun started to dip below the horizon, and she could see her new home. It was the most beautiful thing she had ever seen. It looked far too big for the two of them. *But then*, she thought, *when the children arrived…*

She quickly raised her hand and covered her mouth, embarrassed. She thought about what was about to happen, making this evening the most wonderful night she could ever have imagined in her wildest dreams. She giggled.

"Are you alright, my love?" he asked. Turning to face him, she looked into his eyes again and *knew* she had made the right choice. She leaned over, put a hand on his cheek and kissed him.

"Oi. None of that, if ya please," said one of the guards, wagging his finger like a nanny. The guards all laughed. "The good lord will 'ave me arse if any o' that nonsense takes place afore ya gets home, now."

"Okay, okay, Matlin," Coelric said to the guard. He turned to Talith. "Don't make that one mad," he said loud enough for the guards to hear, "He'll get the paddle on ya, and then you'll not sit for a week."

Still pointing, Matlin, the guard, gave his best squinching nanny face, making everyone laugh.

Soon, they arrived at the front of the house. It was far grander than Talith could ever have dreamed. Standing not far from the edge of the Whispering Wood, she could tell that it was of solid mortar and stone, just like the castle she'd always longed for. There was a road leading up to it with trees all along one side, a large wood and iron door and topped by a slate-stone roof. It was more than she could ever have imagined and brought tears to her eyes.

The guards helped them both from the carriage and opened the door, beckoning them to enter their new home.

"Thank you, gentlemen," she said sweetly.

"'Twas our pleasure, m'lady," Matlin replied. They both went in, but just as the door closed, Matlin said with a knowing and wry grin, "Now you two enjoy the ev'nin'…an' don'tcha be doin' anythin' I wouldn't do." All the guards laughed as they mounted and rode away.

The moon had risen and allowed the stars to shine brighter than Coelric had ever seen. Talith had ushered him away from the bedroom so she could change out of her dress. He stood in the front doorway, sighing at how wonderful the day had been, the dancing, the speeches and most of all, his beautiful wife. He shook his head in disbelief. "My wife," he said out loud, smiling. It sounded strange but pleasing.

"You called for me, husband?" He turned and saw her. Bathed in the shimmering silver glow of the moonlight coming in from the doorway, stood the most beautiful woman he'd ever seen in his life, bare as the day she was born and smiling. She motioned him to the room. He closed the front door, picked her up in his arms and closed the bedroom door with his foot.

It was the height of the silvery moon when the birds began to sing, and the owls hooted. The gentle blowing cool breeze carried one last thought.…

'…finally balance…as it should be.'

It took days to clean up the remnants of the festival, and soon life in the four corners returned to normal. The people worked with a little more vigor now that they'd had a chance to completely let go their cares, even if it were for only a day or two of frivolity.

Coelric and Talith soon settled into their new life. Coelric continued to work with Trellin, and Talith stayed at home to help shape their lives as the wife she had always dreamed of being. It wasn't vastly different from the life she had lived at home, only now…it was *HER* life. It was *HER* home. It was whatever they made of it as they saw fit. She knew there would be challenging times ahead, but she had already lived through tough times and knew they would be strong enough to carry on together, heads held high. Life had been a good teacher, and she learned well how to make do if necessary.

The days and weeks soon passed, Wesley and Kalla would come by from time to time to visit. Coelric was always so glad to see them, and he doted on them as if they were his grandkids. It had come to a point where Talith began to ask him if he would rather wear the apron and serve while she sat, scratched her bum, and burped ale. That always got a laugh until one day, they had come over for supper, and Coelric really did come out of the kitchen wearing an apron and kerchief and really did serve supper. Wesley said that he "did a right fine job" and turned to Talith, asking why she wasn't as good at it. That earned him a vicious scowl from his daughter and a backhand to the arm.

Coelric would return home when his day was done with flowers or a piece of fruit, and she would welcome him by wrapping her arms around him, kissing him and listening to his daily stories. He would eat and listen as she told him about the things she did that day and what she was thinking while he was gone. At night, they would lie in bed discussing their future and becoming parents. They would recount the events of their joining, often laughing so loud that they scared the crickets to silence. But every night they slept in each other's arms and woke with a smile knowing that they both were exactly where they wanted to be.

A full moon had come and gone when, over supper that night, Talith asked Coelric if he enjoyed working beside his father. After all, he had been working for him most of his life, and she had been curious. It was a harmless enough question, but one she had never thought of before.

He stopped eating, looking at her as he put some thought into it and said, "To be honest, love, I never really thought about that before."

He sat back, lifted his cup of mead and took a sip. He held it midair for a second, just thinking. Then setting it down, he replied, "No. On thinking about it, no. I don't really like it at all." He looked back at her.

The revelation brought a smile to his face. Staring at his cup, he shook his head slightly. "No, I don't," the epiphany making him smile even more.

She didn't know if she had done something wrong, but the look on his face made her think differently. "Did I say something, love?"

"Yes, my beautiful wife. Yes, you did." The broad grin on his face almost made her laugh. It was…too happy, she thought. He wiped his mouth and stood. She could see his mind working on what she couldn't know.

"I'll be home later, my lady," he said, bowing regally, then hurried out the door. She looked at the fire in the hearth, bewildered and thought, *Gods all-seeing, what did I do!*

She sat in front of the fire, which had died down to almost embers, waiting for his return. Night had fallen, and the moon shone brightly. He said he'd be back later, but to her mind, later had long passed, and she was beginning to worry. He had been gone for an exceptionally long time, but she willed herself to remain calm.

Just as worry was taking hold, the sound of hoof beats came slowly to a halt just outside the door. *Hooves? We don't own a horse.* She listened quietly, waiting, but nothing happened. Talith stood and went to the door. But as she opened it, there he stood, lip and nose bloodied, tunic torn…and a smile on his face.

"By the Great Mother, what's happened?" She was almost in a panic. She grabbed his arm, pulled him into the house and plopped him down onto a chair in front of the fire. She ran and dipped a basin in water, got a cloth and began cleaning his now bruising face. He sat in the chair and dumbly smiled at the flames.

"So, are ya gonna answer me or just sit and look like a grinning twit?" she demanded, wiping more blood from the crease of his eye. He looked at her and grinned wider without uttering a sound.

Just then, came a knock at the door. Wide-eyed, she looked at Coelric and then back at the door. Coelric silently motioned with his thumb toward the door. She rose, went and swung it open.

"Evenin', lady." She could tell it was Trellin, but the shadow covered him and made it hard to distinguish his features. "Might my son be home, by chance?"

"Well, yes, he is. Come in. Come in." She motioned for him to enter.

"Gods help me. What happened to *you*?" she said, bringing her hands to her cheeks in surprise.

He walked past her and over to Coelric, who glanced up, saw it was his father and motioned for him to sit.

"I done some thinkin', lad, and decided you goin' out on your own be the right thing to do." He pushed his thumb against the corner of his now darkening eye and squeezed the blood from it. Talith stood staring in shock.

"My beloved wife, will ya please get my father a cloth to wipe his face?" he asked, smiling. She scurried off and returned with a basin of water and a cloth, then brought a mug of ale for both. She stood quietly, a stern look on her face, waiting for one of them to speak. Trellin wet his cloth, dabbed at the cut on his face, then dabbed his bloody knuckle.

It was too quiet, and she began fuming. Her eyes darted from one to the other, and when it looked like neither would speak, she bellowed, "SOMEONE BETTER EXPLAIN AND DO IT QUICKLY!" The abruptness and tone made both men jump and cover their heads in defense.

"Alright, alright." Coelric recovered and sat back. "You asked me if I liked working for my da, and what did I say?"

She answered, "No."

Trellin shook his head sadly and repeated, "No."

Coelric said, nodding to his father, "No!" Again, she stood silently waiting for the conversation to continue.

Nothing.

"WELL?" She angrily folded her arms, stomped her foot and jutted her hip.

Trellin looked at her and said, "I agreed," and leaned back.

She looked at Coelric, then Trellin, then back at Coelric, fire blazing in her eyes. Seeing this and knowing women, Trellin seized the moment to make his exit. "If ya don't mind, daughter, I'll be getting' along now. Lots of work on the morrow and the sun'll be up soon." He slowly stood and put his hand on his son's shoulder as he started for the door. "See ya tomorrow when ya come get yer things, son."

Without looking, Coelric replied, "Bright and early, Da."

Trellin gave a nod, leaned over and kissed a confused Talith's cheek, opened the door and started out.

"Make my greetings to the good lord for me, will ya?" As Trellin closed the door, all he said was "Aye."

Talith was beside herself with fury and stomped off. As she reached the back room and fell onto the bed, she heard, "My love for you knows no bounds, my beautiful bride."

Sighing, he leaned forward and raised the mug she had set down. He tipped it and, seeing there was still ale in it, dipped the cloth and dabbed the blood from his knuckles. Then he raised it and drained it in one gulp. Placing it on the table, he leaned back, picked up the cloth again and wiped more blood from his lip. *Well, now, that went better than expected*, he thought.

"So, he agreed?" she asked quietly, stepping to his side. He reached out and pulled her to his lap. "That he did. I had to tell my side of course, but he came around."

"And…this?" She flourished her hand about his face. "Bah, we just had a bit of a disagreement is all."

He held her close and gave her a squeeze. She rested her head on his. "I love you too, daft as you are." She gently kissed his forehead and sighed.

He returned to the stables the next morning, bright and early as he said he would. It was a cool, misty morning, but the sun struggled its way through, nonetheless. He went into the stable house and saw the wagon had already been harnessed and loaded. Trellin stepped from behind it, holding a basket of flowers. Coelric looked at his father with a smirk and a raised eyebrow. "They're for yer wife, ya twit," he said, jokingly. He put them up on the bench and turned to his son, looking him up and down. He smiled and said, "Look at ya." He grabbed him by the shoulders and gave a gentle shake. "Yer a man now, and a damn fine one at that—strong, smart. Well, not that smart." They chuckled. "But I'm damn proud of ya boy. If yer ma was here, she'd be right proud o' ya as well." He gave his son a hug. A man's hug, to which Coelric returned as best he could. "You better make that lass happy, or it's yer ma that you'll be dealin' with."

Coelric laughed. "Ya know I will, Da. She's the world ta me. I'll do right by her, I swear."

Trellin let him go and stepped back; the sadness on his face was telling.

"You alright?"

"Aye, son. It's just…seein' all this, I miss yer ma's all." He looked down so Coelric wouldn't see his pain.

"Me an' Talith are right down the road from ya. Come eat with us when ya feel like. She'd be damn happy ta have ya."

Trellin looked up, smiling. "Ya know," he began, "I always knew this day would come. Yer ma and I both couldn't wait ta see it." He looked down, trying to hide his sadness. "Then she left." He looked at him square in the eyes. "Live and love every day like it's yer last, boy. Because it just might be." He quickly grabbed him and hugged him for just a minute. He stepped back, "Better get to it," he said quickly, turned and walked away.

The road was clear all the way home. It was early, so it wasn't out of the ordinary. He bobbed his head from side to side in time with the clip-clop of the horse's steps. After a short while, he shook his head and chuckled. He wasn't silly very often, but this morning he felt especially good. The sun had broken free, warming his face as the wood warbling thrushes began to sing their happy calls. *That's odd,* he thought. *It's a bit early in the season for the thrushes.*

A little farther down the road, he crossed paths with a small chatter of starlings, scratching and bobbing for seeds. As he passed, they all began to sing and chirp, which Coelric found very strange indeed. Stranger still, they took flight only once he had passed. He shrugged off the oddity and continued the short trek home.

After some time, he slowed the cart in front of the house and hopped down. Dusting himself off, he opened the door and went inside, but as he closed the door, Coelric turned to see Talith standing in front of the fire with the widest smile she had ever beamed.

It took him by surprise. "Um, is everything alright?"

She just stood smiling.

Coelric looked side to side, half expecting something to jump out. Seeing nothing, he took a step forward and asked again. "Talith? Is everything alright?"

Again, she just kept smiling.

As he neared her, he stepped between the two chairs before the fire, and there, just by her side, stood a new cradle, freshly made and neatly bedded. He looked up at her smiling face. Then the truth struck him.

"What?" He blinked, disbelief widening his eyes. "No…" he breathed, half-laughing, half-stunned.

Still smiling, she nodded and threw her arms around him, holding so tightly he thought she might squeeze the life from him. He wrapped her in his arms, took a step back, and spun her around, laughter breaking into tears of joy.

"Oh, I love you so much." They both stood there and cried giant tears of happiness while he showered her with kisses.

"Ahem," came a sound from the door.

They both looked at the entrance with tears of joy still streaming down their cheeks.

"I hope I'm not interrupting anything, my daughter, but ya left this pile of swaddling clothes at home." Tears were streaming down her father's face as well. He entered the house and grabbed them both in a huge hug. "Kalla told me that ye had th' glow an' were holdin' yer midriff a lot. You know yer mother. Sometimes, she just knows. By Hearthmae, I'm so damned happy for th' both of ya."

They stood holding each other, allowing the grand moment to settle in. Wesley sighed and pulled away from them. Sniffing, he wiped his eyes with the cloth he had pulled from his pocket.

"I should be goin' now, let you two have th' day to yerselves." He sniffed again. "Kalla'll be passin' by again ta see if ya be needin' anything."

As he turned, he was doubled by a coughing spasm and almost fell over. Coelric grabbed his arm to help him steady.

"Are ya alright?" Coelric asked, concerned. He'd never seen him do that before.

"Oh, aye. I've been coughin' a bit these past few days. What with th' changin' of th' season, new blooms, th' stables an' all, it's no wonder," he said, wiping his mouth with the cloth and quickly returning it to his pocket. "I'll be fine, lad. Don't ya worry."

Coelric frowned but said no more. Something in Wesley's cough gnawed at him, but he let it pass.

He waved again, heading home, but as he walked, he pulled the cloth from his pocket. Wesley looked at the blood he had coughed up and sighed....

He sighed...

'...and she smiled.'

'...not so fast.'

Kalla came by quite a bit now. She always had a smile and was so glad to help her daughter and give sage advice. Soon, the word spread and even Lord Galgun passed by to see how the soon-to-be mother was faring. Trellin suggested building a shed behind the house so they could move their stored crates and barrels from where the children's room would be. Coelric agreed that it was a clever idea, and they began work that very day.

Day after day, they worked with Talith leaning against the door frame, watching them with folded arms and shaking her head. *Men.*

The two cut wood and worked every day until the moon rose to finish it. Watching the two work together, Talith was amazed at how much alike they had become. Coelric's body had gotten stronger; he was now almost the exact image of his father, tall, strong and handsome. They would laugh and carry on as they hammered and cut as if they were more brothers at play than father and son. Watching her husband work and knowing that it was for her and their children only made her love him even more.

After a few days, it was complete and turned out to be much bigger than they had all anticipated. At almost the size of the main room in the house, it looked more a home than a shed.

"Well, now, you should be house builders for Lord Galgun the way you two carry on." She smiled and shook her head, "Why don't ya just add a hearth and a back room so we can get Ma and Da ta move in with us." Talith shook her head, laughed and walked back into the house.

Trellin and Coelric looked at each other, neither saying a word.

She had just gotten done chopping leeks and potatoes for the evening meal when the relative silence was broken by loud noises out near the lodge. Curiously, she went to the back door to see what it was, and when she opened it, saw both men sweating and hauling stone from the back of the wagon. Confused, she stood there wide-eyed with her mouth open. Coelric glanced up as he tossed a stone and saw her there, staring.

He shrugged his shoulders and said, "Well, ya wanted a hearth, didn't ya?"

Trellin chuckled. "So, when's the family comin'?" Both men laughed warmly and loudly at the shock on her face.

"But…" she just stood watching. The men went back to tossing rocks and singing dirty tavern catches. She shook her head again and walked back inside.

They asked Trellin to stay for supper, to which he obliged. It was a grand meal with ale, fresh venison, boiled potatoes with leeks, and a boule. They ate, laughed and drank well into the night, but realizing how late it had become, Trellin felt it was time to bid his leave. He thanked his daughter for the wondrous meal and left for home.

The couple sat by the fire, she on his lap, and stared at the flickering flames in silence. Coelric felt the weight of the past few days settling into his body, his muscles tight and his back aching. Sleep was calling. As they rose, he stretched, snuffed out the fire, and turned toward the bed…where he stopped, heart now beating hard in his chest.

She stood in the moonlight, bare and radiant, the silvery glow tracing the soft curve of her form. He caught his breath. The light from the window touched her face, making it seem as though the moon itself had chosen her. His heart surged with love. Slowly, he stepped toward her. She opened her arms, and when they met, it was with a quiet certainty. He gathered her close, lifted her gently, and carried her toward the bed.

That night, the shadows danced, and the forest sang.

...The Piper and The Mother shared their joy.

Talk of the town:

"By Hearthmae's locks, it be 'bout time them two finally tied th' knot. Thought she were gonna be an ol' maid till 'er last day."

–Madam Garven

Of Moons and Shadows

Summer gave way to fall, which came cooler than expected this year. Most farmers had become worried as a cool summer usually meant an even harsher winter. Everyone gathered as many provisions as they could to survive the expected upcoming snow, and those who fell short were helped by neighbors and friends. Luckily, the harvests had been healthy and plentiful this year, and the animals bore many young, which was a blessing for the next season.

As was tradition, a celebratory festival was held to honor and thank Hearthmae during the night of the Mourning Moon. It had always been referred to as such because it looked as if the moon were shedding a single shining tear. The four hamlet elders gathered fresh vegetables and grains, cakes and biscuits, which they would place in a cart atop freshly reaped grass. This was topped by the likeness of the Hearth Mother herself and pulled by cows that had recently birthed new calves. Townsfolk would follow the procession to a large glade deep in the Whispering Woods, a place long rumored to be where the presence of the gods and goddesses could be felt.

The livestock were unhitched, and tinder was added to the wagon that was to be used as the sacrificial pyre. The priests of the four hamlets touched their torches to the pyre, and a great flame leaped forth, the flames dancing high into the night sky. They chanted the ancient words of thanks and hope while circling the blaze. Onlookers repeated the chants in hopes of grasping some of the blessings for themselves, which was also tradition.

They continued until the bright crescent of the Mourning Moon was at its peak, then they all began to depart. Out of respect, they walked silently to avoid disturbing the gods or spirits of the woods.

When they reached the outskirts of the forest, they hugged each other, said their goodbyes and returned home for the winter, hoping their prayers would be answered.

Along with their families, Talith and Coelric embraced and said goodbye. It was comforting to learn they lived close enough to visit, which eased Talith's heart. Wesley, however, was looking more frail than usual, a change that worried everyone, even the town elders who depended on him to keep their herds healthy.

Kalla had been a steadfast comfort as Talith's belly grew heavy, reminding her often that she'd be due "'afore th' Long Night Moon. No one's born under th' Long Night Moon, for 'tis a bad omen," Kalla would say, words that brought relief and peace to the soon-to-be mother.

Wesley managed to find them through the throng of departing people. The cough had become much worse recently, and there were days when the poor man wouldn't even leave his bed. Kalla tried her potions and concoctions, but none seemed to work, which vexed her incessantly. All of her knowledge and experience was proving useless. He began to lean more heavily on his walking stick of late, causing him to leave the house less and less. After the blessings and well wishes, they soon departed with Wesley coughing so loudly it resonated through the forest.

"Ya go 'head, my dear. I must speak ta Talith." Kalla gave Wesley a kiss on his pale cheek. "I'll help ya home soon as I can." He nodded and headed home. Talith kissed Coelric's cheek and went to Kalla.

"Yes, Mother, what did you need?" she asked, puzzled.

"My dear, there be many things in this world that're mystical an' 'mazing." She put her hand on Talith's stomach. "Ya carrys that mystery in ya.... Fer you and I be bound to it, more deeply than ya yet knows."

Talith nodded her head, feigning understanding, but had no idea what Kalla was actually talking about.

"One day, you'll understand. But ya first must do this one thing I ask." She leaned closer to Talith's ear.

"You must tell 'em…tell 'em both. They must understand an' carry on." She pointed toward Talith. "Promise me. Promise."

Talith drew back, eyes narrowing as she tried to grasp her mother's meaning. "What are you trying to say, Mother? I don't understand at all. Tell both? Tell both what?"

"Promise me," she said, still pointing.

"Of course, I promise." Now becoming worried, she asked, "But what? What will I tell them?"

Kalla looked deep into Talith's eyes. "Yes." She sounded sure. "Yes, ya will." Kalla leaned in and kissed Talith's cheek. She could see Talith was dumbfounded and confused. She winked, lightly touching her daughter's cheek, then walked away. Talith tried to understand what she had heard, struggling with it for a few moments, but then started for home.

Coelric stirred the remnants of the fire so they would smolder and go out when Talith came in and stood by his side, wrapping her arms around his waist. He smiled and kissed her, but noticed the confused look on her face.

"Are you alright? What did she want?"

She paused for a second. Looking into his eyes, she told him about the conversation she and her mother had and how baffled she was about the message. They talked about it for a while, found no answers and headed off to sleep.

Rays of the morning sun brought her out of a deep sleep. She slowly opened her eyes and stretched, preparing for another day. Apparently, Coelric had already gotten up and was clearing the ground on the far side of the house. He had decided days before that he and his father would build a small tannery building on the other side of the house. It was something he had always wanted to do and, now that he was out of his father's charge, could readily pursue. She slipped on her shoes, drew a shawl about her and went to the hearth to warm herself. The mornings had grown colder as the days inched close to the winter season, and, luckily, Coelric had drawn a fire to chase it away. She put her hands close to the flame just as she heard Coelric talking in a muffled voice outside the house. She bent her head to listen, but could barely hear, so she went to the door and opened it up to see who was there.

Lord Galgun, Trellin and Kalla stood in front of Coelric, with Kalla crying and sobbing heavily.

They all turned toward Talith. "Gods, what's happened?" raising her hand to cover her mouth.

It was Lord Reginald who spoke. "My lady, I must inform you that during the eve your father, Wesley, died at home. I am so sorry." He bowed his head.

She was stunned, uncomprehending. She looked from Reginald to Trellin to Coelric. She had no words. It was Kalla's sob that broke the spell. Her head swam. Seeing her swoon, Coelric reached out, caught her before she fell and carried her into the house. Trellin put his arm around Kalla and escorted her to one of the chairs in front of the fire, where he gently sat her down. Coelric gently held Talith, who had begun to cry uncontrollably, kissed her cheek and simply let her cry.

Lord Galgun put a consoling hand on Kalla's shoulder. "My lady, words cannot describe the sorrow I feel for you right now." He turned to Coelric and Talith, who was still sobbing. "I will inform the priests, and we will prepare the pyre." Coelric nodded without a sound.

Trellin put his arms around them both. In a whisper, he said, "May the Veiled One light Wesley's path to peace." He kissed them both on the forehead and left them to grieve. He leaned over and kissed Kalla's hand. "He isn't gone, Kalla. He awaits you on the path to peace with a joyous smile and love in his heart." She looked up to him, tears still falling. "You're a good man, Trellin Soryn." She sniffed, fighting hard not to sob. "The gods know it." She patted his hand and began to cry. He straightened up, walked to the door and glanced back one more time, sighed, then closed the door.

Two days had passed since the Mourning Moon. Wesley's body had been anointed with oils from the bark of trees gathered from the Whispering Woods, as was tradition. The priests made sure to add a sprinkle of soil from the fields he worked, albumen from a calf he helped birth and a cloth imbued with a kiss from his wife and daughter. They spoke ancient words that would summon the Veiled One's minions to help guide Wesley down the path of peace while gently placing his body upon a cart filled with hay and wood for transport to the pyre.

The oxen were led down the road and stopped at Coelric's house, where the grieving family awaited escort. Upon seeing the cart, Talith and Kalla burst into tears once again. Trellin held Kalla in his arms, trying to console her as best he could while Talith managed to regain her composure, though the tears still flowed freely. The priests wore the deep blue veils of mourning as well as their blue robes and waited as Lord Galgun and his guard escorts arrived. He dismounted, placed his guards in the proper positions and slowly walked toward the family. He kissed the grieving lady's hands and passed on consoling words, then mounted his horse and waited for the procession to begin.

The drummers beat time as they began the long walk to the pyre, with the four bearers leading the lumbering ox and cart. Behind them, the family followed, with the lord and guards after. The only other sounds were the wheels on stone, the heartbroken sobs of the ladies, and the rhythmic march of the guards.

Townsfolk who had known Wesley lined the road, holding grasses, flowers and rye to be cast into the flames as tribute when Wesley began his final trek down the path. As the procession passed, the townsfolk fell in behind the guards, following all the way to the glade in the Whispering Wood.

The cart was placed in the center of the ceremonial circle, exactly where they had held the Mourning Moon ritual. The bearers then led the ox away as the priests took their places at the four corners of the cart and began to sing their sorrowful chant. It was a sweet but ominous sound meant to help summon the Veiled One's minions and declare their readiness.

Through the crowd came a man dressed from head to toe in a white gold robe and a deep blue veil, holding a clay mask above his head. He stood before Kalla, saying the ancient mystical words of transformation, before he handed it to Kalla. She slowly walked to Wesley and gently placed it on his face, kissing his forehead, tears still streaming. She returned to Talith and took her hand. The head priest in white produced a ceremonial torch, which he lit and handed to Kalla and Talith. Together, they took hold of it and walked to the cart, setting it alight at each of the four corners, then returning.

The flames burned slowly at first, then, as if oil had been sprayed, the flames roared and leaped into the sky, sending a shower of sparks cascading into the air. The ladies fell to their knees, crying and sobbing in grief. Behind them, witnessing the fantastic display of flame and smoke, the onlookers murmured.

"The Veiled One, did you see? He took Wesley."

"The gods took him. He's on the path."

"The Veiled One, he's here. Look."

Then, no one moved. No one spoke. The crackling of the white-hot wood reverberated throughout the forest. Shadows danced as the flames flickered. Somewhere deep in the woods, the breeze echoed the whispering cry of the ancients.

It took some time for the fire to die down, and as it did, people passed the flames to add their tokens to help Wesley depart, then went home.

Lord Galgun gave his condolences to the bereft family and made his exit with his guards in tow.

They remained next to the pyre until there were no flames, then quietly left for home as well. Once home, Coelric escorted them to the back room and helped them to sleep. He went into the kitchen where Trellin sat waiting, no words spoken, just knowing glances. Coelric went to the small storeroom attached to the kitchen and emerged with a butt of mead, which he proceeded to tap. He dusted two flagons hanging from the wall, then filled them to the brim and set them in front of his father.

As he took his place next to him, Trellin stood and raised his tankard with his son and both toasted. "Wesley Fielder, may the Veiled One light your path to peace." They bumped their tankards and gulped down every drop of mead, then sat.

They were silent for a long time, each staring into the fire, neither wanting to disturb the silence. Without a word, Trellin stood, leaned over his son's head and kissed him, then hugged his neck and departed quietly so he didn't wake the ladies.

The days passed solemnly. Talith was quietly sad for those days. Coelric did his best to keep a smile on his lady's face, but it turned out to be an arduous task. She missed her father dearly, and it showed. She became increasingly worried about her mother living alone, though. There had been reports of bandit attacks, uncommon as they were, but it didn't allay her fears any less. Lord Galgun's guard detachment, strong as they were, held the ruffians at bay, though they could not stop them all.

A week after her father died, Talith had just finished feeding their cow at the back of the house when she noticed a bright orange glow coming from the direction of Kalla's home.

"Gods, no!" she yelled as she went inside to tell Coelric. She pulled him outside only to see that the glow had grown brighter and the smoke, thicker and darker.

"Go. Go," Talith said, shoving her husband into action.

Grabbing a handful of mane and jumping onto his horse's back, Coelric kicked hard, causing it to rear and bolt toward Kalla's house. As he neared, he saw the raging flames leaping into the sky and seeing Kalla standing well clear of the fire, which brought great relief to him.

He pulled up beside her, leaped from the saddle, and swept her into his arms.

"By the Mother, are you all right?" He was out of breath from the hard ride.

"Yes, yes. I'm fine," she said as the fire continued to engulf the refuge.

"Thanks be to the gods. Talith is beside herself with worry." He stepped back from her and gazed at the fire, which was in full rage.

"How?" he asked as another beam collapsed into the raging inferno.

"I was…cooking when I heard a noise outside. I went ta check, an' two men were trying ta get into th' house." She blinked to keep the ash from getting to her eyes. "When I yelled at 'em, they turned on me an' I knew I were in trouble, so I gone back in an' tried to bar th' door. One of 'em tried ta kick it open, but then it stopped." Coelric frowned as she continued. "Next I knew, there was a sound an' then it went quiet, 'cept for th' fire." She looked back at the house and pointed. "I come out an' wasn't no one there. I don't know what happened after that. I was jus' here lookin' at my house burnin' an' then you come along."

She wrapped her arms around his. "Thank ya', lad. Ain't nothin' ya can do, but I'm glad yer here." He patted her hand and surveyed the area quickly.

After a while, a few townsfolk arrived with buckets, but it was far too late for that. Her house had been completely engulfed, turned to smoldering ash with only a few timbers left standing.

"Well, looks like you'll be staying with us, I think." Coelric looked at Kalla with a smile. "Talith'll be happy. She's been worried sick about you ever since Wesley died." He turned and guided Kalla to his horse. "Did you lose everything?"

"All but what's in the shed," she replied, looking back at the remnants.

"I'll get Father, and we'll cart it all over in the morning," he said.

"Thank ya, son. It's all barrels an' crates. Not too much." He took her by the waist and hoisted Kalla to the horse's back.

They both looked back at what was left and began the walk back home.

When they arrived, Talith came running from the house and grabbed her mother in a huge hug as Coelric sat her down.

"Oh, Mother, I was so worried," she said, stepping back and looking Kalla over to ensure she was all right.

"What happened?" she asked gently, slipping an arm around her and guiding her inside.

Coelric heard Kalla recounting the story to Talith, and the door close behind them. He patted the horse's neck, chuckled and told the horse, "Thus ends the saga of the gallant hero." He shook his head and led the beast into its stable.

The next day, Trellin and Coelric went to the burned wreck that was once Kalla's house. The sun had just peeked over the treetops, but the cool breeze couldn't whisk away the odor of burnt wood and metal. The shed was old and rickety, barely passing for a shed at all, but they managed to load the crates and barrels into the cart without much trouble, then they looked around to see if there was anything else to salvage. They found nothing of note, but as Coelric checked the back of the shed to be sure he hadn't missed anything, he noticed what looked like drag marks and called his father over for a second look. Two distinct sets led from the shed's door, around the side, and into the nearby forest. From what Trellin could tell, being a former soldier, there seemed to have been quite a struggle. As they followed the marks, they saw two separate splatters of thick, dark blood. It looked like it started as a spray but ended in dark black pools that had seeped deep into the soil. The men looked at each other, both puzzled and concerned.

Carefully, they had only taken a few steps into the woods when they stopped, shocked to see two men, tied to separate trees, dried blood coating their bodies and...

Both men's hearts began to pound uncontrollably as fear and panic set in. They stared in disbelief at the things that used to be men, faces contorted into screams of silent agony and eyes wide as if they saw the nether regions themselves. It was surreal. But their bodies...

They ran back to the cart, not wanting to look back. Trellin took hold of the reins, shook them hard, and the horses bolted. As quickly as they could, they retreated, never to return again, their hair standing on end.

Just as they got to the house, Trellin tried to speak.

"Don't..." He never finished as Coelric cut him off sharply.

"Never. Trust me, never," his eyes still staring ahead in fear.

Without uttering another word, the two men began unloading the cart into the lodge.

Kalla opened the door and stood in the doorway watching the men hard at work.

"Thank ya, boys. I thank ya."

They turned to her, faces white as sheets, then went back to work. Kalla, as if knowing, gave a silent smirk and quietly went back inside. Neither one spoke a word of what they'd seen to anyone that night or any other night. What happened this day was so surreal that neither wanted to know if it was real or a dream.

Several days had passed, and Kalla insisted on moving into the lodge even though Talith tried to be adamant otherwise. Being a man of some experience, Coelric now decided it was best and safer to let the women come to terms on their own. It ended in Kalla's favor, of course, much to Talith's chagrin and ire. Even in defeat, Talith ensured her mother had enough blankets, wood and candles to be comfortable.

Things began to settle down both for the Soryns and the town. Coelric finally got his tannery up and running. Kalla began helping Talith prepare for their new child, and life in the town shut down, being well prepared for another cold winter. Even though travelers were sparse, a rumor of the lord's health began to circulate, yet no one knew exactly what ailed him, but all were sure it wasn't good.

On odd days, while working in his shop, Coelric would notice Kalla returning to her lodge with a sack over her shoulder or a small crate in her hands. He had always figured she was collecting remnants from her old home and never gave it a second thought. He felt for her, though. Her life had been a difficult one, to be sure, but through it all, she still managed to keep in good spirits, even with the loss of Wesley and her home.

He loved her, too. To him, she was like his mother, who had passed so long ago. She would chide him when he needed it, doted on him at times and occasionally thanked him for being such a good husband to her daughter. She had become very special, even more than she knew. Every day, Kalla would lay a hand on Talith's stomach and tell her what she could. Like a mystic, she just knew. Several months before Talith gave birth, Kalla revealed that it would be twins and suggested girls. The two were overjoyed by the news.

One day, she brought a friend over, a midwife named Elma, who confirmed the news. Talith beamed with joy and laughed when Coelric shed a tear of his own. He wasted no time crafting a new cradle to match the other and outfitted the room just as Talith wished.

The days passed in quiet expectation, each one measured by the hammering and scraping of Coelric's tools and Kalla's watchful hand upon Talith's belly. All of the ladies had grown much closer since Elma joined them, and, Coelric would never admit it, but the meals had tasted much better as well.

Occasionally, neighbors would visit to see how Talith progressed, saying that she would easily miss the Long Night Moon and not to worry because, with the events past, the gods were done toying with the hamlet and peace would soon return.

Talith had been apprehensive knowing that the day of the Long Moon had finally arrived. Kalla and Elma assured her that all was well and progressing normally, which seemed to make her feel better. That night, they ate a light meal, after which Kalla, according to tradition, placed a plate of food outside the front door. It was an offering to the spirits, the belief being that they would take the food and leave the family unharmed. They all sat about the hearth fire, talking quietly about the babies and what Talith might name them.

Kalla had suggested Aleen, as her mother had been named, and Karil, her great-grandmother's. Coelric selected Tara and Una. He didn't know anyone by those names but liked the sound as he said them. Elma liked Aleen and Una but deferred to Talith, saying it was up to none other than the mother to choose. Then they all fantasized about who and what they might grow to be.

"I hope they just grow to have a better life than I had...up until I met the love of my life," she said, beaming at Coelric, who blushed and looked down. "What is your hope, Coelric?" Kalla asked, seemingly interested.

"I don't know really. I suppose they can be who they really wish to be. All I want is for them to be happy and of good health—no more, no less."

The night finally closed in, and they all went off to sleep. Outside, the night was very dark as the Long Night Moon ominously began to rise, black as pitch yet surrounded by a thin silver string of light. Coelric checked the shutters and ensured the door was barred before coming to bed. He crawled into bed next to Talith and let her lie on his arm. They both heaved a contented sigh and began to wander off into sleep.

The moon had reached its zenith, the silvery darkness glowing ominously over the land. No one witnessed the things that silently walked, the shadows that crept in search of unlucky wanderers, taking them quietly, never to be found. The homes that followed tradition were left alone, the food on the steps being taken instead of animals or people. As for the others, their tales were only told when the sun rose, for good or ill. Talith lay curled in her husband's arms when a restlessness she could not name stirred in her chest, like hands caressing her heart. It brought a sense of ease and calm she had never felt before. It was comforting and concerning all at once.

Then came the pains in her belly. At first, every so often, but then occurring more frequently and more painfully. She began to double over. Coelric, now becoming alarmed, ran to get Elma and Kalla, who grabbed pouches and sacks and made for Talith. They rushed in, saw what was happening and hurriedly ushered Coelric from the room. This was no place for a man, especially tonight.

"Is it time?" he asked, half excited, half scared.

"We'll get ya when it's time. Do not enter, no matter what ya hear," Kalla demanded. "Ensure th' doors an' windows stay shut tight. An' don't open 'em fer nothin', no matter what ya hear."

Coelric knew better than to cross her when she spoke like that. She might be old, but she was never one to be trifled with, a lesson Wesley had taught him long ago.

In the bedroom, where Talith lay in dreadful pain, Elma began lighting ritual candles and oil flasks of alabaster and ebony. Kalla opened the pouch she had brought and removed various powders and vials of unknown liquids.

Another searing pain. "No, it's not time." Talith was scared, more than she'd ever been. "Not tonight, please, Mother. Not tonight."

"Hush, girl. Whether ya want it ta be or not, the Mother has decided." Kalla stayed near Talith's head while Elma took her station.

There was no wind that night, no stars, no light save for the trembling candle at the bedpost. The air was thick with bitter incense, smoke curling like fingers around the rafters, meant to ward off unseen eyes. Talith labored in silence but for her ragged breathing. Elma muttered charms as she worked, words half-swallowed in the smoke; veiled, silent, hidden, the tongue she spoke in was too strange for Talith to grasp through the pain that racked her midriff. Kalla hovered near, her hand steady on her daughter's brow, her other scattering dark powder into the brazier, echoing the same strange words. Each spark hissed as though some vast presence pressed close, listening. Outside, the things that walked the night now gathered outside the window of the room, listening, learning, waiting.

Elma kept demanding Talith push, but her strength was waning quickly. The sweat streamed down her face and from her body. Kalla's calm voice helped soothe her. She drizzled a dark powder on her daughter's forehead, easing the pain. She glanced at Kalla, who, smiling, nodded her head, and she pushed hard once again. More things gathered: shadows, addlesprites…wolfweres, all silent as the grave, as if waiting for the revelation of the birth.

Then it happened. Talith screamed once, blinding pain coursing through her body, then fell silent, not from the easing pain but awe. Elma and Kalla smiled as the shadows that danced on the walls quickly vanished as if afraid. Both daughters came together, one head-first, the other feet-first, as if pushing into the world from opposite ends of a rift.

And both at the exact same time.

Neither the elder.

Neither the younger.

It was at that time the things in the night left the manor, each knowing that something special, something powerful, had happened this night. Each knew that a return would earn them their own journey down the path.

And the night was afraid.

Elma, who was a mature yet not elderly woman with moss in her braid and river-stone eyes, staggered back, her muttering breaking into a whisper: "Twins born in balance…one to see, one to feel."

They were pale as moonlight: eyes like gleaming forged steel, hair as white as frost, no blood, no noise, just breath.

Elma gave no blessing, only this warning:

"This is not a birth. This is an arrival. One child walks with a shadow in her heart, the other with silence in her bones. The smart one will always feel too much. The quiet one will always feel too little. Do not speak of this night—not ever. For if the world ever learns what stepped into it this night…all that breathes will curse the light and drown in its own fear."

Kalla squeezed Talith's trembling hand. Her eyes, dark and knowing, held a truth her daughter could not yet bear. Smoke still drifted through the room, clinging like shadow, and in the flicker of the two red flames of candlelight, it seemed as though something unseen leaned close, watching.…

"There she is." Kalla's smile was warm and reassuring. "You're a mother now, my sweet daughter." She leaned over and gently kissed Talith's forehead.

She tried to sit up, and the ache and pain of birth made her wince.

"Here, let us help." Down pillows were stacked behind Talith so she could sit up to hold her babies.

"Are they alright? Are they…whole?" She was getting nervous.

Elma assured her that both girls were as the Mother intended: healthy, whole and beautiful.

Talith breathed a sigh of relief. "May I see them?"

"We must first…" Kalla sighed, looking at Elma.

"You must. It is the only way." Elma glanced at the girls and smiled. "They must know."

Talith was confused. "Must know what? What are you talking about?"

"It is time. I must pass on what I know, Talith," her mother started. "It is the way of our folk. Our lore and our rites are older than time, passed down by generations. And now it is your turn…to know."

The pain in Talith's belly was forgotten as Kalla's words began to unravel their past.

"We are Valyn, my daughter, the ancient folk of the Whispering Wood and beyond, those who are charged as myth, lore, evil."

Talith was stunned, disbelieving, her mind still swirling from giving birth.

Elma continued. "You think the tales a myth, as do all other folk. They are not. It is real, and it is us. We folk of the woods have existed since before the arrival of humans and will be here long after they depart." Kalla searched Talith's eyes, where she saw wonder, disbelief and confusion.

Kalla continued for Elma. "I, my daughter, am called Kal'La. I am also Valyn. We knew of the coming long before you were born. It was written." She placed her hand on Talith's. "We know you doubt. We know you have questions. It will come to you in due time, then you will see—we promise."

Kalla continued. "The time has now come for the naming, as the time is short. It is yours and yours alone to choose."

"But Coelric, what about Coelric?"

"He must never know. If he hears the words, he will be lost for all time. It, too, has been written." Talith's eyes went wide. "But fear not. He is safe and unharmed." Kalla drew closer and leaned her head sideways. "We have ensured he never hears the words."

Talith's face began to contort with worry and anger. "What have you done, Mother?" she said through gritting teeth. Upon speaking her last word, time stopped. Smoke stood suspended, not moving, the flicker of the candle completely motionless.

Her eyes widened as a voice in her head softly whispered, *Have no fear, little one. He is safe.*

Talith blinked, and everything moved once more.

Kalla and Elma both smiled widely and nodded. "We know Talith. We heard her, too."

Talith didn't know whether to be afraid, consoled or confused. Her head swam. So much to take in. So much to understand.

She felt warm lips on her forehead as Coelric kissed her. "I'm here," he said with a smile. "They are beautiful, so beautiful." Tears began to stream down his cheeks.

The words Kalla and Elma spoke were gone from her head as if they were nothing more than a dream. All she knew was that her husband and newborn children were here, and they were safe.

"You must leave now, Coelric, just for a few moments. We have…woman needs to attend to," Elma said, pointing to the door.

Coelric, nodding his assent, kissed Talith's forehead once more and walked from the room with a smile and a glow about him. He paused at the doorway, peering back one last time. He never wanted to forget this day…or this moment.

"Come now, my daughter," Kalla looked to Elma, who said, "A name, girl, from your heart."

Talith felt that strange restlessness in her chest again. She closed her eyes tightly as visions formed behind them. Shadows swirled and billowed, coalescing into a word. The feeling welled up, and a name came forth.

"Chandra…Dashow"

She didn't know why. She didn't know how. She only knew it was…right.

Elma began to chant, flourishing a silky, black dust.

"Chandra Dashow Soryn." She closed her eyes tightly.

"Born headfirst, mind first, the knowledgeable one, the listener of things no one else hears." Her gaze wandered to empty corners. Her hands moved with unerring purpose.

Elma whispered, "She will know what others fear to know, and she will never fear the darkness."

The two exchanged smiles. They knew.

"And the second, my daughter, what is the second name?" Kalla asked, kissing Talith on her left cheek.

Again, Talith felt the restlessness. This time, there was pain, slight, true, but pain, nonetheless. Behind closed eyes, once again, came the vision of blood, like drips falling into a basin of water and distilling into a void.

She whimpered as a single tear rolled gently down her cheek. "Lyssa Socha."

Elma again began to chant, this time flourishing a silky red dust.

"Lyssa Socha Soryn." She closed her eyes tightly again. This time, she winced in pain.

"Born feet-first, a walker, not a watcher, but her silence speaks louder than words. She befriends shadow. She would be moon-bound, wood-tied, always listening, always waiting.

The midwife laid a cold hand on Lyssa's chest and murmured, "This one will speak with the forest. And when she walks, even the shadows will tremble."

Kalla and Elma shared a glance. Now, there was fear in their eyes and, yes…they also knew.

Kalla moved slowly to the first cradle. With a pinch of black dust, she sprinkled a line across the wooden rim. The powder hissed, then shimmered as though the wood itself were breathing. Slowly, letters formed, black and swirling, "Dashow" etched in glowing pale purple light.

For a heartbeat, the shapes trembled, sliding like fish beneath dark water. They bent, shifted, almost becoming another word.

Talith blinked, and it was gone; only the cradle remained, the name fading like smoke.

Then she turned to the second cradle. She drew out a pinch of red dust and let it fall across the rim. The wood shuddered as the powder struck, flaring briefly like embers. Letters seared themselves into the grain. "Socha," glowed with a dull, bloody light.

This time, the shapes did not drift gently. They writhed, twisting sharply, threatening to splinter into something else. A sharp scent, like hot blood on steel, filled the air. Kalla and Elma exchanged a glance, fear darkening their eyes. The letters burned brighter for an instant, then vanished as though they were swallowed whole. Kalla sighed and turned to Elma.

"It is done."

The shadows outside whispered to the forest. The forest whispered to the breeze. The breeze whispered to the moon.

They had arrived.

Nothing would be the same...

...ever again.

'...and the tables turn.'

Talk of the town:

"Two babes born at dawn? That be good luck, it is. Prettiest pair o' girls ye e'er seen, that's fer sure. Aye, an' them little ones come right with th' sunrise."

–Madam Cheryworth to Madam Garven

"Well now, I hears from Thom's cousin's wife that Lord Reginald's fixin' ta send some o' his tally-keepers down here...though don't ask me why. News travels crooked, y'know."

–Madam Garven to Lord Reginald's Purse Warden unknowingly.

64

"Wesley's gone...hard ta believe."

"Aye. Town won't be th' same without him."

"Good men like Wesley don't come 'round too of 'en. I'll sure miss th' man, I will."

–Local fielders

"Oho! I see two little sparks yet unborn, dancin' about like mischief lookin' for trouble. One'll steal hearts, the other'll steal sleep! And somewhere down the line...someone's goat's gonna go missin'. Aye, clear as crystal that is!"

–Gypsy seer to Madam Garven

"I needs me another ale...."

–the town's sot

Of Growth and Understanding

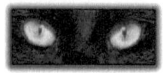

Talith took to motherhood as a cat to her kittens, doting on the children every minute of every day. Coelric's chest remained puffed out like the proud father he'd become. They'd been sternly warned by both Kalla and Elma to never speak of the day of their birth; otherwise, they would put the girls in dire harm, to which they agreed. As far as the town would be concerned, the two beautiful girls were born on the morning after the Long Night Moon, just as the first rays of morning topped the trees.

Two days later, Trellin and even Lord Reginald passed by to see the new additions. They congratulated the young couple on their blessings, thanking the gods that they were born after the omen moon and noting their unique hair and eyes.

Life had become beautiful, though tiring, for young Talith. Motherhood suited her well, and she reveled in the chaos of it. Her lifelong dream had finally come to fruition, and she felt as if she were the luckiest woman in all the realm.

Coelric, busier than ever at the tannery, now drew work from every hamlet and city beyond. His craft was sought after, and soon he'd hired help for cobbling and "scrapping," as he called it, reins, straps, flaps, and the like. Those small requests stole time from his true work, armor and clothing, but the coin was good, and they were never in want.

Yet, for all their fortune, they remained humble. Talith often thought it a king's sum, given the poverty she'd once known, but she could never bring herself to flaunt it. Even the thought of such finery made her feel guilty.

In the years after Wesley's passing, Talith's sisters scattered like seeds. The eldest, Mira, now nearly grown, was soon joined from

Lord Galgun's hall, where she had faithfully served in the kitchens. He was a fine young man who had taken over his father's smithy in the middle part of the city, making Kalla a very proud mother.

The next, Wendi, followed her path not long after, joined while still fresh-faced and eager. Her new husband was a strong man, much like Trellin, who'd been a footman in the king's army but had also been injured in battle. He was heir to his father's stead in Harrowing, two counties past Tantyn. Talith would miss them both greatly, but was so proud of the new lives they'd live.

Only the youngest, Ahsha, remained at Lord Galgun's household. At a very young age, her skill with numbers and keen eye for order carried her above both broom and bucket; she became the steward's aide, learning the household from its ledgers upward. Whenever Lord Reginald visited, he would brag about how smart and efficient she was and how he would groom her to be his purse warden. She would also be assisting the steward with some of his usual household duties.

Kalla began to keep mainly to her home in back, and they began to see less of her as the girls got older. On odd days and some nights, Talith would see her return with a sack full of things, though she knew not what they were, and on one particular day, she became curious and asked her about it. Kalla produced several wild onions, leeks and even yams, which Talith never knew grew in this region. Her concern for her mother's loneliness also began to weigh on her. She seemed increasingly withdrawn, almost hermit-like.

The babies had become toddlers and were roaming all over the house by now, crawling under this, trying to climb on that. It helped that Grandmother Kalla became their new playmate, as it took some of the burden from her daughter. Talith would hear her mother cackling happily as the girls did something new or funny, and the love she'd shown those children warmed her heart, yet she only wished her father were here to see it.

"Your father knows, love. He knows. I'm sure he sees everything and is so very proud of you and the girls," she would say. Kalla missed Wesley as well. She could stare out the window, and when Talith asked if she were speaking to Da again, she would sadly nod and smile.

Once again, spring turned to summer, and summer turned to fall. Barns and larders filled to overflowing, and stock was sheltered to prepare for another winter. As was the yearly tradition, the four hamlets gathered for the Harvest Moon festival with more people than ever attending. As usual, the colorful banners, streamers and flags adorned the buildings, fences and halls. Minstrels, drummers and pipers played and sang wonderful songs of the harvest and of the gods.

There was more food than the eye could see or the stomach could hold, and all types of ales, meads and wines by the barrel full.

Even though it was a grand celebration, everyone saw but never mentioned just how gaunt the good Lord Galgun looked. He smiled and drank as usual but sat in his high seat until he could no longer. To everyone's surprise, this year would be the first and only time he did not give an oration or blessing at the end of the festival, making most residents concerned for his health. In the following months, his decline became visible to all. The healers called it *the Withering*, a wasting of the body that no poultice or potion could cure. All the local priests did their best to save him but, in the end, comfort was all they could provide.

Sadly, just before the first snow, Lord Reginald of House Galgun, Warden of Tantyn and the Whispering Wood, Steward of the Four Hamlets, Keeper of the High Seat, passed into history. He died quietly, surrounded by his family and the few who had served him longest. It was believed by the townsfolk that it was the will of the gods that he had given so much for his people's happiness; there wasn't enough left for himself.

Long beloved and respected by his subjects as the most generous and caring lord in a century, his passing was felt by lords, barons and kings the land over.

Unfortunately, his fame was such that the king insisted he be interred in the city catacombs with other revered lords, depriving the folk of Tantyn their attendance to the "official" funeral rites. However, the priests of the various deities devised a ceremony and erected a permanent monument to honor the land's most beloved lord. As was the tradition, the four hamlets celebrated four days and nights to honor their hero. It had also been attended by many visitors from the city, from other outlying counties and associated territories. It was joyous to see lords celebrating with barons and ladies celebrating with the common farmers as if there were no caste, no titles, and no rank.

On the eve of the fourth day, an official royal carriage arrived at Tantyn Manor. The king's messenger was received by the steward, who then returned to the city just as fast as he arrived. As is usual in most small communities, the word of his arrival spread like wildfire, piquing everyone's interest. Bright and early the next morning, Lord Reginald's personal messengers traversed the entirety of Tantyn, posting bills announcing the upcoming declaration from the king. All were welcomed to attend the official reading at Hearth Hall the next midday, and nearly everyone from the four hamlets turned out. There was great apprehension among the masses as rumors spread that the next lord would be officially appointed, bringing worry to almost everyone. Too many times, this meant a foreign or unfamiliar lord could be selected, bringing drastic changes that could be enforced in any number of ways.

Fear began to grip the throngs of people in attendance, each murmuring, whispering and gossiping. The sound of concerned conversation was so loud that one had to almost yell to be understood.

Inside the hall, Sir Trellin entered at the top of the dais in complete battle regalia. His full harness, replete with gleaming sword, ax and polished mail, immediately silenced the room. He was a magnificent sight to behold. Coelric's chest puffed with pride at the mere sight of his father standing regally at the forefront. He never before realized just how much of an imposing figure he was and how his enemies must have trembled at his approach.

Next, four priests followed and took their places spaced evenly on the lower steps.

Robed in white and green, a wreath of wheat and alder branch adorning his head, the high priest stepped to the lectern, clearing his throat to speak. He unrolled a parchment, its seal broken with care, and quickly read the wording, his voice carrying over the gathered crowd:

"In accordance, and by the appointment and grace of our liege and king, and in accordance with the laws set down by the ancients, hear now the last words and binding order of Lord Reginald of House Galgun, Warden of Tantyn and the Whispering Wood, Steward of the Hamlets, Keeper of the High Seat. Being bereft of wife and heir, yet mindful of the good people of Tantyn and Whispering Wood, he names Sir Trellin of the House Soryn, son of Sir Alwyn Soryn, savior of his life and faithful companion, as Lord and protector of these lands. With the blessing of his liege and in the sight of our goddess, Hearthmae, so it is sealed, so it shall stand."

There was an audible gasp as the villagers bowed their heads. Some wept, others whispered, but most applauded while Sir Trellin himself stood stiff and pale, as though the weight of the words pressed upon his very shoulders. He never wanted this. He had expressed it so to Lord Galgun on numerous occasions, yet here he was, the lord protector of this territory. No longer Trellin Soryn, lord's stablemaster, no longer Sir Trellin, Lord Galgun's second, he was now…Lord Trellin of House Soryn, Warden of Tantyn and the

Whispering Wood, Steward of the Hamlets, Keeper of the High Seat…from this day until the Veiled One claims him.

It had been several years since Lord Trellin's appointment. In that time, the hamlets had settled into a steady rhythm under his rule, the people growing to love and respect him as they did Lord Reginald. His name was often spoken in the same breath as their late lord's, which Lord Trellin found reassuring. He strove to emulate his predecessor, visiting the townsfolk, listening to their troubles, and mediating their quarrels. He took a genuine interest in the families under his charge and worked tirelessly to see the land and its people grow prosperous, year after year.

Life in the Soryn home was no less busy. Lyssa and Chandra had grown spirited and rambunctious, quick to laugh, quicker to cry and always finding new ways to test both their mother's patience and their grandmother's tolerance. They toppled baskets, scattered tools and wore out every pair of shoes Coelric could cobble.

On one occasion, while Talith was in the backyard hanging clothing to dry, Lyssa had managed to open the chicken coop and began to chase them, giggling and laughing while also scattering them across the yard. It took the better part of the morning for their parents to herd them back while Lyssa and Chandra laughed and tried to scatter them again. One chicken would go into the coop and, as Talith left to retrieve another, Lyssa would release it and chase it around the yard again. The young parents would try to be angry but would always end up laughing and playing like little children themselves. Yet, with every scrape and tumble came more stories, more laughter and a bond between the girls that only deepened as they grew. They soon became inseparable. If one went into their room, both did. If one got in trouble, both did. The young parents thought it uncanny, especially for children as young as they.

Their birth celebrations had always been full of joy, family and festivities. Friends would arrive with sweets and pies. There would be fun little games, and the meals would fall nothing short of fantastic. Kalla and Talith would make the girls' favorite stew, a dish called "Gimme gimme." Whenever it was made, the girls would yell "Gimme gimme" and eat every drop, so, from that day forward, the name had just stuck.

Father would always have his cobbler create new shoes for them. Chandra, who had begun to show signs of being a "lady," loved to wear more dainty, lady-like shoes. She would prance and show them off as if she were a lady of the court. Lyssa, on the other hand, liked more practical, lightweight, supple deerskin boots. She was more the boisterous little rogue, always getting into mischief and creating pranks. She loved to sneak up on her sister and parents and startle them, all the while whispering "Gotcha" and running away laughing.

On one particular night, after their seventh birth celebration, the girls lay in bed recounting the joyous events of the day, giggling and laughing at all the funny things that they'd done. The door opened, and Father stepped in, the firelight at his back. The twins thought he looked like a giant shadow standing there, and already being in a giddy mood, began to laugh at how funny it was.

"Alright now, ladies, it's late and time to sleep." He stepped in and gave each a kiss. "I hope you both had a wonderful day."

Excited, they began to speak at the same time, making Coelric laugh. "I'm glad. It does my heart good to know you're so happy." He kissed them both, telling them how amazed he was at how big they'd gotten and, looking back with raised eyebrows, said, "Sleep, ladies." He began to close the door. "I love you."

"Look." Lyssa pointed toward the ceiling.

"What? I don't see anything," Chandra said, squinting.

"There it is again," Lyssa said, still pointing, but this time in a different spot.

In the moonlight that beamed through the window, Chandra saw what looked like shadows, lightly dancing across the ceiling. "It's just shadows from the hearth fire, silly," she said, as the shadows stopped. "Go to sleep." Lyssa looked for a second more to see if they would begin again. They didn't, so she rolled over to sleep. "I guess you're right." As she began to slip into a deep sleep, she thought, *"But there is no firelight."*

'...and this leads to...'

Talk of the town:

"Hard losin' Lord Galgun...but Trellin's takin' th' mantle now, gods guide th' lad."

–Guards chatter

"I tells ye, them lil Soryn imps. Cute as a button... but lil devilkins they be."

–Madam Cheryworth

"Gods my sister looks happy. It's about damned time too."

"Ahsha! That ain't no way fer a lady ta be talkin'"

–Ahsha Soryn, berated by the House Matron

"Pyre burned somethin' hot at th' Mournin' Moon festival this time. Means the fields'll sleep warm, my gran always said."

–An old farmer

"Seems them Soryn sisters done scattered ta th' four winds this year. Fine girls, them. Sure made a good life fer themselves, considerin' where they come from."

–Madam Garvin

Of Secrets and Blood

That year, the hoarfrost came early, coating the land in a soft white veil. The Harvest Moon festival had come and gone, its highlight, Lord Trellin's speech, a heartfelt remembrance of Lord Reginald, gone these five seasons, and his wish for the Mother's blessing on all. With that, the four hamlets readied for the coming cold, praying the gods would once again be kind. Chandra and Lyssa began the habit of visiting Kalla in her lodge when time permitted. Every visit was different and new. It seemed as if their grandmother was always concocting one vial of this or one salve made of that, sometimes cackling like a witch from the tales she told and chasing them about the room.

Kalla, on numerous occasions, directed them on the processes of how to create various things such as sweet drinks, basic dyes and even special tannins for their father.

One evening, they were shown how to make a minty potion meant to soothe stomach ailments. Chandra listened intently and tried very hard to get the measurements just right, but had a habit of tripping over the distilling and mixing process. It ended up tasting abysmal and almost made the poor girl retch.

Lyssa, on the other hand, barely heard a word her grandmother spoke. She deciphered the ingredients and the amounts, just spilling them together as if she'd been practicing alchemy her entire life. The creation was perfect. So much so that Kalla admitted that she would have been hard-pressed to copy it. Lyssa even told her to correct the amount of spearmint extract because the way it was taught would actually cause a stomachache from the amount of acid. Nonplussed at her failure, Chandra would stomp off, much to Lyssa's delight and teasing.

Some days, when Lyssa helped her father in the tannery, Coelric would tell Lyssa how his father taught him to hunt when they had the time. She would listen intently, asking questions and begging him to show her as well.

It was becoming obvious that the girl had absolutely no passion to be a lady, no matter how hard Talith or Kalla tried. They would scold, cajole and try to force the young girl to conform, but Lyssa was as stubborn as her father. She would stamp her foot with arms crossed or intentionally brush past the hearth just close enough to get ash scrubbed into the cloth. One time, while being taught to eat soup properly, she intentionally sneezed into her bowl, covering Chandra with hot gravy. Seeing Lyssa's impish grin, Chandra flung her soup back, and the fight was on. Lyssa, of course, ended up on top of her, scratching and pulling hair. That fiasco earned them extra chores for a fortnight, but even though they disagreed and fought, they would always end up laughing and playing as if nothing had ever happened.

Finally, they had given up and ushered her to Coelric to see what some fatherly guidance could do for her. She knew the art of tanning and cobbling, but ever since he told her the stories of him hunting, her insistence became an obsession that he could no longer ignore. He had fashioned her a sturdy bow, which at first was too large and stiff for her to even draw. He began showing her how to aim, breath and sneak. She took to training like an egret to water, growing deceptively stronger as one boy in town found out after teasing her. For good or ill, it earned her the nickname of "little rogue." Feisty, strong and agile, she proudly wore it like a mantle.

Seeing Lyssa and her father in town, women would scold Coelric, "You should be ashamed, raisin' a young lass like that. And in breeches, no less. Shameful." He would shake his head and say, "Yes, Mum. I can't agree more with ya, but what's a man ta do?" Then he'd wink at Lyssa as they walked away laughing.

That winter, while being taught the finer points of hunting, Lyssa spotted a doe at the edge of the tree line and some distance off. She signaled Coelric to stop. He could tell, with a smile, that she wanted this one for herself and crept forward. She crept closer. Her father was amazed at just how quiet and careful his little rogue had become, the way she used the shadows, the way she avoided crackling leaves and twigs. She had gotten almost a stone's throw away, surely in range of her bow. She stepped into position.... The doe's head shot up, staring right at the little rogue, ears twitching, then fled like it had seen a wolf. She stomped her foot in anger and frustration.

From the corner of her eye, she saw a sudden movement, causing her to look quickly in that direction. Nothing. She would have sworn that something moved. Her father frowned, puzzled. "What happened?" Lyssa lowered her bow. She had made no sound; she was well downwind and had kept to the shadows. They both looked around, perplexed, discussing it at length, but could find no reason, even after she searched the glade for tracks.

Chandra had been setting places for the night's meal when Lyssa passed by, still at odds with the incident. Quietly and with a slight smirk, Chandra teased, "And you were so close, too."

Lyssa stopped, confused. *How did she know?* Another annoying moment for the "little rogue" to wrestle with. She knew, or thought she knew, that her sister had something to do with it. She didn't know how, but she knew she had to get even with her.

The next morning, after they had washed their faces and finished their morning meal, Talith asked Chandra if she would be a good lass and bring in a few pieces of kindling for the fire. She went into the bedroom to pull on her heavy shawl and headed for the back door.

"Have you seen Lyssa, Mother?" She knew her sister all too well. She'd tweaked her nose twice and had a feeling retribution was coming.

"Out with Father tanning a new set of hides, dear. Run along now."

Satisfied, she opened the door and left for the wood pile, which was on the other side of Kalla's lodge.

Reaching down, she selected three good pieces then turned for the house…and came face-to-face with Lyssa, scaring the wits out of her and causing her to fall to the ground. Lyssa, who had an impish grin on her face, began to laugh and point at her sister, who was still sitting bum-deep in the snow.

Chandra fumed as she stood and picked up the wood, eyes squinted in anger. With a huge grin, her sister leaned closer, now nose to nose, and whispered, "Gotcha." She quickly kissed the tip of Chandra's nose and sped away laughing.

Chandra blinked her eyes and bent to pick up the rest of the wood. She never heard her sister walk up; she'd seen no tracks and that kiss on her nose…that was the retribution. She wiped the kiss from her nose angrily, sighed and went back into the house. *I deserved that.*

She stomped the snow from her now-wet shoes, clumsily pushed open the creaky back door and stepped into the warm kitchen. She barely registered the faint scraping sound before Lyssa's voice came from directly behind her ear, "Gotcha."

Chandra flinched, dropping the wood, this time on her toes. She yelped, turned around and started to get angry just in time to see Lyssa throw her arms up in mock victory.

"You've become too easy to scare, my dear, sweet sister." She leaned forward, kissed her nose again, whispered "I gotcha" and ran into the room laughing as before.

"One day, little sister," Chandra warned, "the shadows will tell on you."

Lyssa yelled back, laughing and rolling on the bed, "But not today, Chandy dear!"

Winter was a time of tales and recollections for the Soryn family. With not much else to do, the girls would either play in the snow out back or sit with Kalla and hear stories of their mother or wild tales of the woodland creatures, of addlesprites and the dances they danced to attract people into the woods where they'd be lost for days, of will o' wisps and their sorrowful temptations, though Lyssa never really understood those. Having read all about magical creatures and such, Chandra would sometimes correct Kalla, who would shake a finger at her in warning, "A book don't know nothin', but I do, little girl. Ya be watchin', or I'll send one after ya, I will."

They were playing outside after one such tale. Chandra played the part of the addlesprite because "she knows all about them," and Lyssa played the sneaky hunter. Chandra would hide and tempt Lyssa just inside the woods, making sure to only make the sounds she thought they'd make. She didn't realize the snow tracks she made were always a giveaway for Lyssa, who was already beginning to understand the ways of the hunter. Chandra saw her sister getting closer, so she ran deeper into the woods, still playing the tempting addlesprite. Quietly sneaking along, Lyssa saw her, and they began to chase each other through the snowy bushes and around trees, the hunter determined to capture her quarry. When Lyssa finally brought her sister down after the chase, they realized they'd gone too deep into the woods.

"We're lost, sister. Mother will be furious," Chandra said, looking for a familiar path.

"No, Chandy dear. I'm the hunter," she said heroically. "I can find our way out. It's simple, follow our tracks," Lyssa said, grinning.

They both started looking for their tracks in the snow, but they'd wrestled and rolled around so much that none were readily visible. Their search grew wider with no better luck, and Chandra, who was never pleased with being in the woods to begin with, started getting more scared and clinging on to her sister.

"We are going to get in big trouble, Lys," her eyes still fixed on the ground, searching.

"Ah, I found some tracks." She pointed, "I told you. I'm the hunter, little sister," she said proudly, but Chandra wasn't so sure.

"These aren't our tracks. They're far too large.... Look." She put her foot into the print, proving she was right. "Someone else is out here, Lys." Fear showed on her face now. The game was no longer fun, and they both realized they had to find their way out—quickly.

The sun was going down now, and it was growing darker, adding to their fear. Lyssa took a deep breath, trying to calm herself.

"Father said if you feel like you're lost, look to the sky. The sun falls away from the woods at night." She looked up and tried to find the sun, but it had been blocked out by the trees; her sense of direction had been completely thrown off. They now held on to each other tightly, the fear gathering quickly.

Then, up ahead, a light blue glow appeared from behind a large tree a short way in front of them. They looked at each other, still in the grips of fear.

"What is that, sister?" Lyssa asked, eyes wide.

"I-I don't know." Chandra tried to remember anything from her books about mystical creatures, but nothing came to mind.

"You don't know? You bury your nose in all those books, and now you don't know?" Lyssa was beside herself.

"Hold on." Chandra closed her eyes and thought hard. *Blue glow. Blue glow.* She looked closer and saw the glow was actually from a creature of some kind. It floated from tree to tree, on tiny wings, dimming then shining again. She concentrated, Lyssa, holding her arm tighter.

Then it came to her. "It's a sprite. Yes, that's it, a sprite." She grinned from ear to ear.

Lyssa looked at the glowing creature as it moved. "Will it hurt us?"

"I don't know," she said cautiously. "There are supposed to be many types. It's very hard to tell the difference."

The sprite began to move away from them.

"I think we should follow it," Chandra said.

"What about the other tracks, sister?" She pointed down. "There's still someone here. What if they find us?"

Chandra looked down, then at the sprite. "We should decide quickly. The sprite is almost gone."

"Dammit, let's follow," Lyssa said. Chandra covered her mouth. "Ooh, Lyssa, what you said. Mother would make you chew soap."

"I won't say anything if you don't." The attempt at levity went unnoticed as they both ran after the now fast-moving sprite.

Around trees and snow-covered bushes, the tiny creature went. They did their best to keep up but found that it was outpacing them quickly. They were in a full sprint now and suddenly…the glow disappeared.

As they came to where they'd last seen the tiny creature, Chandra tripped over a fallen branch, sending them both head over heels and onto the ground. They both stood, shaking clumps of snow from their faces and out of their tunics.

"Where have you two been?" Talith asked them. "I've been looking all over for you. It's time to eat." She turned and went into the house.

The sisters looked at each other, at the house and then back again. They hugged each other and laughed so hard they fell back to the ground, not caring how cold or snow-covered they got. "Come in *now*, girls," their mother demanded.

That night, while the girls slept, the man who was leaning against a nearby tree kept an eye on the house until the last light was blown out. The glowing creature that sat on his shoulder stood and flitted back into the woods as he turned with a smile and followed, happy that he could help.

Several times, during that winter and into spring, Lyssa would visit Kalla, mostly by herself, as Chandra had given up on helping her mix and brew concoctions. She had concluded, "It is mindless and absurd, and I gain nothing from it," which reaped her grandmother's ire.

In the meantime, Lyssa's knowledge and interest made her grow very proficient in the art of transmutation, much to Kalla's surprise and joy. She had begun teaching Lyssa how to work with some very advanced potions and compounds, to which Lyssa seemed to grasp with extreme efficiency. When the reagents ran low, they would go into the woods searching for the right ingredients, teaching Lyssa what to look for and what to be careful of.

One night, supper had been cleaned from the table, and everyone had settled down. Kalla excused herself for the evening and asked Talith if she could borrow Lyssa's help for a while. Talith glanced with a hesitant, wary nod, begrudgingly giving her permission. Talith trusted her mother, but, to her mind, had been spending a little too much time with her by keeping her out after dark and keeping her from doing her chores. They quietly walked out to her lodge, and as they entered, Lyssa asked, "What do you need me to do, Gran?"

She turned with a serious look on her face and said, "Lyssa, my dear. I been instructin' ya these past fortnights or so, in th' art an' practice of alchemy."

Lyssa nodded slowly.

"My dear, ya've learned some o' th' most complex and vexing potions known in th' alchemical world. Some're so complex that I had to look over lots o' scrolls an' tomes just ta understand 'em myself. Yet, ya create 'em with a practiced hand, as if ya'd been a grand chymist all yer life. For someone of eleven seasons, yer truly uncommonly gifted."

Her granddaughter smiled. "It's fun, Gran. You make it easy to learn." She walked over and hugged Kalla. "You know how much I

81

like helping you and Da. I always learn so much, and I'm finally better at something than Chandra." She kissed her grandmother's cheek.

"Sit down now, dear." She motioned to a nearby chair.

A scowl crossed Kalla's face as she began to pace.

"What is it, Gran? What did I say?"

She took a few more steps, stopped, glanced at Lyssa, and began pacing again. Lyssa knew not to interrupt Kalla when she paced. She knew Kalla was pacing because something vexed her, and she was deep in thought.

Kalla mumbled to herself, "Young, she be too young, but she knows; aye, she does. Do I dare?"

She stopped in front of Lyssa, her face becoming more serious than Lyssa had ever seen before. Kalla had come to a decision, and she prayed to Alythra, the Crucible, that her choice was correct.

"I'm about to say something very sacred an' ancient. Somethin' that's been passed from countless generations afore. Ya MUST promise ta forever hold this sacred knowledge both in yer heart an' in yer mind an' speak it to none other—NONE other."

Lyssa's mouth immediately went dry as she stared blankly at her gran. What was she doing? What was she asking? WHY was she asking this?

Kalla went silent, staring coldly into Lyssa's eyes, into her mind, into her very spirit.

Lyssa's thoughts were racing. *She's never lied to you. She's never done harm to you. She TRUSTS you!*

She looked into Kalla's eyes and saw purpose, sincerity.

She drew a small knife from her sleeve, black steel, sharp and menacing, and held it out. Without hesitation, she drew the edge across her palm, holding up the bleeding hand for Lyssa to see.

Lyssa met her gaze, then looked at the dagger. Gently, nervously, she took it from her gran's outstretched hand. She opened her own palm and placed the blade's edge against her skin. Trusting her completely, she dragged it across, wincing as blood welled and ran down her wrist.

When she pressed her hand against Kalla's, the pain seemed to fade, replaced by a strange warmth that spread up her arm. Their blood mingled, and with it, something unseen stirred.

"To the gods, I swear it."

She continued to stare intensely at Lyssa but nodded for Lyssa to repeat.

"To the gods, I swear it."

She felt a tingle in her palm.

"To the ancients, I swear it."

Lyssa now returned the stare. She began to see in Kalla's eyes darkness and shadow.

"To the ancients, I swear it."

Kalla's eyes began to glow with an ominous dark emptiness.

"And to the Valyn, my people, I swear it."

A disturbing smile began to form on Kalla's face.

Lyssa almost froze as the visage of a lady became barely discernable.

"We are now one." The lady's mouth moved, but there was only silence.

"And to the Valyn, my people, I swear it."

Their hands separated and, as Lyssa looked down, there was no cut, no blood, no pain.

Kalla's smile broadened. "From this moment on, we ain't gran and granddaughter, Lyssa. We are now sisters, you an' I." She leaned closer and kissed Lyssa on both cheeks.

"What I'm about ta pass on ta ya be th' knowledge of our past, our ancient people, my dear. You an' the Valyn are th' only folk what know o' these mixtures an' how to properly concoct 'em."

She walked to the hearth, then bent and wiggled a loose stone slab, removing it. Underneath was a small square metal chest bound in thick, worn leather. There were three black leather straps secured with brass brads and large brass buckles. She pulled it out and set it on the table. Fumbling with the buckles, she lifted the lid. A ghostly mist billowed from it, engulfing her hands as she reached in and removed a large, heavy tome covered in oilskin. Laying it on the table, she motioned for Lyssa to come to her.

"Open th' tome, Lyssa, an' learn th' wonders within."

She hesitated for just a second, glanced questioningly at her gran, reached over and cautiously opened the tome. As she began to look at the cryptic runes, magical words and symbols, she felt her eyes tingle, almost burn. She began to feel drawn to the tome, into it, and knew she couldn't stop looking. Her mind felt compelled to read every word, to feel them, and she began to turn page after page. Her finger lightly dragged over each page as she read, almost feeling the words, hearing them speak to her in a soft whisper. More, she had to know more. Faster, she turned page after page.

Her eyes remained staring at each page, absorbing every tiny detail, every glyph and rune, searching for their meaning, searching for the one truth. Images began to form, dancing in her mind like tiny entities, each moving in its own unique way. Kalla's image appeared, dancing silently. It stopped, looking at her with a reassuring nod. She faded into darkness, and another appeared. This time, it was her mother; she was dancing an unnatural dance, her arms flailing and her head swinging left and right. Talith's image soon faded into the semblance of an old woman she had never seen before. Gnarled and bent, it finally faded…into a withered and shriveled corpse. Its eyes opened, glowing in an eerie blue. Then it spoke.

This, you know. This, you own. This, you must now live. Everything faded to black.

The tome appeared, floating in thin air amid a swirling gray mist. In her mind, she reached for it, but just then, two glowing red eyes blinked, and the book opened wide. The page edges glowed as if smoldering, its smoke drifting away darkly as if taken by a gentle breeze. The unfamiliar words had been written in aged, cracked blood. The pages themselves were crumbling, as if time had desiccated the ancient parchment. Then, a surreal and ominous glow surrounded the open pages to reveal the final destination. The truth held for so long, for so many generations, each word searing painfully into her young mind.

Everything suddenly went black. She began blinking her eyes quickly, trying to return to the present. Her head began to swirl and her knees, to buckle. Her stomach turned as if she were going to vomit. Gran pulled a chair close and sat Lyssa down carefully.

She looked at Kalla, still trying to regain her senses.

"W-what happened?"

"Dear, sweet girl," she hugged Lyssa's head, "you now have th' knowledge of Zhul'xora Theryxis—the Sleep of the Ancients." She pulled back and sat in front of her. "Tis a poison so deadly, so caustic that once applied, survival's impossible. I dare say it might even slay a god." She glanced up at the ceiling as if the gods themselves were listening. "It be th' most difficult potion ta make an' even harder ta make right."

"But why me, Gran?" She was scared now.

"No, no, no, don't be afraid, Lys." She grabbed her hands gently. "Ya musta truly been touched by th' gods, my dear. What ya've absorbed in one season took years an' years fer me ta learn."

Lyssa stared in disbelief.

"But." She took a breath. "But why would I ever want to use a...poison? Why would I dare even THINK of killing someone?"

"That I don't know, child." She looked at the floor and thought for a second. "Perhaps them gods 'ave a special task for ye. Perhaps yer meant fer somethin' greater. None can say." She looked up and sighed. "Our people handed down this tome from every generation past. There're very few who been chose, very few indeed, but ya been chose as one of 'em. None may know th' reason why. None may know th' purpose it serves, only that yer th' one."

Lyssa thought. "You said, *your people*, Gran. What people?"

She brushed the question off. "Not important yet, dear. You'll come ta know when th' time's right."

Glancing out the window, she noticed the moon had risen and knew Talith would question why she'd kept her daughter so late.

"If yer mother asks, tell her ya been helpin' me sort reagents. She knows how tedious that be an' won't question it no more. Now, run along. It's been a long day, an' I weary."

As expected, Talith asked, and Lyssa repeated Kalla's explanation, which she understood and did not pursue.

That night, as Lyssa lay half asleep, she thought about the face she'd seen, the words that she'd seen spoken and what the message could mean. *"This, you know. This, you own. This, you now must live."*

She fell asleep with the words floating in her mind. That night, she slept a long, peaceful sleep.

'...I'm impressed.'

The next day, the sun rose and began to slowly melt the snow. Birds started singing their beautiful songs, and Lyssa stepped outside to breath in the crisp, chilly air. She loved winter and spring, but mostly winter. It was the end and the beginning, and it always made her feel alive.

Kalla was out by the edge of the forest, filling her small basket with wild berries.

"Mornin', dear. Sleep well?"

"I did, Gran. I did. Better than I've slept in weeks."

She smiled. "Good, good. I got berries for ya if ya want ta come inside." She showed them to Lyssa, who nodded, and they went into the shed.

Once inside, Gran began to wash the berries off and place them into a bowl for her.

"Gran?" Lyssa began.

"I know, dear. So many questions need answerin'. I know." She turned to Lyssa and passed the berries to her. "Only way to answer 'em is ta find out fer yourself an' just do it."

Lyssa listened with rapt attention now. "Should I start today?"

"Depends, dear. First, we gotta see if we 'ave th' reagents. What's yer first lesson?"

"Gather yer reagents. Make sure ya gets em all, or ye'll fail first time off fer sure."

Kalla whipped around and glared at Lyssa, who had begun to laugh. "So, ya do remember." She grinned, and they both had a good laugh. Lyssa was directed to search for the reagents needed, so off she went, searching all of Gran's herbs and powders. She searched drawers, chests and jars. After a long search, she managed to gather all but one.

"Gran, do you have any Crimson Lake water?"

"No, dear. At'll be one you'll need to fetch yerself." She rummaged through a small case nearby and produced a medium-sized vial, which she handed to Lyssa. "Ere ya go. Fill this ta the' brim an' 'ave a care. It's fragile."

Lyssa placed it into a leather satchel she slung over her shoulder and started out for Crimson Lake. "Don't be long, Lyssa Socha. The sundown tonight be ripe for th' mist. Ya know what 'appens then—chaos." She said, wagging a finger at Lyssa.

She sighed, "Yes, Gran. I know. Th' mists meet an' wolfweres, goblins an' addlesprites come out ta sew mischief an' chaos among mortals," she said sarcastically. "I'll be back afore that." She leaned over, kissed Kalla and started out.

As she walked along the forest's edge, she glanced at the sky and calculated how long it would take. "Hah, chaos. I AM chaos," she said, laughing. She decided she actually did have plenty of time to return but picked up her pace, just in case. No sense in tempting the gods.

It was just after midday when she arrived at the lake. There was still snow on the ground, though a lot had melted off already. She knew the tales about it, but for some reason, this didn't look anything like they said. The water was a serene blue-green color and as still as glass. The sun reflected off the water like a bright candle flame, almost blinding her. Here and there, egrets poked the water for small fish, and cattails with their sword-like reeds stood proudly on the water's surface. *Sure is early for these birds. They usually don't appear until mid-spring.*

She sat on a nearby stump to rest her feet and watched as two squirrels chased each other near the lake's edge. She sat near the outskirts of the northern Whispering Woods, and, being so remote, no one ever came there purely due to the legend. She looked around and, seeing no one, made her way to the shaded and more secluded part of the lake where she began to undress. The biting cold raised goosebumps all over yet invigorated her, but she didn't mind. It would be a long walk back, and feeling the cold would make the return nicer.

She slowly tested the water with her toes and waded in up to her knees. *Odd, it's not cold... warm really.* She dove right in, the water enveloping her bare body like a mother's hug. She began to swim parallel to the bank, rolling onto her back, allowing the sun to caress her face and body. Her gaze remained fixed on her clothes; losing them now would be exceedingly difficult to explain...to anyone.

After quickly washing, she stepped out to dry off in the sun before heading back. Locating a patch of early blooming meadowsweet nearby, she pulled some leaves from it, rubbed them together, allowing the sweet, almond-honey scent to permeate the air. She began to rub the oils all over, breathing in the intoxicating smell. It was the only real "lady-like" scent she would ever allow on her body. She chuckled. *If Chandra only knew what I was doing, she'd tease the life out of me.*

She lay bare in the sun, letting the warmth and breeze dry her while watching dragonflies slowly meander by. She loved the different smells of the woods; wet leaves, damp bark and the sweet smell of the breeze floating through the trees. They always made her feel soothed and alive, almost as if she belonged.

Soon, the sun and breeze dried her enough for her to put her clothes back on, but as she was slipping on her breeches, the realization hit. *Damn, the sun's down. I waited too long...* The water began changing color from its normal blue-green...to crimson red...and the mist began to rise. Goosebumps of fear rose on her neck and arms, and she knew she'd lingered far too long. She quickly finished slipping her boots on and looked around for her satchel. It was nowhere to be found. *It was right here. I laid it right here.* She began to search in earnest.

The mist began to slowly rise, and now, worry and concern took hold. She'd always thought the tales had been told just to scare children into minding their parents, but now she was learning the truth. This was no tale.

She spotted her satchel near the stump she'd sat on earlier. *By Velkhar's arse, how did it get there? I didn't put it there.*

Fear began welling up; she made a dash to the stump, clumsily slung the bag over her shoulder and started to run toward home. *Dammit, the water, I forgot the water.* She looked toward home, then at the lake, trying to decide what to do. She'd come here for water, but now she could die if she stayed any longer.

She chose the water over her safety and, turning, ran as fast as her legs would carry her, opening the jar as she went. Falling to her knees and sliding, she pushed the jar into the lake, making sure not to get any mud, stopping it and returned it to the satchel. Quickly, standing and turning for home, she ran into something that had been standing behind her unnoticed. She fell hard onto the ground, knocking the wind from her lungs. Her heart was beating madly now, realizing the danger she was in.

Dazed, she looked up to what looked like a man, but dripping wet. Scrambling to her feet, she realized this man was decaying. Big chunks of flesh were missing from his legs and face, forcing her to an even higher level of fear.

"Oh shite!" she yelled. The thing reached out a decaying arm, and as it did, two fingers fell off its hand as it shambled forward to her. She sidestepped it and made another attempt to head in the direction of home. Her first steps were fast, long strides, but the next were stopped short by hands that reached from the ground, and she tripped, falling face-first in the muck and slime.

Survival was now her only thought. The quickly falling sun was blazing a rich crimson off the water now, the mist now fully developed, and the tales she heard as a child were now coming to life.

Kicking out and severing one hand that still grasped onto her ankle, she got back to her feet, now unsteady in the ooze. She kicked out hard, flinging it back toward the water and bolted once again toward home, not wanting to look back.

The sun had now completed its journey below the horizon; darkness began to take over, and stars twinkled above like knowing eyes. The darkness and fear veiled the rock outcropping in front of her. She struck her shin, creating searing pain and causing her to fall to the ground once more. Two more decaying men pulled themselves from the mud, dripping slime and grass, one to her left, the other to her right. She scrambled to her feet, pain flaring, unsure which way to run. Behind her, the grasping hands of the rising dead, to her front, two more reached out, trying to grab her.

She desperately looked for an escape. Without warning, both corpses started to collapse; one's head and arm snapping off, the other dissolving into a mound of slime and goo. She didn't wait and bolted once again for home, but this time there were no more obstructions. She ran as far as her breath would let her, then slowed to catch her breath and run again, every few strides looking behind, making sure the dead remained there. Within a short while, she was home again, safe and bending over, gasping for air.

"Seen any wolfweres, goblin's or addlesprites, lass?" Gran was leaning against the door frame of her shed, a great grin etched on her face. "Methinks, she seen th' Crimson Lake in all its majestic glory, aye?"

"I…never knew… it was…true." She was still gasping for air. Her lungs felt as if they were on fire. Lyssa swallowed hard and stood upright. "I…thought…it was…just stories…to keep…children mindful."

Kalla chuckled.

"What were they?" She was still breathing hard. "They were…decayed, yet…they walked."

"Those be th' spirits o' th' fallen, lass. Long ago, th' lake was part of a vast bog where a battle took place. Over a hundred men died there, some by blade, some by jus' drownin'."

"When I was trying to run away, I fell, and two of them blocked me." She blinked hard, trying to remember. "For some reason, I can't figure out why, they just…fell apart." She shook her head in disbelief.

Kalla gave a wide grin, as if she already knew.

Lyssa wiped her face with the back of her sleeve. "Never again, Gran. Never again."

"Well, it be too late ta make th' potion this eve. Put th' water in th' lodge…. Ya did get th' water, didn't ya?" She asked with a raised eyebrow.

Lyssa pulled the jar out and showed her.

"Well, at least it wasn't a wasted trip."

'*…almost!*'

The next morning, Kalla went outside to gather wood for the hearth when she was met by her daughter.

91

"I see you're out early."

"Need to make something ta eat, get some stew goin' fer tonight."

With concern showing on her face, she demanded, "What are you doing with my daughter, Mother? Arriving home late last night, filthy as a chimney sweep, so tired she couldn't stand."

"Don't concern yerself, dear. Just teaching potions an' salves. We run outta crosswort, an she went lookin'. Fell in th' mud prob'ly."

Talith looked sternly at her mother. "Mother."

"Talith, I ain't tellin' no tales. We worked with them damn reagents all night. Come look if don't believe me."

The glare she gave her mother would have stopped a charging bull in its tracks, but she shook her head, kissed her mother's cheek and turned back to the house. "I'm heading to town. Do you need anything?"

"I got all I needs. Thank ya though."

Seeing her mother leaving for town, Lyssa ran outside to Kalla.

"Ahh, there she be." She chuckled. "Chased by the dead lately?" She laughed.

Lyssa gave a disgusted look and went in. She now had all the reagents to make the poison. She knew this would be the most difficult undertaking she'd ever attempted, and her nerves began to show.

"Do I have to make it now? Right now?" she asked nervously.

"No, dear. Ya can make it any time ya likes." She smiled. "But the longer ya wait, th' less ya remember. That might not do ya too good now, would it?"

Lyssa sighed, resigned to doing it now. True, she was afraid, but the exhilaration made her want to do it more.

"Go on then. Better get started. Nightfall'll be comin' an' ya needs as much time as ya can muster fer this one." She pointed across the shack. "There's th' extra room. Be sure ta cover any light an don't expect me ta come in at all. Delicate potion, this. Have a care, too. I don't wanna have ta explain to yer ma what killed ya."

Lyssa gave a nervous nod to her gran, gathered the ingredients, alembics and glyphs she had already prepared, went into the dark room and closed the door. Her trial by fire had begun. She just hoped she'd survive the task.

Her alchemy table was set as Kalla had shown her, with each item in its proper place according to need. Lighting a small black ceremonial candle Gran had given her, she started her work in silence; the copper crucible balanced between the alabaster tablets as instructed. She could read the words by the dim light that the candles gave off, but just barely.

She forced her movements to be slow and deliberate, and quelled as much fear and excitement as she could. First, the powdered lotus seed, adding it carefully, stirring very slowly. She kept her breathing slow and measured, watching the simmering liquid turn bright red. *Wait, red?* She looked at the fluid more closely. Red. She looked at where she'd gotten the lotus seed powder. It was the nightshade, and she realized she placed them in the wrong order. *Shite.* She'd ruined it already and had to begin again. *Dammit, dammit, dammit.*

She sighed and opened the door to retrieve more of the lotus powder. "Not too good, was it?" Kalla cackled. She turned to Lyssa and slapped her face...hard. Her eyes flew open in complete shock.

"Dammit, girl, what do ya think this is? Makin' mud cakes?" There was true ire in Gran's face and fire in her eyes. "Yer makin' th' deadliest poison in th' land. This ain't no game." She reached out, grasped Lyssa's shoulders and began to shake her. "Are ya tryin' ta kill us both?" She pointed a finger in Lyssa's face. "Calm, girl, pay attention. Be deliberate in everything ya do. When yer life's in th' balance, ya can't afford ta make no damn mistakes." She hugged Lyssa tightly, praying she'd gotten through to her. "Get back an' try again." It was the gods who willed this, not Kalla. She knew this had to be done...for their people.

Cheeks still burning from Gran's slap and partially in shock, Lyssa got more nightshade and returned to the crucible. She carefully cleaned it in the washtub, thoroughly drying it, then placed it back on the stand. Lyssa rubbed away the pain in her cheek, shook her head to clear the cobwebs and began once more. This time, she spat into the crucible like her gran taught her, which was supposed to keep the heat from searing what was in there.

First, she added the powdered lotus and guano carefully, making sure not to breath the dust. As it began to heat naturally, it hissed faintly as she stirred, each motion carefully done as instructed. Her breath was shallow; the room was sealed tight, as it must be.

Next came the nightshade powder, and it turned the mixture a mottled green color, becoming curdled in the process.

Next came the nightshade extract. Drip, drip, drip and with the fourth drip, the mixture began to thicken. She stopped and set the extract down, but slowly kept stirring. *Now for the scary part.* She took a sash from her pocket and tied it around her face very slowly to avoid disturbing the air around her. Even the slightest breath could ruin the entire thing, and who knew what would happen then.

The urticating hairs were next. Tying them very gently between her thumb and forefinger, she held them over the crucible, knowing she couldn't waver because one unsteady move and the entire batch would be ruined. She carefully took a deep breath and calmed herself, while dipping it in and brushing the requisite three times clockwise. She exhaled as she removed it. *Good, that's done.* She willed her hands to stop shaking.

Then…betrayal. A thin lance of light crept down from the rafters above, striking across the rim of the crucible. She froze. Any sudden movement, even the shifting of air, might unsettle the mixture. The draught did not forgive distraction.

Her pulse quickened, but her hands stayed steady. *No, no, no, no.* Like cold molasses, she gently moved to block it from advancing further. Only then did she allow her lungs to empty, a slow exhale barely audible. The crucible still simmered, unbroken. The work could continue.

She poured in the water to avoid rippling the surface and waited for it to begin hissing. Seconds passed. Nothing. Beginning to bead sweat, her nerves started to show. Still, nothing. She lowered her head in defeat. Then…hissing; quietly at first, then growing louder. She smiled, realizing success, and reached for the wooden images. She placed one atop the other and carefully lit them. The flames slowly gained in strength, and soon the mixture began to simmer in earnest.

She waited patiently, watching the wisps of steam rise toward the ceiling. The text never said how long it should simmer, just that it was to be black as pitch. She peered into the crucible, watching it turn color.

She placed the glass condensing coil over it and immediately saw the vapor begin to wind its way through it and toward the end of the tube. It started to collect as a clear liquid on the other side, so she placed a vial beneath as it slowly began to drip.

Lyssa stared at the fruits of her labor, praying that it was completed correctly.

Soon, the flames died under the crucible, and the steaming process stopped. Lyssa raised the condenser so the rest of the crystal clear, lethal toxin could drip into the vial. She heated sealing wax to make it pliable and stretched it over the top, then etched the sealing symbol into it.

Kalla had been sitting by the fire. She'd silently prayed to her gods for Lyssa's safety. She didn't outwardly show it, but her nerves had become frayed as well. There hadn't been a sound from behind the door since Lyssa went in, causing her mind to race to places she didn't want it to go. She was startled when the door opened, and Lyssa stood smiling at her. She gulped, grateful to the gods that they heard her.

"It's done, Gran. All that's left is to leave it undisturbed for one moon." She looked exhausted.

Kalla stood and went to her granddaughter. "Yer alive, child, an' that tells me ya done it right." She kissed the girl's forehead, then sat looking at the ceiling to thank Alythra.

"There be lessons in this life we needs ta learn: patience, fear, diligence." She leaned back and looked at her beautiful face. "Fer most it comes o'er time, fer you it come all at once an', if it didn't, ya wouldn't be here right now." She kissed her forehead again. "I'm proud o' ya, lass. Truly, I am." She rubbed the mark on Lyssa's cheek, apologizing with her eyes. Lyssa knew. It was a hard lesson, but she knew....and she learned.

Lyssa realized that night had come. After an entire day, she found herself completely spent, so she dragged herself to her room, too tired to even eat. Talith got up and followed her.

"Will you tell me what you've been doing all day?" She was both worried and angry.

"Mother, please, I'm so tired. I just need to sleep." She kicked off her boots and took off her clothes.

"And what is that smell?" She tried to wave it away. "Have you been standing in a wood fire? You smell like burnt yew."

"Mother, please." She slid onto the bed, welcoming the feel of the cool breeze coming from the open window.

"Don't 'Mother please' me, Lyssa Socha Soryn. You tell me where you've been."

Coelric appeared behind her, trying to find out what the commotion was. He gently touched her arms and brought her close to him. "Let her sleep, Talith. We can visit this in the morning."

She glanced back at him and relented. Another glare toward Lyssa, and she left. Lyssa rolled over and began to drift off to sleep.

"You've been busy, sister," Chandra said quietly. She'd been standing in a dark corner, watching the entire ordeal. She'd had a feeling that Lyssa had been into something with Gran, but didn't know what. All she knew was that her sister had never looked like this before, and it worried her—greatly.

"Not now, Chandy, please," she said, exhausted.

"Oh, don't worry, sister. I know you've been with Gran, and it's alright." She walked to Lyssa and placed a hand on her shoulder. "We're sisters, and you know I won't let anything happen to you." She leaned over and kissed her sister's head. "Sleep. I'm here with you."

Lyssa was asleep in seconds, a tiny grin of satisfaction on her lips.

'...huh, well played'

As the ancient formula instructed, the vial lay untouched in the dark room while Kalla watched her granddaughter with a careful eye, saying little of what had been done. It had been many days, and it seemed as if there were no harmful effects bothering the girl, which brought a sigh of relief from Kalla. Breathing dust, smoke and steam was a typical hazard and often took the lives of unskilled alchemists. When the night of the second moon reached its height, she rose from her chair and went into the dark room where Lyssa had brewed the lethal elixir. She took the sealed vial in both hands and crossed to the hearth, making sure not to disturb it too much and placed it under the loose slab at the edge of the stonework. The blackened vial disappeared into the hollow. Wrapped in oilcloth, the tome also disappeared beneath the hearthstone, laid beside the vial in silence. She pressed the stone back into place, brushed the ash smooth and sat once more by the fire as if nothing had stirred, its warmth the perfect guardian for secrets that must never see the light.

Routine had once again come for the family. Lyssa began spending more time with her father in his shop. She'd gotten good with her blade and could now scrape the hide supple without damaging the under layer, and even began teaching herself to throw it accurately. Her father had set up a target against a tree far enough away so a deflection wouldn't hurt anyone nearby. It took long hours and many days until she became proficient enough to continually stick the blade and even longer to hit the center consistently. Coelric was fascinated by her dedication to the craft. Repeatedly. Blade after blade. She trained herself, almost obsessed. When she was asked why she did it, she shrugged and simply said she didn't know. It was just fun.

For some time now, Coelric had felt he'd been neglecting Chandra, spending so much time with his "little rogue." Occasionally, a scholar or archivist would stop by, offering to barter their work for an old tome or book. At first, Coelric declined, until Chandra heard of the offer he'd turned down.

She became adamant that he accept such deals. She'd pout, complain of her boredom, and flash those soulful eyes, which only made Lyssa want to vomit. The sisters nearly came to blows more than once over Chandra's shameless fawning, which Chandra, of course, took as a compliment and used to tease her even more.

Before long, more learned folk began to visit in need of his craft, and Coelric started asking if any had spare books to trade. He knew such tomes were rare and costly, found mostly in great libraries, but he did what he could to keep his daughter happy and reading.

When he presented them to his daughter, she would squeal with joy, kiss him and run off to begin reading. He or Talith would usually end up having to pry her away from them just so she would eat or go to sleep. Her appetite for knowledge had become ravenous, which sometimes worried them both, but still, Talith loved to watch her little lady read. Not only was she quite the sight, but she'd also become highly intelligent in the process, even more so than both of her parents.

One day, to her amazement, Chandra learned that her mother had never been taught to read. Talith explained that, in her youth, they had been far too poor for any sort of learning, and to own even one book would have been like holding a mountain of gold.

For weeks, Chandra patiently taught her mother her letters and numbers, and how to piece them together. Talith tried earnestly, but her daily chores left her little time to practice. In the end, she set it aside, smiling as she told her daughter she would be the smart one of the family.

Her father brought her tomes of history and magic research from some very prominent scholars in the city. She had scrolls and even runic notes from curators and archivists. Coelric never asked questions about where they'd come from; he was just elated that his daughter had them. Over the past few months, she'd accrued a small library of her own of which she was thoroughly proud. Several times, Lyssa would go into the room to talk with her sister, who immediately chased her out for disturbing her reading.

On one very special occasion, an archivist from Caer Bryndwyck passed by needing leather book bindings and scroll cases made. Chandra happened to be in the shop at the time and overheard their conversation, wanting to know what tomes and bindings they were for. The archivist, one Quentus Marrik Powl, Archivist First Order, assured Chandra that she couldn't possibly understand texts of that sort. She stared at him with arms crossed, tapping her foot, waiting for an actual answer, which bristled the archivist. Coelric looked at the man and shrugged, resigned. Quentus sighed deeply. "Oh, as you wish; it is the *Archivum Majora: The Complete and Collected Works of Early Chroniclers of the Valyn Age*, authored by The Venerable Othren Halvek: Keeper of the Codified Ages, of which I'm sure you've never seen, heard of, nor could possibly fathom the intelligence thereof." His smug face showed that he thought himself far superior in both knowledge and standing.

Chandra smiled slyly. "Of course, I know this work," she said. "It is a synopsis of the ancient line of the Valyn people collected and compiled by the Seven Chroniclers of the Great City of Mastramor, each one a separate, yet concise study of the many families and histories thereof. As I recall, it was the Venerable Farthen Maximal that began the Archiva, but due to an unforeseen…accident, shall we say, was unable to continue allowing the Venerable Othren Halvek to complete it in his stead. Though, if you ask me, he should have stayed an Archivist: Less Gray, due to the fact he neglected to add the History of Oak'Mara Treewind and Oli'Va Greenbow, who I think would have been far better additions. Don't you agree?"

Quentus' jaw dropped, staring at Chandra's recitation. He blinked his eyes and turned to Coelric. "Good sir, if you will, please construct these at your earliest convenience." He bowed to Coelric and then, with shock and awe ravaging his face, he bowed to Chandra, making his quick exit, never to return.

Coelric turned to Chandra. "Hearthmae be praised, my beautiful, sweet child. Where…? How…?" He was speechless.

Chandra giggled. "I read it in another book. A man named Gervin Smallbottom said it to a librarian in Ferth Morna, wherever that is. Gervin was a poor minstrel who wanted to make a pompous rich man feel small." She laughed. She asked her father, who was still speechless, "Father, what is pompous? Is that a bad word?"

Spring had come, the snow was now long gone, the planting had begun and more people began to visit Coelric's tannery than ever. People would bring buckets of urine to be used in the tanning process, and Coelric would pay them. The acids and alkalis helped remove the excess skin from the pelts, but Lyssa always hated that part of the process and never could understand how her father could soak his hands in it. They had a giant tub in his shop that she would have to pour each bucket into. The stench, at times, was horrible, but luckily, it was only for a short while.

Occasionally, Coelric would close the tannery early and take Lyssa into the forest to hunt small game. Her skills weren't sharp enough yet to bring down a deer, but she always came home with something for the pot. She'd become quite the little hunter, proud to provide supper for the family, which made her feel strong and important like her father.

One night, a forest wolf made its den in the woods near their home and began killing chickens and dragging them off. Kalla tried to help, but no poisons or deterrents worked. Lyssa and her father set traps and hunted for the beast, but they could never find its lair. It slipped past every effort, even breaking into the tannery and tearing at the hides, costing Coelric dearly. Frustration quickly set in.

Chandra tried to help, as well, but there was nothing in her books, nothing her clever little mind could conjure to help stop it.

One hazy night, after Lyssa had gone to sleep, Chandra took up an adz and stepped out the back door, waiting in the hopes of seeing the beast. The chickens weren't acting any differently, so she knew it hadn't come around yet. She looked to the woods to see if there might be a trail, but admitted that she didn't know much about the woods or how animals acted, not like Lyssa.

How can a wolf keep outsmarting people? she wondered, though deep down, she already knew the answer. "I need to find a way," she said aloud.

'...*As you command, mistress.*'

She froze, eyes darting back and forth, looking for the voice. The words entered her mind as if a cool spring breeze had spoken. "Who's there?" She took a step backward, holding the adze in both hands, ready to bolt back inside. She perked her ears to see if she could hear it again.

Nothing, just the sounds of the night. She looked toward the woods once more to see if it might have been Lyssa teasing her, but there was still nothing.

Just then, out of the corner of her eye, something moved in the shadows. She squinted. It didn't seem like something *in* the shadows.... It seemed as if it *was* the shadows. It moved again, and now, she was sure. Moving from shadow to shadow but being a shadow itself. She was confused, nervous and amazed at the revelation. What did she see? She strained to comprehend.

How was it possible for a shadow to move without someone or something casting it? She slowly turned and went inside to her books, starting to research this new phenomenon. Now awake, Lyssa sat on the bed watching her sister madly turning pages, opening tome after tome. "Something vexing you? You look as if you'd seen a ghost, sister dear."

Chandra kept her eyes on the pages and said, "I might have."

Now Lyssa was intrigued. "Really?"

Chandra looked up and said, "I saw a shadow move. No one there and no animal."

"Must have been the wind then."

"It wasn't wind, sister. There is no wind tonight."

She yanked a strand of hair from Chandra's head, "Then, you're addled." She rolled over laughing, but Chandra wasn't. Her eyes never left her books, and she was in no mood for teasing. Lyssa gave up on her teasing and pulled the blanket up over her shoulders.

"Get some sleep, Chandy dear," she said with a grin. "Maybe you're just tired."

Finding no helpful information, Chandra sighed. *Oh, she might be right*, she admitted to herself. Closing her books, she slipped beneath the blanket, still intrigued with her encounter. Through the window, the forest pressed close and dark. An owl called somewhere in the distance…once, then again…and she turned over, still chasing answers in her head until sleep finally claimed her.

Out at the edge of the woods, two small red eyes blinked in the dark.

Morning came early. Coelric was the first to rise, stirring the shop's fire back to life and setting out hides to soak. Lyssa followed soon after, rubbing sleep from her eyes and tugging the door open to let the pale light in. "Good morning, my little rogue." He glanced up, nodded toward the day's work, and said, "Do well today, and we'll hunt afterward." He went to the urine vat and stirred it, making a horrid smell.

"Father, come quickly!" she almost shrieked.

Coelric rushed to Lyssa, thinking she had hurt herself, but as he arrived, he noticed she was pointing at something. There, in front of the shop, stood the rogue forest wolf that had eluded them for so long. It was large and gray-brown, but it looked…odd, standing there, its eyes wide as if it had seen a ghoul and as stiff as a tree trunk. Its fur had become matted and clumped, and its skin had drawn in as if all the fluid in its body had been drained. Its mouth was open as if it was trying to…scream. It looked as if it might have been dead for an age, but that couldn't have been true, as it had caused mischief just the night past.

Chandra came out to see what all the excitement was. Upon seeing it, she just stood and stared with a puzzled look on her face.

'…it is done, mistress.'

She jumped and looked around. It was the same whispering she had heard before, but this time it sounded as if it were…in her head.

Who are you? she thought.

She waited for a reply, but the voice didn't return as she looked around again, trying to locate it. "Who are you?" Nothing, just like before. She couldn't tell if it was fear or sheer wonder that kept her thinking about the voice. "It is done…mistress." Why was it calling her mistress? So many questions yet no answers.

Coelric pushed the wolf over with his foot, and it toppled easily. He started to examine it to see if it had been arrow-shot or bitten, but there was nothing, stiff as if it had frozen in time. They were all confused and could find no reasonable explanation for it.

Coelric took a shovel from the wall in the rear of his shop. Dragging the stiffened corpse by the tail, he went to bury it in the woods to hide the smell. He tried to puzzle through it all day, but no reasonable explanation could be found.

That night, as she lay staring at the ceiling, Lyssa asked, "Chandra, did you do that?" She was sincere.

"I don't know."

"Did you make the shadow move that night?" She was genuinely curious.

"Sister, I just don't know."

Lyssa was becoming worried about her sister. Odd things were afoot, and Chandra was a part of it; she just knew, though she didn't know if she could help. Lyssa's sleep was troubled with worry, yet Chandra dreamed that night…of two tiny red eyes…that blinked.

In the morning, she remembered two things. The red, blinking eyes and the words.

'…*I'll always be there for you, mistress.*'

'…*ahhh, now I see.*'

Of Loves and Lives Lost

The signs were all there: the new lord, Wesley's passing, Talith's happiness and the children—those beautiful children. Kalla checked and rechecked, trying to ensure she didn't miss anything. Each time she ended up with the same answer.... All the signs were there. Her heart sank. All the years she spent there—friends, family, the tough times and the happy—it all led to this.

She went to the window and stared out at the green of the forest, watching the wind play with the leaves, seeing the clouds pass by, uncaring.

The girls were busy inside with Talith or Coelric. She had everything she ever wanted in life and yet…she was silently alone.

One last walk, I think. A forced smile crossed her lips.

She gathered her shawl and wrapped it tightly around her shoulders. *Heh, why bother? It won't help, not now.*

The door opened, and she stepped outside into the warming rays of the sun, the sweet, sweet smell of the air, the chorus of the singing birds. Kalla sighed with a sad, knowing smile.

She found herself at Crimson Lake, not knowing how she'd gotten here. Her feet moved, and she simply followed, smiling at that thought, *to the place where it all began.*

The mist hung low on the lake's face, its surface like polished glass. Kalla walked all along the shore, tiny minnows darting this way and that as she passed. Damselflies and water boatmen danced and played as if the world didn't exist except for right here, right now.

She remembered the lake as a girl; things were so much different then, before it turned and soured into a bog. Those were the bad days, when the things that bumped in the night were things to truly fear. She recalled how her brothers came to cleanse the bog of the terrors but never returned home.

Kalla looked around, wondering if they were still here. She hoped they went to a better place, not rotting in this mire.

She sighed. A dense copse of trees presented itself to her, and she wondered. Cattails, reeds, tall grass, it reminded her of her innocent days as a wide-eyed, young girl, laughing and jumping, splashing in the water, lying on the ground watching the clouds pass.

Now feeling impish at the thought, she glanced around and saw no one. She removed her worn shoes and waded into the water up to her ankles. The water was cool, and the lake bottom not as muddy as she remembered. She chuckled, stepped out and stripped off her clothes like she did as a child and walked into the water up to her neck. A tear came to her eye as she remembered swimming nude and playing alone, never worrying about being seen or what time of day it was.

She did her best to swim; her body wasn't like it was back then, but she managed all the same. She soaked her hair and reveled in the purity of just being here, not Kalla, not Gran or Mother. She felt like nature itself.

She just was.

Kalla stroked to the shore and walked to her worn clothes, still dripping, feeling the breeze blowing across her wet, aged skin. *I'll miss this. I truly will.*

She smiled again, donning her clothes and praying to the goddess that the girls could one day revel in their lives as she did.

But she knew that wasn't to be. Her time had come. The signs were there, the words were spoken, and Kalla knew she must heed them. One last time, she walked the edge of the tree line, stopping every now and again, watching squirrels play, a deer nibbling at the fresh green grass, picking a daisy to smell its natural perfume one last time. They would stare as if to say goodbye, knowing as well as she that all good things must end.

Kalla finally found herself at her stoop, where she sat and took it all in.

She sighed once more and went inside.

Kalla tried to sleep, but the night insisted the morning not come.

The morning finally defeated the night, and it began with the same routines as any other morning. Lyssa went outside to feed the chickens as always. Talith and Chandra cleaned the crockery, and Coelric could be heard scraping hides in his shop. Kalla called Lyssa to the lodge. She had been acting oddly for several days, showing Lyssa where everything was, as if she'd never been there before. She made especially sure to show her where the tome and the vial were hidden and where all her special alchemical recipes had been stored. Lyssa noticed how she was speaking; it was as if she knew she were going somewhere for a long time, which unsettled her greatly.

"Gran, are you alright?" Worry was evident in her big steel eyes.

"I'm fine, Lys. Why do ya ask?" She smiled sadly.

"It's just..." she didn't finish the thought. Instead, she ran to Kalla and hugged her tightly. She didn't know what was going on; she just had the feeling this was the last time she'd see her. Lyssa looked up into Kalla's eyes, and a tear fell.

"Hey, now, now. None o' that, little one." She brushed it away. "You grown up good, Lys, strong, smart." She smiled a nearly toothless grin. "Ya be smarter than me even." It was Lyssa's turn to smile. Don't be fearin' fer Gran. I'm fine. Now ya run along. I got things ta do." She kissed Lyssa's cheek.

Kalla hugged her and ushered her out, watching her beautiful granddaughter return to tending the chickens. She started for the tannery but overheard Talith and Coelric talking, so instead went into the children's room to see if Chandra was there.

As expected, her little sprite was nose-deep into another book that her father had traded for. "Ahh, there's me little lady," she said with a sorrowful smile. Chandra looked up at her and smiled broadly.

"Hello, Gran. Da got me a new book. See?" She held it up to her, glowing: *The Grand and Ever-Veiled Chronicle of the Elder Crafting of Shadow and Forbidden Articulations* by Grand Professor Calvorys Drosvain, Lord Archivist of the Umbral Conclave and Chronicler of the Shrouded Epochs (Hm.Fic. III)

Kalla had to read it three times just to understand the title alone. "Them scholars be quite proud o' their accomplishments now ain't they?" She let out a chuckle.

"It's really very interesting, Gran. It tells about shadow manipulation and some of the spells and what they do and…"

"Slow down, girl. You'll hurt yerself talkin' that fast." The excitement on Chandra's face made Kalla very proud. She was so smart, not unlike her mother, to be sure and maybe even smarter. Chandra returned to her text, barely noticing Kalla after that. She kissed Chandra's cheek and left, stopping at the door to look back one more time at that beautiful little face. Elma's words were true.… "She will know what others fear, too."

She sighed deeply and left, then went to see if Talith was still in the tannery. The door opened, and Coelric's face lit up into a smile.

"Well now, there she is." He stepped away from the hide he was scraping and gave Kalla a big hug.

"Now, stop that, ya impish knave. What ya be on about?"

"Nothing, Mother dear. It's just a fine, beautiful morning, and I'm glad to see you. Is there something wrong with that?"

She glared at him. "Yer up ta somethin' ain't ya?"

"No, just happy. I can't say why. I just am."

"It has ta be all the piss in here, makin' yer mind addled. Talith know 'bout this?"

He grabbed the old lady and planted a huge kiss on her cheek, then howled like he was mad.

"Oooh, ya crazed dotard, get away," she yelled as she ran from the building.

Talith came in from the tannery to start supper, making sure she had all the vegetables washed and near her chopping block. She began to glide her knife blade across a sharpening stone, preparing to cut and pare them for the evening meal.

Kalla went into the house muttering about her lunatic son. She stopped short, seeing Talith already there, pausing, her eyes sad. Her daughter slowly set down the knife and walked to her mother nervously. "What is it?"

"I told you there would come a day. You'd know when it was?" A tear dripped from her eyes.

Talith knew all too well. Kalla had told her about it just after her joining. "Are you sure? Does it have to be today? You know I don't want this. I don't want you to go." She started to tear up.

"Nor I, love. I wanted to stay until my last days, but it just isn't to be. Destiny awaits." She reached over and hugged her daughter tightly. "I've seen all of the signs. I've checked." She pulled back a bit. "You have to take good care of that man, now. He's the second-best man I've ever known, and I mean that, lass. I truly do."

"I will, I promise," she said, now crying.

"And those girls," she leaned back and took Talith's cheeks in both hands, "they're meant for something special, lass. Mark my words. I don't know what, but they are. Keep them safe." She kissed both of her daughters' cheeks. "And never forget that I will always love you."

"Please, not now." Her tears flowed freely now.

"It has to be. You know it. I know it." She tried to smile. "The Mother calls me."

It was at that time that Talith realized that her mother was speaking using normal words...as she said she would when the time came. This really was it.

Kalla turned and walked outside. Talith's eyes followed her mother out the door and into the backyard. She looked back at Talith, her tears freely streaming down her face and blew her daughter a kiss. She sighed, entered the woods and…was never seen or heard from again.

'…that takes care of that, and now…'

Supper passed quietly. There was no conversation, only the wooden sound of spoons against bowls. The drink tasted bland, as did the food, through no fault of Talith's. The occasional tear trickled down a face, a furrowed brow, a sigh from a broken heart. The girls cleaned the crockery at the wash tubs while Coelric and Talith sat next to the fire, staring sadly at the flames.

"Why did she go?" Coelric asked, puzzled. He hoped it wasn't due to his antics in the tannery. He'd done it before, and Kalla laughed.

"It was the signs, dear. You know how Kalla is. She can be like that." She didn't say why, even though she thought she should. A promise is a promise, and she knew it was for the better.

"It doesn't make sense. What signs?" He racked his brain trying to come up with a logical answer, but found none. "Did she say when she was coming back?"

She glanced up at him for just a second, a tear still falling. He knew, but he didn't want to believe it.

The girls came in, still wiping water from their pruned fingers. They stood between their ma and da, leaning against them. Coelric put his arm around Lyssa's waist and pulled her close. They knew the girls didn't quite understand what was happening, but waited until they asked the questions to avoid upsetting them more.

"I knew Gran was going away. She told me in the lodge—well, almost told me." Lyssa sighed.

Talith smiled. "Mother, why did she go? Will she be back?" Chandra was hurt. All she did was talk about the book she got, and now Gran was gone. She fought back the tears.

"She went to see… " she glanced at Coelric, "her family in the woods, dear. I don't know when she'll be back."

"Gran has another family?" Lyssa's eyes went wide in disbelief. "What family? WE'RE her family." She ran into her room crying, landing on her bed and covering her head to hide the tears.

Chandra stood, puzzled. "I don't understand, Mother. Gran doesn't have another family."

Talith smiled sadly. "It's a way of saying things, dear. Do you understand?"

She thought about it for a minute. "She…she's dead?"

"In a way, dear, yes." Quiet tears flowed down Talith's face. She could tell Chandra was puzzling out what Talith had told her. She could see that Chandra couldn't quite make sense of it.

"Those tales of the Valyn that people tell, are they true?" she finally asked, tears flowing as if she already knew the answer.

"No one really knows, dear. Some say they are, and some don't."

"Which *some* are you, Mother. Tell me, and I'll believe it."

She looked at Coelric, who looked back, eyes asking the same question.

"I think they're stories, my sweet girl. But it would be nice if they were true, now, wouldn't it?" Chandra looked at her questioningly.

"At least Gran would be with people instead of being on the Veiled One's path, right?"

Chandra nodded her head, but Talith could tell she didn't believe a word of it. She kissed her ma and da and went off to bed.

Coelric stood and hugged his wife.

"I didn't believe it either, love, but it was better than the truth." He kissed her again. "Not to worry. I won't ask." They went off to bed themselves.

The night was long. Both girls stared out the open window and held each other close.

"She's out there, isn't she, Chandy?"

"Mother says she is." She thought about it. "I hope so, sister. I truly hope so."

Spring passed, and summer came as any other season did. The long days were filled with ordinary labor; Lord Trellin seeing to the people of Tantyn, Coelric at the tannery working hard as always, the girls laughing in the fields and doing chores, and Talith keeping the house steady as always. For a summer season, life was quiet, even blessedly dull for a change, a welcomed respite from all the past tribulations. People would pass, buying produce from the various small stands along the road and gossiping about some unrest in the city. Apparently, it wasn't anything to worry about, but the occasional sight of city guards riding further afield than usual betrayed all of that. Still, during those early days of summer, the family carried on, unknowing how swift peace and serenity would be shattered.

The deer lowered its head, searching for succulent grass among the weeds. It didn't know she was there. It grazed in the low brush, ears twitching at flies, tail flicking lazily. Lyssa's heart thudded in her chest as she crept closer, her father's lessons echoing in her mind. *Quiet feet. Steady, breathe. Let the bow do the work.* If the shot were perfect, the meat would feed them for days.

Her fingers curled around the string, drawing it back, slowly. Quietly, she inhaled through her nose and held, slowing her heartbeat. Focus. Slowly, she breathed out through her mouth and released the string. It spoke a silent twang and sent the arrow whistling to its target.

Lyssa's arrow struck clean and true; the buck stumbled, kicked once, and went still among the leaves.

Her heart thumped hard in her chest as she stepped from the trees, bow still in hand, boots sinking into the soft mulch. Her very first deer. The smell of damp leaves and earth mingled in the cool air. She knelt, brushing her hand along the buck's coarse hide in quiet thanks, already thinking about the meat she would bring home. She could see her father's proud smile and feel her mother's hug for her triumph.

That's when the crunch of boots broke the stillness. A shadow moved between the trunks. Not a hunter, not anyone she recognized, a man in a guard's well-damaged half-armor stepped out, smirking, a patchy beard framing yellow teeth. The way he looked her over told her he wasn't there for the deer alone.

"Well now…look, boys, pretty little thing's got herself a prize," he said. "Shame it's mine now."

Lyssa stood, fingers tightening on her bowstring. "Last I checked, poaching wasn't in the city guard's duties."

Her voice dripped with sarcasm…a little too much.

His smirk soured. He stepped close enough for her to smell the ale on his breath, his anger boring holes in her. She stared at him defiantly. Before she could blink, his hand lashed out and cuffed her across the face, the sting blooming hot along her cheek.

She stumbled back, catching herself, refusing to give him the satisfaction of seeing her fall.

"That's for your mouth, ya little bitch," he growled, then bent to seize the buck by the antlers. His two comrades chuckled as she regained her footing, standing straight as one of her arrows, still defiant.

"Run along, girl. I'll be sure to tell th' cap'n you was trespassing." Still chuckling, they all turned and left the girl to stew in her anger and pain.

She didn't move…not until he slung the deer over his shoulder and walked from the glade.

One arrow, just one. She began to raise her bow, then remembered the other two guards. *Now isn't the time,* she decided.

She lowered her bow slowly, but inside, something sharp had already taken root. It was like a worm gnawing on her insides. She watched him walk away, memorizing the sway of his stride, the notch in his armor, the way his hair stuck out beneath his helm. She would remember every detail.

Rage built up in her body the more she dwelt on it. That wasn't just a theft. It was food for her family, food they needed, and it wasn't going to be tolerated. She sat for some time letting the cobwebs clear from her head. Grabbing her bow, she pushed herself to her feet and began looking for their trail—a bent limb here, crushed leaves there.

I'll be damned if you steal from me and my family, you churl, she thought with fire in her eyes. Slowly, she searched the ground; any sign would be a start. It was hard at first, but big men leave big prints, and soon she found them. A boot heel sank deeply into the loose soil, then another. She'd finally found the telltale signs she needed to right the wrong they had done to her and her family. Squinting with resolve, she set her jaw and eagerly began the search.

She'd been following their trail since dawn, keeping track of how many, how they moved, what they may have been doing. Two sets of boot prints, one heavier, dragging slightly on the left. She knew that gait, the same swaggering limp he'd had when he stole her deer and left her in the dirt. The trail had become too easy; a careless man leaves careless signs.

The sound of slurred and lazy laughter reached her. She came to a depression where a stream once flowed and slowly slid down the embankment toward the road, silent as the wind.

Through the brush and across the road, she saw him. Back to her, shoulders hunched, head tilted forward as he relieved himself, still chuckling at something his companion had said. The carcass had been dropped not two paces from him.

Her timing was perfect. His companions wandered ahead, too far to notice.

No bow this time. She wanted him to feel it. She wanted him to see her face as she got her retribution.

She slowly drew in breath. In two quick strides, she was behind him. One hand clamped over his mouth, the other flashing with steel. Her movement felt natural, fluid, as if she'd done this a thousand times. The laughter died in his throat, replaced by a wet gasp. A single, savage cut had turned his last breath into a strangled scream in her palm. She leaned closely, her voice low and steady in his ear. "Remember me, you bastard?" Then, like a whisper in the wind, she said, "I gotcha." One more slow, deliberate thrust to the heart, and he went still. She turned him to face her. With his last dying gasp, she saw the recognition in his eyes. It was the last thing he ever saw.

She stood over him, breathing hard, the world around her suddenly too quiet. She knew she must leave now, by the same path she had approached. It would make it harder for them to backtrack her if they even knew how. She knew the deer was far too heavy to drag without giving her trail away.

By the time his friends came back up the road, she was long gone, but his corpse lay sprawled with vacant eyes, a gaping wound at his midriff, and a message in blood they'd understood without a word.

Gotcha!

It didn't take her long to return home. She remembered what her father had taught and made sure to retrace her steps exactly. Lyssa pushed open the door to the house, the hinges creaking in the evening stillness. The smell of the hearth drifted toward her, warm and familiar.

Her father looked up. "No deer today?"

He smiled warmly at her while shoving another log onto the fire. His voice was calm, but there was a trace of curiosity there.

She didn't answer. Just shook her head once, eyes not quite meeting his.

He studied her for a moment, as if weighing whether to ask more, then simply nodded and went back to his work. He knew her mood when her hunt went badly. She'd become sullen and would sit by herself until the anger passed.

Lyssa trudged past him and down the narrow hall, each step heavier than the last. She pushed open her bedroom door, pulled off her boots and threw herself onto the bed, still reliving the incident from earlier.

Chandra was there, sitting cross-legged on the bed as well, playing absently with the edge of a threadbare blanket. She looked up when Lyssa entered. Her eyes narrowed, studying her sister's face, her posture, the tension in her hands.

"Something bad has happened," Chandra said softly, "hasn't it, sister?"

Lyssa stopped. She looked up, their eyes locking across the bed.

Chandra's mouth widened into a small, knowing grin.

"I know…what happened." She whispered, "The shadows told me."

Lyssa's breath caught. She didn't ask what that meant. She didn't have to anymore. Because deep down…she believed her.

Without a word, she crawled across the small space between them and leaned her head on Chandra's shoulder. She shifted, sliding an arm around her sister's back in a slow, protective embrace. Her voice was low, almost like a lullaby.

"I told you a long time ago," she murmured, "the shadows are your blanket. Why do you think you moved so…quietly? Why do you think he never heard or saw you?"

Lyssa didn't answer. She could still feel the moment at the roadside, the air still and cold around her, the bandit's shock at her arrival, and how, somehow, she had been invisible.

Chandra's fingers brushed her hair back. "Didn't you realize, sister? It was in that moment…the shadow covered you."

Lyssa's chest rose and fell, slow, heavy.

Chandra leaned her head against Lyssa's. "Dear sister, I would never let anything happen to you any more than you would let anything happen to me."

The words sank deep, past fear, past the rage and into the place where Lyssa's trust lived.

In that moment, Lyssa understood two unshakable truths: She could kill without thought or feeling, and her bond with Chandra would forever be unbreakable.

Whatever came next, they would face it…together.

The room was still, except for their quiet breathing. From the hall, a ripple in the air, a shift in temperature, the faintest stirring of wind. Lyssa felt it without knowing why. Their mother appeared in the doorway. Her face was calm, but her eyes…knowing. She had read the signs before she'd even stepped inside. She looked at her daughters huddling close together and let the moment breathe before speaking.

"Are you two all right?"

Two silent nods from two innocent faces.

Her gaze lingered a heartbeat longer. A sad, proud smile touched her lips. Then she turned, walking away without another word. The door creaked once as it closed, and then the scent of pine and rain was all that remained.

'…wait for it…'

The rest of the day saw Lyssa deep in thought. Talith asked her several times if she was all right, and each time she said yes, feigning a smile, yet hiding her worry. Coelric asked her once in the tannery, and Lyssa became short with him. It was a rare thing that she got short with either one of them, so she apologized and hugged him.

117

That night in bed, Lyssa thought she heard rustling in the bushes and hooves off in the distance. She'd asked Chandra several times, but even she couldn't hear anything, telling her to be quiet and go to sleep.

The morning started as usual with chickens to feed, wood to chop and household chores to do. Coelric was in the tannery, trimming hides, and Talith was in the kitchen doing wash. The girls were in the main room, helping to clean and teasing each other as usual.

But very soon, their world would be shattered…forever.

"Oi, you lot go round th' lef' side, watch the back." The leader turned to the other men and pointed, "You, ta th' right." He looked at the house. "We'll go in front. When ya hears th' commotion, come in."

They all moved to their respective positions, waiting for the signal. Coelric heard whispering outside the window of his shop. The hairs on his arm stood, and he knew trouble was about to knock. He bolted for his sword and ran to the house, seeing the guards slowly closing in.

He slammed through the door, scaring Talith, her eyes wide.

"Get the girls in back. We've trouble."

Without thinking, she ran into the main room, grabbing the girls by their scruffs and shuffling them to the back rooms. Now scared, the girls tried to protest.

"Shut it." The terror on Talith's face silenced the girls immediately. "Stay here."

Coelric grabbed the wooden crossbar and slammed it into place, effectively sealing the back door. Talith slammed the girl's door, went into the main room and armed a sword they kept at the side of the hearth while drawing her paring knife. She was terrified and hoped what training she'd gotten from Coelric would help to keep them alive. Coelric was already at the front door attempting to bar it, but the door crashed in, knocking him over.

Three large men wearing guards' tabards poured in only to be met by Talith's slashing sword. It laid the first guard's face open, but the second guard parried her follow-through. Talith gathered her feet and prepared to parry the guard's riposte. Coelric regained his feet just in time to block a slash to his head. He thrust at the guard's midsection, but he dodged the attempt and brought his own blade down hard. Coelric couldn't dodge quickly enough and took a fearsome wound to his right shoulder. Talith's edge made the third guard's downward slash glance off, sending him to the floor, where she solidly drove her blade through his back. Coelric switched his sword to his left hand but was not as proficient and tried to slash at another guard who had just entered.

By now, the guards had regrouped and were now beginning to pour in, overwhelming the family. Talith saw Coelric's shoulder gushing thick red blood and began wildly swinging her sword while trying to parry with her knife.

The clang of steel on steel and the roar of battle filled the girls' heads. They clung to each other in pure terror.

Talith felled one more guard with a slash across the leg and a thrust to his face. Coelric began to feel his life draining from his shoulder and went into a berserking rage. His eyes went wild, he roared his battle cry and began to tear into the guards who, seeing the almost maniacal attack, faltered and fell back. It was just enough time for Coelric to lop the arm off one guard and slash at the stomach of another, shattering his mail and spilling his entrails.

But there were just too many guards for the two to defend against. Finally, valiantly, they fell. Coelric had his sword hand lopped off and had been beheaded, falling just in front of Talith, who had been slashed and stabbed multiple times and had fallen in a heap in front of the girl's door.

119

Panting heavily, the leader barked his orders for some men to take post at both the front and behind the house. They were to search the home completely for anything lootable.

One of the guards, a deep gouge over his right eye, kicked the two bodies aside and shoved open the door to the girl's room, where they were huddled together in a corner, wide-eyed and shaking violently.

He looked back out the door to the leader, "Aye, an' look what we got 'ere." A sweaty, greasy grin on his face that gave way to yellow and black, broken teeth. He and two of the other men in the house walked into the room. "Whatcha think, lads. Eh? Give it a go?"

The guard whose eye had been gouged reached out and grabbed Lyssa by the hair and began to drag her to the bed, screaming. Also screaming, Chandra tried with all her might to hang on to her sister, but a sharp punch to the head silenced and dazed her, causing her to lose her grip.

Another man who had gotten his nose broken and his lip cut took a struggling Lyssa by the feet and helped toss her onto the bed. He reached over and held her arms down so she couldn't resist as the other stripped her, still screaming. She kicked and fought as much as she could until another, laughing, punched her mouth, causing a stream of blood to pour out, silencing her as well.

One of the larger men had taken hold of Chandra, punching her repeatedly in the stomach and face. Her pain was so excruciating that she couldn't even whimper.

The other guards had taken their turns as the home now became a torture chamber with the two young girls becoming their entertainment.

Several days passed. There was silence in the house. The men found the kegs of ale and drank themselves into a stupor. Lyssa had been left to die, battered and mauled, on her bed, completely bereft of clothing and bleeding from several places. Several guards lay about the house, passed out and snoring. Chandra had been dragged off down the road by several men, still being punched and kicked relentlessly, the men laughing at each strike.

She wished for death, every part of her body, bruised, broken and screaming with pain.

A cool breeze passed through the window where Lyssa lay. She painfully forced a swollen eye to open. Though her vision was blurred by blood and tears, she could see that the guards were all lying on the floor, passed out. She knew she had to leave, to escape in any way she could.

She tried to move, but every muscle resisted painfully. Slowly, she rolled to her side. Her midriff cramped with the pain from within, but she had to fight through it. She rolled quietly to the floor and found a narrow path between the sleeping guards that might affect her escape. She gathered a part of her torn dress and covered herself as best as she could. While pulling her weight closer to her assailant, a glint of steel caught her attention, a small dagger just out of arm's reach. Muscles still screaming, she pulled her body closer, forcing her bruised arms forward. Her fingers slowly wrapped around the hilt, and she drew it closer. She crawled to the sleeping guard and looked at his face. This wasn't one of them, but how easy it would be to exact her revenge. The pain added to her growing anger as she moved the dagger to the man's throat. His bleary eyes opened, realizing it was her, and just as he tried to stand, the knife slowly, deeply slid across his throat. She stared into his eyes, watching as the life poured from his severed veins. She smiled at him. *That's one.*

She quietly began to drag herself to the next man, who was just outside the bedroom door. Again, her dagger silently slid across his neck. She watched as the life poured from his body as well. *That's two.* But she stopped, staring in shock. Her mother lay next to him, blood-soaked clothing covering her white skin, eyes wide, clouded, dead. She stifled her tears, her sobs. The pain seared through her

121

small body as she desperately tried not to cry. She turned her head. The only thing she knew to do was replace her sorrow with pure anger. Rage came easily.

Another pull forward, and she closed on another nearby sleeping guard, curled up on a chair. Her anger had given her renewed vigor. She stood, her legs nearly giving way from weakness. Her rising rage almost replaced her physical pain. She slowly lifted a nearby, blood-soaked cushion, but in her zeal to exact revenge, her brazen act awakened the sleeping guard. His eyes flew open. Terrified at what might come next, she shoved the pillow to his face and brought the dagger up, plunging it just under his chin and up into his brain. He had no time to resist or cry out, and he sagged to the tabletop, dead. *And three.*

To the best of her recollection, none of the three she had just killed had assaulted her. She would never forget those three until her dying day. She promised herself...she would hunt them down if she survived this. And she would survive, if for no other reason than to exact her revenge—for herself, for her sister, for her family. It had now become a driving force.

Fear coursed through her mind. She must leave...now. She tiptoed to the broken front door and looked back. She saw her father's head staring back at her, eyes as clouded as her mother's. The vision burned into her tortured mind. Tears streamed down her cheeks as she looked away. Her path was clear all the way to the woods, and she made a shaky, headlong dash. She knew she would be safe there. She recalled what her sister had told her just the day before.... *The shadows are your blanket.*

'...thank you very much.'

Of Birth and Redemption

He'd followed the tracks for almost two days. The air had grown warm and humid, carrying the scent of pine and damp soil. Several men, humans by the clumsiness and the confusion of the steps, had been fumbling around as if they'd been lost. Several times they had stopped, and several times they had shifted their course.

Following crushed leaves and small snapped twigs, their trail soon led to a small opening in the trees where, upon closer inspection, he found a young girl lying in a beam of bright sunlight. Her clothing had been savagely torn and was barely staying on her beaten body. *What happened here?* he asked himself, looking around.

He listened to the forest carefully, trying to hear any unnatural sound, but found none. It seemed as if they were alone, so he edged closer to get a better look.

The ranger had seen her before and knew she'd come from one of the four hamlets nearby. To his surprise, he saw that this was the girl with the silvery white hair under all of that caked blood. But why was she here? And why so far inside the forest?

He backtracked her trail and found that her journey had been extensive and hurried. Was she running from something…or someone? He returned to her and closely checked over her body, brushing away dirt and insects. She looked to be about fourteen summers in human years and had been beaten badly, possibly with broken ribs as well as a broken arm. What could she have done to deserve this? He'd seen mauled animal carcasses that looked better than this.

He reached down and gently picked her up, cradling her head with his arm. She didn't stir, which told him that she was seriously injured and in dire need of his help. He quickly made sure he wasn't being watched and walked back to his camp in a secluded, dark part of the forest. It was called the *shadow grove* or *val'syl* by his people and was hidden in a grove of yew and pine, keeping it dark yet well hidden.

Once there, he took the time to create healing salves and bindings to help her regain her strength. He laid her on a small wooden cot covered with pine boughs and a makeshift blanket, hoping to comfort her. He placed a pillow made from the skin of a deer under her head and covered her with the stretched, tanned hide of a forest sheep. He meticulously gathered his supplies along with a skin of water and knelt near her to begin his dressing. The wounds were fearful to him. *How can something like this be allowed to happen to one this young?* He shook his head in disbelief.

She began to stir, eyes barely opening. The light stabbed at her skull, turning the dull throb behind them into a searing ache. Through the blur, the figure above her was more shadow than man. His narrow, pale face carried sharp, cruel lines like the demons Kalla had once described. Almond-shaped eyes glowed gold beneath long brown hair braided in several thin cords. His dark, nearly black leather armor was scuffed but functional.

When her eyes finally cleared, his gaze met hers, and it sent shivers down her spine and cold terror through her bones. The memories of the previous day surged back, and she screamed, scrambling to flee. To her, he was a monstrosity, and flight was her only thought.

He quickly grabbed her forcefully, yet gently, holding her in place and calming her as a mother does to her child.

"I'm not here to hurt you, little one." His voice was soft and smooth. "I swear by the Forest Father, you are safer here than any place in the land." He held her gently, rocking back and forth and continued to soothe her.

He sat her down and tried to comfort her for several minutes, humming a slow, happy tune. Her body went numb as he held her and felt as if she were about to faint, but the fearful shaking didn't allow that.

He knew she was terrified, but he had never witnessed anything like this and didn't know what else to do. He held her for hours, rocking gently, trying to show her she was safe in his arms. It took some time, but he finally felt the tension begin to ease in her body. When he was certain she could bear his absence, he eased his way back and gently laid her to rest. "Please," he said softly, holding out empty hands, "allow me to dress your wounds, little one." She drew her knees up to her chest, still trembling once again, her gaze fixed on him in muted fear.

He sighed, trying to imagine the horror this child must have endured. He knelt closer, holding out the water skin. "Please drink. It is only water." He poured some over his hand to show her.

She ran her tongue around the inside of her mouth, realizing that it was as dry as sand. Her stomach knotted, and she knew she needed the water, but could she trust this man? Another man in armor? Whom she now feared above all else. Not taking her eyes from him, she fearfully shook her head, no.

He glanced down and placed it on the ground within reach, then stood back and sat near the fire he had built to help keep her warm.

Ka'Lohane, please help your Syl'draen, he prayed to the god of his people. He sighed.

There was a small pot sitting on a metal grate where he'd begun to stir herbs and vegetables into a stew. She might run, but if she did, he'd follow. This deep in the Whispering Wood, she would surely become lost, and he had to bind her wounds, knowing that infection could finish her off.

He sat farther away, but her cautious eyes remained locked on him. Lyssa found no trust at all in this man, but he did leave the waterskin. He'd said it was water and even showed her, but she knew even poison could be clear.

Eyes hard fixed on this…person…she cautiously leaned over and quickly took the proffered skin, unstopping it. She sniffed the liquid, dabbed her lips with it and found that it was cool and tasted like sweet, fresh water from an aquifer. She turned the skin up and let the water trickle into her thirsty mouth. The cool water soothed her parched throat, making her instantly feel better, but her eyes remained transfixed. He never moved but continued to create his meal, feigning interest in her. She felt cornered, helpless, trying to decide what to do.

He gave me water and didn't hurt me when I tried to run. She kept staring. *He offered to bind my wounds. He helped me to sleep and covered me.* She began to soften. *But he's a man, just like the others.* Her brow furrowed. *Do not trust him.* She sat, unmoving, staring.

The stew began to simmer when he added diced rabbit and squirrel to the mix, which gave off a wonderful aroma, like the stew her mother made.

Her mother—the vision of Talith, covered in blood, dead eyes staring blankly, her skin alabaster white. She lay her head on her knees and began to cry, rocking back and forth. Her sobs began to shake her body, causing the pain to return. Harder she cried, finally able to release her painful emotions.

She didn't hear him move until she felt his arm gently cradling her shoulders. His body leaned against her, drawing her closer. She let the tears and sobs flow freely, not caring who heard or who was near, hands wrapping around his neck for comfort.

Her father's beheaded face burned into her memory, never to be forgotten. She heard the fighting outside their door as she and her sister clung to each other, praying to the Mother to be merciful. She remembered the terror as the door to their room burst in, and seeing the guards enter. She remembered her sister's scream as they dragged her by her hair and the struggle for them not to part. She remembered seeing her beaten and she remembered…

When she awoke, she was covered in the blanket again. It was nightfall, and the leaping flames of the fire lit the camp in a cheery orange glow. He had been sitting across the fire from her, humming a tune she recognized, one her grandmother would hum while she was working as well.

"I see you've awakened, little one." He glanced up and smiled softly at her. "I've bound your wounds and saved you some food." He was wrapping leather strings around the riser of his bow. She lay there motionless, just staring into the fire.

"You've slept for quite some time. You must be hungry." He motioned to the pot. "Please eat. I will stay seated. Do not be frightened."

Her stomach grumbled, and she realized she had not eaten in several days. She sat up, keeping the blanket wrapped around her, then realized she was wearing a cloth jerkin and breeches.

"Y-you. Who are you?" Her lips hurt when she spoke. She ran her tongue over them and realized they had been split and were cracked from being dry.

He bowed his head to her and said, "I am called Kitikithakis. I am *Syl'draen* or Woods Walker in your tongue." He reached beside him and lifted another skin. "May I?" he nodded to her. She paused a second, then nodded yes.

He slowly, carefully, walked toward her and stretched his arm out to hand her the skin.

She took it and watched him return to his seat behind the fire while she opened it and drank deeply, savoring the cool feeling as it sated her thirst.

"Where…am I?"

"Ahh, you are deep in the Whispering Wood," he said, surveying the camp. "Not a safe place for one so young."

She blinked and drank again.

"Where do you call home, little one?"

"My name is Lyssa. Lyssa Soryn. I'm from Hazelwood, or just outside it." Her voice was soft and weak. "It's in Tantyn."

"I see. Lyssa Soryn, was it?" he continued, "Well, Lyssa Soryn, you are almost two days from Tantyn." He sat forward and began to fill a wooden bowl with savory stew.

"Just Lyssa. Soryn is my family name," she said, staring at the bowl hungrily.

He stood again, leaned forward and handed her the stew. "Please. It might not be as good as your mother's, but I assure you, it will fill you."

She took the bowl, smelled it and found the aroma intoxicating. Her stomach grumbled as she tasted it to ensure it wasn't too hot. It was like nothing she'd ever had, so smooth and savory. She shoved spoon after spoon into her mouth and tried to chew, wincing with each painful bite. He'd begun to speak again, but she paid no attention, trying to sate her hunger.

She held the bowl out to him, hoping he'd refill it. He laughed. "I'm glad to see you like it, although after not eating for two days, anything must taste good right now." He refilled it and handed it back. As she gorged on the stew, he sat back, filled his pipe and began to smoke. To her, it smelled like spearmint mixed with wild cloves, and it permeated the entire camp, making Lyssa feel more relaxed and comforted.

Soon the stew was finished, and she set the bowl on the ground in front of her, and without looking at him, she asked shyly, "You dressed me?"

"Yes, I did." He shook his head sadly. "You have some fearful wounds, young one, but they are all cleaned and bandaged now." He took another puff. "I put a healing salve on them that should be reapplied by first light."

"You didn't..." her voice barely audible.

"Oh, no sweet girl, no." He looked shocked, holding his hands up innocently. "I would never. Please believe me."

The look on his face reassured her that he hadn't. She was beginning to trust him, though not completely. She might never trust a man again.

"If I might ask, what happened to you? Why were you beaten so badly?"

She looked away.

"I'm sorry to have asked. It is not my place." He went silent.

She drank from the skin again. "Are you a man? Your ears..."

She had seen they were pointed, and his face looked drawn in, unlike any person she'd ever seen. And his eyes, she'd never seen anything like them.

"Ah, I am...and I am not." He grinned at her confusion. "I am Valyn of my father, and I am human of my mother."

She smiled.

"I see. You know of the Valyn?" he asked, interested.

"Yes. My grandmother said I was Valyn as well." A barely noticeable smile crossed her mouth.

His eyes opened wide, then they narrowed. "And who might your grandmother be?"

"Her name was Kalla."

He sat back and thought. "I knew of a Kalla, rather, Kal'La. She was said to have had a daughter, Talith, or Ta'Lith." He smiled as he remembered. "How are they?"

She looked down, and he knew he had asked the wrong question.

"Gods, is that what all of this is about?"

She nodded.

"I had heard Kal'La came back to the woods, but I never heard what had become of Ta'Lith."

Tears began to flow again. She began to tell the story with shaking breath. He sat silently, allowing her to tell him the way she needed to, never interrupting. When she got to the worst part, he bade her stop. He understood. There was no need to allow her to be tortured once again.

He said in a somber tone, "I never knew Ta'Lith had children. I had heard there were children born close by and that they were white of hair, pale of skin and born during the Long Night Moon. I did not know those children were you and your sister." He shifted on his seat. "When I discovered you in the glade, I had no idea you were one of them."

He cleared his throat. "Do you know where your sister is?"

She shook her head no and began to sob again.

He was not an empathetic man. No Valyn really was, especially where outsiders were concerned, but he felt for her. He knew her pain, her anger and her hate.

He sighed, "You must sleep. It will help with the healing."

She lay down and turned away from him, still crying.

He sat awake all night. There was something about this young girl that prevented him from sleeping.

The night helped him guard her and keep her safe.

The whisper in the trees told him to help her reclaim herself.

The forest spoke.... He would listen.

'...now, let's see.'

'...yawn'

The weeks slipped by. Kitikithakis tended her wounds each day, cleaning and binding them, making sure no infection ever took hold. Lyssa found herself slowly trusting him; he never touched her except to tend the bandages or check the strength of a mending bone.

In time, she began to enjoy his company, the calm, steady cadence of his voice, the way he answered her questions without hesitation, and the quiet help he offered whenever she needed it. She stayed close to the camp to regain her strength, and her body healed quickly. No bones had been broken after all.

The ranger had earned her trust, slowly, and only in pieces, enough for him to begin teaching her the finer points of woodland survival. He became her mentor in the smallest, most uncertain ways. Not a father, not a friend, just someone who didn't flinch when she did and didn't push when she pulled away. She came to understand, quietly, that he had not only saved her life…he had given her space to have one again.

Questions were asked—not many at first—small ones, careful ones. Answers came just as cautiously, and each learned a little more of the weight the other carried. Neither spoke the worst of it, but they didn't have to. Some wounds don't need words to be understood.

He trusted no human; pain had carved that truth deep, and he struggled to understand her fear, even as he recognized it. She trusted no man, human or otherwise, and the way she watched him from the corner of her eye told him she wasn't ready to decide if he was different. They both knew that if trust ever came, it would not come easily. It would be earned, fought for, and fragile.

So they learned together. Not smoothly. Not cleanly. Some days ended in silence; some began with stiff nods and awkward distance. Other days, something eased between them, a quiet understanding neither dared name. But their strange friendship grew, crooked and uneven as a sapling in winter, strengthening one slow inch at a time.

In that time, he discovered she had an instinct for stalking, for slipping through brush without stirring it, for sensing the forest as if it spoke to her. Teaching her became less instruction and more recognition, confirming what she somehow already knew. Bows and daggers suited her hands best, though she took to spears and staves with surprising grace. Her quickness, her balance, her sudden bursts of fluid motion astonished him more than he ever admitted. Once or twice, she moved so silently she nearly startled him, but still he warned her that she still had much to learn…mostly to settle his own nerves.

In truth, she was becoming as silent as the forest itself, as dangerous as one of its cats. And he found himself both proud…and a little afraid of what she might become. She stayed in his company for months on end. Together, they patrolled the Whispering Woods where Kitikithakis taught her how to find his special trails, which were impossible to find unless one knew exactly what to look for. Repeatedly, they retraced until she knew each trail like she knew her own name. Sometimes, they would go their separate ways, checking and guarding the forest from intruders and interlopers, only to return at later times to compare reports.

It happened one day while checking the northern reaches of the Whispering Woods. She heard the sharp sounds of cracking whips echoing through the forest. Using the shadows and foliage, she followed what had once been a rarely used smugglers' trail to investigate.

Ahead, through the dense thicket, she discovered the figures of armored men carrying pikes, four by her count, with several others following behind them. As she crept closer, she realized the ones trailing behind were enslaved men and women bound together with heavy, rusted chains, driven forward under the lash. Each crack of the whip sounded like a tree limb breaking, each cry followed by another blow, another fall.

NEVER AGAIN! screamed in her head, and her anger began to rise. She started to breathe deeply but calmly, struggling to allay her anger and helping herself to think more clearly. She wondered if any of these men were the ones who carried off her sister, but she knew that would have to wait. Ahead were more pressing matters.

She told herself that this wasn't the place for heroics; the trees and brush were far too thick for her to act, so she followed them as far as she could. She kept to the undergrowth just far enough behind to avoid being seen, inspecting and memorizing every detail about them.

They reached the edge of the woods where she stopped to watch the slavers lead their ragged line toward a crumbling tower.

The sun hung just past its zenith, and a northern sea breeze carried the heavy scent of salt across the plains. The tall grass rippled in waves, whispering with the wind, while deer and elk grazed freely, seemingly unafraid. It looked as if war from days past had caused the tower's destruction; the top crumbled away, the bottom remaining nearly intact, its tattered stone lying strewn around the base like small monuments to a past time.

The enslaved people were led inside. Even where Lyssa was hidden, she heard the jingling and rattling of shackles being removed and replaced. After a while, the cries and sobbing stopped as the guards began to mill about, seemingly waiting for more to arrive.

Lyssa crouched low in a thick knot of brush and young trees, hidden well enough to watch without being seen. From there, she could finally tell the guards apart: two with beards, one long and neat, the other split into a rough fork. The last two were clean-faced, though one of them wore no helm at all. Easy marks to remember once the killing started.

The sun dipped toward the horizon; night wasn't far off now. She felt her agitation coil tighter with every slow minute. She needed to help, she had to, but the distance was too great to cross unseen, at least before dark, and they stood just beyond her bow's reach.

Lyssa searched for a better vantage point, something closer, something with cover, but everything she found was either too far or too exposed. Every option felt wrong. Every heartbeat felt wasted. The helplessness sparked a familiar anger she struggled to choke down.

Just then, the sounds of whips cracking and the wails of the tortured began again, causing Lyssa's ire to peak. This was it. She was going to do something, anything, to help. She could tolerate the abuse no longer.

Lyssa watched them carefully, tracking the pattern. Forkbeard stepped out. No-Helm went in. A few minutes later, Clean-Face came out while Forkbeard slipped back inside—then again, and again.

She timed each pass. It was perfect and predictable, exactly what she needed.

Lyssa crept forward, trading a bit of cover for precious yards. She found a hollow beneath a fallen trunk, settled in, nocked an arrow, and drew the string until it kissed her cheek.

No-Helm stepped out again. She waited for Clean-Face to take his place…but he didn't. Instead, the two of them lingered outside, talking, laughing, wasting time she didn't have.

Her irritation flared, sharp and hot. Enough.

She adjusted her aim, raised the bow a hair to set the arc and released. It sang through the air, but as it topped its arc and began to fall, she became certain it would miss. But, as fate would have it, No-Helm turned and stepped a few paces toward her, the arrow miraculously striking him in the throat. He grabbed at it, not understanding what happened and died just before his body fell to the ground. Her eyes lit up with amazement. She would later learn from Kitikithakis' account that the shot had flown more than two furlongs, a unimaginable feat unto itself.

Seeing his friend fall dead, Clean-face frantically looked Lyssa's way but saw nothing and began to sound the alarm. Defiantly, he marched toward Lyssa, sword in hand, searching desperately yet still seeing nothing. The other two slavers exited the tower, surprised at the body of their fallen comrade.

She nocked another arrow, drew and released another shot in one fluid motion. Her arrow arced and found its mark, embedding itself in Neatbeard's face, sending him to the ground.

The final two slavers knew she'd killed their friend. Blood lust took them over and pushed them forward, bellowing their battle cries. Lyssa's calm ended after she fired her final arrow, which buried itself deeply inside Forkbeard's chest. Though he wasn't killed outright, he crumbled to the ground, gasping in pain. The last man was now almost upon her, bloodlust painting his face.

She knew another shot was impossible and drew her dagger, hoping her skills would be good enough to at least put up a valiant defense. She leaped out from the bushes, crouched and ready to spring, when the last guard collapsed clutching his throat, an arrow protruding from his unguarded neck.

Stunned, she flashed her eyes to where she assumed the arrow had originated, only to see Kitikithakis calmly slinging his bow and walking toward her.

"Even the forest cat knows when to fight another day, little rogue." His face was emotionless yet reassuring.

"I could not let them torture those people anymore. I had to stop them." He could see the anger on her face.

"I know. Sometimes, we must do what we feel is right, no matter the outcome." He knelt at the edge of the forest and pointed to the tower. "You must finish this. I cannot leave the protection of the woods. I am so sworn."

She nodded and headed for the tower, wondering what she would see. As she passed Clean-Face's lifeless body, she kicked him hard in the groin…just to be sure. Her grandfather, Trellin, always told battlefield stories about enemies who feigned death until your back was turned. She wasn't about to make that mistake. When the corpse didn't move, she knelt and checked for anything useful: some coin, a ring and some dried meat. Her grandfather taught her that taking from dead men was akin to stealing from a child. In her eyes, this was no man.

A bit farther down, she came to Forkbeard, whom she shot in the chest. He lay there gasping for breath, trying to remove the arrow, to no avail. She stared down at him with cold, unfeeling eyes.

"Ye little bitch, end it then, go on." Blood was filling the guard's mouth. She coldly stood and watched his life bleed down the side of his face and chest, no expression at all.

"I hope I see ya in th' void, ya bitch. I'll 'ave me way with ya, I will." He said, trying desperately to smile.

She knelt beside him, grabbed the arrow and slowly pulled. He winced from the excruciating pain. She smiled, slowly pushing it back in. He screamed as she pulled it again.

"I hope I see you on the path. And I pray the Mother that the path is long… so I can do this to you for eternity." She spat on his face and shoved hard on the arrow, sending the tip all the way through to his back. The light left his eyes…and she laughed.

She went to the other slavers, stripping them of their belongings then went inside to free those she could. There, shackled to the walls were five, half-starved, beaten, emaciated men and women. The pain she saw in their eyes and on their faces both angered her and saddened her heart. She tried the key that she found on the first slaver and released them.

"Go. Run, before more guards come," she said, ushering them through the door. Night had fallen, and the stars lit the sky like tiny silvery beacons.

"There." She pointed south of them. "There is a village. Someone will help you there. Go now." She made sure they were going the right direction before she turned and ran to the woods, leaving them to make their own way.

She and Kitikithakis silently returned to their camp, where he stoked the fire, and Lyssa placed her booty on the ground for her friend to see.

"This was all I could find on them. Take what you want," she told him.

Without looking up, he said, "I've no need for the baubles of men, little rogue. They serve no purpose for me here." He skewered two coneys and placed them over the now-burning fire to cook.

She shrugged and put them in her belt pouch. "I have a feeling I'll be needing them, then." He nodded, knowing soon she would be leaving.

Slowly turning the sizzling coneys, he seasoned them with freshly picked rosemary and coriander.

"I must say, you have come a tremendous way since we first met, little rogue," he mentioned, lighting his pipe. "You have mastered all I can teach you. So proficient that one might even call you Syl'draen." He smiled for the first time since she met him. "Alas, that is a name only given by the Valyn so I shall call you," he thought for just a second, "*ke'thra*, the cat."

She smiled. "Lyssa ke'thra. I like it."

He frowned. "No, no. You are Valyn, my friend. It is spoken, Lys'Sa ke'thra or, in your tongue, Lyssa the Cat."

She smiled and leaned back. *Lyssa the Cat.* It fit her, and she liked it.

They both sat silently for some time after that. He came to the understanding that her world was not his and she needed to explore the vastness of it. He called her *friend*, but she had to go out among her own people and see what her path had to offer. He knew she was strong enough in mind and body to take care of herself, but he also knew she could not follow.

Two days later, as if Ka'Lohane, the One Who Breathes Life, had spoken to him, she left, bidding farewell to her friend and mentor.

'Interesting play.'

Of Crones and Tomes

The tavern was loud enough to drown out the wind. Dice clattered against wood, someone sang half a verse of a vulgar drinking song before forgetting the words, and mugs slammed hard enough to splash the floor.

Near the hearth, a group of men leaned around a battered table, throwing bones. One of them, lean, red-faced, already swaying in his seat, was halfway through a boast.

"...So, I'm out there in th' woods yesterday, hacking on a pine fer kindlin,' and I hears this howl. Not a wolf, mind ya. Somethin' worse." His eyes got big, and his voice cracked.

The big man across from him grinned, eyes narrowing. "What's the matter, Brennan? Afeared o' the woods? Ya afeared o' owls?" He threw his head back and bellowed in laughter, as did the rest of the table. Brennan's smirk was thin, humorless. He lifted his mug but didn't drink.

"Not afraid o' the woods, mate," he said, his voice carrying just enough to quiet the nearest tables. "Afraid o' what's in 'em."

The big man chuckled, glancing at the others. "Here it comes again, lads. I heard this one afore."

A younger man beside him leaned forward, grinning through ale-flushed cheeks. "Go on then. Tell it."

Brennan set his mug down slowly, leaning in as if the shadows might be listening.

The others leaned in as well, ale sloshing. "Go on then. Tell it." They all went silent to better hear Brennan.

He glanced at the door as though checking it was shut. Then, in a voice just low enough to force them closer, he began:

"You ever hear what happened ta Garrow?" He swallowed hard, as if reliving it himself. "Followed th' old crone inta th' trees one night, he did, thinking he'd steal her purse. Ya 'member he always liked an easy mark. Well, lad ne'er come…ne'er come back." He dragged his hand across his mouth nervously. "Aye, they found his boots by the river, they did…but no Garrow." He drank deeply from his mug. "Just…nothin'. No blood, no…" All of the men stayed silent, trying to discount it but worried that it was true.

Another man laughed, breaking the trance of fear the others were feeling. "That ain't how it went. Me uncle swore she lured 'im up ta that old church. Seen 'im go in but ne'er seen 'im come out."

A third man leaned forward, eyes darting to the dark corners of the tavern. "My granda told me she speaks ta shadows. Heard it, he did. In whispers, an' th' shadows? They move for her an' sometimes speaks back." He leaned back a bit and looked around fearfully. "Maybe Garrow's still with her…just not th' way he was." He nodded to make his point clear.

The first man scoffed. "Bahhh, gossip. Gossip an' lies." His eyes glanced at all of them. "Aye an' maybe so, but I ain't wantin' ta find out. Better ta leave things be." His hand stayed wrapped around his mug, but he didn't drink.

From the far corner, a voice spoke…a voice like dry leaves rustling.

"Heh, heh. Yer all wrong."

They turned. A woman, gray of hair and shawled, sat in the shadows. Her weathered skin, softened by the dim light, her smile grim. But it was her eyes, those dark eyes, almost empty yet staring and cold. Every man stopped as if frozen in time, mugs suspended in air and silent as the grave.

"She let 'im in cause she knew 'is fate," she said, her words slow, certain and looking at no one…and everyone. "She sees it, ya know—all of it. And if she don't like what she sees…"

She smiled a toothy grin and chuckled.

"...ye never leave."

When the serving girl came to clear the mugs, the men were gone, and so was the old woman. They all knew of the mysterious crone. Most called her *the seer, the teller,* and some...*the harbinger.* But they knew one thing: When she spoke, the words always rang true.

"Heh heh. Tellin' story's o're drink." The crone turned back toward town, her gray hair blowing in the breeze and yelling. "Sots, the lot of yas!" She turned back to the road and continued to walk. The days had grown colder, and that made her old bones ache a little more. "Talk, lads. Yes, it is. All talk." The sun was now above the tall trees of the forest. A slight, cold breeze swirled the dried leaves around her aching feet, yet she pressed on.

She knew the time was close at hand. She didn't know what was to be. She just knew it was nearly time. She felt it; in her bones, in the air, in telling smells, the way the land breathed. Aye, she knew. She knew.

She mumbled with every step, looking down, the clicking of her cane against stone and dirt. She stopped. She sensed...something, cursing her eyes for not seeing as they once did. Sniff, sniff.

"Yeeessss," she hissed. "It is time. Oh, thank you, maker. Thank you for this time." An almost wicked grin spread across her wrinkled, weather-worn face.

Her pace quickened. She squinted in the now-failing light. *Where? Where is it? Where is the sign?*

Her eyes darted side to side, hoping, praying she wouldn't miss it. Was that a sound? She stopped again. Sniff, sniff.

Ahh. THERE it was. She could smell it now, faintly at first, but growing stronger with each hobbling step. *Hurry. Must hurry afore I loses it.*

She walked faster, frantically, almost tripping several times, and then...

Narrowing her view, she saw it. There, a mass on the side of the road. She almost ran; she was so excited.

The mass was before her now; small, dirty rags, as if someone had tossed them aside.

A girl, nearly fourteen by the looks of her, beaten badly. Bloody, so bloody and dirty.

The crone let out a shuddered sigh. This was not the way the sign was to be delivered. A tear slipped from her eye. *No, no, no. We needs ta repair this, we does. The maker can't see 'er like this. Must fix. Must fix 'er.* She began wringing her hands as she looked the girl over. *Yes, we will. Fix it.*

The girl moaned and startled the crone. She tried to speak, but her severely wounded face wouldn't allow it.

The woman leaned closer to the girl's ear and whispered, "It's okay, little one. I'm 'ere ta help ye. Yes, I am. 'Ere ta help ye." She reached out a frail hand. The little girl slowly, painfully grasped it as she was slowly, gently helped to her feet. Her bruised and shaking legs fought back as she stood, knees barely holding her up. The crone fumbled in the leather pouch at her side and produced a flask.

"Here ya be, little one. Drink. Yes, drink." The girl, still barely able to move, took it and tried to drink, but the pain in her mouth and her lips only caused her to pour it down her throat, slowly at first, then gulping it down, so fast that dribbles of the fluid fell from her chin. Her head began to spin, slowly crumbling to the ground, gasping at the exertion and pain that racked her body. The crone helped guide her gently to the ground, making sure she didn't fall hard.

"Rest, little one. Ya be feelin' better soon. Yes, soon." The girl blinked her eyes several times to shake the cobwebs from her head. The crone looked up and down the road to see if there were any other travelers, but found none to her approval.

The crone examined her head to toe, only to find that she had been left on the side of the road, a complete mess, both eyes bruised and swelled shut from several brutal blows. Judging by the caked streaks of blood, her nose might have been broken as well. Her lips looked like ground meat, and clumps of hair were missing from being dragged, not to mention the still-bleeding gash across her scalp, her fingers badly scraped, and the nails of both hands and feet looked to have been smashed, by what she could only guess. She looked to the sky, wondering what this poor little girl could have possibly done to deserve this amount of punishment.

"Tsk. Tsk. Tsk." The crone shook her head. *This be a debt owed. Yes, a debt owed. The maker'll see to it.* She pursed her lips and gave a silent curse to the unseen ones who did this.

After several minutes, the little girl began to feel better.

"Here ya go, girl. This'll help th' swells. Drink it down, now. Here, here."

She handed a small blue vial to the girl, who took it and, without questioning, gulped it down. Her eyes suddenly went wide, and she grabbed for her throat. The taste was awful, and she felt like vomiting.

"Come now, girl, ain't ya never had lavender an' yarrow mixed with wort an' cats' milk?" The crone shook her head. "It be common enough. Yes." She took the vial back and tipped it upside down, ensuring it was completely empty. "Give it a bit an' you'll feel lots better. Yes, better." Then she returned the vial to her pouch.

Just as the sun touched the horizon, the girl looked at the old woman and tried to stand. "Oop, oop. There, there, child. Be easy." The crone helped her to her feet and steadied her. "Yer lookin' much better, deary. Can ya walk, maybe? Walk?"

The battered girl nodded, still dazed, and took a few steps just to be sure. The old woman knew her potions were working; the swelling had all but vanished, leaving only the bruising. The blood that had flowed freely from the girl's head and mouth before had now stopped, making her look much better. "Well, let's be going, girl. Not good ta be out after dark near this place. Bad men about, yes, very bad."

The old woman started at a slow pace at first, making certain the girl could keep up. Her first steps seemed pained and awkward, but as she moved, they became steadier. They walked for a few minutes in silence, the woman glancing behind to make sure she was still there.

"What be yer name, girl?" She looked back at her. "Ye can talk, yes? Ya talk?"

Almost a whisper. "Chandra…mmma'am." Her voice was as raw as her torn lips. The name sounded fragile, but it was all she had left of herself.

"Bah, ma'am." She grunted. "I ain't been ma'am in…well, too long a time, girl, too long." She glanced back again to make sure the girl was still keeping up. "I be the crone, Stidyen." She spit. "Huh, crone. They'll see a crone. Yes, they'll see." She glanced back at Chandra again. "I better tend to ya when I gets ya home." She chuckled. "Home." A sideways grin stretched the wrinkled skin of her face.

The ruined church loomed ahead, its thatched roof half-collapsed, stone walls streaked with moss and soot. The air felt heavier here, as if the very ground itself held its breath—dank and dead. The world had forgotten this house of some unremembered deity, but the crone didn't.

Chandra stumbled at the threshold, every bruise on her body aching. Stidyen's hand quickly reached out to steady the girl. Chandra noticed that her hand was surprisingly steady on her arm.

"Come, girl," the old woman murmured, her voice low and certain. "You've nothing to fear, here. This be yer new home now. Yes?"

Chandra looked bewildered. Confused.

143

"Huh." Stidyen looked at Chandra knowingly. "Ya got a mum? A da?"

Chandra's eyes filled with tears that rolled gently down her battered face.

Stidyen looked at the ground and, in a soft whisper, said, "Aye, child. I thought not." She shook her head and let out a sigh of pity, then motioned for Chandra to follow as they both stepped inside.

The dim interior smelled of wet earth and ash. Benches lay scattered, broken and overturned, straw littering the stone floor and leaves swirling with the gentle breeze. Fading sunlight bled through shattered windows and cracks in the decaying walls, painting thin bars of light across the dust.

Stidyen whispered, "Bastards knocked ya witless, they did. S'alright, it be. The lady got somethin' a waitin' fer 'em, you'll see, somethin'." She nodded knowingly.

Chandra's eyes scanned the room and became fixed on something…interesting.

The shadows…they seemed to move. She grabbed her head with both hands and gently squeezed. She felt better.

Not like in the forest, not the slow creep of dusk, these shadows seemed to shift when Stidyen passed, drawing aside like curtains to let her through. It was subtle, but impossible to mistake. Chandra wondered if she was more severely injured than she thought. Her pulse quickened.

They reached the far end of the church, where a crude, broken table stood in place of the altar. Stidyen paused, resting her fingertips on the splintered and weathered wood, caressing it as if it were porcelain. Her mouth moved ever so slightly as she mumbled strange words that Chandra couldn't understand.

Mystically, the air above the table shimmered, folding in on itself without a sound. The shadows swirled in a chaotically twisted dance. A shimmering dark archway bloomed in the empty space, impossibly deep, its edges glowing faintly gold and blue in the dimness. She could feel the electricity in the air, subtle but there. She smelled the sweet ozone as it crackled. Her heart began to beat faster. Excitement crept into her veins. She stood motionless and stared disbelieving, the ache in her ribs all but forgotten. The sight, the sense of pure magic, cleared her foggy mind; she was utterly enthralled, mesmerized by the sheer wonder of the magical rift before her. She'd never seen this before, this…magic. She knew she wanted…more.

Something in the pit of her stomach told her she had just stepped into a different life; new, exciting, powerful. And she was ready.

"Come, child," Stidyen said again, glancing over her shoulder with a knowing wink and smile.

Chandra followed her through the portal.

It was eerily dark, and the odors of herbs, incense and boiling concoctions were almost overpowering. The air was damp, heavy. It caused her to gasp. She quickly looked from place to place, taking in all there was to see. She felt the flutter of excitement well up in the pit of her stomach. Alembics, cauldrons…and books—so many books, tomes, scrolls. Her eyes went wide with amazement and wonder. She stood, open-mouthed. Her mind was awhirl with thought and fantasy. THIS is what she'd always fantasized about. THIS is what the shadows whispered about. THIS is what she was meant to do. Her bruised and battered body tried to slow her excitement, but her sheer exhilaration erased it all from her mind.

"Come, girl. Yes, come."

She slowly turned to where the old lady stood, another vial in her hand. When she got there, she noticed a small pot filled with a simmering red liquid. She'd never smelled this before. It was sharp, spicy and sent pleasant vapors through her nostrils.

"Here," she shoved a small vial into Chandra's hand. "Ya, drip this…drip mind ya, into the pot and wait till it smokes. Then stop an' put this weed in it." She wandered off to the other corner of the room to retrieve something else before the girl could ask her why.

Chandra turned back to the pot and opened the vial. She fought her reflex to sniff its contents for fear it were some caustic poison. She touched her throbbing lip and winced. It began to bleed again. It slowly oozed to her chin as she began to drip the liquid from the vial. *Slowly,* she reminded herself. Once, twice.

"Good, good," the old woman said upon returning. She peered into the pot. "Yes." She slung a small animal the size of a rat onto the table. "Yes, very good." Picking up a cleaver, brought it down hard.

Chandra startled, turned away and shivered. Just as she did, Stidyen glanced at her and began to say something when she noticed the drop of blood about to fall from Chandra's chin.

"Nnnooooooo!" she screamed, her voice echoing throughout the room.

She reached out to try and stop it, but was too late. The drop seemed to almost hang in the air, but fell onto the surface of the liquid just as Chandra looked in. It sparked like lightning then burst into a rolling, smoky black cloud of steam. It seared Chandra's face, causing her to fall backward to the floor. She grasped her face, screaming in agony, writhing on the floor in pain.

"Nooo, no, no, no," Stidyen shrieked.

She leaned down, terrified, and roughly rolled the still-writhing Chandra onto her back, struggling to pull her stiffened hands away from her face. Her wounds had inexplicably disappeared, the swelling abated, and her bruises, gone. She stopped crying out in pain and just stared at Stidyen, frozen.

Chandra's eyes were wide, her breathing fast and shallow, whites and all, had turned black as pitch. Stidyen looked closer and could see they swirled with black smoke and shadow inside. She stepped back and gasped with fear. *By Destiny's grace, th' goddess' child. Could th' prophesy be true?*

After half a minute, Chandra blinked several times, and the smoke disappeared. Stidyen stood staring, trying to understand what had just happened, trying to fathom the very essence of this wondrous and fearful occurrence. Still bewildered, she leaned to help Chandra as the girl struggled to sit up.

"Wwwhat…what happened?" She felt as if she'd been knocked senseless. Her head felt as if it were filled with cotton, her eyes blurred and watery. Stidyen remained silent, still watching.

Chandra grabbed her head with both hands and, rubbing hard, tried to remove the cobwebs.

"What did you do?" Stidyen calmly asked, more questioning than angry. "What?"

Her head finally settling, Chandra looked at the crone blankly. In one impossibly fast motion, her head suddenly whipped backward, mouth and eyes wide. The words came from unmoving lips as she cryptically whispered.

"It is time. She must learn all that can be taught—quickly. The time is nigh. It is your task."

The breath in Stidyen's body left her as if she were gut-punched, her eyes wide with fear, almost terror. It WAS true. The lady had spoken.

Her mind began to race as she gasped. The realization. She knew. She knew the words. It had been written. There would come a time. She would be the teacher. She had a task to perform.…

'…it is time!'

Chandra stirred. She stretched and blinked her eyes, willing them to focus. The room was dark yet cool. The blankets that covered her were threadbare yet warming. The room was unfamiliar, full of unknown smells and sounds. Panic began to set in. *What happened? How did I get here? Where am I?*

A hand lightly touched her shoulder. Terrified, she whipped her head around and raised her arms to protect herself.

"Oh, oh, oh. There, there, little one. Have no fear. You're safe with Stidyen. Yes, safe." She smiled warmly at the girl. "Ye had a terrible night, ya did. A lot o' yellin' an' such." She looked pitifully at the young girl. "Yer safe here, though. Have no fear. No one'll hurt ya here; I promise ya this. Yes."

It took some time, but Chandra began to calm. She looked around to make sure the old lady was right. She saw it was just her and the crone and began to relax visibly.

"Where am I?" She tried to remember her name.

"Stidyen, dear. Stidyen, yes." She stood and went to the small table just inside the room. She lifted a metal ewer, poured what looked like water into a mug and brought it to her. "Here...Chandra? Yes, Chandra, that's right. Here. Drink."

She took the mug from her, looked into it, then back at Stidyen.

"Water, little one, just water. I promise. No harm here."

Chandra sipped it, realized it was water and gulped it down quickly. She handed the mug back.

"Ya want more?" Stidyen asked.

Chandra nodded emphatically.

Stidyen chuckled. "My, my. Thirsty girl, yes, thirsty." She got the ewer and filled the mug again. Quickly, Chandra emptied it and handed it back, wanting more.

"Last one. Don't want to drink too much now. Not good for you, no." She poured again and returned the ewer to the table. Chandra sipped this time, looking at Stidyen. There were many questions, but she was afraid to ask them.

The old lady knew. "They call me *the old crone*, but I be Stidyen though, yes. Most be afraid o' me age an' think me some kind o' witch er a mage. Bah. I ain't neither. Just an old lady. I heal. I makes potions. Folks are afeared...but they want what Stidyen makes, yes makes." She grinned. Her eyes began to shine with excitement. It made Chandra uneasy. She stayed still, wary, silent.

"Ye can talk ta me…Chandra, yes. I listen. I can hear an I can help. I teach. Yes, teach all ya needs ta know."

Having gotten rest, Chandra's mind now began to remember what had transpired the last day. Sheepishly, she asked, "What happened yesterday? The table. That…magic…door."

The crones' eyes widened. "Yesterday? Ya was sleepin' yesterday, girl. Last three days, sleepin', yes."

Surprised, Chandra said, "Three days! It seemed like yesterday."

"Oooh, ya was in a bad way, dear. Bad, yes. But me potions helped ya get better so's we could get ta home an I could tend to ya, yes."

It was then that her stomach growled. Chandra covered her stomach and gave an embarrassed glance at Stidyen.

"Come, girl, let's feed ya. Yer lookin' thin. Uh huh, thin." She stood and reached her hand out for Chandra to take.

Chandra stood, took her hand and followed her into a good-sized rectangular room. When they got there, the aroma of garlic, onion and simmering stew brought back the memory of home. There, she saw a very large, stone hearth on a long wall, easily twice the size of the one at home. A large table made of strong timber sat in the center of the room with several tall, wooden shelves filled with metal and wooden plates, bowls and spoons across from it. Along the far wall stood a wooden cutting block. Old blood stained the wood, and discarded entrails filled a slop bucket underneath, a huge washtub next to that.

Stidyen sat the girl down on a pillowed chair facing the warm fire. She swung out a hanging cauldron from the fire and filled a bowl with hot, deliciously smelling stew and set it before her.

"Here. Have a care. It be hot as liquid metal, but it'll fill ya. Take what ya need." She went to a small cask sitting on a little stoop next to the chopping block and drew some liquid into a mug.

"Here, drink. It ain't water, but it'll keep ya warm," she said, chuckling.

She headed for an arched exit next to the wash basin.

"I got things I gotta tend ta. Make yerself ta home. Ya live here now so it be yer place too, yes." She turned and was gone.

Chandra blew on each spoonful of the rich brown stew. Her first attempt to eat sent a sting through her lips; though no longer split, they were still tender. When she finally managed to slip the spoon past them, the taste struck her with an aching familiarity. It was like her mother's rich, creamy gravy giving way to perfectly cooked carrots and potatoes.

Chewing caused pain in her face, so she used the spoon to mash the pieces, making them much easier to swallow. The meat had been cooked so well that it all but melted on her tongue, and she savored every bite. Before long, the bowl was empty and finding herself still hungry, she filled it again to the brim without spilling a drop. Her mother's stew had been good…but this was the best she had ever tasted.

She lifted the mug beside her to wash the stew down…and nearly choked. The strange sweetness, followed by a sharp burn, blasted out through her nose. She coughed and sputtered, eyes watering as the liquid sprayed down the front of her worn dress.

Stidyen had filled the mug with mead, only mentioning that it wasn't water. Chandra had heard of mead before but had never tasted it, and the heady burn struck her like a slap. She set the mug down quickly, wiped her mouth with a cloth and silently swore never to touch that foul drink again.

Once again, the bowl was emptied and, leaning back with a full stomach, Chandra quickly looked around, stifled a belch, then giggled. Mother would have chided her, then they both would have laughed. The thought made her heart sag with sadness again. She stood and went to clean her bowl and spoon. Finding no place to set them to dry, she got a cloth from one of the shelves, placed it on the table and set them upside down to dry.

Well, she did say to have a look around. Maybe I should find her and ask what there is to see.

Chandra stood in front of the doorway, staring at the black beyond. She could see no hallway and no torchlight. It wasn't shadow, not quite, more like a veil of nothing. Her stomach fluttered. *What is this place?* She wanted to see more, to explore, to know where she had been taken. Hesitantly but with excitement, she stepped through and found herself in a small room with Stidyen.

"Hello, dear. Get enough ta eat, yes?" she asked without looking at Chandra.

"Yes, ma'am. Thank you." Chandra was looking all over the room. This had to be the room where she performed her alchemy. It reminded her of her grandmother's lodge with all her reagents hanging from hooks suspended from the ceiling, jars on shelves and countless books strewn across every surface.

"Ye stop that, ma'am, now. I ain't no ma'am. Ain't been one fer ages I can remember, no." She just kept pouring things and dicing others. "I be just plain ol' Stidyen, yes, Stidyen." She turned to retrieve another reagent. "Or if ya want, Gran, makes no mind ta me."

Glancing at her young charge, she said, "Ya be wantin' somthin'?"

"Yes, ma...Stidyen. Is there anything...interesting here to see? I'd like to explore if that's alright."

"Anywhere's okay. It be yers as well, so go lookin'."

Chandra shrugged. She didn't know where she wanted to go, so she decided to just explore. She turned and looked through the doorway again, expecting to see the kitchen, but it was pitch black. She looked back at Stidyen, then at the doorway and walked forward into the darkness...and found herself in the small room with Stidyen once more.

The old woman raised one brow, the corner of her mouth twitching. "Well now," she said, voice rich with amusement.

Chandra blinked, completely puzzled. *Maybe I got turned around in the dark*, she thought. She turned and tried again. Through the doorway…and again, there was Stidyen, waiting with that same sly smirk.

This time, Stidyen laughed outright. "Round an' round, eh? Like a wee little mouse in a wheel." She laughed again.

Heat rose to Chandra's cheeks. "What happened? I went through the door."

"Aye," Stidyen said, leaning on her alchemy table. "But where ya be goin' to, girl, where?"

"I…" Chandra faltered. She didn't know. She'd only wanted to go and explore.

Stidyen's eyes gleamed. "That's the trick now, ain't it? Where d'ye want ta go? Where?"

Chandra thought hard. Her room, she wanted her room; the meal had made her tired, and she needed a place to rest, to think. She fixed the thought in her mind. She glanced back at Stidyen, resigned that this was going to work, and stepped through the dark.

The thick black void peeled away, revealing her bed. She was in her room.

Her breath caught as she turned in a slow circle, wonder blooming in her chest. Behind her, she could almost hear Stidyen's laugh echoing, soft and knowing.

So, this is true magic. She thought. *I want MORE!*

'…let's try this.'

Sleeping was difficult. She kept dreaming she was back with the bandits, being pummeled and kicked. Part of her had wished they'd just kill her and be done with it. They had dragged her by her hair across the rocky road and dropped her, but not before kicking her in the face. She remembered seeing stars…and two red, blinking eyes.

She sat bolt upright, bewildered and gasping for breath, looking around and realizing she was still in her new room…safe.

'…*never again, mistress Chandra, never again*'

It was that voice…in her head. She squinted, rubbing her temples, trying to remove the memories of the last week.

She exhaled and began to feel better.

She had to know. Who or what was this voice she kept hearing? Was it only in her head, or did she actually hear it?

"Who are you? Where are you?" She looked around again but saw nothing.

She slid out of her bed and went to the basin to splash water on her face. She raised her head and looked at her reflection in the cracked mirror. It looked as if she'd never been touched, yet she could still feel some of the pain around her eyes, jaw and in her ribs. *Stidyen's elixirs. I should have listened to Gran,* she thought, examining each side of her face more closely.

She walked through the portal and was instantly whisked away to Stidyen's location. The room now smelled of spice and apples, making her mouth water. "Ahh, there ye be, yes." She walked to Chandra with a small tin mug and bade her drink. Chandra slowly sipped the wonderful-smelling liquid. "There ya be, lass, cinnamon cider. Good for ya. Yes, good indeed."

She sipped more and found that the smell and the taste filled her head and made her feel so much better, relieving the pain and helping to clear the fog.

"Ya know 'bout potions an' elixirs, girl?" Stidyen asked, not looking at her.

"Yes, ma'am…er Stidyen. My gran made them. She called it alchemy, though."

"Ye ever learn it?" She peered over at her.

153

"No. I could never get the measures right. I got tired of my sister always making me look silly, stupid, at it," she said with a disgusted tone.

"Ye got a sister ya say?" Now she was looking right at her, interested.

"Yes, Lyssa. I'm afraid for her, though. I think they killed her. They were doing…horrible things…" The visions of the men holding Lyssa down became too much, and she burst into tears, sobbing loudly.

Stidyen went and put her arms around Chandra to console her. "Don't ya weep, girl, no. Them men? Have no fear. The anger they sowed. They'll get it returned in tens; I tell ya, tens." She pulled away. "An' that sister o' yers? Oh, lass, she be livin', yes livin'. No, they didn't break her, no. She's stronger than afore. You'll see." Stidyen could feel…something. "Almost stronger than yerself, almost."

Chandra wiped her eyes. "But how do you know?"

"Stidyen knows. Ne'er doubt Stidyen, lass." She winked and raised her finger to assure her, then turned back to her alembics.

Chandra sat and hoped, prayed, Stidyen was right. She began to miss Lyssa so.

She stared into the darkness, a daydream but not, and began to think about that night, the invasion. All the yelling, screaming, blood.

Without realizing it, she began to raise her hands, wisps of dark black, roiling shadow beginning to seep from her fingers. She blankly stared into the past, her anger beginning to rise, thinking of the beatings she had taken. Those men…

She felt nothing but anger—and pain—so much pain.

Stidyen glanced over to see why she'd become so quiet. She looked surprised, watching the girl in amazement and seeing the tension in her eyes. The hand gestures, the flourishes, she knew the girl was weaving and understood things could quickly get out of hand. She watched Chandra closely yet moved closer to stop her if needed.

"There ya go, lass. Let the anger settle. See the shadow. Feel the shadow."

Her voice cut in, and Chandra's anger dissipated. She blinked several times until she could finally see Stidyen clearly.

"Ye have th' gift," the crone said, enthralled. "How long?"

"Gift? What gift?" she asked, confused.

"Ahhh, ya don't know, do ya. Hmmm." She stroked her chin. "Don't know, yet…"

As if she found a missing question, she rushed off to a large cabinet, pulled open the door and began rummaging through scrolls and books. Dust lingered and swirled in the air as she moved from one to the other.

"Ahh, this, yes, this one." She slammed the book on the table, threw it open and began to turn pages quickly.

Stidyen mumbled as she read, running her finger down the page as Kalla once did, turned the page and repeated it. She glanced up at Chandra every few pages and returned to reading. Finally, she stood and began stroking her chin while walking toward the girl.

She paused, thinking. "Do as I say an' don't question," she demanded.

"Raise your hands again, just to here." She raised them to shoulder level, her palms facing each other and fingers bent like they were frozen.

Chandra complied, silently confused but excited.

"Now, close yer eyes an' think about a shadow. Try ta move it 'round in yer head."

Chandra made the attempt with no luck. She squinted and kept trying with no result.

"No, no, no. That won't do. Think, damn ya. See it move, then move it." She watched Chandra closely, wondering if she could.

Chandra took a breath and tried again. She saw a shadow and tried to will it to move, but again, nothing happened. It just wouldn't move.

Stidyen let out an exasperated sigh. Then, she decided to try another method.

"Alright, now. Raise 'em again. Close yer eyes an' think."

Chandra did it, waiting for the next command.

"Think about them men, that first rap to yer gob."

Chandra's eyes opened in fear.

"NO DAMMIT! Close 'em an' do as I say."

She closed her eyes. The memory was very fresh in her mind. She saw the guard, his huge fist moving closer to her small face. She could feel the contact and then the pain. Anger welled up in her chest. She began to breath deeper, faster. She couldn't stop the next punch, or the next or...

"There, slow down now. Keep 'em closed an' let the anger settle. Keep it level."

Chandra heard every word. She tried to do as Stidyen said, but the more she thought, the angrier she got.

"Okay, okay, okay, lass. That be enough." She grinned, now knowing what Chandra's skill was. "Calm, now, calm yerself down."

Chandra dropped her hands and slowly opened her eyes just in time to see a gigantic, roiling plume of shadow dissipate into nothing.

"Did-did I do that?" Chandra questioned, her eyes wide.

"Aye, I'll say ya did, lass. Shadow as I've ne'er seen from one so young—ne'er." She stared at Chandra and began to rub her hands together.

"We've work ta do, my dear, yes, much work indeed."

Stidyen returned to the book she had left still open on the table and began reading. She walked to another cabinet and removed a tome, looked at its spine, removed another, looked at its spine as well and motioned for Chandra to come to her.

"Here." She pulled a wooden chair to her, set the books down and said, "You read these. Do it slow an' let the words talk to ya."

Chandra sat and looked at both books. The first book's cover was ordinary and uninteresting to her. It was all black with writing she'd only seen in Kalla's lodge and an odd symbol.

"Ahhh, I see ye starin' at the big book. What's it tellin' ye?" Stidyen's voice rasped with something between mischief and gravity.

"Nothing. It's just a picture."

The crone sighed, exasperated. She reached over, grasped the back of Chandra's head and forced it forward roughly. "READ! Ya can do it, just open yer mind."

Fear began to grip Chandra. She forced herself to look. She concentrated.

The symbols meant nothing until…they did.

The symbols began to writhe, first meaningless scratches, then shifting, twisting, warping and sliding into place. The black outline boiled like smoke, the circle's heart bleeding red as congealed blood. The pentagram lifted from the page, edges shimmering, letters burning into her sight:

Her eyes grew wide, her fear turning into sheer excitement. *THIS is what I've been searching for.*

The second book was green in color with a triangle filled in black and a gold eye in the center. Her heart began to beat faster.

"Are these tomes…magic, Gran?"

Stidyen looked at her in a way she hadn't looked at anyone in over one hundred years. It was the look of…love.

"Yes…my child." She hesitated at using the word to get her reaction. "It be th' beginning o' understandin' magic."

Chandra glanced up at Stidyen with awe and excitement.

"Ya read, lass, an' let Gran know when ya be done. Aye, we've LOTS o' work ta do."

She walked off and, glancing back, saw Chandra diving into the tomes and reading with avarice.

At first, the way the words were written made it impossible for her to read, being more symbols than writing, but she forced herself to learn, to piece them together. They fought back in the beginning, but then, as if she could will them to abide her command, they became legible, easier to decipher, and most of all, meaningful.

The pages began to turn in a flurry; she gulped down the words as if they were food. Her eyes became transfixed on every word, like hands grasping and taking hold. Her mind stored them, and she could feel the mystical tingle of magic enter her very spirit.

The first book closed. She sat back, eyes closed and mentally reviewed what she read, making sense of every passage, hands moving unwittingly as if placing the words into their proper place. She understood this book as if it had been in her mind from the day she was born. She was MEANT to know this. Her lips moved as she spoke to herself, placing the new information in the right spaces of her mind. Her hands moved faster the more she thought, until the epiphany. The book was finally hers, stored for all time in her lockbox of memory.

Chandra sat forward and opened the second tome. It was not as informative but far easier to read than the other, and it spoke of far more varied things as well. Where the first spoke of mages and scholars from centuries past and how the spells were forged, this one was of anatomy, actual physical manipulation and method.

In no time, both books were read and reviewed. She looked around the room, trying to locate Stidyen, who was nowhere to be found. Her heart pounded faster. Her mind raced. *More, I must know more.*

Standing and looking into the cabinet, she tried to find more tomes that gave her the knowledge that she looked for, bypassing tomes of anatomy, alchemy and mythical creatures. She had to sort past scrolls of all kinds, notes and historical accounts, but found nothing to mention, much to her chagrin.

"I see ye finished both of 'em, yes?"

"I did. Is there more?" Her eyes had a ravenous glint to them.

"Ta be sure, girl, but now ain't th' time. Sleep. Ya needs sleep." She pointed to the hourglass on her alchemy table.

"Ya been at it all day an' night without no food, yet."

"All night?" Chandra asked in disbelief. "It seemed like just a short time."

"Aye, lass. That's where ya gotta be cautious. Power o' this nature can fool ya, suck ye in, get ya lost inside yerself ta where ya ne'er return." She had a very serious look on her face. "Fer centuries, mages an scholars've gone mad tryin' ta absorb all that." Stidyen pointed to the portal like a mother sending her daughter to bed.

"Go get ya some sleep. In th' morn,' ya can start again. I'll give ya something new this time." Chandra, disappointed, stood and went to the portal, thinking of food. Upon stepping in, she found that she had returned to the library where Stidyen stood, hunched over her alchemy table. "Ya needs ta go eat, child."

"I thought about food, but it brought me back here, Gran."

Stidyen stroked her chin and sighed. "Too deep, girl. Ya delved too deep today." She moved to Chandra and placed her hands on the girl's shoulders and looked into her eyes with sorrow. "Ya been reading so much, yer body thinks it be eatin'. Tis th' way o' magic, yes, magic." She turned her around and nudged her to the door. "If ya delves too deep too fast, girl, ya gets lost. If ya gets lost, it grips ya an' sucks ya in with no way o' returnin'." She sighed. "It be my own fault. I pushed ya too hard." She kissed Chandra on the forehead, which she hadn't done to anyone in a century. "Go eat, food this time. Then get ta sleep. In th' morn, we'll see how ya feels then start again…maybe. Just depends."

She sat at the table. A plate of squab seasoned with rosemary and thyme, boiled potatoes and greens sat on the plate before her. She stared at it, words and formulae still drifting through her mind. Hunger battled knowledge, and this time, hunger won. She took a deep breath and tore off a piece of breast and started to eat, the savory rosemary-thyme taste settling her mind and calming her spirit. The more she ate, the better her head felt, calmer, less voracious. She smiled. She'd finally found her purpose, her meaning—to be a mage, not just a mage…a powerful mage. It felt right, and she knew…Mother would be proud.

'…regrouping, are we?'

Talk of the tavern:

"Barkeep'll tell ya…. Two summers back, a whole trapper's party vanished. Only things found were their knives, laid in a line, neat as could be. Crone's mark, they say."

"Oh, shove it, Taerin…. Ya couldn't spot a crone ifn she sat on yer lap an' ordered ale."

"Stuff it. If I could pick yer mother out, a crone'd be a blessing to me eyes."

–Taerin to Kieran before they brawled

"...just stared at us, like she were tryin' to decide somethin'."

"Aye...and then she waved us off, gentle-like. Told us to mind the path."

–two guards on patrol

"I swear, if she wanted us dead...we'd be bones in th' leaves."

"Aye. I ain't ne'er goin' near them woods again...not for all th' coin in th' realm."

"Shadow follows that woman—mark my words."

–two wandering merchants over an ale

"Folk call her a monster, but she saved me cousin last winter."

"Saved him? That crone?"

"Aye. Found him half-frozen on th' ridge, dragged him to shelter, an' set his leg straight."

"Hells...why ain't folk knowin' that?"

"'Cause nobody believes th' truth when th' lie's more exciting."

–Barney to a kindly "old woman"

Of Shades and Shadows

Her dreams were filled with the knowledge she had gained earlier that day: dancing words and phrases, images and symbols swirled and intertwined as if each had life, runes and glyphs wrestled with each other, vying for notice in her hungry mind.

She awoke early and found that Stidyen had already selected more reading for her.

"Come here ta Gran, girl."

She stood before her, and Stidyen placed her hands on Chandra's head. She caressed the crown and the back of her head carefully, softly, like a mother soothing an ache.

"Ya feelin' better today, yes? Better?" She looked into Chandra's eyes.

"I do. I slept well. Better than I have since…"

"Now, now. None o' that. No," she said, waggling a finger. "Did ya eat some? Eat, yes?"

"I did. I don't think I've ever had spiced eggs before, but they were delicious."

Stidyen's eyes narrowed, then, as if speaking to the air, "I told ye not ta be doin' that ya shady halfwit. No. Listen ta me, now."

Chandra looked around to see who she was yelling at.

"Bah, never ya mind, lass. Never ya mind."

"Yer gonna rest another day, yes rest." She turned to put the books back on the shelf.

"Please, Stidyen…Gran. I'm alright, really."

Stidyen looked at the platinum-haired girl, her steel-gray eyes sparkling in anticipation. *Let 'er. She'll be fine, aye, fine.* She started to speak to Chandra, then shook her head. *No, not taday. Too fast, jus' too fast.*

"I told ya, ya dim-witted puff o' smoke, leave out or else," she said to the darkness sternly.

"No, lass. Can't be takin' th' chance. Tomorrow, yes tomorrow I think." She walked to the portal and left.

Chandra's eyes dropped to the floor with disappointment. She wanted more, so much more. She looked at the portal as its shimmering edges dissipated to nothing, Stidyen now gone. She began to worry about Stidyen. Was she addled? Who or what was she talking to? She thought better of arguing with her, not wanting to test her limits just yet.

Returning to the kitchen, a yellow bottle sat on the table with a note. It was from Stidyen telling her to drink it before she did anything else. It was a vitamin elixir that would help settle her mind and help prepare her better for her next lessons. She drank it down and went back into her room, where she tried to sleep again. This time it came quickly and peacefully. Thoughts of Lyssa came to her. They were little again, chasing the chickens, and her mother was yelling, angry at Lyssa more than her. She'd let them out and was chasing them all over the yard. She saw herself joining in, dodging her mother's grasp, her mother's laugh.

When she woke, she had a smile on her face and peace in her heart. She remembered what happened, but the memory helped to ease her mind. Chandra sighed and went to the kitchen, where she quickly ate and went to see if Stidyen had returned yet.

Speaking no words but pointing at the books that now sat on the table, she returned to her work. Chandra excitedly rushed to the table as if the books would disappear before she got there. Magic, it was all about magic now; what it was, how she obtained it and mostly…how to use it.

Still buried in the tomes before her, she never realized that Stidyen had left and returned without a sound. She reminded her once again that night had fallen and she needed rest. "Eat first, lass. Every scholar an' mage makes th' same mistake. They don't eat.

After a bit, their bodies wither, their minds leave 'em, an' insanity causes 'em ta die in horrific ways." She pointed a finger at her. "Yer too pretty ta let that happen. Now, ya listen ta Gran. Eat."

Chandra noticed that her teacher was beginning to repeat herself. The words were almost the exact same as the day before, which puzzled and concerned her.

She looked at her books, then at Stidyen and went to the kitchen where a fine table had been set. She didn't really feel hungry, but, remembering the night before, knew her eating was necessary. When she took her first bite of the succulent pork, she found that Gran was right. The flavor of daisy, coriander and rosemary were like nothing she'd ever eaten, and she found the potatoes flavored with butter and green onion to be the perfect combination of flavors.

A goblet of wine sat to the side of her plate, though she had never been fond of wine, she drank it down just the same. The taste mixed with the food, making her more relaxed and even a bit sleepy. Before long, her stomach was filled and, leaning back, she gave out a sigh of content satisfaction.

She thought of her father, how he'd lean back and belch, causing Mother to glare at him. They all knew she appreciated it, but was too much of a lady to allow it at her table.

Chandra looked around and belched so loudly it echoed.

"I heard that, lass. No lady does that, no," Stidyen said with a chuckle. "But I be glad ye liked it."

Chandra laughed, stood and went off to bed.

Days and weeks passed. Chandra absorbed knowledge from almost every book and tome Stidyen had. The sheer volume of reading she had done was impressive and, even when put to the test, Chandra proved she'd retained every bit of the information contained within. Question after question was asked, testing every aspect of what she'd read. Every answer was correct, every piece of additional information Stidyen added, she absorbed. Where Chandra found conflicting information, her teacher corrected it, helping her to better understand. Stidyen was proud of her, though she didn't often show it. She knew Chandra was smart, but not to this extent. The girl absorbed books faster than she'd ever seen. She also knew this meant one other thing. The girl would become…powerful, too powerful to contain, perhaps, which was concerning to her.

'…I see where this is going.'

The girl was becoming bored with just reading. She wanted practical application of what was being read and started to nag the old woman. When? When was she finally going to be allowed to weave, to actually see the fruits of her toils?

Ya have ta know afore ya can do, Stidyen would tell her. Chandra felt she already knew more than Stidyen and was anxious to prove it to her. After all, she did begin to cast something shortly after her arrival. Stidyen even directed her, and she witnessed the aftermath, though she didn't know what it was. She wanted to finally see and do.

The season had changed to fall. It seemed Chandra hadn't left the home in months, and she'd begun to feel as if the walls were closing in on her. She knew she had to get out and breathe the fresh air, or she felt she'd lose her mind. Stidyen taught her the words to open the portal so she could come and go as she liked, but warned her to be careful.

"Have a care, girl. None can know an' none can follow." She told her what to do if anyone tried and how to protect herself in the old church.

"The building knows, lass. It knows."

Chandra went outside and closed the portal behind. She stepped into the sun and reveled in its warmth, letting it caress her skin. She closed her eyes and took a deep breath of the fresh, cool air; she walked around the old church, looking at all the brightly colored fallen leaves. Fall had always been her favorite season. The colors always reminded her of a raging fire, the yellows, reds and oranges. It would begin to get cold soon, the breeze carrying the smells of drying leaves, wheat and barley ready for cutting and even the faint smell of someone cooking far away.

The sun was nearing the horizon, and the sky was clear. Soon, stars by the score would be shining brightly above, twinkling as if speaking in an unknown language. She dragged a broken bench from the church outside so she could sit and enjoy being a part of nature. Looking to the southern horizon, she could see the road was still far off. It looked like a dark line, cutting her view in half, yet close enough to where she could still see people and carts traveling back and forth.

She lingered in the natural silence for quite some time, never realizing just how wonderful the sounds of nature could be. The sun was now nearly gone, only the dimming light remaining. It was the time when shadows began to lengthen, and fewer people passed on the road. She sighed, feeling the time had passed too quickly, and it was time to go inside, so she stood and stretched.

'…I'm here, mistress.'

Oddly enough, with all the learning she'd been doing, she'd almost forgotten the voice.

I know. I've felt you. It was the first time she was able to speak to it.

'…I'm certain. You have but to ask and it shall be done, mistress.'

She was curious. What was this? Where did it come from, and why her?

'…I am called Malhrun, mistress. I am both shadow and dream. The voice was a whisper, slow and calming.

'…I come from a place you do not yet know, and the answer to the question you have asked since you were but a child is…because you are POWERFUL!'

The last word rang like a raging thunderclap in her head.

You can read my mind?

'…always, mistress. We are one.'

166

She sat and began to puzzle out everything she knew about this Malhrun. She'd never seen him, only heard, and never aloud, only in her head.

Did you kill the wolf that was pestering my father's tannery? She'd always wondered about it. She always thought it was the gods answering a wish or a prayer, but that never sat right with her. She knew there had to be more to it.

'...*mistress commanded. Malhrun obeyed.*'

"So, it WAS you," she exclaimed with a smile.

'...*of course, mistress.*'

"You can hear?"

'...*to be sure, mistress, as any other thing.*'

She began to get excited. She thought about what this could mean, what the possibilities could be.

"Alright. You didn't tell me where you came from, so now, I ask, what are you? I can't see you, so are you a ghost, an apparition?"

'...*I am what you call, a shade, mistress. I am the shadow itself.*'

She thought back to the times she heard him in her head. *It was always daylight. So, how could I hear him?* she thought.

'...*I am the shadow, mistress. Where there is shadow, there I am.*'

"Are you completely shadow or can you just hide in what shadows are present?"

'...*I move from shadow to shadow, no matter where they are. I am as near or far as the shadows are from you, mistress.*'

The sun was gone now; only the dazzling twinkle of starlight remained.

"Can you show yourself to me? It is dark. I wish to see."

She looked around. Then, right in front of her, two blazing red eyes blinked. It startled her for just a second.

"YOU!" She now remembered.

"I've seen you time and again—everywhere, blinking red eyes." The realization brought a flood of memories.

"In Gran's lodge, in our room, in the woods under the moon, when I looked outside, you were there all along." There was a wide grin on her face now.

'...yes, mistress.'

She remembered teasing Lyssa about all the mishaps she had while hunting.

'...yes mistress. You requested it.'

Her face grew dark. "Why didn't you save my mother and father?" The question burned her heart and face.

'...I was no longer attached, mistress.'

"No longer attached?" She became furious. "What does that even mean?"

'...mistress. It is in my very nature to become tethered to the living entity that is deemed to have the most energy. I had been tethered to Kal'La as she emitted more power than anyone...until Ta'Lith entered the world. Her innate energy was far stronger than Kal'La's.'

Chandra absorbed every word. She knew Gran had a certain energy about her, but not her mother.

"Mother had no power. She never made elixirs and knew no spells, at least none that I'd ever witnessed."

'...Ta'Lith denied her power, mistress.'

"But why? That makes no sense."

'...Ta'Lith wanted only life, not power, mistress. The more she denied, the less she emitted and thus her energy was lost. I remained with Kal'La until you were born.'

"How did you know I had more power? I was a newborn. I had no power."

'...you and Lys'Sa arrived with more power than I had ever experienced previously, mistress. I could not connect to either. I became isolated, disconnected.'

"I understand. But why me if Lyssa had the same amount of power?"

'*...Lys'Sa had more power, but she too, denied, mistress. Her ignorance of her own power allowed alteration by another's and, thus, allowed me to become tethered to you.*'

Chandra pondered that, silently, for a while. She had to ask.

"Altered by what?"

'*...I cannot say, mistress.*'

"You can't say or won't say?"

'*...I can...not say, mistress.*'

"What if I wish it or request it?"

'*...I am forbidden by one who IS power, mistress.*'

"One who IS power?" She thought that was an interesting answer.

"And who might the one who IS power be?"

There was a blinding flash of blue-yellow lightning and a deafening clap of thunder that scared Chandra to the ground. She looked at the sky, expecting a downpour, but...the stars were shining. There was not a cloud to be seen.

'*...THAT is the one who is power, mistress.*' Two red eyes blinked in the night.

She suddenly felt bitter cold under her arms and felt as if she were being lifted to her feet.

"You are solid as well?"

'*...Only rarely, mistress. My power drains very quickly. I must go. I am weak.*'

"You said you would never leave me."

'*...I am always here, mistress. As you say, I must rest.*'

"Wait. Why did you say Kal'La and Ta'Lith?" She just realized the name differences.

'*...Because that is their names, mistress. Do you not know your own family?*'

"They are Talith and Kalla. And, of course, I know my family." She was now confused and needed to know.

'*...As you wish, mistress. It is not for me to dispute.*'

169

"But I don't understand."

'…I am forbidden, mistress. You will be told in due course.'

She pondered the conversation. *He said he wasn't attached to save my family, yet we were the most powerful. He couldn't attach to any one power while Lyssa and I were children, even though Lyssa denied her power.* It was coming together. *Lyssa still had the power until…until.* Then it struck her. *Gran left, giving Lyssa and me the power. Mother had no more power, so it got confused. Then the guards…* She swallowed away the pain. *Leaving just me as we separated. It attached to me until Stidyen appeared.* Her brow furrowed, deep in thought. *Now, why was she yelling at it?* Her eyes flashed wide. *Because Stidyen was more powerful until I started reading. It made my power stronger, so it attached to me. Which means…*

'…you are correct, mistress.'

After she'd opened the portal and gone inside, she was met by Stidyen. "There ya be. Getting' air, were ya? Air?"

"Yes ma'…Gran. It's nice tonight, and it's been a while." She smiled at the old woman and began to walk to her room.

"Tomorrow, we begin. Get yer beauty sleep, lass. Sleep."

'…I think introductions are in order.'

Morning came early for Chandra. Excitement kept her awake for most of the night as her mind kept envisioning powerful spells, lightning and fireballs. She had no idea what time of day it might be, so she quickly slid out of bed, put her tattered dress on and went to Stidyen's conjuring circle. She was already there, mumbling to herself, mixing reagents and boiling herbs.

"Ahh, she comes fer training, yes, training." On a lectern that had seen far better days sat an open book, its pages tattered and brown from age. All around the floor were deep scratches, gouged by unfathomable entities, burns and ash. Stidyen looked Chandra from head to toe, pondering the possibilities. "I'm ready, Gran. Really, I am," her eyes bright with excitement.

Stidyen's eyes looked to the pages of the book, then back at the young girl. "We shall see, yes." She pointed to a chair. "Here. Bring it here an' sit."

Quickly, she did as instructed, looking at the crone, eagerly awaiting her lesson.

"Yer 'bout ta learn th' art o' spellcraft, weavin' we calls it, but once ye begin, there ain't no goin' back. Ye'll begin ta weave th' skeins of magical power that makes up th' very air we breathe; th' very blood that courses through yer body; th' very spirit that binds yer life," she paused to let that sink in, "ta begin means surrenderin' yer entire life in pursuit o' that which ya wishes ta become." She stepped down and coldly stared into the young girl's eyes, then whispered in an ominous tone, "Ye'll feel power like ye ne'er felt afore. Yes? Ye'll be pulled to it til ya can't stop. Always more, there be—always." She blinked as if waking from a dream. "Yes, yer truly ready." She looked into the girl's eyes, no, not into…through, as if she could see deep into her very spirit. Chandra could feel the cold from her stare…and she wanted more.

"Will ya devote yer life ta th' realm o' magic an' power? Think first. Ye'll ne'er be th' same Chandra again. Ne'er"

She didn't hesitate. "I want it all. Teach me, Gran."

A knowing grin passed the old woman's face. She knew she had chosen right.

"First's first. Magic be tiny strands o' power floatin' invisible all about ye. There ain't no lines o' lay like them weepy nature weavers say. Them be false teachin's. Lif' yer hand. Close yer eyes. Feel 'em."

Chandra closed her eyes and extended both arms and palms out. She felt a slight tingling all over her fingers, over her hands and down her arms. Her heart began to race.

A smile of wonder, hands moving to grasp each strand, she whispered, "I feel it, Gran. It's wonderful."

"Ahhh, good. That be magic…in its raw shape. Ye've always felt it. It were always there. Ye just ne'er knew what it be." She watched the girl intently, smiling. "Now, move yer hands an' think of a thing, a piece o' black nothing, a ball o' void. See what happens." Her eyes went wide with anticipation.

Chandra saw a black ball in her mind. She began to flourish her hands in a slow, revolving circle.

"Easy, lass. Slow as ye go. Yer doin' good."

She felt the tingling turn to a buzz and began to move her hands faster, heart beginning to pound in her chest.

"Alright, lass. That be enough, now. Slow down, slow."

She didn't want to because it felt amazing. The power flowed through her like a warm breeze.

Her hands came to an abrupt stop. She opened her eyes to see Stidyen almost nose to nose with her.

"When I says stop, YE STOP!" Chandra could see the fire in her eyes and knew she had gone too far.

"I'm sorry, Gran. The power…it just felt so…good. I couldn't stop." She had fear in her eyes.

The old woman softened, "I know, lass. I know. But this be somethin' ye'll have ta take hold of. It'll eat ya alive ifn ya don't. Magic be power," she said calmly. "If ya lose control, it'll kill ya fer sure. Ne'er ferget that." Her calm turned serious. "Ya almost lost control."

Her lessons had now begun. Trivial at first for certain, but Stidyen had to reveal how much the girl knew, how practiced she might be.

The first spells she taught were minor, easy weavings she called magical gestures. They were nothing more than simple spells: lighting a hearth fire with a snap of the fingers or setting candles aglow with a sharp clap of the hands. Chandra all but laughed at those.

Next, Stidyen taught her the finer points of common summonings, minor manipulations of the elements, and even basic illusory abilities. She tried to outwit the girl with improper casting techniques and unassumed shape-shifting. Chandra saw through all of them and even managed to dupe the crone on several illusory tests.

The old woman had never seen abilities of this magnitude in someone so young. Chandra had adapted to almost every method that Stidyen challenged her with and was successful each and every time. What she was teaching would have taken most mages years and years to learn, studying tomes, gestures, proper spell pronunciation, and most of all, using the correct amount of magic. She had absorbed all of this in just a day. True enough, it was lower-level weaving, but the amount she took in was staggering.

They conjured and cast until they both had become physically and mentally exhausted.

"Enough, lass. Enough." Sweat slowly dripped from Stidyen's forehead. Though tired, Chandra wanted more, feeling as if her energy would never wane.

"We must rest fer th' night, lass, yes rest." She was still breathing heavily. "Too much. I showed ye too much." Shaking her head, she walked to the portal and was gone.

Chandra sat, eyes closed, reliving every spell, every motion, every word Stidyen had spoken. She saw each glyph, rune and spell swirling in her mind, fighting for release. She took a deep breath, held it for just a second, then let it slowly escape, calming the magic swirling in her mind and allowing it to settle into its rightful place. Opening her eyes, she smiled as the velvety skeins of magic gently caressed her skin. She now knew she could control it. She now knew who she was meant to be.

The old woman sat at the table staring at the leaping flames of the fire. She couldn't remember the last time she had worked so hard to dupe an apprentice and failed. She became worried. This girl could take every spell she knew, learn it, cast it and still want more. It was not natural. It must be the lady's will. SHE was the one who sent this little girl. It had to be her. There was no other explanation. The woman sighed, resigned.

But the lady wanted her to teach Chandra, teach her everything. She had her reasons, which were not for Stidyen to know. But she knew.

She knew this one would be powerful…and dangerous.

Finally, Chandra went into the kitchen and sat to eat. The meal had already been prepared and was ironically the very stew Talith would make when the season switched to winter.

"This is very good, Gran." Her grin was like that of a little girl, sweet and innocent. "My mother used to make this when I was younger."

She smiled and said, "I know, dear." She glanced up to see her reaction. "I knew yer mum, or knew of her, yes. Kalla were your gran, yes?" She took another bite of the steaming stew. "I knew Kalla, I did. Potions and elixirs, aye, them." She swallowed. "Was it she what taught ya spells?"

Chandra blew on her stew to cool it a bit. "No, Gran. No one told me how. You were the first." She ate a spoonful and smiled.

Stidyen's eyes widened a bit. "No one, ya say?" That raised her brow. "Hmm, interestin' lass, interestin'."

"Why's that, Gran? I did do it right, didn't I?" She began to worry.

"Aye, ya did, too right for someone what just started." She'd stopped eating and had turned her full attention to Chandra now. "Did ya learn yerself, perhaps?"

"No, Gran. Today was the first real time I've ever done this. I thought I had once." She stopped eating as well. "My sister swore I made the shadows move, but it wasn't me."

Stidyen sat silently, slowly mulling over the possibilities. But she had to know for sure.

"Try weavin' one right now. Don't think, just weave." She watched raptly.

Chandra hesitated, trying to understand what was happening.

Stidyen calmly stood and slammed her hand down onto the table, making Chandra jump.

"NOW DAMMIT! DO IT NOW!" Her face contorted into ire, rage. She had to make the child react.

Bewilderment fell entirely into anger. She hated yelling. Her mother never did it, but Kalla once did. It reminded her of that day...*Never again.*

Chandra's mood changed instantly as she stood, snarling with anger. She slid her chair backward and started to move her hands, mumbling unnatural words. They rose over her head, unknowingly yet rhythmically. All she saw was Stidyen standing there, her hands still on the table, and she felt the heat of rage, almost hate. She swirled her hands, intertwining them, flourishing them. If Stidyen wanted her to react, then react she would. Her words became fierce, more pronounced, but still foreign to her ears. She dropped them almost to her waist, palms up as if clawing at the very air around her. As she did, a thick, black shadow began to form. It began to billow and form. Stidyen's eyes went wide. *By the lady...*

The black cloud began to form into the shape of a towering shadow beast, its maw yawning wide to bear fangs like black obsidian. Chandra began her chant, an otherworldly voice even she didn't recognize. "Meeyan trad..."

'...*Not now, mistress. Not now.*'

She tried to fight off the voice in her head, but it broke her concentration, silencing her words and causing the apparition she had formed to quickly dissipate.

Stidyen was completely taken aback.

"By the Lady, ya be a shadow-weaver," she said in awe, wonder...and fear.

Chandra was panting from the strenuous conjuration she had produced, yet still staring at Stidyen angrily. Sweat forming on her brow, she sat heavily on the chair and leaned back, trying to regain her breath and calm herself.

'...Well done, mistress.'

"Where'd ye learn this magic, yes, where?" Her question sounded nervous, worried. Shadow weavers were exceedingly rare, indeed, and having one this young, this untrained, would be unbelievably dangerous. She already had an inkling of what Chandra was capable of, but a full-on shadow weaver?

"Nowhere. I just got angry and saw it in my head. I'd seen the shadows move when I was younger, but I told you I've never done this before." She sat upright, now able to breath normally. "Why won't you believe *ME*!" She leaned back again, taking another deep, cleansing breath.

She looked at Stidyen and asked more calmly, "What is a shadow weaver?" The very sound was ominous to her ears.

Stidyen swallowed hard. She knew she had to tell her. She had to teach her control or else the danger could envelop them both. Her insides fluttered with both excitement and fear. This could very well be the beginning...or her end.

"Shadow-weaving is th' manipulation o' shadows themselves. Th' very darkness 'round ya." She took a deep breath. "This form o' weaving be called Aesh'amon-tu, or One Who Commands Darkness. An,' as I knows it, ye be th' first one ta do this in over two hundred years." She felt her mouth go dry. Was it fear or terror?

Chandra gave the crone a confused look. "But how...? How is this possible? Until today, I've never used any form of magic, let alone knowing what this Aesh'amon-tu was."

"It don't matter, lass." She stood, troubled. "The gods give ye a gift. I guess it be me that'll teach's ya how ta use it."

"When? Tomorrow?"

"No, I must go an' see someone 'bout this, yes, see someone." She slowly walked off mumbling to herself.

Chandra blinked, troubled at the revelation. She leaned forward and cupped her bowl, looking at it as if the answers were written there. She touched her spoon absently, though the stew had already gone cold. Tonight, sleep would not come easily...not after this.

She lay for some time, still deeply troubled and trying to understand. She'd never heard the words, the chant, never saw the shadow before. How was she able to do this? Did the words come from something she read? If they did, then which tome was it? A million questions raced through her young mind, seemingly with no answers.

It scared her...and yet excited her.

Trying to desperately remember the words, she started to have visions. The words, they began to appear in her mind, jumbled, swirling, perfect, then in line, as if...

'...MISTRESS, STOP!'

Her eyes flashed open in time to see two burn marks on the ceiling glowing blue and purple. Wisps of black, inky shadow drifted from the impacts, causing her to gasp.

"What...what happened?"

'...control, mistress. Control.' The shade sounded worried in her mind.

'...shadow orbs, mistress. Even in sleep, you are powerful. Must control.'

For the rest of the night, she would go in and out of sleep, the fear of it happening again never leaving her mind. She tried numerous times to will herself to sleep, but the fear, worry and elation fatigued and strained her very being.

The next morning, she went to the kitchen to eat. This time there was no food, no drink and no Stidyen. She found a loaf of bread and began to eat. It was stale but not crumbling, yet she ate it anyway.

She went through the portal to find Stidyen, but when she entered her sanctum, she wasn't there. The oily alchemical smells that normally permeated the air had been replaced by the musty smell of a dry and dusty cellar mixed with that of damp forest leaves. It was both comforting and ominous.

Curiously, Chandra wandered the room, investigating countless herbs and liquids, studying the various textures and colors. *Lyssa would have fun here,* she thought. A pang of sorrow found its way into her heart. Lyssa. Her heart began to hurt at the memory. One day.

Lyssa. Is she alive? If so, where is she? Could she be looking for me? Stidyen said she was alive, but how could she know?

She began to worry all over again.

Pacing helped to ease her worries, to allay her fears and still keep hope for her sister, but there was still one gnawing fact: she was still missing.

Oddly enough, Chandra had picked up her daydreaming habit from her mother, who would do it unconsciously at times when things became troubled. Unaware of her surroundings, she bumped into the big study table near the bookshelves and almost fell. Chandra cursed herself under her breath for her clumsiness. The pile of books, tomes and scrolls in front of her were dusty and very old, but she could see from the oil lamp's light that they all referenced Aesh'amon-tu in one form or another.

There were many compendia, most of which she'd never seen or heard of before. Curiosity took hold as she peeled a scroll open. The words were ancient and faded, barely decipherable to her dismay.

She set it aside, opened one of the books and tried reading it. A broad grin crossed her face as she realized that they were the words of magic, of mages long past, whose discoveries and inventions were being passed down to those who could understand them. Who could manipulate them? The lighting was poor, so she clapped her hands together once, and the stands of candles burst into flames, giving off plenty of light.

She became lost in knowledge. Once again, her thirst for magical knowledge overrode her will. Book after book, scroll after scroll, she read, absorbing each word and the very heart and meaning of each one, making them a part of her mind, of her very spirit. Time became invisible, unimportant. She absently opened the last scroll.

As if she were being called by the words, her eyes were forced to stare, to understand, to learn. They began to dance as if alive. Mesmerized, she watched as they moved together, forming comprehensible words, explanations, divinations, and conjurations.

It was a spell written long ago. Someone or something wanted her to know, to learn this particular slice of Aesh'amon-tu. She read on. The final words coalesced into a chant of darkness:

Meeyan fastuul mafren uumbraa

She spoke it like she would a common whisper, slow, controlled.

Without realizing it, she stood while reading the scroll. Her eyes had rolled white. Her hands rose as if clutching for shadow; the scroll drifted back onto the table. Her spell was gathering the very shadow that surrounded her. She repeated the words. Again. Again. A musty odor of damp, rotting wood and dry parchment began to fill the room.

The shape of the shadow beast began to reappear. Fully formed, jagged, shadowed fangs filled its maw.

'Iii am yoursss…mistresss. Command…meeee.'

Its words hit her like the midnight breeze, cold and gentle. Her eyes returned, and she saw the shape of the apparition she'd almost conjured earlier.

'Show no fear, mistress, for it is you who commands it.'

Swallowing her rising fear, she raised her head and gave her command. "Return to your plane, servant of shadow. I will summon you again."

'Assss… youuu…commmand.'

It slowly dissipated until there was nothing left.

She had done it. She had called forth a shadow and knew she could command it. It felt to her as if the being almost…feared her.

Her heart pounded with elation. She had done it, something only thought of in her wildest dreams. She drew a chair to the table and began to reread some of the pages. Again, the words began to speak to her. They embedded themselves into her mind as if they had been pieces she had been missing all these years. The more she read, the more comfortable she became.

The odor of ozone and the sound of crackling electricity broke her concentration. She looked up to see Stidyen dusting herself off and walking toward her.

The old woman stopped short at the table, eyes narrowing at the scattered tomes. They shifted from the table to Chandra, then back to the books.

"What be this, lass? Why're these out, hmmm? Why?"

Chandra looked up, confused. "Didn't you leave them here?"

"No," Stidyen said slowly. "I been gone, yes." Her gaze lingered on Chandra, sharp, weighing truth from falsehood.

"They were on the table when I woke up. I thought you'd put them here for me to read." Chandra felt the prickle of accusation. She opened her mouth to protest, but the silence stretched too long.

She closed the book and stood. "Shall I replace them?" she asked, now wary.

Stidyen looked into her eyes for just a second and silently shook her head. She noticed that the smell of the room had changed. *What 'ave ye been up ta, hmm? Yes, what?*

They didn't speak for the rest of the day, each going about their business, ignoring the earlier tension. Chandra continued to read, often searching for another book or scroll on the shelf or in the cabinets. Every time she moved, Stidyen glanced at her in secret, desperately trying to know, to reveal. What was she doing?

'...what are you up to, Lady?'

Talk of the tavern:

"Something's wrong on that hill, I swear it. Went up to gather berries and felt eyes on me back th' whole time. Not beasts...I know beasts. This were somethin' else, somethin' old and restless."

–women's fence-line gossip

"My dogs stopped dead near th' edge of them woods. Didn't bark, didn't whine—just froze an' backed up with tails tucked. That kind o' silence ain't natural. Makes me think somethin' up there be wakin'."

–a local farmer

Of Dreams Fulfilled and Shattered Hopes

The days slowly passed, yet Stidyen remained wary. Though her mistrust abated enough to begin teaching Chandra again, she deliberately withheld parts of her knowledge, fearful that giving too much would leave her weaker than her apprentice. She now had no alternative but to resign herself to the fact that the girl not only had a voracious appetite to learn Aesh'amon-tu in all its forms but hungered for the magic to make it powerful. She herself was not as schooled as she needed to be, so she often left for days at a time, returning with tomes and books that could further Chandra's desires but not before she'd consumed them herself. She was finding it more and more difficult to absorb the foreign methods and teachings, but forged ahead more out of fear than necessity. Chandra's mind had become unlocked, and she began to understand the finer subtleties of weaving these types of spells, how to cast several spells together to get the desired effect and how dangerous these spells could be when woven correctly. Several times, she had conjured effects and beings without knowing how to completely control them. Stidyen would have to step in and correct the error, her chastising growing more unrelenting each time.

Chandra's hubris had grown considerably since her first conjuration as well. She'd begun to attempt spells and summonings without a circle of control and, even more dangerously, without Stidyen's knowledge. In her mind, she felt that she'd summoned and controlled the shadows once; she would do so again…but it became an obsession. She had to know more, to gather all the power she could. She would, sometimes, struggle to contain an evocation, almost in vain, but would, somehow, manage to regain control and put an end to it. From this, she cultivated a great disdain for elemental magic. Though necessary, she found it too limiting, too basic. Malhrun insisted, several times, on reminding her of her lack of skill and that she needed to stop pushing herself so hard. He could see the mental fatigue beginning to exact its toll on her, but felt her power grow with each spell. Sometimes, she would listen; others, she would just angrily banish him.

Stidyen was growing concerned about Chandra's growth in power as well. She was getting fearful that the girl could no longer be contained and that she was quickly becoming an uncontrollable threat. She tried to get Chandra to learn different disciplines; elemental, alteration, illusory, perhaps, but each time she dismissed the thought and returned to Aesh'amon-tu. Against her better judgment, she had even considered necromancy; the idea chilled her blood and stirred fearful memories of her mother. The manipulation of the physical dead, she reasoned, was taboo and ultimately counterproductive; there was no true knowledge to be gained from a corpse.

Shadow manipulation, however, not only offered insight but allowed her to go one step further, to bend the shadow itself. Yet, every refusal, every defiance, drew her back to Aesh'amon-tu, the art she knew best and trusted most. She grew increasingly fascinated by the power and the subtleties of the discipline, the power needed to summon or create, and the ultimate fascination of the entity created. Even Malhrun watched with amazement at the sheer variety of shadows she brought forth. Shades, fetches, wraiths and even a *thal'vess thaleen.*

She had only held one in control for just seconds. Its mere presence caused Malhrun to scream an icy, terrible scream, which caused her to release it. Chandra had no idea what she'd done until the shade explained it to her.

'… *it is a forest terror, mistress. Even the Valyn fear the thal'vess thaleen. It is Forest Veil Stalker. There are but two, both named, and once learned, marks your name for death.*'

183

Chandra now felt she had gone too far, pushed too hard. She couldn't remember if it spoke a name or if she'd even heard it, but she knew her trials had come to an end.

Stidyen's spirit affliction seeped into her already weakened mind. The fear that Chandra had surpassed even her considerable power forced her to think that one day she would have to confront her, that it would be Chandra's will against hers. She'd come to care about the child as a daughter, but now true fear crept into her old bones and, for the first time since she rescued her, contempt.

Today, that bond of master and pupil would shatter.

Chandra read nearly every book, every tome and every scroll available to her. There was but one remaining. It had been secreted away in a chest, locked and chained. When she had asked Stidyen, the old woman chastised her and forbade her even a glimpse. Her words were harsh, hateful and final. She tasked Malhrun with delving into the tome as best he could; she had to know. The wonders and terrors he revealed piqued Chandra's curiosity even more. She must know this magic. She must pass this final test.

Without a second thought, she'd woven her weak elemental magic and melted the bindings from the chest. The acrid smell of burnt metal permeated the air. The chest lid opened easily and, as she peered into the dark bottom of the container, a faint glowing purple aura formed around the tome. It felt bitter cold to the touch as she lifted it out and set it on the table, ominous, almost defiant, yet begging to be revealed.

Once in full view, it began to radiate an eerie purple-black, icy mist, and the eyes began to glow brightly.

As she looked upon the glowing glyphs, ancient words began to resonate in her mind: *Aesh'amon-tu Voth'en-raa.* For One Who Commands Darkness…The Way of No Return.

She gasped.

184

Without warning, the cover swung open on black metal hinges, the pages wildly turning. With hands to either side of the tome, she leaned over and stared into it, the words, they moved, danced…beckoned. She knew this was power. She felt it. She yearned for it. No book she'd read since her first emitted this sort of aura, this power. It captured her, mesmerized her, drew her in.

She was becoming one with the words. It was becoming her skin, her being. Every line shimmered, glyphs rising faintly from the ancient vellum before sinking back, whispering in a tongue she almost understood. She could not look away; each glyph hooked into her mind, tugging her deeper, until she wasn't sure if she were reading the book…or the book was reading her.

Malhrun crept close to her. '…*have a care, mistress. Rule the power but do not let the power rule you.*'

Too late for that. It was far too late. It had become a part of her and she it. They had mystically become one. The script pulsed, veins of violet light threading through the words, as if they drew strength from her gaze. It seemed there was a world beyond the tome, dark and foreboding. She felt it pulling, almost begging her to follow, a large black lake, shadowy entities writhing and dancing, beckoning her forward, challenging her very will against theirs.

She heard Malhrun's words ringing sharply through her skull. She fought back. She must regain her power yet take theirs. She could see it now, a shape. It loomed large and menacing. The black lake began to turn a dark crimson red. As it loomed closer, she could feel its will taking hold of her, but she must not lose. She must take its power to escape. The battle of their wills raged on, each trying to overpower the other.

She fought hard and began to draw back, pulling the entity with her. But it fought back, unwilling to succumb, pulling with even greater strength. She felt as if she were tiring. It knew. It came still closer, draining every ounce of her will. She felt it waning increasingly faster. Just then, the vision of Talith flashed into her mind. She nodded and smiled, then she was gone.

Chandra locked eyes with the entity, its purple eyes oozing glowing power, its open maw sucking in every bit of her will. She smiled, and with every ounce of her being, fought back. She could feel its power being absorbed; it enveloped her, filled her, flowed through her. She felt the entity beginning to weaken. She laughed defiantly, finally knowing and heaved with all of her might. The entity tried to resist, but only for a brief time. It knew Chandra was stronger. She could feel it too, and now challenged it to defy her. Then…it became certain. Defiance was now futile, and without any further resistance, gave itself to her completely.

Chandra's body fell hard against the chair behind her as the tomes' power finally released her. Her ragged dress drenched with sweat, and panting heavily, she desperately gasped for breath. Malhrun covered her with his shadowy body, attempting to help cool her down. He could feel the heat of the battle radiating from her like a stoked fire. For what seemed like hours, she tried to recover her strength. Finally, feeling better, she slowly sat forward and looked at the tome. It was no longer open. The eyes no longer glowed and had shut. The book, now silent.

A faint odor of sweet water and brimstone hovered gently in the air, then dissipated.

She wiped her brow with the arm of her sleeve and reopened the cover. They were all just words, faded on worn and yellowed vellum. She began to reread the pages, first one, then another. No more writhing, no more dancing, the words were only a reminder of what had once been. She smiled and gently closed the book.

'…*you are now… Mistress of the Shadows.*'

Two glowing eyes blinked close to her face, and she felt the shade wrap its cold appendages around her in a dark, almost tender embrace.

There was nothing more to learn. The knowledge she had absorbed since coming here had satisfied her voracious hunger, and for the first time, she felt whole.

She glanced at the shade. "You've known all along, haven't you, Malhrun? You've been guiding me to this point all of my life, haven't you?"

'*... not I, mistress. It just was destiny.*'

She took a deep breath. "I wonder where destiny will lead me next."

'*...where, dammit?*'

Her head sagged under its own weight, every thought too heavy to hold. The struggle had drained her strength as well as her mind. She laid her weary head down on her arms, covering the tome. Her muscles relaxed, and the feeling of sleep clouded her mind. *I did it. I did it and survived.* Her heart felt lighter knowing she'd finally done the one thing she'd always dreamed of. She *COMMANDED* magic.

Ozone and the sound of electricity filled the room, startling her awake. She sat upright, dazed. It was Stidyen. She stood in front of the portal, looking around the room as if searching for something...someone. Turning, her eyes fixed on Chandra sitting at the big table...in front of the tome.

Her brows furrowed, breath coming in ragged bursts.

"What...did...you...DO?" Her words were clear. They resonated through the room.

Chandra tried to shake the cobwebs of fatigue from her mind as Stidyen continued to scream.

"You were WARNED. I TOLD you. What have you DONE?" Her words dripped with venom, and Chandra now knew there would be a confrontation. The hag moved quickly to the desk and snatched the book from under her arms. Stidyen's eyes went wide with realization. "YOU!"

Her expression showed both rage…and fear. She tossed the tome aside, no longer caring about its importance.

She had been forewarned; there would be a day…and it had finally come.

Chandra stood, eyes narrowed, preparing for the unwelcome showdown.

Her voice grew louder with every word, "I told you this was not to be opened. You did it anyway. I told you this was FORBIDDEN! You did it anyway. Why? WHY?" She began to shake with rage.

Chandra didn't want this. She didn't know if she could outduel Stidyen and didn't want to find out. Stepping toward the still active portal was her only respite, and she knew she had to at least try. Just as she reached the magical door, Stidyen grabbed her arm and tried to pull her face-to-face. The old woman was much stronger than Chandra thought, and now she knew this was heading for disaster. Outside, that was her best defense, someplace she could work unhindered. She jerked her shoulder back and jumped through the portal. A flash, a cool breeze of pure magic, and she was inside the abandoned church once more.

Chandra saw that night had almost fallen and quickly ran outside. She stepped behind the building, waiting to hear the crackling of the portal once again, but there was nothing. The bright stars twinkled, and a slow, cool breeze chilled her while she fearfully looked toward the sky. She began to piece together her thoughts. What were Stidyen's strengths? What could she possibly know that wasn't already taught? Should she fight or run? Her mind raced with a million thoughts. But the one thought that made her afraid was…I feel so weak.

The trial of wills took a heavy toll on her mind and body. Her thoughts felt foggy, muddled. Would she even have the strength to duel her teacher? She knew she must; her very life now depended on it.

She felt the cold of Malhrun at her ankle. It reassured her, but she knew it wasn't enough. She stepped into the open and began to summon another shade. Her hands rose quickly, and a bright purple glow began to take shape in her palms. She started to twirl her arms…and was immediately knocked over by an invisible force. Stidyen stood before her, eyes glowing red, breathing heavily, death on her mind.

The moment had come. It was now time for the final reckoning. This would be her final lesson, but would it cost her own life?

Stidyen's hand began to glow and pop with electricity. Chandra's eyes went wide. She dove just as a large bolt of crackling electricity passed her head and hit the tree behind her, splitting it and causing it to smolder and smoke. She glared back at Stidyen, her anger peaking.

"As you wish, hag." Her scowl flashed hate at the old woman. "To the death."

She blew onto her extended right hand, forming a blue-black orb. She threw it at Stidyen with all her might, who barely dodged it in time. The orb burst on the ground near her, sizzling black tentacles of shadow flailing about, reaching for the old woman, but finding nothing. Stidyen regained her footing and raised her hands above her head. A huge ball of bright yellow-orange flame formed, brimstone smoke covering her body. She threw it toward Chandra, who fanned her fingers, creating a wall of black nothing, a shimmering void that swallowed the incoming projectile and disappeared.

"Ya've meddled enough, girl. Time fer ya to see who Stidyen REALLY is."

Chandra wasn't listening. She'd already begun to conjure her minion. It began to coalesce from the very shadow that surrounded her. Small shadowy figures ran into one another, forming a vastly larger entity.

At the same time, Stidyen's body began to grow, slowly at first, writhing and spasming, until she towered over Chandra. She smiled a toothless grin. A flash of intense light belched from her gaping mouth and crashed into Chandra's midsection, sending her cartwheeling into the woods. Her partially formed minion dissipated, the magic it needed to coalesce, disappearing.

Chandra gathered her feet and emerged, unsteadily, from the woods, leaves and dirt sticking to her body in clumps. The crone, still enlarged, sent a thin green bolt to Chandra, who was still off balance. It wrapped around her and began to take the shape of a huge iridescent constrictor, which started to tighten its grasp.

Chandra struggled against the binding snake but found she couldn't move, couldn't defend herself. She struggled in vain, knowing she was caught and at Stidyen's mercy. The crone's shape returned, and she slowly began to walk toward her former apprentice. An evil grin creased her face, drool sliding down the side of her mouth.

"Ya can't win, girl, no." She cackled. "You thought ya had old Stidyen, yes? Not so smart now, are ya?" She stopped, wringing her hands, savoring the moment. Then, speaking to herself, "She said to train ya. I did. She said ta keep ya. I did." She turned to Chandra and yelled, "SHE NE'ER SAID NOT TA KILL YA!"

Her fingers began to twist in a dance of conjuration. Swirling colors of all types began to form into a colorful ball. She held the forming spell over her head as it continued to grow in size. Shimmering brightly, it emitted small crackles of electricity, the smell of ozone permeating the field around her. The spell was now at its height. Pure power was now at her disposal. Her eyes narrowed, glaring flashes of red, and she began to throw it.

Just then, Malhrun, who had been watching from a distance, covered the old woman in an almost invisible cold blanket of weak, almost imperceptible shadow. Her sight being somewhat restricted, Stidyen released the ball of electricity into the air, hoping it would find its mark. It arced harmlessly into the night sky like a tailed comet.

Her loss of concentration allowed the snake constricting Chandra to weaken and fall away. Now freed, Chandra saw her chance.

She blew magic onto her raised hands, creating void orbs, which she threw at Stidyen. Both landed close by, writhing black tentacles grasping the crone's legs, not allowing her to move. Malhrun quickly released her, seeing his mistress begin her ominous spell.

Chandra's breathing shortened, concentration becoming more focused. Remembering her earlier struggle, she forced her very will into her hands and arms as she began to weave her shadowy incantation. Black fog began to permeate the ground before her, covering her entire body in a thick blanket of billowing shadow. Rising, it formed a dense cloud that was visible even in the darkness. As the spell completed, two glowing purple eyes blinked and looked at her.

'*...yesss, my queenn.*'

Chandra pointed at Stidyen. In a deep voice, she growled..."Kill."

It floated toward Stidyen, who was flailing, trying desperately to wave away the shadowy tentacles that held her. Closer it came. She could feel the burning cold creeping toward her. Malhrun weakly gathered himself and stepped aside as the fog reached Stidyen. She shrieked loudly in agony, begging for it to leave her. It hovered for just seconds and then was gone.

Stidyen lay on the ground, motionless, her extremities frostbitten to the point of blackness, her eyes drawn wide as if she'd seen an unexplainable terror. Smiling in triumph, Chandra cautiously stepped closer, ready to cast another spell.

'*...she is alive mistress...but just.*'

Chandra stood over her teacher. There was no longer any emotion.

Stidyen's eyes turned to look at Chandra, no more fear, only sadness.

"You…have taken…my life." She began to shiver. "You…now…own…the power."

Chandra leaned a bit closer.

"She…said you would." She nodded at her words. Her face relaxed into a soft, motherly smile. "Destiny is calling, lass.… from the lake…she calls." She slowly, painfully motioned for her to move closer.

Reluctantly, Chandra leaned even closer.

"You never asked me about my name, who I am."

Chandra said, "No, never."

Stidyen smiled. "I…am the daughter…of Lady Destiny…herself." She coughed, grinning. "And now…Chandra…Dashow…Soryn," She smiled warmly, "So are you."

Stidyen's hand dropped limply to the ground, and she slowly exhaled her last breath.

Chandra's brow furrowed, puzzled, as she stood. A sharp, stabbing pain in her skull caused her to double over, both hands grasping to stop the agony. She became dizzy, unbalanced, falling to her knees as the pain worsened. Blood began trickling from her nose.

Her head snapped back, eyes rolling white, and she emitted a scream that shocked the night. Echoes reverberated throughout the woods, sending birds to wing and creatures running.

She collapsed on the cold ground, unconscious.

'…I'll take that, thank you.'

'…ahh, the Lady plays THOSE rules.'

The warmth of the morning sun felt good on her face. Blinking against the light, she realized she was still lying on the ground. Slowly, she sat up, trying to gather her wits and steady herself, the pain in her head from the night before nearly gone. Still exhausted, she rolled to her knees and stood, realizing that she was still near the woods that had saved her life. The smell of burned wood hung in the air from the tree behind her. She touched the scorched mark Stidyen's spell had left behind, remembering the battle she never wanted to fight.

Stidyen…she turned back to look at her pale body. She nudged it with her foot, making sure she was truly dead. Her body lay lifeless, splayed where her shadow minion had left her. Chandra took a deep breath, reliving the night and the speed at which things had spiraled out of control, the fear she felt when she was confronted with Stidyen's ire. She had been confused and disoriented, but when her minion appeared, oh, the power she commanded. The intoxication gave her the feeling as if she could crush anything or anyone that stood in her way.

Then her eyes squinted with one memory: *I am the daughter of Lady Destiny herself, and now Chandra Dashow Soryn, so are you.*

What did she mean by that? Daughter of Lady Destiny? Lady Destiny is a goddess, and I wasn't born of a goddess. It made no sense at all. She thought about another revelation that Stidyen proffered, *Destiny is calling, lass, from the lake she calls.* What lake? Crimson Lake? The lake is cursed with the undead. None of this made sense to her. She felt her stomach begin to flutter and her mouth water. Turning to the still smoldering tree, she was relieved of its contents, wiping her mouth with the back of her sleeve. *All this and I still wear rags.* She chuckled at the irony.

She groggily stumbled back to the abandoned church and opened the portal. Once inside, her tired legs managed to carry her across the quiet room to one of the small chairs in front of the fire, where she slumped down and tried to gather her thoughts. Her head still felt foggy, as if it were filled with cotton. The usual smells of the room were now absent, and the musty smell of dust hung in the air.

The lake, she thought. *Crimson lake.* She sat up, continuing her thoughts.

She remembered seeing the lake in her struggle with the shadow demon. How the other shades were dancing and beckoning. Were they calling her? Perhaps...no.

She thought more about what had happened.

Did they know? Did they see what was about to happen? Were they telling me to bring Stidyen to the lake? She felt confused.

Kalla appeared like a misty dream. She was smiling and nodding her head, then disappeared.

Chandra jumped, startled awake. She must have fallen asleep without knowing. Looking at the fire that was now just smoldering ash, the thoughts of her dream coalesced.

She needed to take Stidyen's body to the lake.

She lashed together a crude litter from broken boughs and a torn cloth from the church, cursing the work with every knot. The body was heavy, and the ground uneven; each tug sent bark biting into her palms and mud sucking at her shoes. She hated it, the stink of death, the dragging of dead weight, the pointless labor of hauling a woman she came to loath to a place she would never thank her for. More than once, she muttered that she should have left her for the crows, but the lake called, and Chandra knew this burden had become a part of her. Another step in her rite of passage.

Just before the sun reached the horizon, she arrived. There was a slight breeze that carried the smell of wet wood and peat on it. She was wary now, eyes straining to find any movement. She'd read all the tales and the accounts: a battle, the fallen, the curse from the lips of a hedge-mage. Yes, she'd heard them all. The truth, she knew, was about to be revealed.

She dragged the litter, crossing the reeds, bushes and mud to answer the lake's call, but this time she knew she had an ally, one she could summon, one who could protect her. Step after muddy step, she closed on the lake shore, arms and legs now tiring.

Just then, it happened. The sun ebbed, the lake reflected bright light and the water began to change its color to crimson red with a foggy mist wisping above the water's surface. The birds that had been singing fell silent, and the breeze disappeared. Now the truth.

The sound of bubbling mud and splashing made her stop. It began to grow louder and seemed to emanate from all around her. Slowly, she watched as the rotting corpses of soldiers long past rose up from the mire, eye sockets glowing blue and purple. They did not try to grab at her or stop her, but stood, like ancient sentries.

She looked at the lake and decided to chance a step, but none moved. She took a few more steps and, yet again, none moved. Still cautious, she started walking at normal stride, but as she walked, another then another rose from the mire in silent formation like a row of ceremonial guards protecting a path.

Now, almost at the shore, she set the litter down and looked back at the line of undead sentries, who, in unison, turned to face the lake and her. She held her breath waiting to see what they were going to do next. Nothing. They stood like a rotting military unit awaiting command.

Chandra turned to the litter and began to drag it into the water, hoping that it would float. Slowly she pulled, and it remained buoyant, bobbing up and down with every tug.

She heard marching and turned to see the undead soldiers marching toward the shore. She raised her hands to her hips and began the incantation to summon her minion.

But something made her stop and watch as the soldiers stopped in battle formation as if paying a silent tribute. She wondered what was happening but felt compelled to continue. She stepped deeper into the cool water, helping the corpse of her former savior and caretaker quietly float to the center of the lake. It was as if an invisible current had taken hold of the makeshift raft and pulled it along, farther to its center. The crimson of the water gave the illusion of wild flames leaping against the makeshift raft, engulfing it until, as if it were a ghost, it disappeared into the mist. She stood there and stared at the ripples where her teacher had once been.

Chandra felt compelled to speak a eulogy to the wind even though she wasn't practiced nor did she particularly believe in it:

"Lady Destiny, you are the force behind life. Veyra the Unseen, you are the record of it.

Destiny makes choices matter. Veyra ensures they are never forgotten.

Together you are the beginning and the end, and everything in between belongs to time."

She watched the waters calm and the crimson disappear. Then she spoke to Stidyen for the last time.

"You saved my life, and for that I am grateful.

You tried to teach me, and for that I am also grateful.

You tried to take my life…and for that, I too, am grateful.

You've made me who I am.

I will miss you."

Chandra turned from the shore, water and mud clinging cold to her shoes. The undead did not follow. They stood in rigid ranks, facing the lake, silent as stone. As she passed between them, they parted without a sound, holding their formation like eternal sentries, not for her but for Stidyen, the crone. She didn't look back until the trees of the Whispering Wood swallowed the lake from sight.

'…temper, temper.'

She leaned heavily against the stone of the fallen church. The night had been long and taxing both on her mind and her body. Exhaustion took hold, and she knew she had to sit. She thought about her home before, the love she felt as a family, the love for her sister, her friend. She brushed it from her tired mind and cast the portal spell. The smell of a sweet breeze and the swirling, roiling shadow gave way to a new portal. She stepped back, shocked. What had happened? Was this a new portal, or was this a trap? The magic it emitted felt the same. It was conjured the same. Yet...this...

Chandra decided to take the chance and stepped through it, allowing her to enter the conjuring room.

The smell of incense and herbs, which had somehow replaced the musty smell, welcomed her. She stood motionless for several minutes, taking it all in. The ache in her body reminded her that she needed to sit and recuperate. Walking to the hearth, she stirred the fire and sat, reflecting on the past few days, her inheritance of the powerful spell that led to Stidyen's downfall by her hand, the undead and the lake.

She still smelled like wet mud and rot. The void door stood before her. She cocked her head to the side, wondering about something Stidyen had told her some time ago. *She said anything is possible here. Shall we try?* she thought. She envisioned a small spring fed by a waterfall surrounded by trees, and then she walked through the open door. When she reached the other side, it appeared just as Stidyen said.

A small spring, a waterfall, trees, even reeds and cattails. She was amazed. Exhausted and sore, she stepped into the water and found it to be cool but not uncomfortable, the sound of the falling water soothing her head. She stripped off her filthy, ragged clothes and stepped under the waterfall, the water caressing her bare shape, soothing each muscle. She just stood there, no thoughts, no spells. She sighed, releasing the tension of the last several days.

She sat there for a long time, feeling each muscle relax, wondering what to do next. She had become immensely powerful, so much so that she managed to kill the strongest mage she knew. Chills covered her body with excitement, realizing that she now had the knowledge to bend entire towns and cities to her will, to become the ruler of every land if she had a mind to. She could weave the very shadows themselves to do her bidding. The possibilities were endless. A wry grin crossed her face.

Yes, no one can harm me now.

A voice came into her head. *You are my sister, Chandy. We look out for each other.*

The grin left her face, her delusions of grandeur faded, and sorrow crept into her heart. Lyssa. *Where was she? Did they kill her? Was she looking for her?* So many questions flew through her head like comets through the night sky. She had to know. She had to be certain.

She left the bath for her room, stopping to pick up her clothes…rags, water still dripping from her bare body. *The possibilities are endless,* echoed in her head.

She peered at the doorway. "I wonder." She thought hard again and walked through the doorway portal.

On the other side, she was in a room…filled with all different forms of clothing. Proper, fancy, military and even seductive clothing was draped and hanging throughout the entire room. It was lit by wall sconces, smoke lightly billowing to the ceiling. Sitting on shelves streamed gently floating vapors from several oil lamps that burned with the aroma of spicy, sweet incense.

She looked around, thinking of how she wished to introduce herself to the world for the first time. She tried on the seductive clothing and attempted to piece them together with other items, but to no avail. She didn't feel comfortable revealing that much of herself; her mother would have been very disappointed. She tried something more military, but oddly, she felt...weaker, as if all the metal and thick leather were sapping her magic.

Finally, something caught her eye.

She found a dress draped across the back of a chest, black as oil, soft as silk. Excitement fluttered in her chest as she slipped it on. The hem brushed the floor and split high along both legs, front to thigh. Over it she laced a bodice of deep violet velvet, trimmed in black leather, and edged with subtle spikes, the surface alive with filigree. The sleeves matched the bodice, running long and fitted until they spilled into soft purple ruffles, laced along the outer seams. Leaning against the chest and below the dress were boots cut of velveted leather, rising over the knee, cuffed high and laced up the side. They were perfect. Holding them up, giggling, she had a naughty thought.... *These look as if they were made for walking the edge between shadow and sin.* She looked around as if someone might see, sat down, and put them on, feeling the soft leather hugging her shapely feet and legs. She stood and looked at herself in the mirror, smiling broadly. She found a blood-red sash and a black belt with two small golden buckles hanging from a nearby stand. Fastening them quickly, she turned back to the mirror and smiled. *Sultry yet dangerous,* the perfect reflection of who she was becoming. Never in her life had she worn, or even imagined wearing, anything so fine. As a child, she'd only pretended, playing at being a princess, but she had never honestly believed such finery would one day be hers.

Looking around once more, she noticed something on a small side table, a piece that might add a touch of mystery to her new appearance. She lifted it carefully and, after a hesitant breath, dared to place it on her head.

It was a glistening circlet of black gold, set with three large amethyst stones that shimmered in the light. At first, it hung too loosely, slipping over her ears, and disappointment settled in. But as she reached to remove it, the metal stirred, shrinking, molding to her shape, and her disappointment turned to wonder.

Tears welled up in her eyes as she stood there, looking at the young lady she now saw in the mirror. Her medium-length platinum hair glistened brightly in the light, accentuating her ample, nubile body. She realized that she was now an adult for the first time, no longer the naïve little girl who had once graced these halls that she now called home.

She spun like a child in the mirror one last time, smiling and hugging herself. She was free, free to be whomever she wanted to be. And no one could change that.

She inhaled deeply, held her head high and said, with confidence, "Never, my dear. Never again!"

'... *though you are human, mistress, you are...beautiful.*'

Malhrun had been hiding in the corner.

Startled, she looked its way. "Must you always follow me, imp?"

'...*Malhrun must, mistress. We are one.*'

She sighed with exasperation but softened, giving a weak smile and sighed, "Thank you, my shadowy friend. Believe it or not, that means something to me."

From what Chandra could tell, Malhrun bowed to her, which she returned. It may have been a shadow, but she realized it was now her only friend.

She left the room with Malhrun in tow, entering the conjuring room, as she now called it, making it far larger than it had originally been. With a single thought, she had instantly changed a witch's dungeon into a conjurer's study replete with dark woods, exquisitely crafted seating and a library that would be the envy of even the most learned scholars in all of Caer Bryndwyck.

The hearth was now made of well-placed gray stone, two fully armored knight statuettes standing at either end with a large, wooden mantle topped by an alabaster skull that blazed with glowing purple gems in place of its eyes, for effect. The calming scent of cinnamon and sandalwood gently permeated the room in a light, drifting fog. Where the alchemical table had once stood, now rested a well-lit, darkwood table with seating for several. She'd reshaped the library into a comfortable retreat with thick, cushioned chairs and a broad, round table beneath a wrought-iron chandelier. Many bookcases made of darkwood lined the walls and stood like soldiers beneath brightly lit wall sconces. Each shelf held old, dusty tomes, books, scrolls and maps.

Before the great thaumaturgist's circle stood an oaken lectern surrounded by symbols and candlelight. At its edge, a low three-step dais marked the place where portals could be summoned, a purple-and-black carpet spilling from it into a warm, inviting greeting area.

Instead of her home looking like a witch's nightmare, it now looked like the grand entrance to a fine manor, ornate yet not pretentious. She held her arms out, smiled broadly and silently wished her family could see what had become of her, though she doubted they would have accepted her magical abilities.

She strolled about her new home, investigating each detail, each elegance and extravagance. Midstride, she yawned, the excitement of the day wearing on her, and decided to rest for the night, excited to see what the next day would bring. Quickly looking around the room once more, she left for her bedchamber, which she also decided to alter. Again, the room had grown immensely and far grander.

In the center was her four-post bed, made of darkwood, a large purple canopy billowing overhead. Several chests, cabinets, dressing tables and chairs filled the walls. Tapestries depicting nature, animals, Tantyn and even one of her entire family hung from golden rods with tasseled golden ropes. It was far more lavish than anything she'd ever seen.

Now that everything was in place, she felt more at home and at ease. She stood in the center of her new chamber, tears of joy streaming down her beautiful face. She slowly turned once again to take in the beauty of her creation.

Finally, Chandra yawned as she disrobed and fell into bed, burying herself in the thick covers. With a sigh, she was asleep, ready to begin her new life.

'...enough!

Of Fallacy and Epiphany

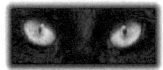

Her dreams began as twisted and horrible memories, recalling the nightmarish war between her mentor and herself, but soon returned to more pleasant ones; she and Lyssa playing in their backyard, Mother laughing from the doorway and glowing red eyes.

She smiled and stretched, looking around her new room. The sound of the waterfall and the fresh smell of clear, sweet water brought a smile to her face, prompting her to bathe and dress in preparation for the new day ahead.

Pressing her shining circlet into place and making one last check in the mirror, she went through the portal to her kitchen, where she found sweetbreads and rose tea already prepared. She loved magic, to be sure, where every whim became reality and comfort was but a finger snap or a step away.

Once she finished, she went through the portal once more and found herself in the study. The sconce-lit bookcases stood like soldiers, side by side, and the large table and chairs beckoned her to come and learn—but not today. No, today was going to be her day, a day to understand the world in a new light, to see it as a powerful mage would, through knowing eyes and the certainty of her skin. She wanted to be among people, to show herself off and let the world know that Chandra Dashow Soryn was here, and here to stay.

Smiling, she went to the portal that led outside, climbed the black carpeted dais and stepped through the swirling black mist.

Outside, the church still lay in ruins, the perfect ruse hiding a wondrous secret. Daylight showed through the broken doorway, and she stepped into it, allowing the sunlight to bathe and warm her body. The wooden bench still sat against the wall, almost in remembrance of days past, so she sat and watched the wanderings of travelers on the distant road. It felt good to just feel the things she'd been missing while under the tutelage of Stidyen. She was a well-meaning teacher and guardian, but Chandra knew it wouldn't have lasted long. Every tome and book she'd ever read ended the same way; the apprentice would always surpass the teacher and move on, though maybe not in the same fashion that she did. The circle of life must always turn as each entity reaches its final destiny.

She sighed and decided to delve into her books to see if there might be some tidbit of learning that would spark a new spell or send her to another level of insight. She went through the broken door and to the altar to open the portal inside when a sound made her turn around.

"Ahem."

She turned to see a figure in the doorway.

"And who might you be?" she asked, squinting to understand the sight before her. It was a figure wearing the fine robes of a learned woman, gnarled hands and tangled flowing hair. It had to be a mage by the glowing staff it held, but the image was not corporeal; more a ghostly figure than anything.

"I am Tefa, sibling to Stidyen…whom I understand you have, shall I say, displaced." The image showed a somber face, but its body language showed aggression.

"She was my mentor, yes. We had a disagreement that went horribly wrong, I'm afraid." Chandra was becoming angry at the mere presence of this intruder. "What business is it of yours, pray tell?"

"Ha-ha-ha. Business. Yes, I suppose it could be called business." Its knowing grin sobered very quickly. "My business, murderer," the image gnashed its teeth, "is that you have killed my only relative, as I have witnessed, and I am simply here to avenge her."

Chandra blinked in disbelief.

"Avenge? You have no idea what happened here that night, nor do you have any right to meddle in this affair." She stepped toward the image. "Now, I say begone and tend to matters that you have knowledge in or face my wrath." She felt her warning would be enough to send this hag back to where it came from.

"Murderer," the term dripped sarcasm, "your wrath is something I look forward to incurring, actually." It smiled broadly. "I can be found in the tower Nightlock-on-the-sea to the north."

"Why not show yourself and have at it here and now?" She was livid.

"You jest, murderer. I will not duel on your soil where you sway advantage. I propose neutral soil. The tower is not owned and far from my advantage, to be sure." It bowed. "I look forward to seeing you soon, murderer. Please, come prepared. I'd hate to make short work of the shrew who killed my sister. I am *so* looking forward to your pain and suffering. Until then." It bowed again and disappeared.

'...*mistress, I urge you, be wary. This is not Stidyen.*'

Chandra balled her fists with rage. *How dare you threaten me in my own home!* Her ire forced her pale skin red as she returned inside to prepare. She wanted to be certain of her victory. She searched for any information at all on this Tefa. Who was she? Where did she come from? What sort of mage was she? Every tome she checked led nowhere.

Tefa is her sister. There had to be at least something mentioning her.

She sat heavily in her chair, desperately trying to come up with an answer. Where else would there be information? Leaving the church could be disastrous for her, as she didn't know how true to her word this hag would be. He could be lying in wait right now.

'...*mistress, perhaps Stidyen's room?*'

Chandra looked at the blinking eyes in the corner in disbelief.

"Malhrun, my sweet shade, if you were human, I might kiss you." She smiled, heading for the portal.

The swirling shadow dissipated as she stepped into the old woman's room, only to find that it was...appalling, to say the least.

A pile of molding straw lay on the floor in one corner with a tub of fetid water nearby. Creatures dusty and stiffened by age hung from the ceiling, and a pile of rancid clothing lay mildewing in another corner. Next to that stood an old, rickety bookshelf full of rotting books, letters and scrolls.

One by one, she leafed through them, each letter opened, and each scroll unraveled, only to find nothing of note. Frustrated, she grabbed the side of the bookshelf and pulled it down, screaming with frustration. She turned and kicked at the straw, sending it flying in all directions when she finally saw it. Still half buried in the rotting straw was a thin, small diary. Her eyes lit up, hoping this was the key she was looking for. She picked it up and portalled back to her table. Sitting, she opened it, finding a letter inside that read:

Sister,

It does my heart good to know you are well. I am glad to see you have found another apprentice. I hope this one fares better than the last. My studies in elemental weaving are progressing slowly, though I may have had a slight breakthrough. If you could possibly send another vial of the curative elixir, I may yet complete my study. Please send my regards to Mother.

Tefa

This was the information she needed. She is an elementalist. Chandra knew she could defeat fire, water and cold, though electricity might prove to become somewhat troublesome. She removed several books from the shelf and began reading about the finer points of elementalism, their advantages and limitations.

Several hours passed when, finally, her reading had covered enough to make this harpy pay for her insolence. She sat with a smile, envisioning her downfall. Sister or not, she knew this had to be a telling fight. She had quickly learned that, though mages were few, their eyes could be far-reaching. Another aspect of her craft she would have to investigate.

She searched her shelves and chests for a map of the local area and found that the Nightlock on-the-Sea tower was just north of Morowyck and west of a small fishing village on the Sea of Tears coast. It looked to be on a headland, high on a cliff, yet in the open with plains surrounding it. No place to hide this time, no protection. She frowned; the harpy's choice turned out to be impeccable.

She sighed. This was truly going to be a test, but she was also sure this would certainly end in her favor. She was Aesh'amon-tu. Where there were shadows, there was power.

It was time. She straightened her clothing and made sure her circlet was straight and left out to accept Tefa's challenge.

Outside, she looked for Malhrun, who was nestled in a dark corner.

'...*you are ready, mistress.*'

"I have no doubt, my little friend. We should go now," she said, looking outside.

'...*I cannot, mistress.*'

She turned toward the shade, miffed. "And why not? You are tethered. You must go," she said, looking confused.

'...*the plains are without shadow, mistress. I would, as you say, die.*'

"You followed before. Why is this different?" She had to know. This was not like him to disobey.

'...*before, mistress, I used the shadows of the woods' edge or even your shadow to stay close. Using yours this time would prove useless and could be my undoing...as well as yours.*'

"Oh, this is absurd. How am I to keep you close otherwise?" she asked angrily.

'...*perhaps your pouch, mistress. I would not be safe, but I could assist from there...somewhat.*'

Chandra rolled her eyes, exasperated and opened her pouch as she watched him climb her body and disappear.

"Are you happy now, imp? Can we go?" she asked sarcastically.

'...no, mistress, I am not.' His glowing eyes blinked as she shut the pouch. She almost giggled, imagining the little shade pouting.

Chandra closed her eyes, envisioning her grandmother's old shack. Her arms began to move in a clockwise motion, creating a swirling, black portal, the inside rolling into itself like smoke from a fire, yet shimmering black and purple. Stepping in, she found herself behind her mother's burned-out house in Mapleton. Using any portal always made her feel somewhat queasy, but traveling any lengthy distance made it so much worse. She gasped for air, trying to keep the urge to vomit at bay and walked toward the tavern where a wagon had been posted. *Tavern?*

She had never known there to be a tavern in Mapleton. Her mother had taken her here to visit friends on many occasions. This was a farming community, small, quiet, nothing more than that. The Broken Plow looked to be freshly built, with new solid timbers, painted shutters and a door that still sat on working hinges. She shrugged and went in to see that it was almost empty, save some weary travelers and several carters and wagoners. What little bit of conversation silenced as she stepped toward what looked like a well-traveled wagoner. Looking at the beauty that stood before him, he gulped, not believing his luck that a woman such as she would even consider nearing him.

"Might I be helpin' ya, lady?" he asked shakily.

"Good sir, you will take me to Nightlock on-the-Sea," she demanded.

His eyes widened. "Lady, I be goin' ta Caer Bryndwyck with a load o' meats fer Lord Balamore in the Guild Ring."

She glared at him, annoyed, and he shrank.

"I believe this should suffice." She produced a sack the size of a skull and set it on the table in front of him.

"Tell Lord Balamore you had more pressing business and let us away—now." She turned and walked outside to the wagon.

They looked at each other, dumbfounded, as he followed her out waiting to be helped into the seat. He had never encountered a woman of such refinement before and felt completely out of sorts. She held out her hand; he steadied her as she climbed up and sat. He rushed around to the other side, climbed up, and they were off.

The ride was long, and the conversation nearly nonexistent. He did his best to strike up a conversation with no luck. She found him an idiot and, above all else, smelly. By the time they had arrived, the sun sat very low on the horizon. She climbed down without help and dismissed the driver with a look of disdain and a wave of her hand.

With the wagon-driving lout behind her, Chandra surveyed the proposed battlefield. She was correct; this location was perfect for a full-on mage's duel. Ahead stood the old tower, stones weathered and worn white by nature and time. The top crenellations had crumbled and lay strewn about the ground, weeds and small scrub partially hiding their existence. Beyond that came the loud crashing of waves from the Sea of Tears, angry and throwing great clouds of mist into the sky. She noticed that the wind strangely blew from behind her, which could play into her favor depending on how the battle progressed.

Malhrun had been correct in his assessment; the plains were so flat and barren that no shadows existed. The wind-swept grass stood knee high and would have been little help to the shade. Her hubris waned as she realized that she might be out of her element here. She started toward the tower, thoughts of possible spell combinations careening through her mind. She felt no fear, only apprehension. She had only taken part in a single duel and, if not for Malhrun, might not have even survived that. She knew she had to be far more careful and aware this time than last.

Chandra closed to just over bow range when a booming voice bellowed, "She accepts the challenge." She stopped cold, searching the tower top to bottom yet seeing no one.

"Prepare yourself, murderer. The Veiled One lights his path for you."

There was a bright flash, and Tefa stood at the broken entrance of the tower.

"I was sure you would cower in your hole, murderer." She smiled. "At least now you can meet your death with some semblance of dignity." The tip of her staff glowed with a bright green light.

Chandra tensed, waiting for any movement she might make.

Then, without warning, a bolt of ice slammed the ground just to her left, making her jump. Shards of ice sheared holes into her dress, slashing the leather of her boots and nicking her skin, but just slightly. Tefa must have been on the tower's roof when she cast. She'd been veiled; Chandra never saw her; it was her spectral image at the door that drew her attention.

Dammit all, she thought, regaining her balance, but looked up just in time to see another bolt of ice coming straight for her head. She instinctively ducked as it passed over and slammed into the ground behind her. Chandra knew she was wasting time now. She attempted to weave a shadow bolt, but nothing happened, to her dismay.

Another ice bolt slammed the ground to her right, this time barely missing her. The shards of broken ice cut into her dress once again, nicking her leg, causing a cold, searing pain. She could feel the small shards freezing into her skin like pieces of searing metal. Chandra knew now that she was in for a much tougher fight than with Stidyen. Fear began to creep into her spine as she tried to form a shade to defend her.

'*...NO MISTRESS. NO SHADOW!*' she heard Malhrun scream in her head.

Chandra searched for Tefa on the roof but realized she was no longer there. What spell could she use that didn't require shadows? She could think of none and felt defenseless. Then, from the right side of the tower, a ball of rolling flame the size of a fist flew directly toward her. Chandra sidestepped, allowing it to pass by, and moved toward the tower, her eyes still fixed on her enemy.

Tefa stepped into view and conjured another fireball, larger this time, and hurled it toward Chandra's head. It streaked forward, this time faster, but Chandra again sidestepped it with ease. Tefa ducked behind the tower for cover, laughing now, loudly, darkly, demonically.

Chandra now understood why. The two fireballs that landed behind her caused a wild flashfire that was growing still larger, fanned viciously by the wind at her back. She turned and saw that, at the speed it was burning, she would be engulfed in no time.

"Shite, shite, shite." She looked left and right for any escape but could find none. Her only hope…charge toward Tefa and weave a terror spell at close range. She just hoped she could close on that hag without being killed herself.

Chandra lowered her head and ran to the opposite side of the tower, hoping Tefa wouldn't see her, but out she stepped, huge grin on her face. Chandra now knew this had been a trap, and she had just walked into it. She veered just in time to avoid being hit with a bolt of electricity. Now gasping for breath, Chandra reached the tower and pressed herself as close to its stone as she could.

Which way? Dammit, which way?

She remembered that Tefa was on the left side, so she thought to move right, thus avoiding direct contact and another trap.

'…*go left, mistress. Go left.*'

She faltered.

'…*go NOW!*'

She turned and quickly heeded Malhrun's direction just as another ball of flame sailed close and scorched the wall where she had been standing.

Chandra once again knew she was outclassed and that her life was in dire straits. She was now totally defenseless.

"Try, damn you. Try," she yelled at herself.

211

The flames of the flashfire closed in; the smoke now began to sting her eyes and fill her lungs. She would have to move to the back of the tower to avoid the flames, but that would mean running into Tefa if she were there. The shrew could be inside for all she knew. Chandra looked out to the sea. Through the smoke, she could see the sun was about to dip below the horizon; if only she could buy herself just a bit more time for it to go down completely...*then this witch is mine.*

She took a deep breath and continued to slip around the left side of the tower...and ran right into her. Luckily for Chandra, Tefa was looking the other way and never saw her coming. She knocked the witch to the ground, her head making a dull thud as it hit the tower hard, causing her forehead to open up. Chandra managed to regain her composure faster than Tefa and began to weave a simple shadow spell, hoping it would work. The fallen elementalist looked back at her with fear in her eyes, realizing she had now lost her advantage. Chandra would make that fear turn to terror as she released her spell, sending a purple flash that seared Tefa's face. Her eyes opened wide, body paralyzed, a painfully terrifying scream piercing the smoke-filled sky.

As her shriek began to diminish, wildfire blew in from around both sides of the tower. Chandra was now in trouble, trapped on two sides by fire and a cliff in front of her. She might yet win the fight but could still die in the process. She looked at Tefa, then the fire. Without further thought, she grabbed the witch by her robes, lifted with all her strength, heaving Tefa as best she could onto the fire in an attempt to use her as a bridge. She leaped onto her chest, but just as she crossed, the inferno set Chandra's dress alight, forcing her to tear off her lower skirt in full stride. Stumbling forward clumsily, she avoided the wind-swept flames, dodging the smaller spot fires behind.

Unfortunately, in doing so, she lost her concentration, and the spell's effects dwindled. Tefa found herself suddenly alight, screaming as she rolled to her feet and tore off her robes down to her smoldering underclothes. Spotting a gap in the fire, she ran through it, clutching her head as she tried to escape, pain twisting her face. The last shards of sunlight were disappearing, and Chandra began to feel the full energy of the shadows gaining strength.

Tefa tried to find the tower's entrance by circling back around. There, just in front of her, she spotted it. She tried to reach it but saw Chandra's hands swirling as if weaving another spell. Chandra saw Tefa falter and try to ready one of her own.

That decision proved to be her enemies' downfall. Tefa stepped back, trying to distance herself, her spell now almost ready, but her heel caught a stone from the crenellation, causing her to fall hard.

Seeing the mistake, and now smiling, Chandra knew Tefa was finished…until the body hit the ground, revealing that it was another apparition. The real mage had circled to the opposite side of the tower. There was a blinding flash as Tefa's laughter cut through the crack of thunder. Chandra's shoulder recoiled from the searing bolt of lightning.

She staggered, clutching her arm, numb, useless, and realized the illusion had fooled her completely.

'…*release me, mistress. I can help.*'

Chandra opened the pouch, allowing Malhrun to leap out. It immediately melded with the existing shadow, glowing red eyes now narrowed in anger.

'…*she's retreating to the other side, mistress.*'

"Get her."

'…*it is not possible, mistress. There is light there.*'

Anger now took over. A plan suddenly came to mind; this time, she knew it would cost Tefa her life.

Chandra moved to the left of the tower and began loudly whimpering.

"The fire. Stop, Tefa. I yield, please." Malhrun's glowing eyes caught a glimpse of the woman now moving slowly toward her.

'*...she comes, mistress.*'

Smiling, Chandra now began to summon *him*, the one being she knew who could rend this woman's mind and torture her beyond belief.

Her hands flourished until the spell was complete.

"Please, please, I yield." She sniffed as if crying.

Then, as the final word of her chant was spoken, *he* appeared. In the shadow, next to Malhrun, who bowed in supplication to the giant shade, stood the very shadow demon Chandra forced to submission. Tall, powerful. '*Commmaannd mmmeeee, missstresss.*'

The sun was now fully extinguished, and only the emptiness of the dark remained. The energy from the shadow demon was almost overpowering.

Tefa rounded the corner and stood directly in front of him, Chandra to its right, smiling broadly.

Pouting, she said, "Please, no more. I yield," mocking her. "I need no false images, pretender."

Tefa stepped back in disbelief. Malhrun, thinking she was preparing a spell, violently wrapped her in cords of freezing shadow. She let out a shriek of pain, the shadows burning through her underclothes and into her flesh. She struggled to free herself with no hope.

"Hold, murderer," she said through gnashed teeth, trying to keep the pain at bay. "I know the words my sister uttered to you in her dying breath." She smiled a knowing smile. "You know of the Daughter of Destiny," she rasped, "but know now, that I am her sister, Tefa...Fate. By killing me..." she grinned through the searing pain, "...you've become what the grand lady has always set before you...Death."

Chandra smirked.

"Kill her," were the last words she heard as the demon entered her body.

Tefa stood paralyzed, eyes wide in a scream of silent terror. Her skin contorted unnaturally as the demon destroyed her from within. She withered as if being drained of all fluid and began to crumble to the ground.

Chandra spotted the remnants of her skirt and walked toward the front of the tower to retrieve it. She tied what she could around her waist as the demon came to stand before her, awaiting its next command.

She looked at the withered corpse and smiled. Her home called to her. She would listen, saying over her shoulder, "Destroy it."

The powerful demon stopped, turned and, along with Malhrun, began to echo a blood-chilling scream of energy.

"STOP!" commanded Chandra, spinning toward the tower.

Both shades immediately went silent.

'...*what is it, mistress?*'

"Do you feel it, Malhrun? Energy."

Malhrun was silent, then, '...*I do, mistress. From the tower.*'

Chandra dismissed the shadow demon and walked to the tower, sending Malhrun inside to investigate.

'...*I see nothing, only an empty ornate pedestal, mistress.*'

"An empty ornate pedestal?" Chandra frowned, deep in thought.

'...*mistress?*'

She looked up to see Malhrun's glowing red eyes. It was searching as if seeing something that wasn't there.

'...*strands, mistress, woven. Magic, powerful but weak.*'

Chandra thought she had felt it earlier, but simply dismissed it as the energy from Tefa.

'*Powerful but weak? That makes no sense...unless.*' She looked around, trying to feel which direction the strands were leading, but could not because her senses had not yet become as refined or attuned as Malhrun's.

"Malhrun, be a dear and follow the strands as far as you can. I must know what this is." She was puzzled. Other than Tefa, what could be this powerful, to leave a magical trail that could linger this long? She had read about this type of power, but this would have to be enormously strong…or ancient.

She followed the little shade until night gave way to dawn. With daylight rising, Malhrun would have to hide, making the search impossible to continue. Turning to get her bearings, she spotted the far-off shoreline of the Sea of Tears while off to the west stretched a line of trees, which told her she was closer to Straggler's Bog, a place she didn't want to have to go. The tales she had heard and read would make even the mightiest knight wither in fear.

The night-long search, the battle and the previous long day finally began to take its toll on Chandra. She had never done well with fatigue. Lyssa would constantly tease her about it, and considering she knew where the strands led, decided to create a portal home to eat and rest. The bog wasn't going anywhere, and she was sure Malhrun would enjoy not being trapped in a pouch any longer.

'…*most assuredly, mistress.*'

Her home was warm, a fire still burning cheerfully in the hearth, and the diffusion of spiced and fruity aromas instantly began to soothe her entire being. She breathed deeply, filling her lungs with much-needed calm. She opened her pouch, releasing a now happy shade and retired to her rooms to eat and wash the smell of smoke and sweat from her body.

The feel of the cool water brought reality back into perspective. She realized that her obsession with magic made her sometimes forget that she was human, a being in need of sustenance and sleep. Like a bolt of lightning, Stidyen's words echoed through her mind, *"Eat first, lass. Every scholar an' mage makes the' same mistake. They don't eat. After a bit, their bodies wither, their minds leave 'em, an' insanity causes 'em ta die in horrific ways."*

Chandra shook her head and laughed. Even after death, the old woman was still teaching her lessons. She found that she really did miss Stidyen. Ever the stodgy taskmistress, the woman had a softer side she rarely let show, but when it did, it reminded her of Kalla—and love.

Leaving the warmth of the spring, she dried and headed for bed. Snuggling deep under the covers, she wandered off to sleep. At first, the dreams were of her and Lyssa, chasing each other around the house, Mother soon joining in and laughing. A smile crept across her face while still deep in sleep. Then she dreamed of those tiny red eyes. They seemed to comfort yet concern her.

Then, like echoes from the past...

'First's first. Magic be tiny strands o' power floatin' invisible all about ye. There ain't no lines o' lay like them weepy nature weavers say. Them be false teachin's. Lif' yer hand, close yer eyes. Feel 'em."

Unknowingly, her arms reached out. She could almost feel the strands coursing through her fingers in her dream. Then, still sleeping, whispered, *"I feel it, Gran. It's wonderful."*

Ahhh, good. That be magic. He mouth moved as she slept.

Then Gran said, *"Ahhh, good. That be magic...in its raw shape. Ye've always felt it, just ne'er knew what it be."* She watched the girl intently, smiling.

She watched me, smiling, her mind screamed.

Her eyes flew open, and she sat bolt upright. "She watched."

A knowing grin formed on her face, pulling the covers from her and making a mad dash for the portal. Once through, she ran to the library and began to look for a certain tome, large, old, older than the others. Where was it?

"Ahhh, there." *The Principles of Ionic Conduction* by Scholar-Primus Celan Arctis. She drew the book from the shelf, slamming it down hard on the table and opened it, looking for a specific page. Madly, she flipped pages, sometimes backtracking to be sure.

At last, she found it. *"... Of the strands that energize a path to the emitter of such power, the current, being the more potent phase of magic, is ionically charged; its trajectory remains ever discernible."*

That was it. She finally knew the missing piece. SHE was the conductor. SHE was the second part of the strand.

'*...excuse me, mistress.*'

Her thoughts began racing. *It must have become interwoven when I arrived. There were three strands, but when Tefa died, her strand dissipated but mine remained entwined. That's how Malhrun detected it.* She slammed both hands down on the table, making Malhrun jump, startled.

'*...excuse me, mistress.*'

"But why can't I feel it?" Her face contorted, straining in thought. Then, "By Velkhar's bollocks, I know why." She looked up. "The staff. The staff is the conductor. Tefa had a green-tipped staff. It had to be conducting energy from the item inside the tower to her." She stepped back and sighed. "I can find Tefa's source if I use her staff." She let out a deep sigh of triumph. "Now, I just have to return and find it."

'*...MISTRESS!*'

"What. What. WHAT, Malhrun. What in blazes do you want?"

'*...you are bereft of clothing, mistress.*'

She looked down at her bare chest, realizing the tiny shade was right...

and laughed.

Talk of the Cat's Rest Tavern and Inn:

"Swear I saw lights dancin' over the plains—not lanterns, not lightning—bright streaks, then a boom that shook dust from my rafters. Whatever was happenin' out there, it weren't no farmhand playin' with torches."

–banter between inn patrons

"You see that blaze out by Nightlock on-the-Sea last night? The whole sky lit up red as blood. Folk're sayin' something powerful was throwin' fire 'cross the open plain. Didn't look natural—not by any stretch."

–local farmers

Of Life and Death

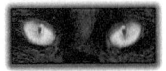

The swirling shadow of her portal cast an ominous glow as it formed. Chandra stepped through and found herself almost directly on top of Tefa's undisturbed remains. The smell of burnt flesh and grass permeated the air, reminding her of the battle fought just the day before. The flashfire looked to be more brutal than she had experienced, burning a swathe from the tower clear to the beach.

"Malhrun, search the tower for the staff," she commanded.

'*...as you wish, mistress.*'

Chandra curiously looked over Tefa's remains, something she had only done once before. She moved Stidyen's body to the lake, but had never actually searched a corpse and was not about to now. She had no qualms about creating the dead, but refused to handle them. There appeared to be various rings and a necklace, but all proved to be nondescript and worthless to her. She had read about the looting of bodies but found it not only detestable but far beneath her, so turned her attention to more important things.

'*...the staff is here, mistress.*'

"Can you retrieve it for me? I don't want you to weaken yourself, though."

She found that she had become more concerned about her shadowy friend. It was now a big part of who she was, and found that relying on it had become important to her.

'*...I can, mistress. The night allows far more endurance at its darkest.*'

She looked to the doorway and watched the shade carrying the staff to her. She took it in her hands and felt the power resonating through its wooden length. As the tip began to glow, she could see the gnarled darkwood had been harvested from an aged tree, by the feel, one older than old. She stood with it by her side and felt the glow of the tip's energy, pulsing. Green light bathed the surroundings with an ominous hue, almost ghostly, mystical.

She turned to Malhrun and said, "I can see them, Malhrun. I can see the strands now."

Its red eyes blinked, making her feel more at ease.

Just then, the green glow darkened, leaving only the many-faceted and malformed crystal atop the staff. There was now only the dim, silvery glimmer of moonlight bathing everything in an eerie, ghostly blanket of light. She stood, confused, wondering why it had darkened.

Would the staff come back to life? Then, her hand began to hum from the vibration of the darkwood. She glanced questioningly at the shade, who could do nothing more than blink.

Chandra looked back at the staff just in time to feel the massive force of…nothing, pure nothing, a void of such magnitude that it completely enveloped her, pulling her into itself, bending, stretching, and twisting her, yet she felt nothing.

As fast as it appeared, it was gone, leaving only her and the staff, its tip now pulsing with the purple-black glow of shadow.

"Maaalhrunnnn, what just happened?" She remained still if afraid to move.

'…a moment, mistress.'

She could feel the shade washing over her as if investigating her very being.

'…I sense the staff is now…you, mistress.'

"The staff is now me?" she asked, concerned.

'…yes, it is, how you would say… attuned to you.'

"Attuned? You mean…" she thought for just a moment.

'…what you feel, it knows; what you think, it acts upon. It is you, mistress.'

She stood quietly as Malhrun's words sank in, letting her thoughts sort through the possibilities, what she could do, how she might do it. Then, without warning, the answer came. She summoned the image of an orb of pure darkness and unleashed it toward the tower, catching Malhrun completely off guard. The orb tore through the air, a black sphere of pure emptiness that struck the wall and erased a great section of stone, sending the tower crashing down.

She glanced from staff to the shade, impressed.

There were no words spoken as she turned and walked toward Straggler's Bog, following the mystical strands of power dancing above her head.

She smiled.

'...well, that was different.'

It was now dusk, and a chilly wind began to blow from the south. The season would be changing soon; the leaves had already started to turn, making the forest seem as if it were on fire. Chandra loved the reds, yellows and oranges of fall. It always felt serene, like it was made specifically for family and friends, for celebrations and memories, for renewal. This would be the first season in her new abode, and she so wished her sister were here. As she followed the magical trail, she wondered what she and Lyssa might be doing if things had remained the same. Gathering wood for a fire, preparing for the harvest festival in town or maybe simply sitting in front of the fire with Mother and Father, sharing memories of Kalla and Wesley. She sighed.

'...we have arrived, mistress.'

Her vision came back into focus to see they had arrived at the edge of Straggler's Bog. She really didn't wish to go there, but she had to know what the mystical thread led to. For good or ill, it was necessary.

"Stay close, little one. I have no idea what lurks." She took her first step into the unknown and wondered... *What is happening?*

There was no trail, no discernable path; walking was slow and constantly impeded. If not for her knee boots, her legs would have

221

looked as if they had been scratched by an angry wildcat. Bushes and limbs grabbed and tugged at her as if warning her to turn back. Several times, she stopped to catch her breath from the constant struggle to delve deeper.

The twisted energy remained over her head, winding over felled trees and around stumps and bushes. Still, she forged on, hoping the journey wouldn't be in vain.

Finally, she came to a nearly invisible trail seemingly made by wandering animals.

'...*mistress, listen.*'

She stopped and held her breath to hear better.

"I hear nothing, little one."

'...*exactly, mistress. It is silent.*'

She listened again and found the shade was correct. Not a bird, insect or animal could be heard, only the breeze moving through the barren trees. She looked around and saw nothing. Even the sunlight was hard-pressed to pierce the tree-laden canopy, though the branches carried no leaves to stop it.

She found this to be tinged with foreboding and a dreadfulness she had never felt before. Everything surrounding her signaled death; yet, she knew her trail only led forward. The muck that surrounded the trail she followed, the fallen and rotted trees, the cypress knees, all began to fill her with a sense of dread unlike anything she knew.

"I don't like this, Malhrun. The energy still leads us, but I don't know that I want to continue. It isn't fear; I sense...death." She looked around, hoping to see anything other than death.

'...*a tower ahead, mistress—not far.*'

She looked down at the shade, who was now barely discernable, and hoped he was right.

They traveled no more than half a league when a tall, black tower loomed in front of them. It stood in an open glade of fouled bushes and trees like a monument to an evil god.

The walls were slime and moss-coated up to the second-floor lancet windows, the black stone dripping dew as if weeping. The front gate looked to be rusted and broken, revealing a rotted wood door held only by one rusted hinge. There appeared to be a circular courtyard around it, but surrounded yet by the muck and slime of the bog itself.

Chandra glanced warily at Malhrun, wondering if the remaining distance to the tower would be worth the walk.

"It looks as if the strands lead into the tower." She looked around to ensure she was not mistaken.

A loud but whispered voice called out from the tower. "Wwwhy hhhave yyyou cccome?"

Chandra took a step back, not believing what she heard.

"Wwwhy hhhave yyyou cccome?" The voice sounded both mystical and eerie.

"I have come in search of a missing item, taken from Nightlock-on-the-sea tower," she said, head held high.

"Yyyou cccome iiinnn vvvain. Leeeave," the voice insisted.

"I'll leave once the item is returned," she replied, eyes narrowing. She tried to see where the voice could be coming from, but found nothing.

"Find it, little one," she commanded.

'...yes, mistress.'

She watched the shade continue down the trail and decided to slowly follow.

"Leeeave nnnoww ooorr bbbeee llllost fffor aaalll tiiime," the voice warned.

Chandra continued to walk, daring the voice to stop her. With her staff in her left hand, she prepared a minor void orb in her right hand as a quick defense.

In her head came Malhrun's report. '...he is here, mistress. He is alone, and the ancient is here as well.'

He? What he? A mage? Malhrun could hear her annoyance.

'…a master of the dead, a necromancer, mistress.'

She stopped in mid-step. Necromancer, master of the dead. She remembered the undead from Crimson Lake—the stench, the silence, the feeling of pure evil. She knew this was not the sort of magic she wanted to test, but the draw of the mystical thread forced her to go on. She took another step, eyes now affixed on the tower. She wouldn't make that mistake again. Another step, another. Nothing moved.

'Yyyou hhhave bbbeen wwwarned!"

'…MISTRESS, BEHIND YOU!'

She whirled around to see a walking abomination trudging in her direction. She threw the void orb and watched as it devoured the corpse into nothingness. She prepared the simple orb again, turning back toward the structure. From both sides of the tower rose two more corpses, both clad in rusted armor and brandishing long spears. They looked to be standing sentry on either side of the gate, almost daring her to enter.

'…mistress, they are everywhere, human and animal alike.'

Chandra looked around only to see the rotting bodies of armed soldiers and even animals clawing and digging their way from the mire, all glowing yellow eyes fixed on her. She took a deep breath, preparing for the fight she now faced.

'Stay there. Keep note of the ancient.'

She threw the void orb once more and devoured another corpse, now realizing the orbs would be useless with so many undead rising. She tried to find a break in their numbers to get a better idea of how to breach the tower, but found none; there were simply too many. They continually clawed their way from the muck and mire with seemingly no end in sight. They were now on the path and trudging slowly toward her, chunks of this and parts of that falling indiscriminately. She was glad to see that they walked so slowly, but their sheer numbers would make her movement very difficult. She began weaving a shield of pure darkness and tried to push her way toward the tower gate. There was still a good distance to move, but she forced herself to try.

Three human-sized corpses moved to block her way, chunks of rotted gore dripping from them. She pushed her shield into them, sending each into oblivion, but each time the shield made contact, it became weaker. She pushed into another, making it disappear as well, but the shield finally collapsed, leaving her defenseless.

Chandra veered to the left of the path to avoid the mass of human corpses attacking her, only to run into an undead alligator, its rotting maw dripping ooze, trying to kill. She quickly produced another orb and slammed it down onto the animal's midsection, causing its hind end to disappear. Its maw snapped down just missing Chandra's leg, yet still relentlessly pulled itself closer, attacking, now followed by three more.

Chandra couldn't believe what she was seeing. There was no end to them. The stench of rot was now becoming overpowering, causing her to nearly retch several times. She ran past the decaying creatures farther into the bog, but off in the distance, she could see even more rising from the fetid water, this time what looked to be armored knights on rotted horses. Her heart was beating hard in her chest.

She closed her eyes and began to weave. "Meeyan fastuul mafren uumbraa."

A large shadow beast appeared in front of her, ready to be commanded.

"Kill," Chandra demanded and pointed to the mass of corpses near the front of the tower.

Let's see what happens now, she thought to herself.

She continued to move, not giving the undead a chance to get close.

The shadow beast quickly floated to the walking rot, pulverizing each one as it attacked. She grinned and began to summon another, but noticed that with each hit, the beast, not unlike her shield, got weaker.

Another beast was summoned and sent to help the first, which was now nearly gone. She moved again as a rotted soldier tried to slash her with a rusted sword.

This isn't working, she said, now becoming angry.

She began to weave another shield, just in time to ward off two more soldiers. They had gotten too close, and she knew she had to move quickly or be overrun.

'...he is on the roof, mistress.'

She ran for the trail again, seeing the decayed corpses had followed her into the bog, thus clearing a small path. Finally reaching it, the necromancer showed himself just where Malhrun had said. Chandra didn't have time to get a good look as a spear tip found its mark and pierced her arm. She let out a scream as the blood began to pour from the fearsome wound. She pointed her staff at the rotted man, sending offal splattering into the bog with a bolt of lightning, a spell she hadn't used since Stidyen taught it to her.

The bolt ripped through her attacker, arced to a second, then a third, each exploding in a flash before the lightning burned itself out.

She felt herself getting weaker from her wound and from the amount of energy she had been expending. Stidyen's voice echoed in her head, *If ye use up yer energy, then ya got nothin lef' ta fight with. Then ya be dead.*

Still holding her arm, another spear tip found Chandra's leg, nearly dropping her. From nowhere, Malhrun appeared, a huge, winding rope of shadow encircling the four corpses that now surrounded her. It squeezed hard, splitting them in half. She could see the attempt had quickly drained his energy, yet he continued to help as best he could. She limped toward the tower, the necromancer now cackling like an old woman.

"You were warned. You must now pay with your blood," he yelled, then began laughing again.

She stopped, looked up at the tower roof and saw him. A middle-aged man clad in black robes, a red hood, and a spade-shaped beard. His toothy smile angered Chandra, reminding her of one of her childhood attackers.

Her breathing became heavier as the ire washed over her body.

She raised her staff over her head and flourished her wounded right arm.

The necromancer, peering joyfully over the wall at the bleeding Chandra, now shuddered at the terrifying words she began chanting.

Chandra's eyes rolled white as she began to chant…

"Khar'eth vel umbra, sen'dar uth vel'tar.

Nael'nith sero, mal'aruun sha'reth.

Bythra vel'nar…Raneth-cha, en'sath dravh."

The necromancer, now almost in tears at his understanding, mumbled the words that would put an end to his world.…

"From silence, shadow rises; from shadow, purpose binds.

Through will unbroken, the servant wakes.

By the bearer's call…Raneth-cha, take form unseen."

He bowed to Chandra in defeat as he witnessed the enormous shadow demon she had just summoned.

As she commanded, "KILL!" a rusted spear pierced her lower leg, sending her to the ground in sheer agony. Malhrun sped to her aid and covered her with his bitter cold, hoping to preserve her life until help arrived, if ever it did.

The shadow demon, Raneth-cha by name, witnessed his master's wounding and fell into a wild rage. It turned and let out a piercing bellow of pure energy that destroyed a swath of undead before it.

It turned toward the tower and bellowed again, the waves of power slamming the stone walls, causing each to crack, split and explode, sending it crashing to the ground, debris flying in all directions. Several hit Chandra, but Malhrun's energy proved enough to repel them and keep its mistress safe.

The pain in Chandra's body became severe, blood still flowing, though not as fast. Realizing the debris was no longer falling, Malhrun did his best to freeze her wounds in an attempt to staunch the bleeding, keeping Chandra from falling into lethargy.

As the final pieces of the tower came to rest, Chandra looked around to see how many of the undead would send her down the path, but instead witnessed the complete demise of the necromancer's entire horde. One by one, the rotting foes fell, the mounted knights crumbling into large piles of goo, the walking dead following suit.

'...fear not, mistress. The necromancer is no more, as are his minions.'

She must have fainted because when she finally opened her eyes, sharp rays of light began to show through the bog's canopy, making the carnage easier to see. She was still racked by pain, but her bleeding had miraculously lessened to just a trickle. Malhrun was near but huddled into a tiny mass of shadow, barely the size of a boot. Chandra painfully opened her pouch, allowing the shade some shelter from the deadly rays.

Raneth-cha must have been guarding her this entire time as he was huddled in a crevasse of broken stone, still looking in her direction.

"Thank you, my friend. You honor me with your protection. I now release you to your domain," she said, tears welling in her eyes.

'...fear not, mistress. You are safe.'

"The ancient, is it still here?" She tried to sit up.

...the ancient is destroyed, mistress, lost for all time.'

Her shoulders sagged at the news. She would have liked to have seen what it looked like, but was glad, still, that sort of power was rendered unusable to all. She doubted even she would have been able to resist that much of a temptation.

Using her staff, she struggled to stand, being careful not to anger her wounds to bleed again. She steadied herself with it and flourished her hand, creating a portal home.

"Come, Malhrun. The day has been long, and I need rest." She limped to the portal and stepped in.

She released her friend from the confines of the pouch. It tried to use the portal to locate any healing elixirs or potions Stidyen may have hidden away, but found that he was not attuned to that sort of magic. Now having lost a lot more blood, Chandra staggered to the portal, images of Stidyen's restorative draught now clear in her mind.

She was taken to a room filled from floor to ceiling with row upon row of shelves, each stocked full with various potions, tonics, elixirs and the like. Her heart leaped, knowing she would once again be whole.

Reaching for the nearest, she took it down and tried to identify which type it was.

Oh, no. There's no writing. No labels. I don't know what they are.

In the back of her mind, she could hear Gran and Lyssa cackling at her alchemy mistakes.

Why didn't I listen? Why didn't I try harder? Am I now about to pay for my arrogance?

Weakness began to creep into her mind and body. She could feel her legs weakening.

Malhrun, I must try, she thought.

She staggered back to the portal. As she passed through, the red blinking eyes of Malhrun flashed inches from her face.

'... in your pouch, again, mistress. I can pass then.'

She opened the pouch, letting it in, then fell through the portal. It shimmered as she passed, only to find herself back in the receiving hall. Her mind had become muddled from blood loss, and the thought of the draughts fled her mind. She was weakening quickly now.

She gathered all of her strength, stood and, picturing the colored vials, fell through the portal once again, this time finding the correct room.

Find it, little one. Help me.

She had never asked for help in her entire life, not even from Lyssa, but this time it was her very life she needed help saving. The toggle to the pouch flipped open, and Malhrun floated immediately to the far side of the room, gathering up the proper draught and bringing it back to her. As he arrived, she could see that the exertion cost him much more energy than she wanted him to expend.

It was a tiny vial, barely the length of her thumb. She looked at Malhrun, not wanting to question him about its contents. She would have to put all of her trust in it. She pulled the tiny stopper and turned the vial up, emptying its contents into her mouth. The taste was horrible, sapping the rest of her strength and energy, her head coming to rest on the floor.

She didn't know how long she had been there. When her eyes fluttered open, she could see the dimly lit room and the shelves. She was still in the potion room. Carefully, she began checking her body by wiggling her fingers first, then hands, feet and legs. There was no pain, so she sat up, now leaning against a wall. She quickly searched for Malhrun.

"Malhrun? Are you here? Are you alright?" she nervously called out.

'…I am here, mistress—always.'

She let out a loud sigh of relief. She could almost hear it smile. If she were able, she would hug the life from it in gratitude.

'…it is Malhrun's duty to serve mistress.' He paused.

'…but I…love?… you as well.'

Tears began to fall from Chandra's face.

Malhrun understood why.

'…*that was underhanded.*'

Talk of Murwyck:

"Lights flickered over that bog again...sickly green ones this time. Didn't last more'n a heartbeat, but it were enough ta make th' hair on me arms stand. Ain't natural, whatever's lurkin' in that muck."

–local fishmonger

"Old folk always said Straggler's Bog were cursed...but last night proved it. Air turned cold as a cellar, and I swear I felt somethin' watchin' from the reeds."

–off-duty guards Alyster and Bartholemew

Of The Cat and The Fox

It had been raining on and off for nearly two weeks since she killed the slavers. Spring had always been the wettest of the seasons. Farmers loved it, but right now, it did nothing but add to her utter misery.

Lyssa returned home, but the bastards had burned it down after they… She tried to bury the thoughts. She sifted through the rubble and ash to find anything useful, but after all this time, there was nothing—nothing at all. Pilferers took what was usable, and nature washed away the rest.

The tools in her father's tannery had melted from the extreme heat or rusted to uselessness, and even her grandmother's house yielded nothing but ash and memories. Then she remembered the loose stone in Kalla's lodge. She sifted through the burned debris and managed to locate it. Though it was weathered into place, she banged on the stone, loosening it, and there lay the tome and the vial of poison Kalla hid there for just this reason. She knew the tome must be safeguarded at all costs, so stuffing the vial into her pouch, she located the old trail she and Chandra used to play on as children and hid the tome in an old fallen tree. That tree still bore the mark they'd carved into it as children, so she hid the item inside and covered it until she could return. Using limbs, leaves and sticks, she camouflaged the spot to look as natural as she could, enough to fool any passerby.

Lyssa remembered crying so much in the last year that there were simply no more tears to be shed. At times, she felt dead inside, numb from the inside out at the thoughts and horrors she'd faced. They had stolen her family, her mind, and her body and all they left her with was ashes and anger…pure, unadulterated anger. She felt it well up inside like a flame. It started small, but it stoked as she recalled her past. Her parents' screams as they fell to the bandits' blades…her sister's screams as they pummeled her relentlessly and dragged her from the house…and her own screams as they…

The flames in her heart turned into a raging inferno. She whipped her head backward and screamed as loud as she could. Birds flew in fear, and animals bolted as she spewed all her rage and sorrow from her lungs. When she finally ran out of breath, she collapsed to the ground near the tree, breathing heavily, curling into a ball, and falling fast asleep.

As Lyssa's eyes flitted open from the dim sunlight, she tried to gather her wits. She didn't know how long she'd been there. A day? She had no way of telling. All she knew was that it had stopped raining, and the sun warmed her awake.

She sat up and looked around, but something was wrong, very wrong. She was obviously still in the forest, but nothing looked familiar. The tree where she hid the tome was gone, as was the trail. Standing, she looked for markers like the ranger had taught her, but found nothing. *Where am I?* She remembered screaming and falling asleep. She was awake enough at the time to remember if she'd gone wandering, but was sure that wasn't the case. She reinforced that by searching for her tracks, yet none were to be found. Her stomach grumbled from hunger, and her pouch had no food. Then she remembered what Kitikithakis had taught her about a sort of fungus that was safe to eat, but she couldn't remember which one it was.

She searched for some time, at last spotting a large tree with an odd-looking fungus growing nearby. It was about the size of her fist, white and looked as if it were made of hair. This was it. He called it *lion's mane* and told her it was safe to eat, but it was very hard to find near them.

She sat beneath a nearby tree, her stomach still growling, and picked it up. After blowing off the dirt and insects, she bit off a small piece and chewed. The taste wasn't as bad as she'd expected;

oddly, it reminded her of the fish her father used to bring home from the market.

By now, it had almost reached midday. Lyssa stood, stretched the stiffness from her muscles, and continued to search for Tantyn. From the pattern of the trees and bushes, she believed that she was close and could possibly find it by nightfall. Off she went, hoping the direction she chose would lead her to her desired destination.

After walking for some time, voices in the distance drew her toward a well-used road. She stayed hidden until she was sure it was safe to reveal herself. When she finally crept to the edge of the woods, it was clear this wasn't Tantyn, or anywhere near it. The buildings looked different, the people dressed differently and the roads ran the wrong way. She was utterly lost—and alone.

The throngs of people amazed her. She'd never seen this many in one place at one time except for festivals back at the four corners. It then dawned on her. This was the outskirts of Caer Bryndwyck. She'd never been this far east before, but she'd heard Uncle Trellin and her father speak of it from time to time. Inside the city walls, it was supposed to be magnificent. She and Chandra used to imagine what it might look like and pretend they were princesses riding in a royal carriage, waving to the crowd. She gathered her courage and started to walk toward the nearest building. There, she sat against it and watched all the people walking, conversing and going about their daily lives in awe and wonder.

"Here, dear. Gods help ya."

An older woman reached down and pressed two silver coins in her hand, and kept walking. She looked at the coins, then back at the woman. *Now, why did she do that?* She shrugged and shoved the coins into her threadbare breeches and continued to watch. Most people who passed by her would glance and walk away with their noses in the air. Lyssa couldn't understand why they would do that either. *What is wrong with these people?*

She sat there for most of the day trying to take it all in. It was so overwhelming. She saw a man in full studded cuir-bouilli armor pass by. He had two swords on his hips and had a rather fine bow strapped across his back. Lyssa had seen a bow like this before. A man had come into Father's tannery wearing armor like that, wanting repairs. She had asked him about the bow, and he told her it was from a yew tree, which confused her as she thought he was saying it was her tree. He would say "No, yew" but she kept pointing to herself, causing her father and the man to have a good laugh at her expense.

She finally understood when she asked her grandmother about it, and she explained that yew was a type of pine tree that was strong but poisonous.

"'Ere, lass. Get yerself from the road," an older man told her. "Dang'rous men what do harm ta lone children 'bout lately." The man had dropped a single gold coin in her lap. He winked and walked away.

She started to wonder why people were giving her coins. She didn't ask for any. Father always told her not to beg, but she never understood exactly what that was. She came to realize that at the age of fourteen winters, she really was naïve to the outside world. Her family had never traveled, though Father had always spoken of it, but somehow never found the time.

Just then, a boy, a bit older than she was, walked by and kicked her thigh.

"Oi, bitch, ya best be walkin' afore I crown ye one. I'm workin' this part o' town. Steal from me again, an' they'll find yer body down th' road. Now, git." He balled his fists threateningly and motioned for her to leave.

She stood and walked back behind the building and into the woods. She was so confused. She wasn't working. She was just sitting and minding her own business. As she walked deeper into the woods, Lyssa heard steps behind her. Instinctively, she crouched to the ground and moved deeper into the shadows. Luckily for her, the time of day was in her favor. Whoever or whatever was following her would have the sun directly in their face. The shadows had grown longer, which gave her more room to hide and more of an advantage if anything were to go wrong.

She patiently waited, the sound getting closer. It was the boy who threatened her. His ragged clothes were as threadbare as hers, and he was filthy from head to toe. He was also holding a small knife whose edge gleamed sharply. Lyssa got nervous, realizing she was in an unfamiliar place, unarmed and now being hunted for no reason. The fear was beginning to turn to anger. She began to see the bandits in her mind's eye. Lyssa closed her eyes and willed herself to be calm and think.

The sun was at her back. That gave her an edge. He was unaware of where she was, another edge. She was hidden and could see everything he was doing. This was starting to look good.

"C'mon out ya rat. I got som'thin' for ya." He looked around. "I know yer here, I can smell ya." He stepped closer, still unaware.

Her breathing slowed, eyes focused on him. Just a bit more...

He stepped closer. If she leaped now, she had him face-to-face.

Wait. Just like Da said. Pick your moment.

Her father was no hunter by any means, but he knew enough to make a hunt worth it.

The boy stopped, looked around and turned his back to Lyssa, who was still hidden.

It happened in the blink of an eye.

She leaped and wrapped her arms around the boy's neck, catching him in a choke hold. He startled, lost his footing and fell backward, dropping the knife.

Lyssa wrapped her legs around him and squeezed with every ounce of her strength. He tried to resist, but every time he moved, her grip tightened like a snake. He continued to struggle.

She squeezed again, this time feeling her strength beginning to wane. The boy's body was weakening quickly.

She knew she had to keep hold, or this was going to turn bad.

He was almost limp now. *Just a bit more.*

He went completely limp, but she kept hold just a bit longer, until her strength had completely drained, making sure this was truly the end of it.

Completely exhausted, she rolled out from under him, gasping for air, staring at the sky. *What have I done?*

When she realized that she had just killed him, her nerves began to race, and her hands began to shake. It reminded her of the guard she killed a year past, the very one who caused her entire world to crash down around her. She scrambled to her knees and looked around to ensure no one was near, muscles tense like a coiled snake, ready to jump in any direction just to be free of this place.

Pssst.

She jumped at the sound. She looked in the general direction but saw nothing.

Pssst.

She looked again. It was a girl about her age dressed in rags and just as filthy.

Lyssa dove for the knife and held it in front of her menacingly. She knew how to use it well enough to get herself out of trouble if she needed to.

The girl came out of the shadows and stood. She was about Lyssa's height and build, but she had thick, long, brown hair and big brown eyes.

"Quick. Ya gotta get rid of that." She pointed to the body while looking behind her.

Lyssa didn't know what to make of this.

"Come on. I'll help."

The girl quickly checked the boys' pockets, finding a small pouch of coins and another knife, grabbed his legs and, with a nod of her head, motioned for Lyssa to grab his hands.

"Just a little bit that way," she motioned with her head to a place behind Lyssa, "there's a gully. We can toss him down there and get outta here." Lyssa nodded, and they both began to shuffle their feet to the gully.

Once they found it, they swung his body over the side and watched as he limply rolled to the bottom. They crouched down and listened for any movement. Lyssa could hear no other sound but the woods themselves. The girl grabbed Lyssa's hand and began to run deeper into the underbrush, urging her along as fast as they could go. After a few minutes, they came to a dense copse of trees where she motioned Lyssa inside to a small lean-to and a fire pit. There were a few sacks and a bedroll laid out under it with boughs of pine used to camouflage.

She plopped down onto the bedroll and motioned Lyssa to sit. "We're safe here. No one comes out this far because of the wood folk."

Lyssa looked around again and sat. "I'm Ashby. Ashby Brimmer. You can call me Ash, though. It's just easier." She grinned.

"I'm Lyssa Soryn." She felt alone.

"Well, Lyssa, ya look thirsty. Here." She tossed a flask to her.

She opened it and, without thinking, began to drink deeply. Her eyes snapped open as she realized this was not water at all and began to choke. She regained her composure as Ashby sat laughing.

"It's mead? I thought it was water," she said, wiping the mead from her face and nose.

"Water? I don't drink water. Fish spawn in it."

Lyssa looked at Ashby, understood that it was a joke, and they both started to laugh.

"And don't worry about that ass. He had it coming, and nobody'll miss him." She rummaged around in a sack and handed Lyssa some dried meat and a biscuit. "Here. It's no tavern out here, but it's food."

"Who was he? Why'd he want to hurt me?"

Ashby blinked in astonishment. "Really? You don't know why?" Lyssa shook her head no.

"Look at you. You're beautiful." Ashby raised an eyebrow. "Get it now?"

Lyssa dropped her eyes.

Ashby looked at Lyssa, somewhat confused. She could see there was far more to it than this, so she took a chance and decided to ask.

"Look, I don't know you. You don't know me, but we're both alone and in dire need of a friend." She smiled at Lyssa. "Ya do need a friend, don't ya?"

Lyssa nodded, she really did.

"Okay, so what happened?" Ashby looked at Lyssa seriously. "Don't be afraid, you can tell me anything."

"I don't know where we are," she said shyly.

Ashby paused in disbelief. Was this girl serious?

"Yer near North Caer Bryndwyck. Outside of it, really." She took a bite of the meat. "Where ya from? Where's home?"

"From Tantyn, Four Corners."

"Tantyn," Her eyebrows raised. "Girl, ya be a distance from Tantyn. How'd ya get this far out?"

She sat silently.

"It's okay, Lys, you can tell me. It can't be all THAT bad, can it?"

Her eyes brimmed. "It's that bad."

"Son of a bitch...No."

"Aye," She nodded and began to cry.

"Fuck."

The word hit home, and Lyssa began to sob harder. Ashby quickly went to Lyssa, put her arm around her and began to rock back and forth to soothe her. She couldn't imagine that horror and did her best to comfort her new friend. Lyssa told the story of that day and the nights after, and how she mysteriously ended up in this area. Ashby sat and listened quietly, letting her unburden herself. Neither letting go of the other.

They stayed like that the entire night, each holding the other, each crying tears of sorrow, pain and loss. It was along night.

'...you can try...'

In the morning, when they awoke, Ashby kissed Lyssa's cheek. "I'm not going anywhere." She smiled. "We'll look out for each other, okay?" Lyssa turned red with embarrassment. The only ones who had ever kissed her cheek were her parents, Kalla or her sister. This was new to her, and she really didn't know how to take it.

It was early enough in the morning that only a few people were milling about. Ashby showed Lyssa the entire town, where the fruits and vegetables would be easiest to steal, where to cop a drink or two, and the best hiding spots if they were chased. This was all new to Lyssa. She had never stolen anything in her life, and thinking about it made her heart pound heavily.

The sun reached its height for the day. The square was full now, the sounds of market callers trying to persuade people to visit their stalls. The girls were becoming hungry, and having few coins meant they'd have to steal to eat. Ashby tried to persuade Lyssa to try it, but she was just too afraid of getting caught, so Ashby did it herself.

"Now watch me. Don't follow though."

Ashby passed by stands and people, milling about, poking her nose here and there, making it look as if she were out to purchase something. Several ladies, who looked fairly well-to-do, were huddling around a fruit stand, grabbing and arguing. The king must have allowed a small amount of apples to be released to the town because they began to squabble about who was going to purchase what.

As the finger pointing and hand waving continued, Ashby quickly flicked her hand out, grabbed an apple and pocketed it. She then coolly walked behind another and nicked two apricots. Into her pocket those went. She continued to another stall that sold dried meats, where she managed to slip a couple of hunks of beef into her pocket. While she headed toward Lyssa, she made the time of day to an older lady, laughing and then calmly walked to where she had left her now amazed friend.

"See? Easy. The trick is that you gotta look like ya belong there and you're gonna buy somethin'."

They walked down an alley and behind the cobbler's shop, sat and shared the food. Lyssa ate hers as if it were the last lot of food she'd ever get.

"Easy, Lys. We've got all day for more."

Lyssa looked embarrassed as she licked her fingers. "Sorry," she said with a grin. "The last few weeks have been…tough."

They watched the throngs of people go about their daily lives without a care. Lyssa wished her life were like this—walking with Mother to town to purchase supplies, working with Father in the tannery, or even chasing Chandra and playing tricks on her. Back to normal and without a care. But apparently that wasn't the path the gods had wanted for her.

She'd have to grow up the hard way, life teaching her hard lessons, for good or ill.

Just as the sun touched the horizon, Ashby stood and stretched. "Too bad neither one of us can pick a lock." She had a broad grin on her face.

"Now's the best time, ya know. It's when the night and day are almost one. Makes things harder ta see outside."

"I know," Lyssa replied. "This is when I usually do my best hunting."

"You hunt?"

Lyssa nodded.

"I never learned that. Mother wanted me to be some sort o' lady." She laughed.

"My sister was the lady in our house. I never liked it, those silly dresses and lah-di-dah girly things." She shook her head in disgust. "Da would take me out sometimes, but we never did get much, rabbits and squirrels mostly. Sometimes, I'd get lucky and take home a wild sheep." She remembered the day she almost got the deer, but Chandra used a shadow to scare it off.

"I don't remember my da, my ma neither really. I was passed around from one part of my family to another. Everyone always argued that they didn't want me or they'd try ta put me in a lost kids home. I got tired of it an' left. Never went back." She sat quietly, remembering. Lyssa put her arm around Ashby and put her head on her shoulder.

"Looks like all we have is each other, Ash." She shook her gently. "That's alright. We're all we need, right?" She pulled her close, and they hugged the pain away.

Ashby rubbed a tear away and smiled at Lyssa. She knew she'd found a good friend that she could trust. Maybe things would start looking up for her now.

She took a deep cleansing breath. "Oh, well. Where was I? Oh yes, the stands're the best place to nick coins, other than pickin' that is."

"What's pickin'?" Lyssa asked.

"Why, pickin' pockets, of course. Ya never done that either?" Lyssa shook her head no. "Huh, you really are outta place then, aren't ya?" Ashby laughed.

"So how do I get into a stand?" She had genuine curiosity on her face.

"Ya sneak up ta the back of one, see if there's a lock, pick it and take what's there, but ya gotta run afore someone sees ya."

"How do you pick a lock? I've never seen that done."

She looked at Lyssa with a strange look. "You never lived in a city or big town before, have ya?"

"No, never." She looked sad. "Tantyn and Hazelwood aren't big at all, farming towns mostly, nothing like this."

She made hand gestures to match her description. "Well, ya take these two thin strips of metal, stick 'em in the keyhole, jiggle 'em around 'til the lock opens."

"Huh." Lyssa thought about that, and it didn't sound very hard. "Do you have some...pickers?"

Ashby chuckled, "They're called picks. I got a set, but they're real hard to get if one breaks."

"I could give it a try if you don't mind."

Ashby thought a second. She wasn't particularly good at it anyway, so breaking them really didn't matter to her.

"Sure, here. Give it a try." She handed the funny-looking strips to Lyssa.

She looked at them, trying to figure out how they could possibly work. They were odd shaped, one was curved just at the end, and one had a sharp bend at the end like a pick. Placing them in the fold of her boot, she got ready to give it a try.

"I'll sit here, but if you get seen, run yer arse to the old cellar. I'll meet ya there."

Lyssa nodded and started off.

The moon was crescent, so the light was low, making it much easier to go from shadow to shadow. She crouched low then searched the area. Nothing moved. Keeping to the shadows, she slowly made it across to a tree near three of the stands that stood alone from the others. To her, they looked like big wooden boxes with a makeshift cloth ceiling and an angled tabletop. She darted to the back of the nearest one, where she saw that there was no lock, just a door. She quietly slid it open and found two leather bags tucked into the far corner. Not bothering to open them, she tied the drawstrings together, slung them over her shoulder and sneaked to the next stand. Again, there was no lock, but inside was a small wooden box the size of her hand. Glancing around carefully, checking for movement, she slipped it into her ragged tunic so her belt would keep it secure inside without it slipping out.

Again, she searched the area and saw no movement. Quietly and still crouched, she went to the third, but this time there was a lock. It looked old and rusted with a large keyhole, and though she jiggled it, it remained locked. She studied both doors, trying to see how they pulled open. To her surprise, there was a hasp where the lock secured them together and four hinges, two on each side. She reached for the picks and realized…the doors pulled out, which meant the hinges were accessible from outside. Grinning at the uselessness of it, Lyssa shook her head in disbelief. She quickly felt around in the poor light and found a thick, sturdy twig. She lightly jiggled the door to avoid making too much noise and found that they were loose on their worn hinges.

Sharpening the twig on a stone, she worked it into the hole beneath the hinge while jiggling the door at the same time. Sure enough, the hinge pin began to slide up. She grabbed the top and pulled. It came right out. The next hinge came right out as well, and the door pulled out easily, revealing the contents inside.

A medium-sized box sat inside, about the size of a bucket. It was heavy, but she managed to tuck it under her arm, peek around the stand, and, seeing no movement, slipped through the shadows to rejoin Ashby. Hiding behind a tree, she spotted her crouched at the corner of a nearby building. A guard rounded the corner, making his rounds, lazily scanning the street. She waited until he turned away, then darted to another tree and across the road. Circling the building, she reached out and tapped Ashby on the shoulder, making her jump in surprise. "By Skippin's boots, how did you get here? I never heard you coming."

"Come on."

Lyssa moved low and quiet as a mouse with Ashby in tow.

Ashby followed her new friend through the woods, amazed at the way she slinked past trees, bushes and ravines. When they got back to the lean-to, Ashby lit a small fire as Lyssa set out the pilfered booty.

"How'd ya learn ta move like that, Lys? I had the damnedest time following ya."

"I sort of grew up in the woods. I had two good teachers." She smiled.

They sorted through their loot, amazed at their fortune.

"Gods, you got a lot. I usually just nick a few coins and run."

"There was only one lock. Oh, here." She handed the picks back.

"Didn't you use them?"

"No, the doors at the third stand were easy to open. Didn't need them."

Lyssa turned to the first pouch and opened it. Nothing much there, a few notes and a spoon. She kept the spoon and emptied the rest into the fire. She tossed the bag onto the bedroll.

She opened the second pouch and found several apples and some raspberries. She shared them with Ashby and went on to the small box. It was a plain wooden box with no markings. Carefully shaking it, she heard something rattling around in it.

"Want it?"

Ashby took a final bite of her apple and motioned for Lyssa to keep it as juice ran down her chin. She tossed the core into the flames and watched the sparks fly into the sky; the sweet smell of roasting apple core mixing well with the smoky smell of the fire.

Lyssa banged it on a rock, and it broke open, revealing three ornate rings with nice gems mounted in them.

"There we go," she said triumphantly and rubbing her hands together.

One had a large sapphire stone atop a silver band. She gave that to Ashby, who tried it on all her fingers, finding that her thumb was the best fit. She smiled broadly at her new bauble.

"Does this mean we're joined now, Lyssa, my sweet?" she said in her most sultry tone.

"Ashby, my love, my heart swoons for you." They both threw their heads back and laughed like little girls.

Next came a multi-stone ring. Lyssa pocketed that one. The last was like the first, only an emerald. Lyssa went to give it to Ashby.

"You keep it, Lys. You took it. Keep it."

Lyssa's eyes lit up. She put it into her pocket and tossed the box into the fire, where it slowly began to burn, sending small sparks up into the cool night air.

The last box had a lock in the center and was made of metal. It wasn't especially thick, but there was no way to break it open without making a lot of noise.

Ashby handed back the picks.

"Looks like you'll need 'em after all."

Lyssa laid the box on its back to make the lock more accessible and visible. Taking the picks in hand, she put the bent one in first to check the top. The other was only bent at the tip. She poked it in and started to feel around. With the bottom one, she felt it sink down, so she stopped and held it there. With the top one, she felt a catch, pressed it and then turned, hearing the click of the lock opening. The lid swung open to reveal its bright metallic contents.

Their eyes widened as a multitude of coins spilled out of it. They glanced at each other in awe, then back at the coins. They were mostly silver, but there was gold as well, and the box had been almost full. They each took turns running their fingers through it as if they'd discovered a dragon's horde. With smiling anticipation, they decided to wait until sunup to count and divide it.

Ashby placed the box in the back of the lean-to; they both crawled into the bedroll and went to sleep, ending a very busy day.

'...*bored*'

The next morning, they were greeted by the warming rays of the sun peeking through the trees. Lyssa stretched and went to stir the coals of the fire back to life. A light fog hung over the camp, giving the flames a cheery glow.

Ashby groaned and stretched herself awake.

"Get your lazy bum up. The day's calling." Lyssa smiled and gave the coals another stir.

"Lazy? I'm not the one wakin' the whole forest up snorrin'," she said, moving closer to the fire for warmth.

Lyssa looked at Ashby, faking shock. "Ashby Brimmer, how dare you?" They both laughed.

Lyssa sat next to her as Ashby removed the box and set it between them, anticipating vast riches.

"I guess now's as good a time as any."

It was a particularly good haul. They gleefully separated the coins by type and stacked them in neat rows. They joked and teased until the counting was done, where they each hefted seventy-three silver and twenty-two gold regal marks.

"Someone's about to have a horrible day," Ashby joked as the stand owner would come to realize. But at least today the girls could have a satisfying meal and perhaps purchase some new clothing. Lyssa's rags were in horrible condition, and neither of them had eaten a decent meal in weeks.

Then, from nowhere, "Teach me to pick, Ash."

"What? Why?" she asked. "I thought you were afraid of getting caught."

"I am, but after last night, I sort of…it felt good—exciting." She looked to her feet, embarrassed.

"Well, I guess I can do that."

They took their time and ate. It wasn't much of course: random potatoes, boiled, reheated squirrel stew. At the time, it was a banquet, usually the best they could hope for, considering.

She spent a good part of the day teaching Lyssa how to slice a string, how to bait and switch and even how to tip and palm. She caught on very quickly, almost too quickly. She wanted to go out that very day and try it, but Ashby reined her in and insisted on waiting.

"Greed, Lys, it'll get ya caught ev'ry time. Ya gotta be patient."

She knew that. Her overexcitement usually ruined her hunts as well. Too many times, she would draw the string and, instead of releasing her arrow from the crouch, she would stand, startling the prey or completely missing her shot. She grudgingly agreed and promised to wait until the next day.

The sun was past its height, and they decided to head into town to purchase new clothes. Lyssa's were so threadbare that certain parts of her anatomy began to show through, making her very self-conscious and Ashby's weren't much better. She'd attempted to sew various private areas so many times that they began chaffing. She knew of a tailor whose shop was on the north side of The Guildway ring and close enough to The Crown ring to not be overly expensive. She nudged Lyssa and said there were also "other nice places to visit." She knew what that meant. Theft might suit them here, plus the hideouts were closer in case of trouble. They stood in front of the Velvet and Lace tailor shop. It was a quaint little shop along the main road nestled between a leather specialty shop, 'Alvoora Leather Marigs and Such' and 'Farthings Scents and Apothecary' along the main road deciding if they really wanted to go in, especially looking as they did.

"I feel a fool going in like this, Ash. The tailor will laugh us out."

Ashby chuckled. "Then again, he may feel so sorry for us that he gives us the clothes as charity, no charge." They both laughed and decided to take a chance. The door opened. They stepped in…and all eyes turned directly onto both of them. There was a moment of silence. Both girls looked down at their clothes, then back at all the patrons.

Ashby put on her toughest face, which was more cute than tough and yelled out, "Oi, mind yer own churlish business, ya cox-combs."

Most heads turned back to what they'd been doing, but some looked down their noses and quietly cursed them before going about their business.

The proprietor remained behind his counter, helping a customer, yet kept a clear eye on the girls in case of theft.

There were all types and shapes of clothing that hung from pegs, racks and dummies. Ashby took her time finding several styles of clothing, touching the fine types of cloth, hose, bodices of brocade and velvet that hung with colorful chemises and other undergarments. Across the shop, Lyssa looked through various tunics, breeches and even liripipe hoods, which she had only seen once during a wedding at four hamlets. A jongleur wore one and made it spin around as she juggled, much to everyone's joy.

Ashby decided on linen undergarments, which the tailor's wife helped to properly fit in the back room. She found them suitable for her needs and finally purchased them along with a tunic and breeches. Both the tailor and his wife, though surprised that she could even afford them, scolded Ashby for dressing like a boy yet gladly accepted her coin. "A little lady should never wear breeches. It isn't right." The husband nodded.

Lyssa purchased linens, which she found rather clumsy and uncomfortable, but accepted them, begrudgingly.

They stepped into Alvoord's leather shop, only to be rudely shooed out. He sneered at their "uncouth rags" and lack of breeding. Ashby, who wasn't entirely sure what uncouth meant, took offense. On her way out, she slipped the man's coin purse from his belt…and a pair of fine shoes for good measure.

A few minutes later, walking down the road, she flashed the stolen prizes at Lyssa. Her friend gasped. "I didn't even see you do it!"

Ashby just winked, looping her arm through Lyssa's as they strolled away.

She knew of a more skilled leather tailor whose pricing was better, though his selection wasn't as good. They made their way across The Guildway, almost to the main road and found The Poignant Cuir. Ashby told Lyssa that she'd gotten several *special* items there, and the proprietor, one Borrick Pyle, was known for his *fair* dealings.

Lyssa smiled and was eager to see what the man had to offer. Inside, leather goods of every kind hung from pegs and rafters. Hides larger than she was tall were stretched across the walls and stacked on tables, ready for cutting. Her father's shop had never been this large, but what he made was far better. She saw a doublet on a fashion doll that she really liked but knew she didn't have the coin yet to get it.

"Greetings, ladies," he said with a professional grin. "Welcome to The Poignant Cuir. What can I help ya with?" Ashby smiled and winked at Borrick, who remembered the lovely girl from past dealings.

"It is so lovely to see you again in my humble shop. Might I assist you with a purchase or two?"

The other patrons turned to see who the silver-tongued owner might be speaking to, only to see the two ragtag-looking girls. They issued quiet, derisive snorts as they turned to continue their business.

Borrick looked Lyssa up and down, professionally sizing her, and quietly stated, "Ye wants a good sturdy doublet, not heavy but well made, several inside pockets and supple so's not to chafe." He looked around. "I got one, but it be costin' ya."

Ashby stepped in and showed Borrick the fancy boots she stole. "I believe your wife ordered these the other day, good sir." His eyebrows raised, seeing the excellent quality of the boots and knowing just where they came from.

"Oh, thank you for delivering them, young lass. I have your payment right here if you'll follow."

He led them to the back room. "Those and fifty gold, not a silver less." Lyssa began rummaging through her pouch when her friend touched her arm.

"Not to worry, Lys," she said, revealing the stolen pouch she took from Alvoord's and produced the fifty gold coins. Borrick's eyes lit up. She placed two more coins in his hand and nodded to the leather breeches lying across the chair near his counter.

"Those, too."

He smiled. "Those be fifteen."

She grinned. "I know a man who knows a man, Borrick. I think his name begins with Rohd and ends with Garneky." Borrick's face went pale white.

"Um, er, two gold it is fer a deal well struck, aye?"

"You, my friend, are the sweetest man I know." They walked out into the shop where Lyssa took down the doublet and breeches, smiling with pride as she removed her tunic for all to see. The four customers watched in shock. A wife covered her husband's eyes and ushering him out the door, another woman grabbed her husband by the arm and dragged him out, while the last man stood and stared, a wide grin on his face. Ashby began to draw her dagger while staring at the man who, seeing this, decided it would be safer outside.

Lyssa removed her tattered breeches and started to put on her leather pants with as much zeal as she could muster.

"Lyssa Soryn, what by Hearthmae's tits are you doing?" Ashby said loudly and nearly laughing. She looked up at Ash and realized what she had been doing, smiled and turned around. She'd never had leather of this sort, even when her father made her first pair.

Her new clothing was made from black suede with latticed leather across the chest and two small slit pockets. There were ten ebony eyelets, five a side, strung with thick leather lacing that stopped mid-chest. The arms had suede reinforcing on the elbows with rigid cuffs. The breeches were long and snug but not tight and laced up the sides of the legs. She almost squealed when she saw herself in the cracked mirror, jumping up and down like a little girl.

She hugged Borrick, thanking him profusely and then hugging Ashby tightly, kissing her on the cheek. Then she went back to admiring herself in the mirror again.

Borrick had never seen anyone so excited over something as trivial as a doublet and breeches. He stood scratching his head in wonder. Ashby noticed his confusion, so she leaned over and told him a fast version of Lyssa's life trials. He looked at her wide-eyed and, feeling sympathetic, said, "Ya know what…Lyssa was it? Ya needs a decent pair o' boots too, methinks."

He went to the back of the shop and produced a matching pair of suede boots; low, soft heel, knee-high and flip-topped.

"This should do ya," he said with an ear-to-ear grin.

Her eyes went wide. "I can't pay for these. I don't have the coin."

"Young lady, ya pay me back when ya can. I'm always here, so come find me when ya get back ta town."

She didn't know what to say. Tears of joy filled her eyes, and she went and hugged him again. Ashby looked at Borrick and mouthed *thank you* to him. He nodded back.

Lyssa felt as if she were walking on air in the first new clothes she had purchased herself. She walked arm in arm with Ashby down the road, prancing like a filly, not a care in the world.

They went into the Copper Chalice tavern on the north side of The Guildway. The smell of polished wood and spiced wine filled the room. Large kegs lined the wall, showing patrons the variety of wines available to them. There were even firkins of mead stacked on the far side of the serving plank, also many to select from. A well-maintained stone hearth had a large blazing fire burning, though there were few customers just yet. The girls selected a table close to the fire, both sitting and facing the entrance. The tavern maid asked what their drink of choice would be and brought both quickly. Lyssa decided to pay for the flagons in advance to ensure another round, leaned back and propped her feet on a chair.

"Ahem." Lyssa looked over at the tapster, who was motioning for her to get her feet off the chair. She shrugged and did so, earning her a nod of approval.

"Huh, never had that happen before."

Ashby replied, "And just how many taverns have you been in, young lady?" They both laughed and spent the rest of the evening drinking. Lyssa loved the mead. It was heady with strong hints of honey, spice and apple. It tasted far better than what she'd had before. She liked the taste and grew fonder of it the more she drank.

Soon, the excitement of the day caught up with Ashby. She yawned and suggested they get a room for the evening. Lyssa agreed, insisting on paying for one room for the night. She used a good bit of coin for a room with a stout rope bed, straw ticking beneath a feather mattress, a wool blanket folded at its foot. Ashby was impressed. She'd never been in a bed as fine as this in her life.

They lay in bed talking about the events of the day for just a short while, giggling like little girls. Lyssa silently thought about Ashby. The way they got along and teased was just like her and Chandra. It was as if she'd found another sister. She sighed and then fell fast asleep.

The morning came, and they left their room for food, both famished and calling for a large meal. They were quickly running out of coin with all the extravagant spending, but insisted on one last huzzah before heading back into the world of normalcy. They decided to stay in the area and see how observant their marks might be. After all, this was a fairly well-to-do section of the city, and pockets surely would be filled here.

Many guards were out patrolling the streets that morning, and Ashby could tell that people had become less aware of their surroundings because of it. They roamed from stand to stand and stall to stall, brushing against each other at times, which caught Ashby's eye, making her smile. This could be particularly good for the girls.

It was decided that today, Lyssa could test her skills at picking. She didn't feel confident at first, but Ashby assured her that if it all went bad, she could outrun nearly anyone with her abilities and hide in an abandoned cellar across town. The guards' armor made them far too heavy for a chase, and none carried bows or crossbows, not in the city.

Lyssa stayed nearby and let Ashby work the crowd. The market smelled of dust, sweat and warm fruit; the place moved in a lazy weave of elbows, haggling and bargaining. Ashby darted her eyes at their target, a richly dressed man with a small pouch dangling closely at his side. She gave her a small nod and drifted away, leaving Lyssa alone with the mark. There was no hesitation. She'd watched the way Ashby angled her shoulder, the little pause that made the man's back turn. Lyssa mirrored it exactly. She moved like a shadow sliding into a gap, shoulders relaxed, eyes on the back and scanning to ensure no prying eyes were on her. No one was paying attention. It was as if she were hiding in plain sight.

Snickt! One quick cut, the pouch came loose, she palmed it and turned to walk away. She slipped between two men arguing with one another about meat pricing, past a woman holding a child and past another stand, where she casually took a silver pendant hanging loosely from a peg.

She continued walking, pretending to peruse the wares of a seller dealing in cheap baubles. Right next to that, she noticed a leather-tied pouch sitting at the edge of the table where a woman fussed with her scales. Lyssa looked, paused and shrugged. Her fingers hovered, then closed. She didn't pinch or yank; she eased the pouch outward like she was nudging it toward the woman, slipped it under her sleeve and stepped back, humming a happy tune she'd learned from her gran.

The woman looked over, frowned at nothing, then turned back. Lyssa's heart thudded in her throat for a breath and then eased. She met Ashby behind the fountain in the center of the square and handed over the pouch like it had always been hers to give.

"See?" Ashby said, grinning. "No drama, no fuss, quick and clean."

Lyssa grinned, dangling the second pouch. "Not to mention how profitable."

They both laughed, hugged and returned to the Copper Chalice, where they ate a bounty once more.

Aside from her sister, Lyssa had never actually had a friend. Ashby had become her best, and it was blossoming.

The next day, they returned to the fountain where several people sat and rested their feet. The day was warmer, and there seemed to be more vendors than normal, which, of course, attracted more people. They looked for their next mark and found one, but this lift was smaller, and it felt more dangerous because it required closer proximity. A traveling tinker sat nearby on the fountain steps, his leather satchel slung over one shoulder, fingers warm on his pipe. He smelled of iron and horses and the faint hint of spilled mead. Lyssa circled him the way a cat circles a sleeping dog, paying no mind yet taking in everything.

She crouched at the edge of the step and let her elbow brush his knee, a careful, accidental contact that left him unbothered. Her hand, warm and steady, slipped behind him and found the pouch tied to his belt. It was lighter than she expected. Two quick tugs, one practiced twist and the knot came free. She pinched the pouch between thumb and forefinger and pulled it inward.

A coin slipped from the bag, hit the stone and made a tiny, traitorous metallic sound. The tinker paused, head turning, and Lyssa froze. The man's hand went to his pipe, then his gaze slid past her and settled on a hawker's tired face across the square who had bent down to retrieve his dropped coin. He took another puff, and the moment passed, allowing Lyssa to breathe again.

She rose with a stretch, then moved away before the tinker noticed. Ashby caught the pouch and flipped a coin to Lyssa like a teacher giving a gold star.

"Good hands," she said, but there was a new note in her voice, approval, yes, and something like concern. "You're getting greedy."

Lyssa's grin was all teeth and heat. "Greedy tastes good."

"Aye, Lys—and makes ye lose yer head."

Lyssa looked into her friend's eyes. It was no jest. She nodded and winked at Ashby, accepting the advice.

'...Lady, please'

They next worked the north square. It was alive with color and clamor: minstrels strumming, jugglers tossing, merchants hawking. Amid it all stood a man who didn't belong yet fit perfectly, dark hair streaked with gray, a neat goatee framing a smile that charmed as easily as it disarmed.

His coat was fine cut, boots polished, gloves tucked just so. He looked like a wealthy patron enjoying the day's entertainment. But Lyssa's eyes locked on the leather pouch at his belt; fat, heavy, almost daring her to take it.

Ashby had melted into the crowd, leaving Lyssa to test her courage. Her fingers tingled as she approached, weaving between laughing children and clapping hands. She slowed, matched her pace to his, then let her shoulder brush his arm like an accident. Her hand slipped to the pouch. The leather was warm, supple and tied with a simple knot. Easy.

She didn't see the slight upturn of his lips. Didn't notice how his eyes followed her reflection in a polished kettle across the stall. He knew.... Yet he allowed it.

Lyssa lifted the pouch and pivoted away. Adrenaline surged, her pulse roaring in her ears. A voice cut through, loud as a screeching owl, not his, but some hawker's wife who had seen everything.

"Thief! Stop her!"

Her angry face and pointing finger singled Lyssa out. There was no mistake. The shout cracked the crowd open. A guard wheeled around, spear raised and sprinted after her. Others joined, pointing, yelling. Lyssa's blood ran cold. Her eyes darted left and right, searching for an escape. The cellar. She bolted.

Down an alley, her supple boots slapping stone, a barrel toppled, a dog barked, the guard's curses chased her like arrows. She vaulted a fence, wood splintering under her hands, she rolled, lessening the impact, then dove beneath a wagon axle, mud streaking her doublet. A heartbeat later, she was crawling, scrambling, lungs burning, until her palms struck the familiar cellar door.

She yanked it open, dropped inside, slammed it shut. The world above muffled to a dull roar. She heard the guards run past, mailed shirts jingling and clanking, cursing, then directing. Her breath came ragged, her fingers clenched around the stolen pouch—safe. She leaned against the wall, trying to ease her breathing, willing her heart to slow—or so she thought.

A single lantern burned in the cellar's corner, casting long shadows. From them stepped the man with the goatee, boots pristine despite the alley mud. His coat was still immaculate, his eyes amused.

It was him.

Lyssa froze, eyes wide, back pressed to the damp wall. She placed the pouch in her tunic pocket. He inclined his head, smile faint but razor-sharp.

"Not bad," he said softly, voice rich, measured. "But you'll need to run faster than that…little cat."

His smile was disarming, presenting straight, white teeth and happy eyes.

"Oh, have no fear. You are not in any danger." He slowly walked toward Lyssa. Her eyes darted left and right, searching for an escape.

In the blink of an eye, she leaped toward the exit, but, just as quickly, he stood before her, blocking her way.

"You are fast. I must credit you that." She leaped for the dark corner, spun and drew her dagger in defense.

"Good. When all else fails, bear your claws and prepare to defend," he said, slowly moving toward her calmly, "but you should spread your feet more and lower yourself just a little." He demonstrated by lowering himself into position. He stood and said, "It allows for more spring when you leap." He cocked his head to one side. "Grip needs work as well, but otherwise, very talented."

The dust hung in the air. Her eyes began to tear. She blinked. He leaped. She saw him just a second too late. He grabbed her hand and twisted it, causing the dagger to fall from her hand. He stepped in and placed his body between her and the fallen weapon. She countered by rolling in the opposite direction. Her hand now twisted from his grasp, which allowed her to regain her footing and draw the other dagger from her boot.

He grinned and clapped. "Well done, little cat. Very well done." He stood and began to dust himself.

Still crouched, ready to strike, she growled, "What do you want?"

"What do I want?" He grinned. "Why, I want my coin back, if you don't mind."

She tossed the pouch from her pocket. "There." The small sack landed with a metallic thud, causing a small puff of dust. "Now, let me go." She kept her eyes fixed on his hips. She knew whichever way they went, his body had to follow. It gave her a slight advantage.

"Very good, little cat." He motioned for her to stand. "Up, up, up. That'll be quite enough for one day, I think."

Her eyes stayed fixed on him. One move and she'd bolt for the exit. "What do you want?"

"You've impressed me, little cat; your patience, your instincts, your abilities." He turned and dusted off a nearby chair. When he sat and crossed his legs, he steepled his fingers beneath his nose in thought.

"Have you killed?" Now his eyes returned the stare, waiting for her reply.

"I'll ask again. What...do...you...want?"

"Hmm. We shall have to work on that." His hands fell to his lap. "So, I require an answer, little cat. So, we may proceed with my proposal."

Proposal? He wants to have a joining? She looked bewildered.

He let out an exasperated sigh, still waiting.

"Yes, I've killed." Her stare hardened.

"And how did you do it?"

She was becoming confused. Why was he asking? Did he see? He wasn't a guard, so why was he questioning her?

"I strangled him."

He nodded his head with approval. "And he was larger than you, I take it?"

"Yes! Get to the damn point."

His grin widened. "In a moment. Your friend is arriving."

Ashby came bounding down the steps. "By Velkhar's arse, Lys, what happened?" She stopped cold and stood staring at the man sitting in the chair across from Lyssa.

"Umm." Ashby was confused. How did this man get here so fast?

"Have no worry...Ashby, I believe it is. Correct?" he asked with a toothy smile.

She stood silently and nodded.

259

"So, now I have the cat and the fox."

Lyssa and Ashby exchanged glances.

"Ladies, please, if I meant you harm, neither of you would be here right now."

"Alright, then. For the last time, I ask, what do you want?"

"Ah, to my proposal then." He stood with hands behind his back. "Consider me an executor of...contracts, let's say."

The girls looked at each other, puzzled.

"In other words, I receive a request with payment or the assurance of payment and execute the request per the terms." Ashby stood stunned. However, Lyssa caught on immediately.

Her eyes narrowed, her grin widened, "Sooo, you're an assassin."

He touched his nose and winked at her. "Ex-actly."

She grinned at him broadly. "And what's this proposal?"

Ashby's eyes widened, not believing that Lyssa even asked.

"I will train you, hone your already impressive skills to razor-sharp perfection, and you work for me."

"Gods no. I be a thief, not no killer." Ashby instantly became nervous.

Lyssa, on the other hand, beamed. She knew she was made for this. Her knowledge of poison, her physical skills...and the possibility of finding the men who ruined her life.

She paused, deep in thought.

"I'll give you until sunset on the morrow, ladies." He walked past Ashby and toward the exit. "We'll meet here no matter your answer. No pressure."

"And what if it's no. You kill me?" Lyssa's body tensed.

"Absolutely not. My business requires me to move on to my next contract. I haven't the time to delay."

He walked up the steps, saying over his shoulder, "Until then, ladies."

'...shall I raise the stakes?'"

The girls slipped back to their camp in the woods; that part of the city was no longer safe. A cool breeze swept through, and they huddled together beneath a threadbare blanket Ashby had stolen from a clothesline on the way. The fire crackled softly, its smoke carried off by the wind, scattering tiny sparks into the dark.

"What do you think, Ash? Could be good for us."

"Lys, I don't know. Theft's what I'm best at. I don't think I can stick someone less I have ta." She lay her head on Lyssa's shoulder. "I ain't gonna do it, Lys." She paused. "And I ain't sure you should either."

They sat silently for a while, staring into the firelight. The yellow-red flames danced gently, quietly; every so often, a pop would send stray sparks into the air.

"I'm not cut out for stealing, Ash. It was fun at first, but now…" she trailed off, thinking. She didn't want to leave her friend behind. Ash had turned into a sister, family. She couldn't leave her family.

"I'll sleep on it some more if you want. We'll figure something out. I promise."

They snuggled under the lean-to, Lyssa's arm over Ashby, holding her closely. The nights were getting colder now, and warmth was becoming a difficult commodity to find. They needed to find a way to leave this life, something lucrative yet safer. Ash was all right with theft and moving from place to place, but Lyssa wasn't comfortable with theft. To her, it was like taking the last morsel of food from a starving family. She excelled at it, but it never really sat well with her. Of course, she knew being a cold-blooded murderer would find her head on a chopping block just as well, but the pay might be better if she joined the assassin. Unfortunately, that would mean losing Ashby if she chose to go her own way. Sleep for her came slowly and troubled. The choices were convoluted in morals, family and loyalty. Too much to think about, and the more she did, the less sleep came to her.

Before she knew it, the sun broke over the horizon. Ashby was blowing on the ashes, trying to heat a spark to flame. The air was cold but not freezing yet. She piled some twigs on the coals and, soon, a small fire jumped to life.

"I got some hen from last night if ya wanna heat it," she said, blowing the flames hotter.

Lyssa rolled from the bedroll, wrapping the blanket around her. She took the hen, jammed a stick through it and held it over the flame, watching as the fat began to sizzle.

They quietly ate, neither looking at the other, yet both still thinking of their futures.

Soon, the hens were gone, bones tossed down the nearby hill as refuse. They wiped their hands on an old rag and stood to stretch. Realizing they'd done it in unison, they began to laugh. Lyssa walked to Ashby, hugged her close and said, "Bugger it, Ash. I'm with you." She gave a tooth-filled grin. "We'll rob every stand, pick every pouch and run off rich till our days end." They both laughed and swung each other round and round.

Still laughing, they made their way to the road, planning their next move. They were going to make their rounds of this town, abandon camp and head to the next. Hopefully, they would nick enough coin to pay for a room in the next town so they could case it and start anew.

It would be more dangerous for certain, but The Crown ring would yield the best possibility for coin. The most aristocratic in all the city came here. Every rooster with a name, every hen with a title came to show their worth. The prize was almost too much for them to resist. They noted the apparel most people donned. Poofy this, flowing that. The girls laughed at all of the silly clothing and how everyone walked, noses in the air and fancy language. Just for fun, they wandered through the crowd as they were waiting to hear what ridiculous nonsense those fops would spout. It took no time for the looks, as if their very presence were an affront to their senses.

A man and woman walked by and glared at them. Lyssa held out her hand as if to beg.

"Oh, begone, foul churl. Your sort should be skirted away as common refuse. Come, dear, we've better things to do."

"Oh, please, sir. Please. Me mum's entertainin' some men at me home an' me da's besotted again. Please help." It was all Ashby could do to keep from bursting out with laughter.

"Oooh, faster, my love. Don't let them touch me." They all but sprinted away from the girls as fast as they could.

They fell to the ground laughing, much to everyone's surprise.

And then came the guards.

These were no ordinary guards. Their armor sparkled, and their weapons gleamed. They had the kings crest emblazoned on their tabards, signifying they were the King's Talons, the personal guards of the king himself. Ashby knew it and pulled Lyssa to her feet, who was still laughing.

"Shut it, Lys. This ain't a game no more."

The captain sported a blue comb on his helm, like a brush. His armor was golden-hued, whereas the others were silver.

He stood tall before the girls and nodded his head. "You seem to be misplaced, ladies. If you look over your shoulder, you will clearly see the road leading to The Guildway. Please be kind enough to find yourselves walking in that direction." His manners were impeccable. He flourished his arm in the direction of the road as a real gentleman, which made Ashby almost blush.

"Oh dear. Yes, sir, by all means." Ashby curtsied and, grabbing Lyssa by the arm, started back toward The Guildway. The guards remained until they crossed The Guildway walk, then went about their patrol.

"Velkhar's arse, Ash. What was that all about?"

She stopped and looked deep into Lyssa's eyes.

"Those are not the guards you want to taunt. They can go into any part of the city and capture or kill whoever they want." She looked over Lyssa's shoulder. "They command all the other guards in the city and cannot be attainted unless by witness or in their court."

Lyssa looked at Ashby, confused. "What's attainted?"

Ashby blinked at the question. "You're serious."

Lyssa stood looking blankly. "Of course. I've never heard that word before. What is it?"

She rolled her eyes. "You farmers... It means disgraced, blamed."

"Ahh, I see." She smiled. I wonder..."

"NO, Lys—not ever." Ashby was serious. Lyssa hadn't seen her like this since she met her.

"Oh, all right...this time." She hugged Ashby. "Come, little sister. So many pockets, so little time." She threw her head back and laughed. Ashby did not. She was becoming worried about Lyssa; greed was becoming a problem now. They needed to leave before something bad happened.

They headed for the south side of The Guildway and, after half a day, came away with more gold than they'd ever nicked. A lord's ransom for each, which they were quick to spend on food and clothing. Lyssa returned to Broddick's shop to settle with him and even purchased a new doeskin hooded cloak to match her finery. Ashby bought a weaved leather sash and new boots.

After their feast at the Copper Chalice, they talked about the proposal the man in the cellar spoke of. They began to refer to him as *the assassin*, as he never proffered his real name, and knew the time was short before they had to meet him with their answer.

"I'm out, Lys. We got enough. Let's go to the next town and live there a bit. Please?"

She sounded like she was desperately begging, and the look in her eyes confirmed it.

"For you, anything, Ash." She leaned over and kissed her cheek, smiling.

Ashby's face beamed as she grabbed her flagon and raised it high. Lyssa followed suit as they toasted to a new life and laughed.

The cellar door was already open, signaling that the assassin was already there. They carefully stepped down until they reached the bottom, a lantern lit in the corner sending a flickering glow around the room.

"Nice to see you again, ladies." He beamed a toothy smile. "Have we come to a decision?"

They looked at each other, then back. Lyssa cleared her throat.

"We've decided. If you please," she didn't want to upset the dangerous man, "we'd prefer not to join you. We're not meant for that sort of work, see, and we'd prefer to leave this place and go elsewhere." Both of their faces showed their nerves.

The assassin looked down and rubbed his hands together.

He sighed his disappointment. "Well, that's disappointing." He stood slowly, rubbing his knuckles. The girls looked afraid.

"As you wish, ladies. Though it pains me, I must abide by your decisions." He bowed to them and started for the stairs. "If you will excuse me then."

"You…you're not going to kill us?"

He stopped and looked back at them. "Do you wish me to kill you?"

They looked at each other, puzzled. "Um, no," Ashby replied.

"Then enjoy your day, ladies." He bowed again and was gone.

They looked at each other in disbelief, chuckled at such an odd occurrence and headed back to the Chalice.

As they walked down the road arm in arm, Lyssa sighed, content. For the first time since her sister, she honestly believed that her life was getting better, and she could finally be happy.

They spoke to the tavern owner and passed on that they were going to leave in the morning. Considering all of the coin they'd spent there in the last few days, he gave them a room free of charge for the night. Both girls kissed the man's face, much to his wife's chagrin, and headed off to sleep.

Morning came swiftly. Both girls awoke at the same time, dressed and went into the common room. The owner was already up and asked if they wanted to eat, but they declined, stating the road was calling. He was sad to see them go but wished them well and said they'd always be welcome at the Copper Chalice.

The road was clear this morning. A light mist hovered, and rays of sunlight peeked through the moist leaves of the woods. They decided to walk today, to breathe in the sweet, clean air and revel in the beginnings of their new life together.

As they laughed and bounded ahead, giggling like sisters, they were stopped by three large guards walking in the opposite direction.

"Oi, whacha girls so damn 'appy 'bout, eh?" The guard was heavily bearded and smelled like days-old ale.

The other two were short, almost too short to be guards, which raised Lyssa's suspicions immediately. One was blonde and the other ginger, and they, too, reeked of ale.

Ashby nudged Lyssa to keep moving on, which she gladly obliged, and they passed the men.

"Oi, ya not 'earin' me? I said, watcha laughing 'bout?" They turned to the passing girls and put their hands on their swords.

Lyssa stopped, placing a hand on Ashby's arm. She turned to them and said, "We're just going home. We didn't mean any harm." She pulled Ash's arm so they could move away from them.

"Ya makes one more move an' yet get th' blade."

They stopped and faced the guards. "Please. Our family is waiting for us."

The bearded guard stepped up, looking them both up and down. Lyssa had seen this before. She whispered to Ash, "This is going to get bad quickly."

The other two guards spread out in an attempt to surround them. The bearded one grabbed Ashby by the arm. "'Ere now, lass. I think I'm gonna take ye in." He flashed a greasy smile at the other two, who began to move in on Lyssa.

"Not a good plan, lads," Lyssa said, beginning to crouch.

The men stopped and looked at the bearded one, who grabbed Ashby by the neck and pulled her toward him, now gnashing his teeth angrily. "Get 'er, boys," he yelled out. Ashby shoved her assailant and tried to run. The other two guards lurched forward to attack Lyssa, who crouched low and rolled out of their reach.

"Run, Ash," she yelled just as the shiny dagger embedded itself into the back of her friend's head. Ashby didn't have any time to react. He drew his sword and moved toward Lyssa.

Lyssa became numbed, shocked. Rage instantly boiled up, clearing her mind. "NNNoooo." Her scream pierced the morning's silence.

The day of her assault flashed in front of her eyes. Survival took hold, every motion becoming automatic. *NEVER AGAIN!* roared in her head.

Her first victim was the bearded one. Her dagger went from her boot to the man's face in one motion. The cold steel embedded itself just under his left eye and protruded from the back of his skull. She didn't stop to see him fall. She was already rolling left away from the other two who had tried to change course. Ginger slipped on the loose gravel and fell face-first to the ground. Lyssa reacted to this by leaping straight ahead and slamming her body into the attacking blond man. The force of her attack knocked him backward with her on his chest. They landed on the ground hard, knocking the wind from his lungs. She drew her dagger from its sheath and buried it deeply into his head, over and over. She heard the metallic note of a sword being drawn behind her. She rolled forward, twisted and crouched low just in time to see the last man lunging at her. She easily sidestepped the attack and came to a standing stop, her eyes boring holes into him. He turned and came to a stop facing her.

"Yer gonna die, bitch. Ya know that right?"

She was breathing hard. Her muscles were tense but warm. She smiled at him.

"My friend, you can't kill me." Her smile sent a chill up his spine.

"Oh, and why not?"

"Because the dead can't fight," were the last words he heard from behind him as the glinting steel of the poniard held by the assassin slowly entered his body, pierced his lung, then his heart. The man's eyes went wide as he slowly slid down the length of the assassin and onto the ground.

Lyssa ran to Ashby, picking up her lifeless body. She pulled out the dagger from her head and tossed it away, then gently cradled her. "Why?" she asked, holding Ashby in her arms, rocking back and forth. She made no sound. Her body was numb. *It happened again.*

He walked to her, not uttering a word. She looked at the assassin with silent tears streaming down her cheeks and continued to rock. He placed a gentle hand on top of her head and nodded for her to follow. She lifted Ashby's limp body and followed the man into the woods. They entered the camp where she set her friend down, looking at the assassin. He nodded, and understanding its meaning, began to carefully wrap the body in the bedroll.

By the time he returned to camp, Lyssa had already completed her task and was scraping dirt away for the grave. He handed her a sword to chip away at the hard dirt and used helms taken from the road to clear out the hole. Before long, it was done. Lyssa stood over her friend, her sister, and looked down on her.

"I loved her," her voice low.

"I know."

"She was my sister."

"I know."

"I want revenge."

"I know."

"Teach me."

He took her in his arms and gently hugged her.

"Oh…I will."

'…I believe the scales have tipped in my favor.'

Talk of the town:

"Three guards dead on the Guild Road this mornin'. Whoever did it walked off clean."

"Aye, an' I overheard th' others sayin' whoever cut em' down weren't no drunk brawler, neither. Too clean, too neat."

–two patrons drinking in the Copper Chalice

"Road was closed half the mornin'. Guards whisperin', but no one's sayin' what happened."

–a road-weary merchant in the Hounds Rest Inn

"Bah, they earned it."

–Borrick Pyle

Of Prowess and Hubris

By the time they had reached his manor, the sun had just touched the horizon. White billowing clouds gently floated overhead, their images reflecting on the lazy flowing King's River behind the manor. The humid smell of pine hung in the air like perfume, making her feel more relaxed.

They followed the narrow road through the trees toward his manor. It sat deep in the woods, the canopy hanging so low it nearly swallowed the path. The house stood well off the main road, a perfect place for privacy.

Behind it, the river meandered quietly, its current hiding any comings or goings from view. From a distance, the trees disguised the manor completely, making it seem like nothing more than a humble cottage.

The stableman came out to greet the assassin and hold the reins as they dismounted. The man bowed to Lyssa and gave a smiling greeting, then led the horses into the stables.

"This is your new home…and training ground." He raised an eyebrow at her. "Tomorrow I will find out what other skills you possess so I may know where to begin."

She was exhausted. The day had drained her, leaving her hollow and aching, dragging her thoughts back to *that* day, the one she never wanted to remember.

"You have free run of the premises, of course," he told her. "All that I ask is for you to have a care in showing yourself to the outside world. I have privacy here, and I'd like to keep it."

She nodded her head, still looking around, trying to take it all in.

"If you would follow me to your room."

He led her inside, through a large, heavy wooden door, down a hallway and into the receiving room. The smell of pheasant permeated the air as they entered, and a fire burned on the hearth with several swords and daggers on stands upon the mantle. Fine, cushioned chairs were set close to the hearth, and a desk sat off to the right of it near the corner.

He showed her around the entire manor, which was far larger than she had initially imagined, then led her to the dining room. Inside, there was a long, darkwood table with ten chairs around it, each shining and well-cushioned. He seated her alongside him while he sat at the head.

An older lady came in carrying goblets and a carafe and served them both.

"Lyssa, this is my maid, cook and very good friend, Elda."

"Nice ta meet ya, Lyssa. The good lord 'ere jests. I work for him." She smiled at Lyssa as she poured her wine.

"I'm sorry, Elda. I don't drink wine." She was almost embarrassed.

"Oh, 'ave no fear, dear. I'll get some mead for ya then."

When she returned, she set a mug of mead down on the table and informed the lord that the main course would be served shortly.

"Little cat, I know this is difficult, but I must know. In as much detail as you are willing, what led you to this moment?" His face was serious but genuinely curious.

She looked down at the table, then at him. This was more difficult than she'd imagined.

She sighed and took a deep swallow of mead.

Just as she was about to speak, Elda returned with two large plates of pheasant, boiled potatoes, some odd vegetables and a basket filled with bread. There was a small plate with a yellow-white substance she'd never seen before. He informed her it was called butter, which caught her interest. Elda smiled and buttered a piece of bread for her. When she tasted it, she smiled from ear to ear, having never tasted it before.

The rest of the meal conversation was mainly the lord's expectations of her concerning her training. If at any time she wanted to stop, he told her it would be possible; however, it would entail a move, blindfolded, to another kingdom or duchy, as he couldn't risk being identified. He assured her she would not, in turn, be killed herself. He understood her nervousness when he imparted that bit of information.

"It is what we do, little cat. You must live a secret life now." He took another bite of pheasant and chewed. "I will teach you to use a bow in more ways than was meant, how to use daggers, rapiers and swords, how to hide and move silently."

She nodded, listening to every word he said, absorbing all expectations. He answered all of her questions.

The final bit he gave her was that she had to cleanse her mind of her burdens. That meant telling him all about herself, including the attack.

She tried to insist on Elda being there with her, but he declined.

"You must become strong, not only of body but of mind." He motioned to both. "You must throw morals away to do what must be done. You must not allow anything to affect your judgement, or you risk making a mistake and dying yourself."

She began to second-guess her decision to follow this man. It meant debasing herself and becoming an unfeeling killer, and that went against everything her family believed. She then thought about all the men she'd already killed. Guards, boys…possibly even her best friend.

When the meal was done, he escorted her to the cellar where they could speak in private. Elda went about her business, cleaning the meal from the table and had been left specific instructions not to disturb them in his study.

Once there, they sat, and she cautiously told him about what had occurred years prior, in great detail. She expected him to become angry when she came to the assault, but he sat, stone-faced and unmoved as she continued. When she came to the end of her story, she wiped away the tears, drank from her mug and sat silently as did he. For several minutes, he just sat, looking at Lyssa, which began to make her uncomfortable. Picking up a quill, he dabbed the ink pot and began to write, glancing at her every so often. Closing the journal, he sat back and propped his legs on the desk.

"Now that you've told your tale, how do you feel?"

"I'm sad, angry and I'm confused. Why are we doing this?"

He paused for a second. "I've gotten to understand you. To know you. I've listened." He lowered his feet and sat forward. "Your training has just begun. Your first lesson: Be careful what you divulge. Too much and it can be used for coercion, extortion or even your becoming entrapped. Always listen… carefully."

She stared blankly at him.

"In this short time, I've located your weakness…weaknesses…there are several, and have already planned your death."

She blinked at his words. Her chest tightened. All that remained in that moment was the gaze in this hunter's eyes, and the knowledge that she had too easily become his prey. She had trusted too readily.

"You will learn all there is to know to be an…assassin, for lack of a better term." He sat back. "Personally, I prefer Justiciar." He paused for effect. "Starting tomorrow, I will test your various skills." He became very serious. "I require you to push yourself to the very edge of human ability. I need to know the level of training you will need, how far you can be pushed and how much you can endure."

She nodded her understanding, unsure of it's depth.

"Get sleep. Prepare to become a weapon. Always be aware." He stood and began to walk past her. He stopped by her side, bent down and kissed her head. "I am truly sorry for the horrors you've had to endure. No human should have to weather that."

She looked up at him. He showed genuine sorrow for her.

"Let that burn into you. Let that become your driving force for perfection, for one day, you will exact your revenge. Have no doubt."

He brushed his hand over her delicate cheek, then went upstairs. She sat for some time, thinking of his words. The story she told him did make her burn inside. She knew she must use it, learn from it and, he was right, allow it to drive her to perfection.

Her bed was soft and warm, better than any she'd ever slept in, including the Copper Chalice. Her sleep, however, came in waves of terror, sweating, seeing Ashby and finally lying awake. In her dreams, Ashby kept asking Lyssa *why?*, something she kept asking herself as well. In the soft moonlight coming through her window, she wondered if she'd ever be able to have a good night's rest again. She lay awake, staring at the forest across the river.

Then came the faintest of scratching sounds, just outside her door, or was it inside? It was hard to tell. Was there another attack?

Slowly, she began to edge toward the wall. She carefully reached under her pillow for the dagger she'd been sleeping with since her assault. The smell of pine that had been blowing with the evening breeze had changed. It now had the scent of sweat, very faint, but there.

She began to sit up, her back against the wall and feet tucked in front of her, dagger at the ready.

Without warning, the bed suddenly pulled away from the wall, and a dark figure appeared in front of her. She caught a glimpse of a silvery blade coming toward her. She let herself fall to the floor and rolled under the bed. Whoever it was landed hard on the bed and was struggling to get to their feet, so she pushed off the wall as hard as she could, bringing the dagger up hard, hoping to slash her attacker. The blade struck home, but she didn't wait to see her result.

She scrambled to her feet, ran out the door and into the dimly lit kitchen, where she placed the table between herself and the door, waiting for her attacker to arrive.

She was ready. *Never again*, echoed in her head.

Breathing heavily, she felt her heart thumping in her eyes. Every muscle tensed for the attack.

The assassin carefully walked in, clapping slowly but loudly.

"Well done, little cat. Well done."

"You!" She was incensed. "Why?"

He looked down at the gash she had put in his heavy leather trousers.

"As I said last night, your training started today. I told you to always be aware." He smiled, impressed.

"I could have killed you," she said, placing the dagger on the table.

"Then, why didn't you?" he asked, brows raised.

"I-I just wanted to escape."

"And there it is." He bowed to her. "Always defer until you have the advantage." He smiled. "You did just that. With more training, I believe you would have found an ambush point and killed me as I entered, but one step at a time."

He walked to the little pantry near the hearth and retrieved a small basket of various fruits. He set them on the table and bade her eat, then stoked the hearth fire.

She shook her head, now distrusting him.

"There is trust, and there is madness. I would not poison my own apprentice. Such folly serves no purpose."

The fire started sending a bright orange-yellow glow into the room. The new wood he'd placed on top crackled and spat, sending sparks and smoke drifting up into the chimney.

He selected a bright red apple, which looked remarkably like the type found in the king's orchard, and took a large bite from it. He smiled as he chewed, then offered it to her.

She took it, clearly still wary of his tricks. Carefully inspecting it, she took a bite. The sweet, juicy flavor was like nectar to a bee as she quickly gulped it down.

While she was eating, he removed the heavy leather leg coverings she had slashed.

"Well done here as well," he said, inspecting the deep gash they had sustained. "I dare say, if not for these coverings, I would be unable to produce offspring." He chuckled.

She, however, did not; her eyes still slits of distrust.

He understood his error. He looked at her sternly as she chose another apple and began to eat it. "That was meant to happen, was it not?"

She frowned angrily and nodded yes emphatically.

He gave a resolute nod, storing the incident in the back of his mind. *She's deadly, no denying that. And not afraid to kill. Good. Let's see what her other skills are,* he said to himself.

He'd seen her fighting skills on the road. She'd managed to kill two heavily armed guards with daggers and alone, yet. The third, she would have taken easily as well, and he admired her confident bravado. She rolled and danced like an acrobat and was as fast as a striking adder. Her senses were good; he'd been fully silent, but she knew he was there in the room. Her tragedy had made her a weapon out of necessity; her survival skills were a testament to that. She needed to curb her emotions, though. They could serve her…or be her downfall. He'd need to work on that.

"Please eat your fill, little cat. When you are finished, meet me outside, and we'll begin." He took another apple and left.

Lyssa was not going to leave by the front or back door. She knew the test was still on, she knew he was dangerous, and she knew she must survive.

'…dance, puppet, dance.'

She thought about the best way to leave, one that he wouldn't expect. He knew his manor inside and out, so escape would be nearly impossible. She took another bite of apple.

She thought about her room last night. *Bed near the window, slid from the wall. Nothing there. Lying in bed staring out the window. Cool breeze. Wait.* She stopped mid-bite. *Cool breeze from the river. The manor backs up to the river.*

She stood and walked back to the room, which was still in disarray, and looked out the window. She felt the slight breeze on her face as it blew from upriver. She smelled the pine drifting in, mixed with wet wood and mud. It was a long, straight drop into the water from here, though. She could climb, but the rock face didn't afford much purchase. She could also jump in. It would be dangerous; she'd have to leap a distance to clear the rocks, but she knew she was capable.

Realizing that an escape had been found, she quickly dressed in her leather clothing and tucked her dagger into her boot, making sure to tie it to avoid losing it in the current. Her platinum hair blew as the breeze hit her face while she climbed onto the window ledge. It was still dark, and she knew there was no way for him to see her, so she prepared to jump. One more peek…

And there he was. Across the river, and he was raising his bow. She leaped with all of her might just as an arrow ricocheted against the wall. She splashed into the water, leaving barely a ripple. *If I surface on the other side, I'm dead.*

Her survival instinct kicked in. Her actions became second nature. She held her breath and let the river carry her downstream for just a minute. Running out of breath, she raised her head until it just broke the surface, looking for him. *Clear.* She raised up just enough to refill her lungs, then submerged and swam toward shore. She slowly crawled from the river and, spotting a nearby hiding spot, bolted to it and crouched low.

Daylight began to light the woods around her. The sound of nearby birds chirping let her know he wasn't close. From her vantage point, she could see the back of the stables. She ran to the corner and squeezed her back as close to it as possible. She peered around and saw him standing at the center of the small courtyard.

His bow was slung over his shoulder, and his hands hung by his side. She untied her dagger and brought it up, blade down, trying to hide the glint of the steel. She knew she must get behind him, downwind, to have any shot at the kill. She moved very slowly, checking each step, ensuring exact foot placement. This man was exceptionally good at his trade, and if she were to have any chance at all, she'd have to use every sneaking skill she'd ever learned.

Moving heel then toe, she stepped on any rock she saw, using any patch of clear dirt.

She was close now. He'd been searching for her, she knew. He remained oblivious, but she knew his eyes were alert. The road to the manor loomed before her now. So close. *Well, within bow shot, but not dagger,* she thought.

She reached down and picked up a tiny pebble. Using her thumb, she flicked it back from where she came and waited for him to look that way. It landed and made a slight sound. He didn't look. She was getting frustrated; *They always look, dammit.* He took two steps toward the house. This wasn't working. She had to find a better spot. She moved backward to another tree and again tried to circle him. The teacher began to whistle a simple tavern chanty. He had to know she was there. His body language was an almost dead giveaway. Still, she had to try.

The sun was only a brief time from peaking over the horizon. She returned to her tree, willing to risk everything on her skills.

One final deep breath.

She bolted to her left, startling him. *Did he know?* She switched direction and sent herself into a roll; so very close now.

She stood, for only a second, reared back and threw her dagger at his hip. He turned just in time to see it.

She rolled again to her right and crouched low. If she had to go hand-to-hand, she would, but only as a last resort.

Her dagger cartwheeled through the air, striking her target in his midriff. As it struck true, it rang a metallic sound and fell harmlessly to the ground.

He turned to face her.

His eyes were wide, but he had a wide grin. The sun broke over the horizon, and small beams of bright light lit the courtyard. He began to clap loudly.

"Well done. Well done." He motioned for her to join him. "That was very impressive, young lady, I must say."

She slowly went to him, still very wary. Was he baiting her closer for an attack, or was this the end of the test?

"Let us go inside and go over your trial, shall we?" He motioned her to the door. She let him lead, not taking any chances. *Madness? Huh.*

Once inside, they went into his small study just off the dining room. Before he sat, he removed his tunic and removed the two padded metal plates from his chest and back, setting them on the floor. He reached into his pants and removed another padded metal plate; only this one had a large dent in it. He looked at her, brows raised, impressed and set it down as well.

They sat close to the warming heat of the hearth fire, and he began. "As you could tell, I knew your escape method."

"How?"

"It was the only logical route. However, I did not consider your keen eye. You moved just as I fired. Well done, there."

She kept her eyes narrowed on him, absorbing each word as if from a text.

"I waited for you to surface, but you didn't. Another excellent choice."

Just then, Elda came in with juices and water.

"By the gods, what happened in that back room?" Her words were terse, her eyes glaring at the assassin. "I have to clean that up now." She began to fill two mugs.

"My apologies, Elda. Young Lyssa had a dreadful, terror dream. It could not have been helped."

She turned sorrowful and concerned eyes at Lyssa.

"Oh, my dear, I am so sorry." She put a warm hand on Lyssa's face. "I hope yer alright now. They can be such horrible things."

"Y-yes, Mum. I'm fine now. Thank you. He helped me through it." She smiled shyly.

She turned to the lord, "Yes, he is a good man, if not sloppy at times." She glared at him, then turned and returned to the kitchen.

He sat back and continued his critique.

"Where were we? Oh, yes. I'll be very honest with you. I didn't hear you until the pebble fell." He shook his head. "Never do that. It may work on a peasant, but not a seasoned killer."

She had known that would be a mistake, but she didn't know what else to do.

"A suggestion. When in that sort of situation, if surroundings permit, crouch low and stay in place." He sipped his drink. "Make a very slight sound. A click, a chirp, anything but very slight." He raised his eyebrows. "A normal person would turn, then investigate, thus bringing themselves to you. Spring. The kill is yours."

She hadn't thought of that. It made perfect sense. Kitikithakis had taught her something similar to that, but she didn't think it would help in this situation.

"And finally, the attack." He leaned forward. "Were you trained in acrobatics?" His question was genuine.

"No. I do it because it feels...natural."

He sat back. "Natural. Huh." He thought a second. "The way you move I've seen before but only attempted by minstrels and jongleurs. They are difficult, to say the least. Yet, you perform them as if you *are* the movement. Extraordinary."

That brought a smile to her face.

"Now about that dagger. You most definitely hold great disdain for men, I can tell."

He took her dagger from his boot and handed it to her. "Your aim is…well, let's say, quite focused." He chuckled.

"In conclusion, you have learned a lot since your tragedy. Survival has obviously deemed it necessary. What you do and the way you do it is out of the ordinary as well, yet highly effective, things it would take others many years to perfect; I dare say, even I may not be able to replicate." He smiled. "I now know all I need to help you." He took another sip and sighed. "Ahhh, my little cat. Silent, unseen, deadly." He chuckled. "My little Lyssa the Cat."

She thought back to her time with Kitikithakis. He used that name as well…the Cat, *keth'ra.*

She liked it… a lot.

He let her rest for the last part of the day. They sat outside under the warm sun, enjoying the singing warblers and wrens, watching clouds pass and sharing general conversation. The days had started to grow colder; winter wasn't far away now. Trees were beginning to shed their leaves. The reds, oranges and yellows made the season explode with vibrant colors. The seasonal direction of the wind was changing, now following the river north. It became easier to sense the sweet smells of falling rain on the crisp air. She excused herself and went inside to try to recover some of the lost sleep from that night. With Elda there, she assumed a test wouldn't be feasible at this time, so she relaxed enough to drop off. Once again, Ashby invaded her sleep. Could she have stopped it? Would it still have happened if they'd accepted when he first asked? So many questions tortured her mind, and yet none could be answered.

She sat up to find that night had passed. She'd been asleep all night and didn't realize it. She dressed and went into the kitchen, where Elda stood stirring the cooking pot.

"Good morning, dear. Hungry?" It seemed she always carried a smile.

"Please, yes. I feel like I haven't eaten in days."

She brought a boule with butter and a chunk of goat cheese that smelled of dirty feet but tasted wonderful. It didn't take her long to finish eating and head back to her room to splash water on her face and wash her hands.

Elda passed on a message that the assassin, lord as she called him, would like to speak to her in the courtyard when she was ready. Lyssa thanked her and headed out to meet him, taking a hot roll on the way out and winking at Elda. She wondered if Elda knew what work the assassin did, or whether she even cared.

As she opened the door, she saw him standing under the lamp post speaking to another man and decided to wait for their conversation to end before she went to him. The men clasped arms, and Lyssa moved toward the bench, but as she got there, the man said, "I'll send word when I can." The assassin replied with "Be careful" and sat down next to Lyssa.

"A friend?" she asked, smiling.

"A messenger," he said, "The alderman of Mayfare would like us to assist him with a problem, but didn't impart enough information," he replied.

They sat on the bench and discussed the upcoming trial. He explained that it was a test of endurance that entailed shooting her bow at three different targets, climbing over the stables and swimming across the river. Once on the other side, she must again use her bow, fire at three more targets, then return in the same manner.

The sun had finally reached its height, billowy clouds starting to roll in, casting intermittent light on the course. He allowed her time to prepare, and when she had, he gave the signal and off she went. Her archery had become much more proficient, learning most of the finer points from her friend, Kitikithakis. The targets had been placed at different intervals, a target on the wall of the stable, another on a tree at the edge of the river and one extraordinarily long shot on the far side of the river. She hit the first two, easily placing the arrows just inside the center circle. The third arrow soared over the river, but a breeze caught it mid-flight and sent it just to the target's edge.

She strapped the bow to her back and began her run to the stable, easily ascending it and landing with a graceful roll on the other side. The river wasn't moving very fast, but she knew rivers could lie. The undercurrent could be wild, so she ran upriver just a bit and leaped in. She was right. The undercurrent was faster but not so much that it carried her too far downstream. The weight of her bow and leather slowed her, but just barely, the resistance being easily compensated for. Crossing to the other side, she found another bow and a quiver of arrows. Looking back across, the other targets became easily discernable. The first arrow found its mark dead center, as did the second. As she drew the string for the third arrow, however, her mentor stepped in front, making the center impossible to hit. *Shite.*

She had to think quickly. She ran downstream just a bit until the circle became visible and fired her final shot. Without seeing if it hit, she dove back into the water. This time, the current allowed her to come ashore directly behind the stable. Again, the resistance didn't hinder her, though she began to feel her muscles burn.

Then, she immediately spotted a problem as there was no feasible way for her to gain enough purchase to leverage herself to the roof. Still in a full sprint and without thinking, she headed straight for the wall. She figured that there was only one way to scale it; she needed enough speed to run up the wall just a few steps and hopefully grab the roof, pulling herself up the rest of the way.

She leaped, her foot landed solidly, allowing for another step. It landed, and she pushed off, her momentum slowing quickly. One final step and she'd be there. Her foot landed…and slipped. Still, she pushed off. Her fingertips reached the lip of the roof. She tried to pull up but felt herself slipping back. Planting her feet in desperation, she pulled with failing arms and pushed with her legs, bounding to the roof.

Now gasping for breath, she forced herself forward, fell off the roof and rolled, sloppily making her way back to the shooting spot. She shot her first arrow, center circle. She drew the second arrow and realized her heavy breathing wouldn't allow her to concentrate on the circle at all. She breathed in, held her breath, hearing her heart beating in her ears, and gently let it out until she needed to inhale again, then she released. The arrow found its mark center circle.

She drew the third arrow and prepared it to fire while narrowing her focus to see only the circle at the far side of the river.

"SHOOT!" came a booming voice in her ear as she released. The arrow flew wildly into the air, landing in the river and floating downstream.

She doubled over, breathing heavily and trying to gasp for air.

He calmly asked, "You know why I did this?"

She nodded, still trying to catch her breath.

"To the bench then." He walked off, hands behind his back, leaving her to stew in her failure.

They sat again, her clothes still dripping river water, her platinum locks now stained brown from the mud and grime of the river. He explained why too much focus wasn't good. Things get missed when your focus is too narrow. You miss key details that could get you killed. He commended her archery skills and her acrobatics, giving bits of advice as he went. The sun had gone down just a bit. The breeze had begun to get colder. He directed her to do it again. This time, he made the targets much smaller. The circles had become no larger than supper plates. This time, she had missed four of the six targets. Again, they sat as he calmly explained her errors.

The sun had now reached the horizon. The shadows grew long and hid the targets. She discarded the bow on the bank before swimming, as the resistance had become almost unbearable. Her arms and legs began to feel rubbery from fatigue, causing her to make multiple attempts before finally getting over it. By the time she got back, her tutor had already been sitting on the bench waiting for her while paring a ripe red apple with his dagger.

She sat heavily, still gasping for air. He sat silently, legs crossed and picking his nails.

"Huh," was the only thing he said.

"Yes… I know… I know." She swallowed, trying to clear the dryness from her mouth. "This was a lesson…" More gasps for air, "…in prior planning."

He slowly turned and looked at her, surprised.

"I…" she swallowed hard, "should have dropped the bow…" a few more gasps, "…on my first attempt."

She sat back, her breathing steadier.

"I was…too arrogant…and sure," she glanced at him. "It cost me…in the long run."

"Well done, little cat. Today, you learned many things in one lesson." He turned his body to face her.

"Arrogance will kill you; never be certain. Only your death is certain. Concentration is a good skill, but too much will force you to miss minute details. Endurance can and will save your life, and lastly, acrobatics is good but only to be used when necessary. The toll is too great and, again, will kill you."

She wearily nodded her understanding.

"You've had enough for one day, I think." He stood and helped her up. He looked at her face. "You've done a wonderful job today." He kissed her forehead. "What you deem failures are actually your greatest accomplishments. Know…" he started to walk to the manor, "that you've learned your lessons well." He opened the door and looked back at her. "Welcome to the world of the justiciar, young lady."

'...the Cat worries you?'

The days slipped by in a blur of sweat and repetition. Each sunrise brought another trial, and each sunset found her body stronger than the day before. Her lungs no longer burned from the river; her legs carried her farther, steadier. Her arrows found the center ring with quiet certainty. Even her steps, once steady but clumsy, now whispered against the earth, soft enough that more than once she startled him, drawing only the faintest smile from his lips. When she moved, he could see the cat within, and he smiled.

One evening, as twilight set, he beckoned her to follow. "No trial today," he said. "Today, you learn the rhythm of the dance."

They watched as his stableman crossed the courtyard, lantern in hand; not a mark, not a kill, just a moving figure.

"You will not touch him," the assassin said in a deep voice. "This is a lesson in restraint. Watch, breathe, count." He emphasized each step as a nod.

She led, and he moved with her, murmuring in time: "Step. Wait. Step. Wait. Now pause. Let him feel alone." Her eyes stayed glued to her target, ears perked for his direction. "Close the gap. Breathe when he breathes. Halt when he halts."

Her dagger was in hand before she realized it. She became entangled with the thrill of the hunt. The distance closed, each movement measured against his whispered cadence. She came so near she could smell the man's lantern oil. One more step and the blade would have found his back.

But his gentle touch stopped her.

"Not yet, little cat." His breath was a whisper against her ear. "Death is the final note. You must learn the music first."

The stableman moved on, none the wiser. She slid the dagger back into her boot, pulse hammering in her throat. She glanced back at him and captured a glint of approbation in his eyes.

For the first time, she understood, an assassination was not just the strike. It was a dance of shadow—and she'd become incredibly good at dancing.

Talk of Bledlee:

"Whole town hears the shoutin' at night. Man comes home reekin' of ale, fists first every time. Hate watchin' it happen...hate bein' powerless more."

–Bledlee resident

"That drunk's at it again, dammit.... Poor wife and kids takin' the brunt. Someone oughta do somethin' 'bout it."

–Bledlee tavern keep

Of Beginnings and Endings

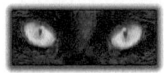

The next day was the first day of snow. The sky had turned a soothing shade of gray. Flakes the size of her mother's biscuits fell silently to the ground, covering it in a thick, fluffy blanket. Her tutor decided to put off physical training for a while and instead switched to mental training for the time being. He had many tomes and books covering a variety of subjects from metallurgy to alchemy.

He was especially taken by her extensive knowledge of alchemy. She knew of things he'd never seen before, let alone attempted. She told him how her grandmother had been an accomplished alchemist and taught her everything she knew. However, she did neglect to mention the "special" brews and concoctions she'd encountered and had sworn to protect.

They began to train in his cellar: hand-to-hand fighting, cutting techniques and disguise. She learned how to use someone's footsteps in the snow to hide her presence and to escape. She learned equestrian and horse care, which she'd become very proficient at. She loved the feel of the horse's strength beneath her and the way the wind blew through her cropped, platinum hair.

The one thing that surprised the assassin the most was Lyssa's love of fishing. They would sit on the tiny dock behind the stable with a firkin of mead and just fish silently, the lazy sound of the river passing by and the wind driving the light snow through the trees. That kept her grounded by reminding her of family, of the times Father and Mother would chase them around the back of the house, of her and Chandra lying in the snow and making ginger cookie impressions. It had been some time now, but the sting of tragic loss had eased only a little; it would never be fully forgotten, not really.

She and Elda became much better acquainted. They would pass on stories of their past, though Lyssa didn't have many. She even learned her way through the kitchen somewhat, once preparing a meal that the lord enjoyed immensely, thinking Elda had made it. They all laughed at his reaction when they divulged the secret.

Once, in his cellar, they sat in the seats close to the hearth fire. The yellow-orange flames radiated a warming heat that chased away the slight chill of the season. She had become more comfortable around him, though she still considered him somewhat of a threat. They sipped wine and mead quietly and, after a while, began to speak of more personal things. She came to understand him more, finding him to be quite pleasant in this relaxed state. He had a wife at one time, who died while being robbed outside The Commons of Caer Bryndwyck. When the guards failed to investigate, allowing the killer to escape, he decided it was time to bring the fight to the corrupt. He insisted that he never killed anyone just for money, though it was a lucrative occupation, but rather took only contracts that imparted justice and righted the wrongs people had done to each other, not only what the wealthy had done to the common folk, but what they would do to themselves. After all, he was not some mindless murderer, yet he was no hero either. He mentored on the theory that killing was still killing, but that his was more acceptable both to himself and to others.

She asked him how he felt about her, and he politely said he had no physical interest at all, though he did hope he didn't offend her. Since his wife, there had never been nor would there ever be another, which set her mind at ease even more. In an offhand manner, he did admit that if he were to think about another relationship, Elda would be his choice, due more to comfortable familiarity than actual love.

He then asked about her, what she liked, and what her family was like. She bluntly said she hated every man alive. She tolerated him at best out of respect more than like. There were very few exceptions, but the truth still stood. He asked about Ashby. She sighed and said that she came to love her immensely as a sister, but he thought there was more to it by the depth of her sorrow. He knew Lyssa was a lost spirit trying to find her way in the world, and he insisted that he was going to help her in any way possible. He told her that there was a reason for everything, that nothing was plainly random. If she could read the signs, then the reasons would become clear.

She also spoke of how she missed not only her family but mostly her sister Chandra. By her telling, they were the same people cut from separate cloth. She loved to get dirty and do things men did, much to her mother's chagrin, and how Chandra loved girl things. She said they always teased each other but stood by each other's side no matter the consequences. It was at that time he understood her sorrow for Ashby. It was more a remarkably close companionship, a sisterly connection, than a lover, with whom he could readily identify.

On occasion, they would ride into town and stalk people. She retained her lessons very well and learned from her mistakes. She began to have trouble with criticism, but took his suggestions to heart as a means to an end.

Once she had stolen some dried meat and a tiny meat pie. As she walked down the road, he came up and berated her for almost causing herself to be noticed, which is something no justiciar should do. He berated her all the way back to the manor, where he finally explained his reasoning. She understood and never stole an item again…unnecessarily.

'…my turn to cut?'

The day had come for her training to be taken to new heights. He had retained a contract that would be fairly simple to execute. This one was about method, and he was certain that she could carry it out without much trouble in the form of a husband who was a drunkard and enjoyed abusing his family. It had been rumored that he'd already put one child in the ground from his violence, and the requester, he never wanted names, needed this task done quickly and discreetly. Coin had been sent in payment, and all that needed to be done was to carry out the request.

They went into the town of Bledlee, which was the next town to the south and west of the manor by a half day, and purchased a room in the Stag & Lantern, the local tavern and inn. The assassin had paid the master a bit extra to keep his presence silent, to which the master agreed immediately with a nod and a wink. Lyssa surmised they had done business before by how easily the terms had been agreed upon.

Out into the square they went, arm in arm, posing as an old father and young daughter. She added a long brown cloak to her leather ensemble, which kept her platinum hair under cover, and he walked hunched over and sported an ornately carved wooden cane, which sheathed his steel dirk inside.

He allowed her to perform the entire contract on her own, with him only guiding her as needed. The sun was up, bright rays of light peeking through high white clouds. Smells of cooking meat, spices and several stands of baked items permeated the air, making her stomach grumble. She knew this was a trial and remained focused, searching for her target through the crowd of people.

She bought her *father* a small pie that they shared and waited for their mark to appear. They sat for a good part of the day on a small bench in front of the tavern, watching people barter and chat, which Lyssa compared to The Guildway of Caer Bryndwyck, but not nearly as large.

Both sets of eyes carefully searched for quite some time until Lyssa whispered that she felt too exposed, so she helped her father stand and continued into the crowd. Until now, their luck had been poor, and even her mentor agreed to return to the tavern so they could try again in the morning. She opened the door for her father to enter, but as he stepped through the door, he was run into by a patron leaving, causing him to fall to the ground. The man was covered in food crumbs and stunk of body odor and sour ale.

"Move yer arse ya bent codger." He spat at the old man and kicked him.

"No, please, sir. He is old. You'll hurt him." Lyssa pleaded genuinely.

The drunk man reached out and cuffed her on the side of the head, knocking her over as well. Flames lit up in her eyes. *Never again!* screamed in her mind. She began to reach for her dagger, but the old man grabbed her hand. "Oh, my. Please 'elp me up, dear." She quelled the ire and remained in character, helping him to his feet. "Ye alright, Da?"

The drunkard kicked the old man again. "Next time I'll mash yer skull, old man," he said, staggering away. Lyssa helped him into the tavern and sat him down at the nearest chair.

"I'm going to follow him," she whispered.

"Be careful," he replied.

She left the tavern and stepped into the square only to see that she'd already lost him. She calmly walked from stand to stand as if perusing the wares on each but still failed to locate him.

Barkers attempted to call people to their stalls and fishwives roamed selling eels, fish and who knows what else. She'd almost given up hope when, down a side road not far from her, he was spotted turning a corner. She carefully headed in his direction, not letting her eyes stray.

He stumbled and fell several times, but she halted and allowed his antics to play out. At times, she would stop and take a bite of food to keep up her disguise, then return to following the man, making sure to stay out of his sight.

Down two alleys and over one, she finally located the man's house as he stumbled up the broken steps. As expected, it was in the poorest part of Bledlee, run down and in complete disrepair. Staying just far enough away to be inconspicuous, her eyes took in every detail of the area, each crack, each light, broken board and in which direction his neighbor's homes faced.

Then she heard the sounds— him beating his family, yelling curses and breaking things. The yelling and cries echoed well down the street. Her ire rose, but she knew she had to return and pass on all the information as soon as possible. Leaving the house, her anger nearly boiling over, she knew that his time would soon come. Patience.

They sat at the table, sharing a coil of sausage and drinking ale as the laughter and talk grew louder, the patrons beginning to file in. The smell of pipe smoke, stale drink and sweat began to overpower that of their food. The assassin was a complete professional, staying fully in character and hunched over his plate as they discussed the upcoming execution. As he spoke, he would cough as if the fever were overtaking him and continue. Their final plan was to lure the family out of the house and eliminate the abuser. They would remove the body, toss it into the river, and no one would be the wiser.

Morning came, and the tavern was silent except for a woman and her child who were eating. There was no fire in the hearth as of yet, but the tables and floors had been wiped clean. Lyssa and her mentor dispensed with their personas and, as they passed the master at the serving board, the assassin tossed three coins to the tavern owner.

"Remember what I said." He winked at the owner, who winked back, and they left.

The sun was not long from peaking over the horizon now. A cold breeze swept through the square, which was barren except for empty stands and a few cats that had been scrounging for dropped scraps. He followed Lyssa as they trudged their way down the alley, disguised as besotted drunkards, to their target's house. The stench of stagnant water and feces overwhelmed Lyssa's senses. Speaking no words, they checked up and down the alleyway, then moved as one up the wooden steps. Each step was taken close to the edges to ensure there would be no squeaks; none that could wake anyone. She tested the door, and it pushed open easily, barely making any sound. Stepping silently and keeping their bodies close to the walls, they checked each room quickly yet carefully. The kitchen proved empty, so they continued down the hallway. The first room they came to was the children's room. Both were huddled on a pallet of straw in the far corner, curled into a tight ball close to each other. The blanket covering them was so tattered and threadbare that it was mostly useless.

They checked the next room, where, inside, they found the wife. She was grasping her knees in the corner, her head resting on them, but they couldn't see if she was sleeping or not. The assassin mouthed the words *'find him'* to Lyssa as he slowly entered the room.

Lyssa crept into the final room. There, lying on a pallet of rotted straw, was the target lying on his stomach and covered with a horse blanket. The stench of urine and feces made her wonder if she'd found his room or the privy. She winced at the odor.

She leaned back to see if the assassin was watching. He was. Lyssa pointed to the man's position in the room and motioned that he was still asleep. The assassin turned to the mother and motioned for Lyssa to return to him. When she got there, she saw the assassin, gently holding the woman close. She'd been brutally battered; cuts and large, painful bruises covered her arms and legs. They could plainly see that she'd been crying as dirty tear streaks lined her face.

"This one is mine, little Cat," he whispered. His face had turned to stone.

He looked at the poor woman with saddened eyes; he reached into his jerkin and produced a small pouch of coins.

He whispered to the lady, "Take this, get your children and leave this town…today."

The woman's eyes went wide as she took the pouch, wrapped her arms around his neck and began to cry.

"Thank you, sir. Thank you." As she pulled back, Lyssa could see the tears flowing like a river. She stood and hugged Lyssa as well, deep sobs racking her chest.

"I will never forget you."

"Please, lady, please forget us. Go, now. Start a new life."

The woman hurried to her children and gathered them up in her arms. On the way out, she grabbed some tattered blankets to wrap around them and left.

The assassin stood and, in full voice, said, "*THIS* is where I teach you the finer points of the kill."

They entered the room, not caring if he woke.

"Now," he started pointing at the man, "when you come upon something like this, the best thing to do is get the job done quickly and quietly."

He squatted down and pointed to a place just under the man's ear. "A quick dagger thrust here," he poked him, "ends the target's life painlessly—not a sound."

He stood up and kicked the man in the face. The man angrily began to curse as he woke, blood streaming from his nose.

"But since he's awake now, we have to do this another way."

The man shakily tried to scramble to his feet.

"The first priority is to always…" The drunkard threw a punch, "…keep them silent." The assassin jabbed the drunkard's throat.

The man grabbed his neck and fell to his knees, trying desperately to breathe.

"Now, if you should happen to get them to this point…" He grabbed the man by his hair and jerked his head up. "…then you have several different options at hand." He walloped the man, breaking his jaw.

Lyssa stood, taking it all in and nodding her understanding.

"Most would just go for the kill."

The man's eyes widened, still grasping his throat.

"That would be the preferred method, but I favor this," he began, drawing his fist back. The man raised his arms to try to ward off the attack but failed. Her teacher slammed his fist into his captive's throat once again.

The man collapsed, gasping for air through a crushed larynx.

"They expire much more slowly this way, and it is far more painful as well. I do not recommend this, as it is considered…well, barbaric." They stood and watched as the man gulped like a fish for several seconds, then finally died.

"Huh," was all Lyssa said.

"Shall we?" he asked, pointing to the door.

"What about the body?" she asked, still looking at the corpse. "We were supposed to dump it in the river." He looked at it, then her and shrugged.

"Sometimes, plans change. Remember that a plan is nothing more than a list of things that can go wrong." He pointed his thumb back at the dead drunkard. "That is a perfect example."

They walked down the alleyway and back to the square.

She asked, "Why did you give her the coin? That was your pay, wasn't it?"

"As I said at home, Lyssa. I am not a cold-blooded murderer."

They continued toward the tavern.

"I knew when I read the contract what sort of creature we'd be seeing. It was worse than I surmised, I must say, but the contract was fulfilled nonetheless."

She thought about his words as they went into the tavern.

It was still mostly empty, but a fire had been stoked, and the heat started to warm the room. There was a table nearby, close enough to warm their bones, so they sat, each in a chair facing the door. After the two lit their pipes, put their crossed feet on the table and sat back, the tavern maid came out with two platters, each with seasoned eggs, a small boule, butter and juices.

"Madam, I thank you, but I didn't request food."

The tavern owner walked up, holding two rosemary chickens and set them on the table in front of them. He silently looked at them both, put his finger to his nose and winked.

"No charge, mate." Then he whispered, *"We thank ye,"* and he walked away.

The two looked at each other and began to feast.

After a few minutes, Lyssa spoke. "You know," she said through a mouthful of chicken, "they know who we are now." She swallowed. "We can never come back."

Her mentor washed the food from his mouth and set his mug down.

"My dear, there are some things you must understand." He picked up an egg. "There are good folk and bad folk."

He bit the egg in half and chewed for a second. "Trust that the bad folk will always be known in any town."

He finished the other half of the egg and said, "Trust, also, that the good folk will always know when the bad folk are gone."

He nodded to the tavern owner. "He knows." He sipped his drink. "And he's grateful."

"But he'll talk." She was more questioning than worried.

"No, little cat, he won't." He smiled at her. "We've just earned this town's respect." He broke off a chicken leg.

"We are now invisible to these good people; have no fear." He winked assurance at her.

"I don't understand. How did we earn the *town's* respect? He can say what he wants, and then we're the foxes being hunted." She bit into a chicken breast.

"People talk, to be sure." He stopped and licked his fingers. "I don't normally reveal this, nor do I usually know who the requester is, but I will reveal this just one time."

She stopped chewing and gave him her full attention.

"The purveyor of this contract was, indeed, the tavern owner himself." He let that sink in.

"Sometimes, people feel helpless to act, which is just how the owner felt. A paying patron of his brutalizes his own family. No one sees it, but everyone knows. Justice can't be legitimately served." He took a sip from his mug. "That, my little cat, is where we come in. Problem solved."

They took their time and ate quietly, savoring the food. The fire warmed them, and the comforting smell of its smoke helped them relax for their upcoming journey home.

"He will speak only enough to satisfy the townsfolk." He belched. "We are safe here."

She thought about his reasoning. When the logic became apparent, she nodded her understanding, then continued to eat.

She'd learned a valuable lesson that day.

Sometimes, people and situations are not what you expect.

Talk of Bledlee:

"I seen two folks walkin' out that door after—quiet, calm. Whoever they were, town owes 'em a drink."

"Aye, Mikle, ya be tellin' a truth there, mate. Whoever it were what walked outta there, they done Bledlee a kindness. Mark my words."

"Finally, someone shut that bastard up fer good. 'Bout damn time someone had the guts. I'm drinkin' this one to 'em both."

–relieved Bledlee townsfolk

"Saw his wife an' little ones slip out before dawn—bless 'em, hope they never look back. Best thing we can do now is torch that cursed house an' forget it ever stood."

–tavern owner to a patron

"Funny thing...there were an old man an' a young lass in town that mornin'. Left right after th' trouble. Nobody'd e'er seen 'em afore, yet folk can't help wonderin' if it were them what sorted that bastard out."

"Could be coincidence, Bray. But two strangers leavin' the same hour th' drunk bastard got his due? Makes me think ye might be right?"

–the cobbler to his neighbor, Bray

"Bless ye, Hearthmae…. Thank ye for guidin' that poor wife an' her young'uns out safe. Keep 'em warm, keep 'em fed, an' keep their road gentle from here on. World's hard enough without men like him."

–Madam Conly

Of Might and Mercy

The next few weeks passed without much excitement. The changing of the season brought new life to the world. The forests began to return to green as new buds stretched their leaves, birds began to chirp and sing as the snow melted and dripped to the muddy ground. Small plates of ice flowed down the river, ushering in the upcoming heat of spring.

The Cat soon realized that she was becoming a woman, almost overnight. When she spoke to her surrogate mother and now friend about womanly things, Elda said that in the brief time she had known her, she'd grown into a fine young lady, even if she didn't act like one. Elda would laugh, and Lyssa would act hurt.

In the past few years, her steel-gray eyes had more twinkle to them like bright little stars, her hair glowed like radiant platinum, and her body began to bud into a woman. Elda informed her that she'd be attracting more attention from men, much to Lyssa's disdain. In her motherly way, she understood as Lyssa finally trusted her enough to tell her of her past. Elda reminded her that it was Hearthmae's way, her will, and every woman was expected to join at the altar and bear children. When Lyssa replied that she was never going to be touched by a man again, Elda understood but looked at her sadly. Life had been cruel to her, and because of that, it would force her to miss the best part of life—motherhood.

The assassin had come and gone on several occasions— business, as he called it. Lyssa knew they were contracts and was eager to fulfill one of her own.

He returned on horseback late one night as Lyssa was just completing her normal archery training sessions. She met him near the stables and saw, as he dismounted, that he'd been injured, quite severely. She ushered him inside, cursing and complaining, trying to send her away. He stated that Lyssa had been spending too much time with Elda; she was becoming more like a nervous grandmother than a justiciar. That earned him an extra application of stinging tincture when she tended his wound.

She removed the blood-soaked, makeshift bandage he'd applied to reveal that it was, in fact, a deep, clean slash wound that extended from the elbow almost to his wrist. Luckily, he hadn't lost mobility in his wrist, or that might have ended his career.

She applied a salve her grandmother had taught her to make, a blend of powdered pine, willow bark, birch leaves and several other herbs. Then came the liquid tincture, a sting so sharp it nearly brought tears to the big man's eyes…and a wry smile to Lyssa's face.

Inside Elda's stitching kit, she found a small, curved bone needle. *Elda's done this before,* she thought. *That's no sewing needle.* Carefully, just as Kitikithakis had taught her, she drew each wound closed and tied off the stitches, finishing with another dab of tincture to keep them clean.

She began to wrap it just as Elda came in, insisting on inspecting it. She was impressed and asked for the ingredients to the salve, which made Lyssa silently proud. The assassin looked at them both impatiently as if they were exchanging cooking notes. As she finished tying the bandage, causing the assassin to wince, Elda produced a page and quill, jotting down the procedure for Lyssa's remedy, earning them a shake of his head in disappointment from the lord.

Supper had been served: roast pork haunch with an apple glaze, stewed potatoes and peas with mushrooms, and a dessert that Lyssa had never seen before. It was wonderful. As normal, Lyssa ate far too much. She knew she'd be swimming the river several times tomorrow to work this off.

They retired to the study just off the dining area and sat in front of the comfortable fire, sipping their drinks and smoking pipes. Lyssa had become accustomed to the pipe. He'd produced a mixture of dried lavender and raspberry leaf, which she found calming, as well as dried mugwort, which was more common. The smell of the fire smoke mixed with the lingering aroma from supper began to make her sleepy. She leaned back, removed her boots and warmed her feet as he went to his desk. Sitting on his cushioned chair, he produced a small vellum scroll from a drawer. It was tied with a black string and sealed with a red wax seal, unbroken. He turned it over and over as if struggling with a crucial decision that vexed him.

Clearing his throat to get Lyssa's attention, he called her over.

"I find that it is time, little cat." He set the scroll down and pushed it toward her with a single finger, as though it carried more weight than his entire hand could bear. His jaw stayed set, but his eyes betrayed the thought already gnawing him— this very well could be the last time he handed such a thing to his apprentice.

"I've thought about this one for quite some time, wondering if the time was right and if you were truly ready."

She listened to him intently.

"The last contract that you and I fulfilled proved to me that you very well could have learned everything I had to teach you. What you've learned before me, and what I've taught you will be the tale of your true, telling skills."

He straightened his back as if proud to be giving his apprentice her first contract.

"This is your time to prove who you are. This is your time to show your mettle. This is your time to succeed...or die."

His seriousness never changed, making Lyssa wonder what was in the note. He looked into her eyes, never blinking, "You have an arduous task ahead of you, young lady. My injury prevents me from accepting this time." He nodded his head for her to open it.

She looked at him, barely able to contain her excitement. She would finally be able to prove herself after all this time. She looked at the rolled page, the red seal showing the impression of a skull impaled by a dagger, then picked it up with a nervous hand.

He placed his hand over hers, causing her to pause.

"Before you break this seal, you should know that once it is broken, only you can carry out the request. If you do not, then it is you who will be next on a request." He nodded to her to make her choice.

She looked at him seriously and, without hesitation, broke the seal. Unraveling the page, she read the words:

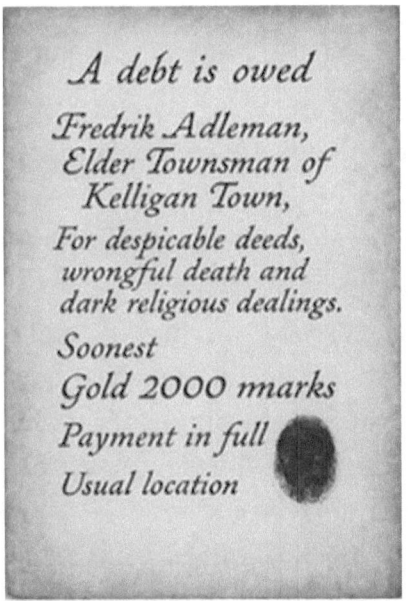

A debt is owed

Fredrik Adleman,
Elder Townsman of
Kelligan Town,

For despicable deeds,
wrongful death and
dark religious dealings.

Soonest

Gold 2000 marks

Payment in full

Usual location

She read the page three times, then she looked at her teacher.

"How long do I have to complete the request?" Her tone was like that of a professional who had done this sort of thing many times before.

"Soonest," he said. He could sense her nervousness.

She looked at him for another second.

303

"Right." She was truly alone now. It was hers to succeed or fail. She'd been handed a challenge by her mentor that she only knew as the assassin.

Succeed and live; fail and die.

'...perhaps a test.'

She had been riding for almost two days, passing the tiny village of Wortham along the way. The sun had been covered by slow-moving gray clouds that continuously threatened rain. Occasionally, off in the distance, flashes of lightning streaked across the sky, the low rumble of thunder soon following. The cool wind had been blowing enough to bend bushes and rattle trees, so she pulled her cloak tighter around her shoulders to help block it out.

She allowed her black mare to pace itself, being in no particular hurry to cross the scrublands. Once they'd topped the low hill, she finally caught a glimpse of the town, where disappointment set in.

The town was dreary; she could think of no other way to describe it. The buildings were gray and dingy. Almost all of the split-rail fences along the road were broken and rotted. Though the fields had been planted, rye and some wheat by the looks, seemed to have fallen to disease and lay rotting haphazardly about. Some of the haystacks had fallen over, and she even saw rats running from stack to stack, eating all they could.

Still, her horse plodded on, indifferent to the wind. In the distance, a few figures fought the gusts, working what little crop remained in the field. Though they tried to reap, the wind only toyed with them, scattering their harvest across the furrows.

She soon reached the outskirts of the town, where it looked just as run down up close as it did from afar. The clouds began to look angrier, the smell of rain permeating the air along with it. The wind picked up, carrying the foul stench of rot and death. She wrinkled her nose but pressed on toward the stables. At first glance, the place looked abandoned, until a man stepped out as she dismounted.

He looked emaciated but not sickly and wore dingy clothes that hung from his body like a scarecrow. He smiled a toothless grin.

"Can I help ya, lord?" he asked, taking her reins.

She dismounted, turned and took down her cowl.

He realized the error and said, "Oh, beg pard'n, lass. Me eyes ain't as good as they were." Embarrassed, he bowed in apology.

"I need to stable my mount. I don't know how long." She said, pulling her gloves off.

"I kin keep 'er here, but we ain't got much feed."

She looked at the poor man. "How much do you charge to stable horses?" she asked.

"Well, normal 'bout five silver regal mark a day. Lately, no one can pay, so I takes what they offer."

She flipped him a gold mark. "Find good feed, no rye. Keep him safe and clean, and there's another gold when I get back."

His face lit up. "Aye, lass, aye. I'll do me bes'. Ya can believe me."

She replaced her cowl and looked hard at the man. "Perhaps you can help me."

Looking down at the ground, he said, "Dunno, lass. I kin try."

"Could you direct me to the Elder Townsman, Fredrik Adleman?"

"Aye, he'll be in th' town hall taday." He shook his head as if he had more to add.

"Aaand?" she asked, impatiently.

"Well, see. He ain't in too good a way. None of us be." He turned and spat. "Seems we got a blight abouts. Ev'ry ones leaving 'cept them what got it."

Lyssa looked carefully at the man. She'd seen illuminated plates in books and written accounts in tomes that mentioned the worst of the blights and diseases, and this man didn't look like he had one.

Kalla had explained some of the earlier ones that had whittled the populace ages ago, but even that didn't fit.

"You look alright to me, a bit starved but healthy otherwise."

"Aye, I feels fine. Jus' no one 'ere ta reap or pick th' fields and slaughter th' animals."

She nodded, paused, then turned and walked across the road to the inn, where she opened the door to peek in and see if it was occupied. Inside, behind the ale board, stacking firkins atop big kegs, was the innkeeper. He met Lyssa at the counter, wiping his hands of grime.

"Aye, can I help ye? Ain't got much ta offer but what I got be good." He smiled.

"What, by Hearthmae's locks, happened here?"

"Ahh, aye. The towns got a blight o' some kind." He said, standing back a bit.

"Huh, you and the lady look alright. Stableman said everyone left town because of it."

She looked around the place. It was fairly clean and straight; a fire burned in the hearth, lanterns had been lit, and, by the smell, they had some food being prepared.

"Oh, aye. Damnedest thing, too. We jus' got done with the town's festival last moon. Everyone's fine afore, but after, they all come down sick somethin' awful. Seems whatever ails folks can drive 'em mad too."

His wife spoke up, "Aye, remember that hierophant? Kernen, I think it were? Was fine as flour afore th' fest but a week after…" she whistled, "mad, I tells ye, jus' plain mad." She looked at her husband, afraid. "Then a ranger or some such come here an' put the good man down." She shook her head. "'Twas a mercy, I say."

Lyssa felt something odd was happening, but didn't have time to play the part of the healer.

"I need a room for the night and some food if you have any."

"Aye, we have both. Not many rooms or plates been sold lately, so ya got the run o' th' place."

She looked at the innkeeper, then nodded to the corner where she went to sit. There was a round table with three chairs around it next to the hearth. She took off her cloak and laid it across the chair, and sat with her back to the wall, her platinum hair glowing. Removing her wooden pipe from her pouch, she leaned over, retrieved a small twig from the fire and lit it, sending small rifts of sweet smoke into the air.

She leaned back and, closing her eyes, exhaled a stream that rolled into the air and hung like a bank of fog.

If the town is sick, then Fredrik might already be dead. She thought. *Velkhar's bum, what then?*

She took another puff, eyes absently scanning the room. She knew she was being overly cautious at this point, but it had become a habit.

Never trust the obvious, rang through her head. The assassin's words were like a bell in the fog, forcing her to stay vigilant.

The tavern maid came to her table with a plate of hard cheese and eggs. It wasn't a lot, but she was grateful for it anyway. She picked one up and bit into it; the flavor was bland but not inedible as the maid returned with a mug of mead and set it down, smiling.

Lyssa held up a finger to get the maid's attention, "A second." She swallowed, then washed it down with the mead. "Might you know of a Fredrik Adleman?"

The tavern maid nodded. "Aye, he'd be in th' town hall 'bout now. Have a care, though. He's sick too. Most folks here are."

Lyssa nodded her thanks and filled her mouth again.

Outside, the wind picked up, blowing the now falling rain against the walls and making a loud tapping sound. The innkeeper continued with his business of stacking the kegs and, once done, tended the fire.

"Ya come from far 'way, if ya don't mind me askin'?"

Lyssa glared at him.

"I meant no harm, lass. Jus', ain't been many folks about ta talk ta of late." He stirred the embers and began to walk off.

"I'm from Tantyn. Been on the road for too many days, it seems." She wiped her mouth with the back of her hand.

"Tantyn? Never heard of it. That east?"

Lyssa shook her head. "No, south." She took a bite from another squab.

"I'd ask why ya come here, but 'tain't my business. Just glad ta see a new face." He smiled and returned to the counter.

After a little while, her meal was done. She leaned back, lit her pipe and allowed her food to settle before scouting the town. She'd have to be vigilant, as there were very few people walking about, so the chance of being noticed was highly likely.

She scraped the ash from her pipe, tapped out the remnants, then stuffed it into the pouch. She stood to stretch, then headed for the door.

"I should have paid earlier, my friend. My apologies. What do I owe you?" She took out a small bag.

"Bah. Food and th' room fer later? Say, five silver marks'll do. Can't spend it nowhere anyway."

"I'll tell you what. I'll pay you this." She placed a gold mark in front of him. His eyes lit up. "There's another tomorrow if you forget I was here. Deal?" She looked into his eyes.

Without blinking, he replied, "Oh, by th' gods, aye. You'll not hear a chirp outta me." He palmed the coin, turned and walked to the kitchen around back.

She knew he wouldn't speak, and even if he did, who was he going to tell?

She pulled on her cloak, flipped up her hood and went outside. It had grown darker, and the rain still fell, though the wind had died down to just a breeze. She looked around at what used to be the town square but saw only broken carts, weeds and puddles of water.

The vendor stands that once stood around the square were now broken, and their cloth coverings waved in the wind like ragged banners from long ago. Whatever blight was on this town had been here for some time.

Across the square was a building she could only assume was the town hall. It wasn't exceptionally large, but it had far better construction and looked much more stable. There was a faint light coming from a side room, so she headed that way. The faint odor of death carried in the wind, making her want this contract over as fast as she could get it done.

Rain dripped from her hood as she reached the front door. She tested it to see if it was barred, but it slowly creaked open, making her cringe. *If they didn't know I was here before, they do now.* She shook her head, disgusted.

She stopped for a second. An uneasy feeling that everything about this contact was wrong crept into her bones. To be sent to a diseased town to kill an apparently evil man associated with a dark god just wasn't sitting right with her. If Fredrik had still been alive or even in his right mind, he would've known exactly who she was and why she'd come.

She put the feeling behind her and unsheathed her dagger. If it came to this, then she wanted to be prepared. Inside, the breeze, mixing with light swirling clouds of dust, blew in from broken panes and the open door. To her, the image was surreal, like an ancient burial tomb. There were benches to the left and right of a central aisle with a large, box-like lectern on a stage in front of her that was battered and aged.

She started to walk down the aisle and gasped when she saw that there were corpses on every bench, stretched head to foot, piled on one another, the stench of death now hitting her like an anvil. She wanted to retch, but she swallowed it down and continued forward, trying to block the smell with her hand and having little luck.

She stepped carefully between the bodies, doing her best to avoid the puddles of rot. Each corpse was in a different stage of decay; some freshly dead, others half-liquefied, and one so desiccated it looked mummified.

If he was here, as the stableman and the tavern maid had claimed, she meant to end it quickly. Moving with care, she crept toward the lectern for a closer look. An open book rested on it; a crude message scrawled across the page in charcoal:

In back.

She dropped her cloak, crouched and drew her other dagger. If this was an ambush, she was ready. Her heartbeat quickened, eyes narrowing as her body tensed. She checked the dusty floor for footprints but found none. Each step was careful, measured, as she moved toward the open door that seemed to lead to the rear of the hall.

Peeking around the corner, she saw a narrow hall that opened into a room. Moving with the silence of a cat, she hugged the wall, each step carefully placed. At the end of the corridor, her eyes swept the space beyond: tables cluttered with books, pages fluttering in the breeze, chairs tipped over and, in the far corner, a bed.

If the rumors were true, then this very well could be him. Perfect timing. If he slept, there'd be no fight, only the quiet work ahead.

She edged forward, patience her only ally. Too fast, and the floor would betray her; too slow, and he might stir. *Patience, silence.* She carefully moved closer.

She was close now. Two steps, and she'd be on him. She paused, listening, his breathing steady, unaware. Time to move.

"You've come…haven't you? Finally…an end." His voice was sickly and raspy.

Lyssa startled as she was caught off guard. *How did he know?*

"You've come…."

"You know who I am?" She stayed crouched. This man was still a threat, and she knew it.

He rolled to face her. His face was drawn in and as white as a bleached sheet. Blood was caked around his eyes, nose and mouth, and sweat dripped from his face. He reached out toward her to reveal that he was gangrenous from fingertip to elbow. The stench was like that of fermenting cheese, making her eyes water. She'd never seen anything this horrible before.

"Doesn't matter who…you are. Matters only that you'll finish…what this accursed disease began." He coughed again, spewing vile sputum onto his blanket.

"Please…no more fever. No more madness."

Lyssa's hand tensed on her blades. At this point, she knew she was in no danger of attack.

"I was sent to kill you…not to grant you mercy."

The man exhaled a ragged breath. "I know. I sent the contract."

Lyssa's eyes squinted, confused. "You? Why?"

"I'm dying. It hurts, so please, have mercy and end this."

It made sense to her now. He made himself out to be evil so the contract would be settled before he suffered much more.

"You see," he started to shake, "under the lectern, it's yours.… Just finish this."

Tears began to roll down his cheek, the pain evident. "Kill me. Mercy or not, it's all the same. Just…let me sleep." He began to convulse.

Lyssa paused, then exhaled. She quickly put both daggers into his chest. He was so emaciated that there was almost no resistance as the blades sank deeply.

He stopped convulsing and exhaled his last breath, a smile passing his lips.

Then a realization hit…

I didn't kill a man. I buried his suffering.

She stopped at the lectern and retrieved the payment, not bothering to count it; the amount no longer mattered. All she wanted was to leave. Ignoring the rest of the town, she made her way back to the stables. There was too much death today. She needed to clear her head and be gone from this diseased sepulcher.

The rain continued to fall; the cold began to bite. She no longer felt it, coming to terms with what she'd seen and an understanding of what it was like to be repulsed by the aftermath of death. Never had she ever seen that part of it before, and she knew that it wouldn't be her last.

She rode until the sun set and found a secluded copse of trees off the road, tied her horse, sat under a tree and slowly nodded off to sleep. It was troubled, with visions of corpses floating on the water. At the hazy end, it was the assassin who laughed.

Once again, her life had changed.

'...oops'

In the morning, just as the first rays of sunlight appeared, she saddled her horse, mounted and continued her journey home. The rain stopped overnight, leaving puddles and mud on the road. The sky was clear, and the day proved to be warm. Lyssa liked it when the roads were clear. She could let her thoughts and memories wander uninterrupted; it always made the day seem so much nicer.

Off in the distance, the tiny village came into view. It looked like a humble little farming village, not unlike Mapleton. She remembered going there once with her mother, meeting her friends and seeing how vast the land was. At her age, it seemed as if the world had no end, and one could get lost in their own backyard.

When she finally reached Wortham, the Cat found a small inn that had tables and benches outside. Lyssa didn't have anything to eat when she awoke, so stopping in sounded wonderful.

A small tree stood outside the inn where her horse was tied. She sat at the table beneath its branches, letting the sunlight find her face. Warm rays caressed her skin as she drew a deep breath, clearing the lingering scent of decay and yesterday's ruin from her lungs.

A young girl walked to her side, dressed in a tavern girl's clothes.

"Um, excuse me, mum, but would ye care fer sumpin ta eat er drink?"

Lyssa looked at her cute pale face, big brown eyes and brown hair.

"Why yes, I would, my dear. What would you suggest for this fine morning?" She leaned closely and smiled her warmest smile at the girl.

"Well, me Da says th' eggs 'n 'shrooms be good." She wrinkled her face. "I ain't fond o' shrooms meself."

She looked sneakily left and right. "If'n it were me, I'd get me a slice o' pig haunch. Da just cooked it up this mornin' so it's still hot. Oh, and some lef' over stew." She grinned. "Most folks don't like it, but it's always best second' time 'round."

"Well, sweet girl, I'll have just that." She pulled her small pouch out and produced two silver marks. "Here, this is for you. Don't tell anyone."

The girl's eyes went wide. "Thank ye, mum. I won't tell no one." She shoved the coin into a small pocket in her dress, then ran off to get her customer's fare.

While waiting for her food to arrive, she surveyed the area. There were several fields that were overgrown with barley and wheat, a few solely for animals and one that was filled with pear and plum trees. This little village was in for a large bounty this season by her reckoning.

The young tavern girl arrived with a big grin on her face, a small plate in one hand and stew in the other. She set them down just so and asked if Lyssa needed anything else.

"Thank you, no. This will do for now."

She gave her best curtsy, then turned and went back inside.

The pork haunch smelled wonderful, the plum glaze was sweet, and the stew was made with pork, vegetables and small apple slices for more flavor. The meal was fit for royalty, which was very rare for this part of the kingdom. It had been almost a week since she'd eaten like this, and every bite tasted perfect. It made her anxious to return home and enjoy more of Elda's cooking.

The little girl came by again, this time with a flagon of mead that was nearly as tall and heavy as she was, setting it on the table and trying her level best not to spill a drop.

"This be plum mead. Da said this be free o' charge bein' yer th' first patron taday."

She smiled at the girl. "Give your da my thanks." She raised the flagon, toasted her father, and took a gulp. It was sweet with a mild fire as she swallowed.

"Oooh. This is quite good."

Without being asked, the girl sat down and started to chat with Lyssa. She told her she was nine winters and had lived with her family in Wortham all her life. Not very many people stopped, even though many passed through. One time, she said the king and his people passed by, and it was like a giant parade. There were soldiers, knights and ladies, all sorts of banners and flags. She was almost giddy telling Lyssa the story, which brought a smile to Lyssa's face and made her think of better days.

When she asked Lyssa about what she did and what her childhood was like, she spoke about her sister, the festivals they had, Lord Trellin and the woods she used to hunt in. The little girl listened with rapt attention, asking many questions and comparing Lyssa's life to hers.

After a while, her father called her inside as Lyssa was just finishing her stew.

"I'm sorry, miss. I hope Tahny didn't bother ye."

"Oh, no, no. Don't jest. She is a sweet, lovely little girl. You should be very proud of her."

"Aye, miss. I am. She's all I got. Her mum died two seasons past." He looked down at his feet. Lyssa knew his heart still hurt from it.

"You two look very happy, though." She held out two gold marks and slipped them into the innkeeper's pocket. "Here, you take good care of your daughter—for me."

He smiled. "I can't take this. Th' meal don't cost that much." He tried to give it back.

"It's to help you and your daughter out a bit. Don't waste it." She stood, patted his shoulder and winked.

The innkeeper nodded his thanks as she mounted and rode off. Her stomach felt as full as her heart when she nudged her horse to a trot.

The day had turned warm just as she'd thought. She raised her head to the sun so it could warm her skin. Speaking to the tavern girl made her feel good inside, and it helped ease the ache she had for missing her sister. She thought about the many pranks they played on one another, running through the tannery while her father yelled at them, even the time Lyssa started a mud fight with Chandra out behind Kalla's shed. The thought made her chuckle out loud. For the first time in her life, she felt like...whistling.

'...whistling?'

By nightfall, she'd reached her adopted home. As she trotted up the road, her eyes fixed on the assassin sitting on the bench in front with his arm still in a sling. The moonlight cast a silvery hue, making him appear almost ghost-like.

She handed her horse to the stableman, lifted her bags and slung them over her shoulder. He had a relaxed look on his face, a jug next to him and a goblet in his hand. He looked so relaxed, in fact, that it made her wonder just how much he really did drink.

"I see the prodigal slayer returns." He sipped from the silver cup. "You're alive, and that's a comforting thing. I guess my training helped." He raised his goblet to her.

She sat next to him and laid the bags on the ground. She opened a flap and passed a medium-sized pouch to him.

"It was a travesty." She reached over, intercepted his goblet and emptied it.

"Alright?!" He waited for her to finish, confused.

"The entire damn town was diseased." She reached over and picked up the jug of mead. Tipping it up, she took a full draw from it and swallowed hard, a small trickle of the liquid running down her neck.

He sat patiently, expecting the rest of the report.

She nodded. "When I got there, there wasn't a damn person in sight. I went to the inn and asked where I could find Fredrik."

"That was…bold," he said sarcastically. He started to say something else, but she cut him off with a raised finger.

"That's not the best. They told me where he was, so I went to the town hall. I walked in and, by Velkhar's arse, the place was filled with corpses, reeking, dripping corpses." She took another swig. "A bunch of rotting corpses."

Wiping her mouth with the back of her hand, she continued. "Worst damned stench I've ever experienced. Entrails, bloat, body fluids all over…I almost retched." She took a deep breath as if to purge the stench from her lungs.

"And was he among them?" His interest was piqued.

"In there? No. He was in the next room, covered in a blanket and covered in gangrene." She drank again.

"That was no assassination. It was a mercy killing. He wrote the contract for himself."

"Huh." He pondered that for a second. "I have to say, I've never encountered a contract like that before." He looked surprised.

He held his goblet out, and Lyssa filled it. "To your first contract, easy as it was." They both drank.

He took up the pouch, removed several gold marks and handed it back to her. "Your contract, your pay."

He leaned back and looked to the night sky.

"You know, with the successful completion of this contract, little cat, your future is now your own," he said. "Every contract from this day forward is yours, as is the coin." He nodded to her. "If you stay here, which you are more than welcome to do, we are partners. The contracts are four parts yours and one part mine, and in return the same." He showed her a broad grin. "After all, one must pay the piper, so to speak." He stood and turned for the front door. "Think about it, if you will." He opened the door and went inside.

It took some time for her to mull things over. She was never really sure what life would be like outside the manor and away from her mentor. Of course, she remembered her former life with Ashby, but it was different now. She'd grown accustomed to his teachings and critiques, even though they sometimes annoyed her. He did have a way of getting under her skin, but that was just another test, a lesson in control. He'd said a year ago when they first met that he would train her to be a weapon. In his eyes, that is exactly what she'd become, but in hers, she still saw a scared little thief who had just lost her best friend.

She still missed her sisters. Oddly enough, they had become one and the same. Each had their special quirks that fit well with hers, each had that special sisterly love…and each had tragically disappeared.

She couldn't leave yet, not until she was satisfied with herself, in her own abilities, satisfied that, when she finally did go out on her own, there would be no more reason for the voice in her head to scream *Never again* in fear.

She went inside and stopped at the front of the door to his study. He was there, behind his desk as usual, poring over maps and books, searching for some form of missing knowledge. He glanced at her, but she just stood there looking at him. He nodded his head and returned to his work. They both knew each other well enough by now that no words were needed, not now.

She headed off to bed, awaiting her next contract.

Talk of Wortham:

"Have ya seen that young lass spendin' time with th' tavern keeper an' his girl? Sweet one, she is. Nice seein' decent folk come through Wortham."

–a milkmaid to the herdsman

"They say Kelligan Town's dyin' slow, wells dryin', fields goin' fallow. Don't think it'll last another winter. Why, I walked through just last week…quiet as a graveyard. Even th' dogs didn't bark."

–town cartwright

Of Doubt and Rumors

Days passed quietly. She kept herself busy by training as always, but she couldn't help feeling closed in, trapped almost. She knew there was a world out there, a big one, but she had to test herself one more time before she would allow herself to go. Perhaps the gods were testing her patience again; she couldn't tell, but she did know one thing: it was taxing both mentally and physically.

Finally, at supper, as they sat talking about her training and being critiqued, yet again, she boldly stated, "I want to locate a contract on my own."

His brow raised at the statement. "Do you think yourself ready?" He tipped his goblet to drink.

She stared at him, somewhat unsure but desperate to prove herself.

"By Skippin's pipe I am."

The comment caught him completely off guard, making him laugh while drinking and sending wine across the table. Her eyes went wide at her comment, and she even had to laugh, knowing that's not the way she meant it.

"Well, alright," he said, wiping his mouth with a cloth. He sat back.

"You're certain, because if you take a contract on your own, I can't help you. It would be completely up to you to see it through."

"I want this. I'm bored here." She looked down at the table and, in a lower tone, said, "I may want to leave after it. I don't know, but I just have to know."

"I see." He thought for a moment. "Alright, as you wish."

He stood. "There is a drop off behind the tavern in Merchant's market. You know of the market?" She nodded even though she didn't. "Look for the large tree in back, and you'll find the mark. If there's a contract, it'll be there." He thought for a second. "You do know the mark?"

She shook her head. He'd never spoken of it before. He stood and went into his study, then returned with a piece of torn parchment. He handed it to her and said, "Remember this. I'll only show it once, and you will burn it afterward."

She looked at the simple etching. She understood how others might see it as nothing more than a random mark scribbled by someone, but to her, this would be the beginning of a new life.

She nodded, turned to the fire, and made certain it burned completely.

She stood and headed to fill her saddlebags for the trip. He stopped outside the kitchen on his way to the cellar.

"Remember your training, little cat. I know you can do this…." He smiled, "after all…I trained you." He winked and was gone.

The moon was high on this clear evening. There was barely a breeze, and the humid air hung heavily, carrying with it the smells of the forest. She loved when it was like this because it helped her stay alert and helped keep her calm. She rode her black mare north on Merchants Road, directly toward the Wayfarer's Respite. She'd never been there but heard the assassin talk about it quite a few times. She veered off the road, leading her horse on foot just far enough inside the woods that it wouldn't be seen from the road. From there, she stayed in the shadows until passing the inn and reaching the back of the tavern. The large tree wasn't difficult to spot, being the widest of them all.

She walked to the opposite side and found the mark by feel. It was just above a hollowed-out knothole and, as she felt around inside, she came upon a folded piece of paper, which she removed.

Slipping it into her pocket, she started heading to her horse when she heard a twig snap. She instantly froze in place, holding her breath to locate the sound.

She waited. Minutes went by. Nothing. She took a step slowly forward and carefully set her foot down, then took another just as slowly. Nothing. Another step, and there it was, just off to her left rear. It sounded fairly heavy, but she couldn't tell what it could be. She slowly pivoted on the balls of her feet to face where she thought the sound had come from and waited. The wait was now truly annoying her. There was something there, but it seemed to be playing a game with her, and she didn't like it. Still, she kept her patience, crouched, and was still very alert.

There it was again, this time to her left front; she was behind it now. Slowly pivoting again, she faced the sound. Her hand slowly slipped down to her dagger, removing it but keeping the blade close to her arm so it wouldn't reflect the moonlight.

It had now become a cat-and-mouse game, something she was particularly good at according to her master, and she would win. *Patience, little cat. Let the prey come to you.*

The moon was now behind her when she heard it again, but this time it was moving toward her. *Ahh, there you are.*

Her eyes readjusted to the darker light and saw that it was the shadowy figure of a man. He, too, was crouched, which told her that this was no ordinary person. It was a hunter of some kind, and great care had to be taken if the outcome were to favor her.

She remained still and watched as the figure neared. *Do I kill or wait?*

Her body said kill, but all she heard was her mentor counseling patience. She would wait. Her eyes followed the shadow, but he didn't move. Her training was paying off as she'd been crouched for what seemed like an hour, yet her muscles had not cramped nor even fatigued.

It moved close but passed by her, close enough that she could smell the sweat of a man. Still, she remained motionless.

Whoever it was had gotten impatient and stood up straight and said, "I don't know who ya are, but ya took me contract. If I find ya, I can assure ya, yer dead."

Is that right?

He started to make his walk toward the road when she leaped like a wildcat, her left arm wrapping like a snake around his neck as her dagger sank deep into his back while knocking him down. She knew he'd fight, so she stabbed him three times in succession before she rolled off and faced him in a crouch. He didn't move.

"Stay silent. Let the prey come to you," were the last words he heard.

She heard the whispered exhale of his last breath before she finally stood. This was something she never expected, yet she was alive. She took a deep breath and began to move the man into the woods. Before she went back to her horse, she checked his body: a pouch, bag, paper and a nice pair of studded bracers. She took them even though it wasn't something she wore, more as a prize than anything. Returning to her mare, she reflected on her attack, at just how lightning fast her reflexes had become. She was impressed with her abilities but remembered there was still a job to do. Carefully, she led her horse back down the road toward home to separate herself from the fight in case someone got overly interested.

She found a tree inside the woods once more, tied off her horse and took a nap until daybreak.

The sun woke her up. She was surprised she slept considering what happened the night before, but she felt refreshed, alive. Standing, she stretched and, remembering the paper that she took from the dead man the night before, opened and read it.

It turned out to be nothing more than a note from a lady declaring her love for him. She chuckled. *Never trust a man.*

The bag was small yet held a bit of coin, but the pouch was the prize. She delved into it and found a whetstone and oil cloth...*That helps,* lockpicks....*Ashby would love this. And what do we have here?*

She pulled out two small vials, remarkably similar to the ones Kalla used for her caustic creations. She unstopped the larger one and carefully sniffed. It smelled familiar. Kalla trained her in discerning the various scents of a potion to understand what its ingredients were. From this one, she smelled ginger, probably highly concentrated, nightshade, of course, monkshood and oddly enough, buttercup. *Buttercup? Why buttercup?* She thought about that one for a minute. What did Kalla tell her about that?

"Ahhh...you bad little man."

She remembered what Kalla once told her: *Buttercup smells sweet, but it be among th' most toxic things ta mix with any poison.* Lyssa recognized the herb at once...highly concentrated, used not for mercy but for torture.

When added to drink, Kalla had said, it caused writhing pain in the gut and burning welts in the throat as it went down. At this potency, just a few drops would do. Death would come slowly...and brutally.

Yes, this was not a good man. And she was glad she was the one to end him for even she would never use such a concoction to kill someone...unless, of course, it were...

She brushed the thought from her mind.

The smaller vial was nothing more than a common blade poison, and a fairly weak one at that. She dropped it to the ground and crushed it underfoot.

She placed the new vial in with the Zhul'xora Theryxis poison and closed her pouch.

She took a deep breath and removed the contract from her pocket, almost afraid to read it. She knew it was too late to turn back now. She had killed for this, and now it was up to her to complete it.

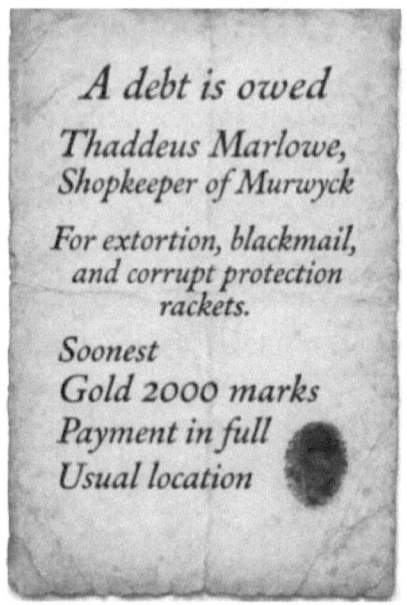

A debt is owed

Thaddeus Marlowe,
Shopkeeper of Murwyck

*For extortion, blackmail,
and corrupt protection
rackets.*

Soonest
Gold 2000 marks
Payment in full
Usual location

Two thousand marks. She smiled.

This was going to be a tough one. Not only was this far away, but she read that Murwyck was considered to be in a free march and overseen by a brutal lord, surely not one to be trifled with. She would have to be very careful. *Am I going to be able to do this? He warned me this might happen.* She was in it now—up to her neck. She was confident she could do it. *Soonest.*

It would take her at least three days by horse, so she would have plenty of time to prepare herself. Her hair would have to change, the way she walked, everything. All of his lessons flooded into her mind at once. *You can do this. Patience. Confidence.* She had to trust him. She had no choice.

As she remembered, if she took the road from the assassin's manor and traveled west over the Argent River, she would come to the hamlet of Bakerston. She could sup there and continue north, which would lead her to the outskirts of Tantyn.

Just before daybreak, she thankfully left Tantyn, never looking back, and took the road to Wortham, where she arrived at midday.

She liked this town. The little girl, Tahny, served her here with her da at the tavern. With plum mead still lingering in her mind, she tied off her horse and sat at the table under the same tree. She kept her hood over her face to surprise her little friend.

Tahny, still dressed in her tavern maid dress, came out and asked the hooded person if they would like food or drink.

Lyssa turned to her and said, "Tell me, little one, do you still hate mushrooms?"

Tahny looked suspiciously at Lyssa. She'd heard the voice before but couldn't see her face.

Lyssa pulled back her hood and smiled. Tahny let out a squeal of joy and wrapped her arms around Lyssa's neck in a big hug. She picked her up and swung her around, laughing.

"You came back; you came back."

"Tahny?! You alright out there?" her father yelled.

Lyssa put a finger to her lips, "Shhhh."

Tahny grinned and kept silent.

Her father came outside and saw Tahny standing next to a leather-clad figure who looked quite menacing.

"I'm sorry if my daughter caused any trouble, friend."

Lyssa turned around, and recognizing his guest, said, "By all that's good, look who's back. Welcome, welcome."

They all sat and talked for a while, as there were no other patrons just yet. They told her about the news from Kelligan Town, which, as it turned out, was not good, and she told them about what adventures she was able to.

Her father, Vergil, brought out squab with leeks and potatoes, and they drank mead, talking for hours. When she had eaten her fill and was ready to leave, Vergil refused her coin, telling her he was simply happy that a friend had finally passed by. Lyssa hugged Tahny, quietly slipping silver coins into her dress, shook Vergil's hand, then left to continue on to her contract.

She spent a little more time with them than she wanted, but it did her heart good to get out and be with people she knew. The road north would lead her to Murwyck, but it would take a day and a half, depending on the weather. She came to a fork in the road, the left fork leading to Kelligan Town. She was tempted to go just to see how bad it had become, but the memory of her last visit quickly changed her mind. She wondered if she would ever visit there again.

The rest of the ride toward Murwyck was uneventful except for the accursed rain. The farther north she went it seemed the harder the rain fell. There were times when it seemed the rain fell sideways, the drops feeling like stones pelting her face. She came upon the road west, leading to Murwyck. There was a copse of trees not far from the town, and they decided to take shelter there. She cut out a small lean-to and tied off the horse, cutting a small shelter for it as well.

As rain pelted down, she began to think about the contract. She knew her hair would have to change color, and she would have to change her persona. The boot black would help there, but she had no clothes to alter her look. She would have to buy ladies' clothes while there and hope this Thaddeus person didn't own the tailor shop. Lady's clothes... she cringed at the thought.

The boot black did the trick; every strand of her hair was now covered as well as her brows. The broken piece of mirror she kept in her pouch saw to that. For the first time, she realized that she had...freckles. They were noticeably light, but she had them, nonetheless. She grinned at the thought and still felt they gave her an extra cute sort of look.

She made sure her head and face were covered by the hood of her cape and entered Murwyck, eyes ever alert.

The main road looked like it would lead to the center of the small town, where homes and businesses encircled the square. It seemed odd to her that houses could be intermingled with businesses. None of the other towns she'd visited looked like this. They all had separate areas allocated for businesses and living. She noted that there were only the two main roads, one north-south, the other east-west. Alleyways separated the various other sections; blocks, she overheard them called.

The people seemed to be dressed as any other farming town, in seemingly handmade clothes, though much finer, except for the fishmongers. She knew who they were not only by their dress but by their smell, each one of the sea and fish.

She found a stable and left her horse there, making sure to pay only what the master required. She didn't want to raise any suspicions here.

Looking down the road again, she spotted an inn called, oddly enough, The Cat's Rest. She smiled at the irony as she stepped inside.

It seemed to be like any other inn, a spacious serving and receiving area with an ale board and a fat man standing behind it. There was a hearth at the far end, ablaze, and several tables nearby. It was early enough in the morning that there were few patrons, and those present were quietly eating.

She paid for a room, making sure to play the part of an out-of-place visitor by dropping a coin or two nervously and apologizing for it.

Luckily for her, it was in the back and had a lone window that looked out toward a wheat field in case she needed to disappear quickly. She noted that the shutters pulled inward and contained a latch as well.

Her bed was a plain, straw-filled sack with a thick blanket and a straw-filled pillow. She pulled the bedding from the wall and located the seam, which she separated as best as she could and placed her bags inside for safekeeping. Once that was done, she checked the coin pouch on her belt, making sure it was secure, and left to find a tailor.

Outside, the town had come alive, herders moving stock, wagons piled with straw and grain, even a cart reeking of fish. Looking north, she spotted an iron hanging sign reading Farman's Stitchery, which she assumed was the tailor.

She headed that way, passing a leather shop and a place she'd never seen before, a Title and Scriptorium. She made a note of it, then continued on to buy her clothing.

Inside Farman's, she saw that it resembled the tailor shop on The Guildway in Caer Bryndwyck. Several clothing stands were showing the finest dresses, small busts displaying various forms of headdress and pegs upon pegs of finery and accoutrements. Not being the lady Chandra was, she had absolutely no idea what to look for. She slowly perused each item, wondering not only what to get but how to even match them.

A commonly dressed woman tapped her on the shoulder and asked if she could help Lyssa, who turned with a shy, lost look and said, "Oh, please. I'm completely lost."

They spent the best part of an hour piecing together clothing that fit and was outwardly acceptable. She found out that the woman's name was Imelda and her husband was, of course, Farman. They'd only come here from The Glen due to the ongoing conflict, and their children had grown out of the home now. Lyssa decided that since Imelda proved to be chatty, she would ask her about someone a friend mentioned to her in passing, one Thaddeus Marlowe, saying that she thought he was a charming man who made her laugh.

"Oooh, ya stay away from that one, dear." She had a warning look on her face. "Aye, that man be charmin', but it be hiding some dangerous goings on, I'll say."

"Really? My friend Elda said he was an exceptionally fine man who treated her very well." She tried to act like the other ladies she knew.

"Fine man, aye, but men say he's black as pitch under that smile. Ya be takin' care if ya meet him, now." She brought the clothing to her husband so he could tally the cost.

"Now, Farman, ya be givin' this one a fair price, ya hear me?" She winked at Lyssa and went to the back.

Farman tallied the cost, and Lyssa paid it, thanking the man so much and telling him he had an absolutely lovely wife. He smiled proudly as she left for the inn.

Once in her room, she stripped off her leather armor and donned her new finery. Unfortunately, there was no mirror, so she had to do her best to ensure things were in their proper places. Her dress was nothing more than an overlong tunic with a woven sash and keyhole collar. She'd gotten a long green shepherd's-knit shawl and chemise undergarments. She found that they itched in places she didn't like and were all but comfortable. *How can Chandra wear these things?*

She entered the receiving room and sat at a table next to the hearth, yet far enough away from the other patrons that she could still hear gossip. She asked the ale wife for a mug of juice if they had any, and water if they didn't. The woman soon returned with water, and Lyssa sat back and did nothing more than listen.

She'd been there long enough to drink another mug of water when the name she was looking for finally passed someone's lips, Thaddeus Marlowe. She listened intently, and other than learning he was a *"deceitful bastard,"* also learned he was the proprietor of the Title and Scriptorium up the road. She also learned he had a weak spot for lovely ladies, but that usury was his primary business.

Interesting, she thought. Her mind began racing, forming the beginnings of a plot. She returned to her room to retrieve her dagger and some coin. She carefully strapped her dagger to her calf and slipped the coin into a dainty bag she purchased at the tailor shop.

Stepping outside, she looked to the Title and Scriptorium. *How can I learn more about this man?* She stood, deep in thought, not paying attention to her surroundings.

"Ahem," she heard to her left. Blinking her eyes, startled, she saw a very well-dressed man standing in front of her. His clothing was impeccable, his hair black as pitch, as was his well-groomed beard.

"Pardon, lady, but you're blocking the doorway." His voice was smooth as silk and very courteous.

"Oh, dear. I'm so sorry, m'lord." She bowed and stepped aside so he could go in.

"I'm sorry, but you must be new in town, lady." He smiled kindly.

Could this be him? She did her best to blush and said, "Why yes, I just arrived this morning." She glanced up and down the road. "I wonder if you can help me."

"But of course. How may I help?"

"I'm looking for...dear, what was that name?" She paused for effect. "Oh yes, a... Thaddeus Marlowe. Might you know of him?"

His eyebrow raised suspiciously. "Why everyone knows of good Master Marlowe. If I might be so bold, may I ask your reason?"

She had to think quickly. "A dear friend of mine, Elda Soryn, asked that if I ever visited Murwyck, to please tell Thaddeus hello and that she still misses him."

"Well, lady, you may tell Lady Elda hello and that I miss her as well." He grinned and bowed.

"My apologies for being mysterious, but I, lady, *am* Master Thaddeus Marlowe." He took her hand and bent to kiss it. "It is a pleasure to meet you..." He paused for her answer.

"Oh, dear...Lyza, m'lord. Lyza Socha."

She tried to curtsy but stumbled, and he caught her quickly, helping her back to her feet. She glanced down shyly at her misstep.

"Be at ease, lady. Would you care to join me? I'm just stepping in to eat."

"Oh, I simply couldn't," she said, looking away.

"I'm being forward. I apologize." He bowed. "I own Title and Scriptorium up the road. Please come see me if you have a mind to. I am so looking forward to being in your company again."

She smiled and tried to curtsy, but this time let her coin pouch slip to the ground. Her hands went to her mouth at the error, but he reached down quickly, unconsciously weighed the bag, and handed it back to her. *You're good,* she said to herself.

"Have a care, lady. Bad sorts about this town." He winked and went inside.

Lyssa knew he would be busy for some time at the inn and decided to see what was available in the tannery shop.

It was called The Split Hide and looked to be more of a general-use leather shop than clothing or armor.

She always loved the smell of tanned leather, and this place reminded her of her father's tannery. Hides of all colors and sizes had been stacked on tables along the far wall, and a desk separated them from the leathercrafter, who was hard at work punching holes with an awl.

She walked along the walls looking at assorted items, straps, pouches, and several types of footwear.

Out of the corner of her eye, she saw Thaddeus pass by, bid her thanks to the leatherworker, who'd barely noticed her anyway, and went to visit him at his shop.

The Title and Scriptorium was unlike any shop she'd seen before. There was a long desk just inside with two large candles set atop stacked books. On the left and right walls were rows and rows of little boxes that contained notes and things, each one labeled with a number.

Behind the desk sat a man of small stature, who was writing madly in a ledger of sorts.

"Ahem, pardon me, sir, but I'm looking for Master Thaddeus." She spoke as sweetly as she could.

The man picked up a small hammer and banged three times on the table, loudly, never looking up from his work.

Master Thaddeus came in from the other room and, seeing her, beamed a smile.

"Well, lady, I did not expect to see you again so quickly."

"Nor did I expect to be here so quickly." She put on a sad face. "It seems you were correct in your warning." She forced herself to cry. "My purse has been stolen, and all my coin is now gone."

"Oh, there now. Come to the back. I can surely help." She walked around, and he placed his arm around her shoulders to console her. It made her want to draw away, but she fought the urge and played along.

He nodded to the little man, who stood and went outside.

Thaddeus led her to a seat at a large round table stacked with ledgers, with more books and ledgers piled high on the surrounding tables. He brought her a small goblet of wine. She detested wine but thanked him all the same.

"Now, how can I help?" he asked, smiling.

"I needed that coin to pay for my room at the inn for several more days, it seems." She sniffed. "My husband will be coming soon, and I can't even pay for my meal." She covered her face with her hands.

A wry smile came over his face. "I can help, lady. Unfortunately, I would have to charge you extra for loaning it to you until your husband arrives. I'm sure he'll be able to repay me. Am I correct?"

She grinned behind her hands. "We are not wealthy folk, lord. I don't know if we have enough coin."

He sat back quietly and steepled his fingers under his nose for effect. "Well, there are…other ways, I suppose." He glared seductively at her now, making her skin crawl.

"Whatever do you mean, m'lord?" she asked incredulously.

"We could come to an accord." He raised his eyebrows suggestively.

"I would never do that to my husband. I am not that sort," she said, insulted.

"Or I can just wait until he arrives and inform him you've been…busy…around town." He flashed her a knowing grin.

Her eyes went wide, feigning shock and embarrassment. She sat silently, playing into his hand, then sighed as if she knew she was trapped.

She lowered her head in shame and asked, "What do you want of me?"

His smile changed to that of triumph. He had her and now wanted his prize.

"You will meet me tonight at the inn, where we will take my carriage to my home outside of town. There you will pay my due, and we will consider this matter settled. Do you agree?"

She quietly nodded her head in mock shame.

"Leave me now, but speak not a word of this to anyone. If you do, then consider your life forfeit. Understood?" Again, she nodded, ashamed.

She stood and left, defeated.

Once in her room, she clapped her hands like a little girl, excited at her luck. Lyssa was prepared. Her dagger had been coated with the Zhul'xora Theryxis poison, the stage had been set, and her target had been fooled…she hoped. Gathering her bags and clothes together, she climbed out the window. She looked around carefully, found a haystack in the field, and buried them inside. She made sure her dagger was tied to her calf, smoothed her dress, and climbed back into her room, where she slept in preparation for the next step.

When she awoke, night had come. Laughter and loud talking issued from the receiving room, so she left out to see if Thaddeus had yet arrived. There he was, standing at the door, a knowing grin painted on a smug face. She wanted to kill him now, where he stood and in front of everyone, but that was not how it was to be done.

She lowered her head as she walked to him, where he placed his arm around her shoulder and led her to the carriage. He gently lifted her in and sat beside her, motioning the driver to leave. Not a word was spoken for the trip's entirety.

His home was not at all far from the town. They could have walked, but that was not the type of person he was. He was the sort who liked to show off, to show how much more affluent he was than others.

She saw that there was a small gathering of trees that surrounded a pond close to the house, which was actually quite nice compared to the black hearted man she was with. *Patience. Let the prey come to you.*

They went inside as the carriage left. Inside the home was finery like she had never seen before, far nicer than the assassin's home, tapestries, finely crafted furnishings and a library with so many books that Chandra would have gawked. He led Lyssa into a nice area where a lavish table was set in front of a large hearth fire. Ornate wall sconces gave off a bright yellow flame, making the entire room look warm and inviting. A male servant stood waiting as Thaddeus sat Lyssa and went to then seat himself.

"I hope you enjoy this, lady. I entertain with only the finest spiced meats and wine," he said proudly. She said nothing, only stared at her food.

"Please. It will not be as horrible as you think." He dismissed the servant. "This I promise."

She looked at him with a tear in her eye.

"Lady, you have my word. I will not make any attempts on you or your husband life after tonight." He tried to look as sincere as he could, but Lyssa saw right through his lie. She wouldn't have been surprised if he didn't try to kill her after the deed was done anyway.

"If you swear to never speak of this to anyone, I will not resist." She looked sincere.

"On my honor, lady. I swear it." She saw the wry grin. She knew. He would try to kill her when it was over, she was certain of it. She stifled a laugh.

Instead, she smiled and began to eat. The conversation was almost interesting; he weaved his lies like a spider weaves a web. Lyssa was spinning hers as well; at certain points, he even seemed interested. It soon came to an end as he stood and walked to the front door.

"Ahh, but the moon is beautiful tonight, as are you, lady." She stood and went to his side, putting her arm around his waist. She almost vomited, but managed to swallow it back. She began to lead him to the pond.

"Oh, what is this here? A pond? How lovely." She almost skipped to it, leaving him behind. She reached down to touch the water while sneaking a glance back. He was taking his time walking to her, leering, so she carefully removed her dagger and slipped it behind and into her sash.

She stood and turned to him just as he arrived. He reached for her, but she gently pushed him back, smiling. He stood, looking at her in the moonlight.

"Beautiful," was all he said.

She loosened the ties to her tunic seductively and slowly lowered it to her waist, revealing her bare breasts and milky skin. She smiled shyly at him.

He moved toward her and went to take her in his arms…then felt the point of a dagger at his manhood. He stopped, shocked.

"I'm not as versed as you in extortion." Her dagger found its mark, and the grin vanished. He froze, terror washing the smugness clean from his face. Lyssa tilted her head, steady, unblinking. "But I'm certain you understand this."

The blade sank to the hilt. He tried to scream, but the toxin immediately began to take effect, paralyzing him and preventing his cries for help. She slid the blade up quickly, opening his gut and spilling entrails. He took one last breath and collapsed to the ground.

She stood staring at the house for a second, noticing just how beautiful it actually looked under the bright moonlight.

She sighed and dragged his body into the pond before pulling up and relacing her tunic, cleaning the blood from her blade and tying it to her calf once again.

She strolled to the house to see what might be available to pilfer. The servant wasn't there, and, looking about, she located several small bags and purses of coin as well as a lovely hunk of pork. She took them all and walked back to town, savoring their spicy taste and licking her fingers clean.

Upon returning to town, she recovered her saddlebags and went to the stable to reclaim her horse.

"Th' black mare be yers, right Mum?" The stableman remembered her.

He brought her around and handed the reins to Lyssa.

"What is the cost, good sir?" She opened her purse.

"That comes to naught, mum." She looked back at him.

He shook his head without any visible emotion.

She silently took the reins and, not saying another word, walked the horse to the edge of town where she mounted and rode off.

Her first contract was now complete. Her payment had been located at the usual place, and the road became her home until she returned to Wortham. She felt satisfied with herself now. She had accepted a deadly challenge, adapted to it and finally, completed it all on her own. Was she ready to be on her own, to accept contracts and perform as expected, to rule her own life and live it as she saw fit? The answer to each question turned into a resounding yes.

She sighed. There came no thoughts, no feeling, only her, the horse and the breeze.

Yes, the world of the Cat had now become wild and spacious.

She smiled and bowed her head.

Mother, Father, Kalla...please be proud.

Her return to Wortham was welcomed happily by Vergil and Tahny. She decided to stay for a few days to let the road wear off and enjoy visiting with real people for a change before continuing home.

She sat in the corner as always, smoking lavender-raspberry leaf herbs, feet propped atop the table and a flagon of mead at her feet. She found it comfortable here. She genuinely liked Tahny and her father. They were a common sort, but there was nothing false about them. They were exactly who she perceived them to be.

Best of all, they loved life.

There were times Lyssa witnessed the little games they played, going unseen by others. She watched her father's eyes light up when his daughter smiled at him. She could see the pride he had in her. Lyssa began to wonder if they had a future here. What with the bandits, mercenaries, and common thugs that presented themselves day to day, it's a wonder they were still alive in this place at all.

She took a deep draw from her flagon and set it down. Another puff, the sweet aromatic smoke billowing to the ceiling. She was relaxed enough to notice the smoke. Odd. She hadn't done that in ages, it seemed.

Lyssa went outside and fed her horse, brushing it down and combing its mane. She loved this mare. This was one of the only places she really felt free. Tahny came out, and Lyssa showed her how to brush and comb it.

She was like a tiny sister now. They both laughed, and Lyssa would tell stories of the faraway places she'd been. Tahny would always listen with rapt attention, excitedly asking questions. Late at night, when the tavern closed, they sat under the stars, talking as if they were family, which warmed Lyssa's heart. She put Tahny down to sleep that night and nearly cried when the little girl hugged her neck.

In the morning, she sat and ate with them before opening. She spent the rest of her time that day walking around the tiny town. There weren't very many people, but those there were turned out to be kind and helpful. They seemed to be hardworking and looked out for one another, very much like Hazelwood and Tantyn.

She felt happy. A small town, with little ways and little to worry about, it made her smile and filled her heart with love. Something she hadn't felt since Ashby.

The sun started to set. She had moved her mare to another spot with better grass and went to sit in her corner.

"Here, Lyssa. Father said to give this to you." Tahny beamed a smile.

"Here, give this to your father, and if he says no, then you keep it." She handed her a small purse of coin. The little girl smiled and ran to Vergil, showing him the purse. Lyssa pretended not to see, but he told Tahny to return it. As she headed back, she stuffed it into her pocket while covering her mouth as if she had done something naughty.

Tahny whispered, "He said to give it back, but I put it in my pocket."

Lyssa leaned close. "It's our secret, right?"

Tahny nodded emphatically, then went to serve another table.

Lyssa leaned back, a grin on her face, and filled another pipe. She scratched her head, then noticed her fingers had come away black. She chuckled about forgetting to clean the black from her hair after her contract.

Pulling the hood down above her eyes, she took a draw from her flagon, savoring the plum mead Vergil made. It was sweet and heady, relaxing her even more.

Customers had begun to fill the tables now. Smoke and raucous laughter became the order of the evening. Bawdy jokes and tales, more lies than not, filled the room.

Lyssa just sat quietly, keeping an eye on Tahny like a mother hen.

A rather large man, already drunk by the sound of him, told Tahny to bring him a flagon of ale.

"Ya ever drunk so much ya wake up wearin' someone else's boots? Aye, well, I woke up wearin' *his wife's!*"

The other men around the table laughed and spilled ale on themselves and the table as Tahny returned.

She tried to put the flagon on the table just as the man moved, causing her to drop it on the floor. The man roared, "What th' blazin' imp's arse are ya doin' ya tiny wench?"

He reached out and cuffed Tahny in the head so hard the poor girl fell. Vergil's attention had been elsewhere at the time, and he didn't see the act. The other men at the table all chuckled but knew what he did was wrong.

"C'mon now, Fen. She ain't but a little girl. Ya shouldn't oughta swat 'er like that."

"Watch, I don't swat you like that, mate." He finished his mug and tossed it at Tahny. "Get me another an' make it quick."

Lyssa had seen enough. She slowly stood, tapping out her pipe and replacing it in her pouch. She walked to Tahny and helped her up, "Go to your father," she whispered.

"Oi, ya sow, leave off 'er." The man gave Lyssa a shove.

Lyssa's glare found the drunkard, sharp and venomous. With Tahny safe at her father's side, she turned for the door, but before leaving, she looked back, a hard, wordless challenge that dared him to rise.

She stepped outside and instantly became one with the dark.

"Oi, mate, she looked at ya like ya was scat." His friend laughed.

Another taunted, "Aye, mate, a damned lass, no less. Ya be a piece o' shite, mate." He nearly fell out of his chair laughing.

Vergil took his daughter into the back room and took up his mace to defend her if needed.

The drunkard stood, now thoroughly angry and embarrassed, and stomped for the door.

"No damn wench gonna' call me shite then jus' leave." Outside, he looked left and right for Lyssa.

"Get back here, ya shite bitch. I'll see yer arse in a grave, I will."

A hand shoved his chest. The breath left him. A tree struck his back. The glint of steel followed by tremendous pain in his throat. As his eyes closed for the last time, he heard only these words....

"Meow."

Vergil and the men stepped out to realize it was already too late.

The drunkard was pinned to the tree by a single dagger in his throat. None remembered her face save Vergil. None could prove it was even her.

Yet, no one heard a sound.

Some say it was the Cat. Some say it was the Valyn in the night. None said it was the black-haired lady.

But Tahny knew—and smiled.

Lyssa sat on the bench for some time, pondering what her future might become. Where she might go, what she might do. Her first thought was to return home. She changed her mind to that. There wasn't any sense in stirring up the ghosts of her past. It was dark. The stars shone brightly. A comet passed by, and she knew.

It was time.

She thought about searching for her sister, as it had been two years since the tragedy, and she had no idea if Chandra was even alive. The last she saw, her sister was being dragged away to who knows where. She chased the image of that day away and took another drink. No one in Tantyn would know. All they could possibly know was that there was a tragedy, the family was destroyed, and the property was razed to the ground.

I have to know. No matter what I find...I have to know.

No, it would have to start somewhere in the direction of where she last saw the guards. The four hamlets were three leagues from the city, and the Poor Road skirted the Whispering Wood. It had been more than two years since she'd seen her ranger friend, but perhaps Kitikithakis would know something, or might have even seen something himself. She decided to go to the river, wash the road dirt from her body and try to sleep.

'...patience, my dear'

In the morning, Lyssa entered the dining room where her mentor had already been eating. He was in his resplendent red and gold robe, which she liked. It wasn't often she was able to catch him this relaxed, and it made her smile. He was more refined than that, but it did her heart good to know he was actually human. He motioned for her to sit, and Elda brought her some food. Herb-boiled eggs, cheese and a boule. It had become her favorite, especially the way Elda prepared it.

"Another lovely day, is it not, little cat?" he said through a half full mouth.

"It is, my friend." She knew he was up to something.

"Have we decided on our future?"

"Yes, actually." Lyssa took a bite of egg, savoring the unique spices. "I'm going to search for my sister." She picked up a bit of cheese. "You've taught me well," she acknowledged with a nod, "but I feel I've been remiss in my search for her." She took another bite of the savory cheese.

He glanced at her. "You know she might be dead, of course." His eyes were actually sad.

"Yes, that's true, but I have to know." She took a drink of water.

He went to his desk in the adjoining study then returned.

"This is the mark of the assassin." He sat. "We have no guilds, like the smiths or thieves, and we are few," he looked into her eyes, "very, few." He produced a small black ring from his tunic pocket and set it on the table.

341

"A gift from teacher to apprentice." A fatherly smile crossed his lips.

"If I am proud of anything, I am proud of how far you've come." He put his hand on hers.

"You started as a young, wild thief and have grown into a dangerous and quite fetching woman." She smiled and blushed.

"I'm still deeply sorry about Ashby. I think she would have been a particularly good justiciar as well, but not quite as good as you, of course." He took a deep breath and sighed. "If nothing else, you should cherish her memory. Her passing made you so much stronger. Remember always, she will be forever in your heart." She started to speak, but he stood and went toward his personal chamber, where he stopped just before entering and looked back at her. "Be warned, though. You may call yourself justiciar…" He went in and just before the door shut, he said, "but you will also be the hunted."

The new justiciar sat and thought about that for a second. She would *be the hunted*. She's always been the hunted, it seemed. The ring sat in front of her, almost begging that she pick it up. It was different, a type of black metal she'd never seen before. The image contained two black adders, entwined tightly and striking a single, many-faceted heart of garnet.

Lyssa slipped it on and found that the fit was perfect. She sighed and went to her room to gather her things, just taking a few bags she could easily hang from her saddle. She went into the kitchen and bid farewell to Elda, telling her how she'd been more like a mother to her than a friend. The aroma of her cooking made it hard to leave, knowing she'd miss her fine meals. Elda cried and gave her a hug, wishing her well on her journeys and that she was welcome to visit her any time.

She mounted her horse and nudged her onward, looking back at what had been her home for the last two years. The plain, dirt courtyard where she'd trained and had been counseled, the lazy yet dangerous river behind the humble white manor, it had been a pillar in her life when she desperately needed one, balancing pain and normalcy when there was no hope to be found.

Justiciar, she thought, staring forward down the road to her future, wherever it would lead.

'...now the fun begins.'

Of Family and Fury

Her path led her north, up the rocky and rutted Merchants Road toward the city that she'd been away from for the last two years. From here, she would turn west and go to the place she dreaded most, Tantyn. No longer afraid of the memory of her home, which had been razed to the ground long before. No, she was afraid Hazelwood had forgotten her. Would Uncle Trellin remember her? Would he even want to? For that matter, was he even still alive? No news from Tantyn had passed her ears in years. So many questions. The biggest one was. *Do I dare?*

The large cottony clouds slowly drifted across the bright sky, and a light breeze carrying the songs of birds in the nearby trees. For some reason, it just seemed brighter, happier today than on other days. She set her worries aside for now. The day insisted that she pay attention to it.

She allowed her mare to pace itself; she was in no hurry to really go anywhere. Her life was now hers to do with as she saw fit, and that was to find her sister.

The Merchants Road stretched east, wide and dusty beneath the fading sun. On its north side stood an inn, the Hounds Rest and a tavern, the Wayfarer's Respite; sturdy, timbered buildings that marked the only true permanence there. She had been there once before, but it was only at night and only from the rear. She wondered if her victim was still in the forest where she hid him. Covering her mouth, she stifled a laugh.

Across the road rose the smithy, its stone walls dark with soot and smoke. Around it sprawled a scatter of tents and makeshift stalls, some twenty or more, lined in rough rows where traveling merchants hawked their wares to any soul with coin to spend.

As it happened, a momentary glint caught her eye in the form of twin daggers displayed on a small wooden stand. Curious, she stopped her mare and, upon closer inspection, noticed just how beautiful and different they were. She slid down and tied the mare off on one of the wooden hitches to see the wondrous weapons better. They seemed to have been hammered from a strange sort of steel she'd never seen before, black of hilt and blade, which was unique to be sure. The oily metallic smell of the forge permeated the air, and the high-pitched clang of the hammer pounding steel told her the smith was there and hard at work. There were several other sizes of daggers, poniards and knives made of various metals, but these were black as the night, not too long, not too short, and they looked as if they'd been made well-balanced. Now thoroughly enthralled, Lyssa wanted more information about them.

"Oi, you the owner here?" she asked the big smith. The man was a giant, coal black hair and beard, sweat pouring off his face and well-muscled arms, a true giant among men. His maul of a hammer clanged once more as he looked up from his work with a friendly smile that greeted her.

"Aye, lass, I am. Vernus the smith at your service." He raised his hammer in greeting. "What might I help ya with?"

She nodded her head toward the weapons. "The black daggers, they for sale or ya just showing them off?"

"Every weapon an' piece of armor's for purchase if the coin's right." The hammer banged heavily on the anvil as he set it down and walked to haggle with her. He picked them up almost reverently and held them out for her to see.

"May I?" she asked, reaching for one.

"Aye, lass, give it a go."

She took one from his hand and felt the weight. Surprisingly, it wasn't heavy at all, perfectly balanced as well. She flipped it in the air, caught it by the blade with two fingers, let it fall forward and spun it quickly. Then she batted it in the air with the back of her hand, caught it with her other hand, flipped it behind her back and finally grabbed it midair with her right hand. Turning her head, she threw it at a narrow awning pole across the shop. It flew with exact precision and stuck fast.

The smith was amazed at her demonstrated skill.

She retrieved the blade and noticed it didn't have a single blemish on its edge. Walking back to the smith and nodding approval, she asked, "What metals?"

"Umm, it's be a new metal I seen when I passed through Helhaven an' over Viper Pass half a year past. They said it were th' strongest they ever seen, an' ya know how them Helites love their steel."

She stared at him blankly, waiting for his answer.

"Oh, sorry, it's a new kind o' steel but made different. They said th' iron fell from th' sky. Honestly, I don't know th' truth o' that, but it was like no chunk o' iron I ever seen afore." He scratched his head. "Th' old smith there, Morgrim Steelshaper, I swear he be part dwarf, that one, said ta hammer in carbon an' black sand powder an' fold it over an' over. So, I looks at 'im funny an' he says, then quench it in whale oil," he looked confused, "Whale oil, if ya can believe. So, I says, I ne'er done that afore, so I gives it a go." He puffed out his chest when he finished, clearly proud of his accomplishment. "I'll be buggered if it ain't the toughest, hardest metal I ever made. I even wrapped th' hilt in special leather, an' th' quillon's inlaid with gold." The man couldn't have been prouder of this work.

"Special leather?"

"Aye. I'd rather not say what, if ya don't mind, thought." He looked nervous.

"I didn't mind before, but now I do." She glared at him.

He looked around, leaned close and whispered in her ear. "It be th' skin of a man."

She almost laughed. "Skin of a man? You expect me to believe that?"

"Look. This old crone comes by a fortnight ago, give me th' shivers looking at 'er, like she was some sorta witch. She says I got somethin' what needed wrapping. I laughed an' says, aye, I got lots what needs wrappin.' She says there be somethin' special, then she hands me this leather an' walks off." He held out the dagger's hilt first. "Damnedest thing be, when I made these, I did run outta leather right then an' I figures, why not. No one'll know."

Lyssa raised her eyebrows, impressed. "Have you made any other weapons or armor in this fashion?"

He shook his head. "Gods no. Th' process took up near a year fer both, an' that odd metal be damned impossible ta find round here."

"Huh." She turned them over in her hands, still testing the balance and weight. "And the price?"

The smith stood proud and tall and said, "Oh, I can't let 'em go for less than, say, three thousand regal marks gold at least."

Lyssa glanced sideways at him, silently flipping them repeatedly.

He noticed her reticence and decided to haggle for them, which he swore he'd never do. This woman, he could plainly see, knew her weapons, was very interested and, as he was hoping, would bargain a fair price.

"Um, well, perhaps that's a touch high. I think two thousand and a half might be more reasonable."

She flipped a dagger into the air and caught it by the blade as she stared at him.

He looked down. "Two thousand?" He looked up sheepishly.

"Sold." She reached under her cloak, produced a medium pouch, and set it in his hands with a smile. He grinned and nodded, satisfied with himself.

With the deal finished, she turned to leave and saw two scabbards of black leather, gleaming black buckles and guilt with gold. She picked them up, looked at the smith and winked. "Same leather?"

He nodded yes. Her presence made his hair stand on end and made him feel glad that this one was going about her way.

She tucked them into her belt and said, "For a deal well struck," and walked off.

The Wayfarer's Respite had been standing for almost one hundred years and was owned by the same family, being passed down from generation to generation.

Lyssa walked in and looked over the room. There weren't very many people, and all that were there seemed to be talking about other merchants or haggling over unknown wares. She looked across the smoke-filled hall and found a nice, quiet, dimly lit corner to rest herself and have a flagon. She chose a table that was next to the lit hearth, where she could use the dim light to hide some of her features and see across the entire room. Crossing her feet on her table, she leaned back and lit her pipe, letting the smoke collect in front of her.

'...every Little Cat needs claws.'

Chandra's sleep was uninterrupted; the sound of water falling into the spring in her room was soothing and comforting. She could recall no dreams and stretched her lithe form lazily, deciding whether to leave her bed or just stay and sleep the day away. The smell of fresh falling water from the spring filled the room. Mixed with lavender and gardenia, the aroma was intoxicating.

She peeled off the covers, washed and dressed. She reveled in her new attire, spinning like a child dreaming of being the princess in a faraway land. Twirling once more, skirts flaring, and in the mirror of the water, she did not see the Queen of Shadows, but the little girl who had once longed to be that very princess.

She passed through the portal and found herself in the receiving room, where the smell of cinnamon and clove mixed with the smoke from the fireplace filled the air. She sat and thought about her day. What would she do? Where would she go? She could remember no pressing business prior to her duel except for her studies on shadow manipulation.

'...*mistress.*'

Malhrun sounded somewhat distressed, which was very unusual.

"Yes, Malhrun. What is it?" She pulled up a chair near the reading table in her library. She opened the tome, *Ars, Praxis et Imperium Tenebrarum*, the very tome that she used to gain her dominance over the ultimate shade, and began to read the now mundane wording.

'...*mistress...*'

"Malhrun, speak."

'...*I feel... I feel...a strange energy.*'

She glanced in his direction. Its glowing red eyes were squinted as it slowly moved toward the wall near her. It pointed '...*this way, mistress. It comes from this way.*'

"It's just the magic of the portals, silly shade. Leave me be." She turned back to her reading. The sconces on the wall flickered, and light black smoke spat toward the ceiling.

'...*Yesss, this energy is strong.... It is you...but not you.*'

Chandra looked up from her text.

"Whatever do you mean?" she asked.

'...*there is another—very strong.*'

She frowned, thinking.

She closed the tome and sat deep in thought, thinking who or what it could be. There were no oddities of fauna nearby. There were no mages from any discipline this far away from the city. She would have felt that herself. She even went as far as to suggest the Valyn, but no one had seen or heard from them in centuries, even if the locals thought the lore was true.

Leaning back in the chair, it was hard to come up with an answer.

'... mistress, I cannot. The tether will not allow me.'

Chandra had forgotten about the spirit bond that she had with Malhrun. When it attached its spirit to hers, its binding became an unbreakable force unless a stronger power was near. Where she went, it went. It could no longer stray any lengthy distance from her.

"Dammit," she said, looking at the shade. "From which direction does it come?"

It left again for just a minute. When it returned, it faced in the general direction of the city.

'... from Bryndwyck, mistress, from the city.'

She paused, thinking. "From the city?" She began to pace again. "There are only five mages in the city at any one time."

'... six, if the healer is considered.'

She glared at him. "Yes, six." She raised two fingers, "Two are in the Tower Arcanum." She flipped up another. "One in the employ of the queen." She raised two more. "And the last are in the Scriptorium Regius."

Malhrun's eyes narrowed.

"Yes, yes and one at the cloister." She shook her head. "I never thought a shade could be so obstinate."

Malhrun moved to a section of the library that was deep in shadow and disappeared.

She sighed, exasperated. "It seems I must travel to the city." She smoothed her dress and began preparations.

'This should prove...interesting.'

With several years of research and testing behind Stidyen's back, Chandra had recently forged a spell she never really thought helpful. She called it "Arcanum Noctis Equi" or Secret of the Night Horse, but she never quite found any use for it, except perhaps for long journeys, which were exceedingly rare for her. She usually weaved her shadow door when she needed to travel, but it proved ineffective for places she'd never visited. Not unlike Malhrun, she had to have a connection to the visited location for the door to be effective, and even then, the connection could be lost over time. The shadow-mare proved very useful for this function, though it would fade at sunup.

Once she emerged from the shadowy portal, Chandra pulled her hood up to cover her hair, snapped her fingers and a glistening black horse appeared. It was large with a flowing black mane, glistening hooves and eyes like a fiery forge glowing brightly and quite beautiful to behold. It was barely discernable due to the remaining sun, but as night drew closer, her mare grew stronger.

It knelt for Chandra to mount, then rose, and they set off at a steady trot toward Caer Bryndwyck. The sun was sinking, and the lengthening shadows seemed to bow in fealty to their beautiful mage.

It wasn't long before she came upon a traveler whose cart wheel had fallen off. An old man was trying to remount it and apparently having little luck.

"Oi, miss, If if ifn' ya c-c-could, when ya gets ta t-t-town, will ya s-s-see if th' smith w-w-w-would be kind enough ta c-c-come gimme a ha-ha-hand?"

Chandra stopped and inspected his mishap. Without saying a word, she began to ride on. In a flash, she heard the bushes rustling. Three men leaped from the woods, one grabbing her reins, the other two to her side.

The cart owner smiled and said, "Ya shoulda s-s-said ye'd help. W-w-e m-mighta let ya go then."

Chandra smiled at how the man spoke. "W-w-well n-n-now, p-p-perhaps you're r-r-right."

The three brigands laughed. "Aye, I sees what yer talkin' about now, Nigel. We shoulda let Graner do th' talkin."

Nigel laughingly replied, "Y-y-yes. I th-th-think yer r-r-right, Trask."

The cart owner's face turned red as a beet with anger.

Nigel spoke calmly, not really taking the robbery seriously now, "Look, lass, we don't wanna hurt ya. If'n, ya got some coin we'll be takin it from ya, if ya please. Then we let ya go, no troubles."

Chandra sighed. "Oh, alright."

She turned to the rump of the horse. "Please pay the men if you will."

The men looked at each other, puzzled.

The shadow-steed shifted, tail flicking, and left its coin upon the earth.

"Here you go, friends—your payment." She smiled. "Oh, I would accept my coin were I you. The alternative could be…messy." She wrinkled her nose.

Her gaze turned to the man holding the reins. Her steel-gray eyes flashed only once, and the man let go, his face contorting with pain. The others, not noticing, took a step toward Chandra.

In a calm and even tone, "Gentlemen, I warn you one last time." Their faces now turned red with anger and malice as they slowly started toward her.

Just then, Trask stumbled from the front of her horse, face now drawing in as if all the moisture had left it.

The brigands looked at him, then at Chandra and back with growing fear in their eyes. Wisps of shadow exited his ears and entered his nose. He grabbed his head with both hands and began to scream a silent, yet terrifying scream, still moving toward his comrades. Horror reached her assailants' faces as they looked at Chandra, who was now smiling.

"I did say messy, didn't I?" She grinned. She turned her horse to face the men, who were now stiff with terror.

She laughed at the sky, clapped her hands, and Trask's head burst like an overripe melon, showering them in a rain of cranial viscera that looked far less valuable than the horse's coin. Nigel fainted. Graner shat himself, and the cart owner dashed into the woods screaming in horror.

Chandra shrugged, unimpressed and rode for town, allowing her shadowy mount to walk at its leisure.

'...surely you can do better.'

The sun was just below the horizon when Chandra reached Merchant Town. Just outside of town, she snapped her fingers once again, and her mount dissipated, watching as the last strands of woven shadow disappeared into the sky. It was always a wonder to her how a ragtag town sprang up from Merchants Road when The Guildway had plenty of space for all the stands and more. *What people will do for coin.*

She walked into the bazaar to peruse wares, passing several jewelry stands, each seller trying desperately to persuade the beautiful woman to their stand for bragging rights. She casually passed them, continuing along each row, glancing, smiling and reveling in the attention.

'...*mistress, I am not wrong. It is here, so near.*'

Growing bored and hungry, she headed for the Wayfarer's Respite for some sustenance. Passing the smithy, the large owner looked up, surprised.

"Back again, I see?"

Chandra looked at the man, puzzled.

"Again? I just arrived."

"Then, m'lady, there be a doppelganger on th' loose 'cause I just seen ya go into th' Hound just afore sun's touch."

Chandra stared at him for just a second, wondering if the steel dust had gotten to his brain. She thought for a second. *Could that power be here and not in the city?* She looked around, trying to find an obvious answer yet finding none. *I don't feel power here, so it can be no mage. Could Malhrun be mistaken?* She glanced at the smith, who shrugged, and continued her search.

'*...closer still, mistress.*'

Across from the smithy stood another jeweler, one who'd clearly seen better days, puffing on a clay pipe. He peered through an oversized burning-glass, so convex he had to squint to study his work. His tools gleamed in the light, each one handmade; Chandra could tell at a glance, for she had never seen their like before.

The piece she examined was a mail gorget, its fine black steel rings so small they shimmered like silk beneath her fingers. It was light, supple and beautifully made, fastened at the back with golden clasps.

The jeweler looked up from his glass, his breath catching at the sight of the woman before him.

"Can you set a stone here?" she asked, touching the center of the gorget.

"Of course, my lady," he said, leaning closer. "How would you have it set, and what sort of stone shall I use?"

"A black claw with golden tips for talons, I should think," she said, holding it with one hand.

"Absolutely, lady. I can have it for you in a touch less than a fortnight, I think." He smiled.

She placed a small leather sack on the table next to him that clinked loudly.

"One twice as large if by sunrise." She smiled, turned and walked away.

The man's shoulders sagged almost in defeat, and the smith said, "Aha. She'll be right irked in the mornin', I say."

The little man smiled. "Says you." He moved aside the item he had been hard at work on and began to hammer out the beautiful lady's setting.

"Now, back to this power." She looked around, searching for an unseen and unfelt mage or sorcerer. Seeing nothing, she decided to continue on to the Wayfarer's.

'...is this going somewhere?'

Chandra walked into the tavern. The smell of pipe smoke, body odor and stale wine filled the air. As she entered, the raucous laughter and song quieted somewhat as all eyes followed the lady's elegance and splendor through the room. Men leaned to whisper lewd comments, women slapped their men, while other women looked jealously on.

She looked about the room, over and through people, searching for an empty table on which to eat and drink her wine, but she found none. She did notice in a corner a dark figure, feet on the table, a flagon close by and smoking a clay pipe. She sat alone at a large table with two empty chairs, the only one suitable for her, so she approached to seat herself and possibly strike up a conversation, an uninteresting one at that, she thought.

"May I?" Chandra asked, grabbing the back of the closest seat.

The person sat staring at her.

She huffed. "Let me rephrase that so you can better understand. I'm sitting here," she demanded.

As she pulled the chair, in a single motion, a black dagger flew from the stranger's boot, cartwheeled into the air, and landed point first in the table. The dark figure puffed on the pipe without a sound, blowing smoke in the woman's direction.

There is something...familiar...about this one, Chandra thought.

"Do I know you? Have we met?" she asked.

"Who wants to know?" It was a gruff female voice. *I know that voice,* she thought.

Chandra concentrated. *Yes, very familiar.* She tried to place the sound.

Leather doublet and boots, dark clothing underneath, she couldn't figure it out, until…

Chandra squinted. A tiny piece of hair hung from the dark hood along the dark figure's face. It was platinum white.

IT'S HER!

Trying to keep her tears and overwhelming excitement at bay, she thought quickly.

"You know, it wasn't your shite archery skills that scared off that deer."

There was a long silence. *How is that possible? No one knows that.*

"And the next time you're faced with a flying book, I should think you'd duck."

The stranger's boots landed hard on the floor as she quickly stood.

"CH-CHANDRA?" The question rang so loudly that the entire hall went silent.

"Gotcha," she said, smiling.

The stranger pulled the hood from her head to reveal her platinum white hair and steel-gray eyes, which were now welling up with tears. There was no mistaking it; her sister was alive and standing before her.

In unison, they both said, "SISTER!"

Finally, after all these years, through all the hardships and pain, the Cat and the Shadow had found each other.

They wrapped their arms around each other in a tight embrace that could only be given by long-lost siblings. Their tears began to flow freely, neither wanting to let the other go for fear of losing them again. For a heartbeat, the tavern was gone, no smoke, no laughter, no eyes watching. There were only sisters.

…And the tavern returned to loud laughter, music and frivolities, paying no further mind.

'…DAMN! DAMN! DAMN!'

The sisters lingered at their table long after the laughter had ebbed. The tavern maid kept their cups filled without a word, too wise to intrude on what was clearly no common meeting. When at last the master of the Respite asked them to leave, their twin glares silenced him quicker than any blade or spell. With a grumble, the candles and torches were put out as he locked the door, leaving them to the shadows and the fire's dying glow. Through the night, they spoke in joyful tones, voices tripping from laughter to tears and back again. They spoke of Stidyen's cruelty and how the crone fell to dust, of crimson lakes and whispering woods, of Kitikithakis and the day he earned her trust. Old quarrels were teased, old wounds reopened, then healed again, and each memory seemed to weave the years spent apart into nothing.

When dawn crept through the shutters and the innkeeper returned, the room was empty but for the scent of smoke, the echo of laughter, and a heavy pile of coin glinting on the table where the Cat and the Shadow had sat.

They walked through the Merchants' Bazaar arm in arm for the entire morning, hawkers' calls sounding like crows calling in the new day, not perusing but walking proudly among the people as if to show each other off. It was the first time in many years that the girls could feel their hearts, each beating together with the love they felt, grown long ago. The smells of cooking meats, treats and the hammering of the smithy filled the air, but for them the world had stopped, their life beginning anew.

Chandra returned to the jeweler she had commissioned to see if he'd done what she wanted. She knew it was an impossible task when it was set, but still had to check if for nothing more than to tease.

Through the flags flapping in the breeze and the throngs of people milling about, he saw her approaching. He stood in front of the gorget she'd chosen, with a dejected face.

Seeing his downtrodden face, she smiled and said, "Ahh, tsk tsk. I paid you for your skill, but it seems you've failed." Chandra pouted at the old man. She was still arm in arm with Lyssa.

She turned to the Cat and said, "See, sister? Coin cannot buy all things, it seems."

Lyssa smiled wide and pointed.

The old man was now grinning from ear to ear. He held up her gorget to reveal the claw-shaped setting with glinting gold talons.

She gasped in amazement. "That was an impossible task. How?"

He bowed his head. "Lady, when a woman as beautiful as yourself asks for an item as special as this, the impossible becomes possible."

Lyssa rolled her eyes, "Oh by the gods, Chandy, do you EVER stop?"

Chandra looked at the man and fluttered her eyes. She took the gorget in her hands and spread it out to see it in full light.

"My good man, I am both amazed and impressed. It is not only exactly as I described, but also perfectly matched as well."

Lyssa shook her head. She'd seen this a hundred times before. Chandra and her wiles, which always made her want to vomit.

"And m'lady," he held out a closed hand to Chandra, "after seeing your beauty, I absolutely had to match it with a very beautiful gift."

Chandra held out her hand. He dropped something heavy into it.

She opened it to reveal a rather large purple stone, a many-faceted amethyst.

"It will fit perfectly into the setting."

She placed the stone into the setting, and the claws clamped down on it hard, not allowing the gem to slip from its grasp.

"Thank you. It is gorgeous." Chandra blushed, much to Lyssa's amazement.

She handed the gorget to Lyssa, who wrapped it around her sister's neck and clamped it tightly into place. Lyssa's breath caught in her throat as she saw a slight swirl of shadow inside the gem. She looked at her sister, then back at the gem. *What is this about?*

Unknown to her, male heads within proximity had been turning, watching her every move with longing. She made their hearts beat faster as she twirled to show her sister.

She turned back to the old man, leaned over and kissed his forehead.

"Friend, I cannot thank you enough."

She produced a large bag of coin, from where even Lyssa couldn't say, and carefully placed it into the man's hands. "The pay I promised you, it comes well earned."

"Oh, no, please, lady, this is far too much. I would never ask for so much." He tried to return the bag.

"My friend, you have more than earned it. I insist." The sisters turned and walked away, chatting about her new purchase and how lovely it looked.

They never saw Velkhar grin, rolling his gold coin over his knuckles.

'...pay attention, Lady.'

The ride back to Chandra's home felt like a dream neither wanted to wake from. Lyssa's black mare moved with easy grace beside the shadow-mare Chandra had conjured once more with the snap of her fingers.

The road went unnoticed, the sisters excitedly chatting the entire way. Soon, they came upon Chandra's church façade, where they dismounted and went inside. Chandra told her sister to lead the horse inside, where it wouldn't be seen. Lyssa began to wonder what sort of prank Chandra was playing on her until she stood before the broken altar and summoned her swirling shadow portal. Lyssa was caught in stunned speechlessness. Magic. Her sister really had become a mage. Her eyes moved from portal to Chandra and back, completely astonished.

"Dear sister, you look as if you've seen a ghost," she grinned, "or a shadow." She began to laugh.

"Y-you've done it. You…you're a mage." Lyssa could find no other words.

"I had to do something with my time if I was to ever find you, sister." She took Lyssa in her arms and hugged her tightly.

"I missed you so much, Lyssa Socha." She looked her square in the eyes and said, "Don't you ever leave me again…please."

After their long embrace, Chandra invited her to her new home. The sisters stepped through and, in a purple-black swirl of shadows, left their cares and the world behind.

For the first time in years, they simply lived. They feasted like royalty on venison and fresh bread, laughing at how they both picked the same cuts from the platter. They sat late into the night before the wide hearth, Lyssa with her lit pipe and Chandra with her silver goblet of perfect wine, letting the firelight dance across steel-gray eyes that mirrored one another. In the mornings, they bathed in the spring-fed pool, the water warm where it gathered and cold where it fell from the stone, their laughter echoing against the cavern walls. Afternoons were spent in idle talk, teasing over old memories; Lyssa swearing Chandra had once nearly drowned her in the pond near their childhood home, Chandra countering that it was Lyssa's fault for never learning to swim properly.

Three days passed in this rhythm, the sisters content to relive and rediscover. No plans were laid, no schemes plotted, only stories told, and long silences filled by the comfort of presence. But on the third evening, as shadows stretched long across the floor and the fire in the great hearth burned low, Lyssa's tone shifted. She leaned forward, her voice quieter, carrying a weight different from their reminiscing.

"There's someone I think you should meet," she said at last, her eyes narrowing with intent. "He is simply called *the assassin*."

"The assassin?" Chandra looked at her as if it were a joke. "Isn't this where you say gotcha?"

The flicker of the flames caused the shadows to dance.

"Sister, this is no joke." She became serious. "Most of what I know I've learned from him." She looked at her hands as if there was blood on them.

"After my time with Kitikithakis…"

"A lover?" she asked with a wry grin.

"Be serious, Chandra." Her eyes narrowed.

Chandra stopped kidding. She knew she'd trodden on a very delicate subject for her sister. "I'm sorry, sister. Continue."

"Kitikithakis was the ranger in the Whispering Wood who saved my life."

"After…you know?" Chandra asked.

"Yes. I didn't trust him at first, but he bound my wounds, fed me and clothed me. I still owe him everything." She started to trail off but caught herself.

"Anyway, after Kitikithakis, I met a waif named Ashby." She smiled.

Chandra leaned closer, wondering where this tale was about to lead.

"I hadn't eaten real food in days. Mushrooms, bark, that's all I could find without a bow." She took a breath.

"I sat against a shop, and people dropped coin to me, thinking me a beggar."

The fire popped, sending sparks soaring into the chimney. Lyssa leaned in and shuffled the logs to burn better, then sat back and folded her arms.

"Not long after, a boy threatened to hurt me if I didn't leave. I didn't know why, so I just left and went back into the woods." Her eyes narrowed again, but this time there was fire.

"He followed me. I heard him, so I hid, like Da showed me."

Chandra smiled. "Aye, right up until I moved the shadow," she said, laughing.

Lyssa glared at her sister, and Chandra knew the next time she would incur her wrath.

"Okay, okay, continue."

"He had a knife, and I knew he was going to hurt me." She remembered the sound echoing in her head, *Never again.*

"I waited until he turned his back on me, and I strangled the life from him," she said as if it were nothing.

Chandra looked at her sister, trying to decipher truth or jest.

"A girl named Ashby, Ashby Brimmer, found me, helped me hide his body, then hid me away. We became best friends after that." She looked sadly into the fire.

Chandra knew there was more, so she pressed. "What happened to her?"

"We were stopped by some guards and they killed her."

Chandra could see the anger and hurt in her expression. She laid her hand on Lyssa's. Lyssa held it before she continued. "I slaughtered two, and the assassin killed the third. From that day, I was his disciple."

Chandra considered her stories. Was she as confident and as dangerous as she portrayed? She never knew her sister to spin lies, especially about herself.

"I think I'd like to meet this assassin. He sounds fascinating." She smiled at Lyssa.

She'd never realized the horrors her sister had seen. Yes, Chandra had been beaten, but it seemed Lyssa had a much more horrible life than she. If her path in life really was this hard, then Lyssa was probably telling the truth, and she was VERY dangerous.

"Fascinating, dear sister? I dare say, he could make one of your shadows tremble."

Chandra swirled a finger in the air, and a swirl of shadow grew into a small floating image. It hovered and squeaked out a tiny growl.

Lyssa looked almost amazed.

"So, your magic goes further than common tricks?" Her eyes went wide with amazement.

"Oh, yes, dear sister, and sooo much more." She gave her a wry smile.

'...*mistress, may I?*' Malhrun was always near but rarely spoke when others were present.

"Of course."

Lyssa knew of shades and how they appeared from nowhere, but this was her first real encounter with one.

'...*I dare say, mistress, the sisters are equal but so different. Each their own destiny.*'

"Destiny, Malhrun? Our destinies are locked, dear friend. We, as sisters, are fated to lives on the same path. Nothing can or will ever break our bonds."

It seemed as if Malhrun bowed his agreement.

Lyssa was very interested in the little shade.

"Is it smart, sister? Can it think?" She had become genuinely intrigued.

Chandra looked at Malhrun and allowed it to answer for itself.

'...*I am shadow. I know what is and what was. Mistress commands me. We are one.*'

He blinked his red, glowing eyes.

Lyssa was highly impressed.

"Well, that is cute, Chandy. You have a pet shade." She laughed.

The shade angrily leaped from his shadowed corner toward Lyssa. Her eyes flicked toward its movement and, in the time it takes to blink, raised her dagger to Chandra's throat. "Little shade, you may know me as the Cat. Believe it when I say I play dirty and I never lose."

Seeing his beloved mistress in harm's way, Malhrun fell back to the shaded corner, bowing his apology.

Chandra was shocked at the speed and precision with which her sister attacked. No fear, no thought, pure reaction...and—toward her.

Gods, what did she have to live through to make her this way? She had no time to even react, which told her Lyssa was one to be very wary of, possibly even feared.

"Sister, do that again, and my shadows may not be...forgiving." She glared at Lyssa, who slipped her dagger back into its scabbard.

"Never fear, sister. You know I could never harm you." She grinned. "Oh, by the way...gotcha." She stuck her tongue out to mock Chandra.

Chandra's eyes were slits of ire. *You got me this time, sister. Your luck may just run out,* she thought.

'...you're getting sloppy, lady.'

It had been some time since they ran around Kalla's house laughing, lying in the grass watching the clouds or even chatting at night as their family slept. They had both been molded by the past, each growing in their own manner, learning different things and walking their own paths. Chandra could only imagine Lyssa's path. When last she saw her, unspeakable things had been done, and she knew Lyssa was not the same girl that she'd grown up with. Outwardly, she was Lyssa, a beautiful girl, passionate about her family but aloof and mistrusting. Inwardly, she was wild, fierce...lethal.

Chandra wondered if Lyssa still felt the same about her as in the past. It had been so long. Was there still love, or was it cool tolerance? She wanted to trust, to believe, but the years had changed them both.

Lyssa knew that she'd overstepped her bounds. She'd never threatened her sister like that before, and she began to feel her stomach knot at the look in Chandra's eyes. She may have been trained as a killer, but she still loved Chandra immensely.

"Chandra Dashow. Sister…" Lyssa began.

Chandra knew that when her sister used her name, she was serious.

"Always know this. Yes, I am damaged and, yes, we've been apart for many years." She looked deeply into Chandra's steel-gray eyes, "I will always love you more than life itself, no matter what, and I will never, never willingly harm you."

She removed her daggers and held them in front of Chandra.

"This one is *Claw*, and this one is *Fang*." She held each to her lips and kissed them. "On pain of death, I swear it."

She stood and held her arms out wide. Chandra stood, and they embraced.

Lyssa whispered into her ear, "We are all that's left. Without each other, we die."

She kissed her sister's cheek and smiled.

Chandra pulled back. "I love you as well, Lyssa. I trust in you."

She pulled away…and tweaked Lyssa's nose. Lyssa grabbed it and looked at her sister.

"Gotcha," she said playfully.

The sound of the waterfall and the scent of lavender helped them sleep peacefully in the feather bed, which Lyssa hadn't experienced since her tragedy. The comfort of each other's presence allowed them to sleep the night through as they had done so many years ago. When the world was so different.

'…well, isn't that cute.'

The sisters rose at first light, refreshed, and after a simple meal, they mounted up. The ride to the assassin's manor took the better part of a day, quiet save for the rhythm of hooves and the wind through the grass. Each kept her thoughts close, the conversation light. Chandra's eyes often drifted to her sister, wondering what kind of man could have earned Lyssa's trust. As the sun tilted westward, the manor came into view; stately but not ostentatious, its strength in bearing rather than walls. A lone stableman hurried to take their reins as they dismounted, the look of awe as Chandra's steed disappeared, leaving the sisters to face the doors of the place where the assassin waited.

"Welcome back, mistress Lyssa. The lord is inside," the stableman said, bowing.

They walked to the large double doors of the manor, Lyssa announcing their arrival with the bronze knocker.

The heat was beginning to subside, yet the air was still heavy and smelled of pine and cedar.

The door opened, and Elda met them with a great smile.

"Lyssa, how wonderful ta see ya, lass." She smiled ear to ear, took her in a big hug and motioned for them to enter.

"And who is this beautiful young lady?" she asked, still smiling.

"Elda, this is my twin sister, Chandra." She beamed a proud grin.

Chandra curtsied lightly. "Pleased to meet you…Elda, was it?"

"Yes, dear. Please follow me. He's in the study."

They walked down the hall and into the dining room. Chandra marveled at the comfortable elegance of the manor, the likes of which she'd never truly seen.

"The lord will see you now. Go right in." Elda took her leave as the girls entered the study.

Chandra's eyes widened at the sheer number of books, tomes and scrolls in this room. The firelight gave the entire room a cozy, lived-in feeling.

The assassin stood and smoothed his tunic.

"Ahh, little Cat, I'm so glad to see you again." He leaned over and gave Lyssa a friendly, welcoming hug.

"And who might this lovely lady be?"

"This is my twin sister, Chandra."

Chandra curtsied as he took her hand and kissed it. Lyssa grinned as she saw her sister actually blush.

"By Hearthmae's eyes, you live. It is a pleasure to see you both. Please sit."

He went to the doorway and said, "Elda, will you please bring wine and…" looking back toward Lyssa, grinning, "a flagon of the new mead I brought back yesterday."

He returned, sat behind his desk and flipped over a few velum pages. *This one is no ordinary lady. She has a…presence.*

"Please excuse me for saying, but from little Cat's recounting, I honestly thought you were deceased. I'm glad to see I was wrong." Chandra thought his smile disarming.

"To what do I owe this honored meeting?" he asked, sitting back.

"There's no significant business to attend to. Oh," she said, tossing a small pouch on his desk, "a jeweler in the Merchants' Bazaar wanted me to give this to you."

He raised an eyebrow and picked it up.

"Well, more like I took it in tribute to you." She laughed.

He investigated the pouch and removed two silver marks. They were odd shaped, octagonal, with an imprint of a bearded face.

Concern crossed the assassin's face. He turned the coins over, firelight glinting from the metal.

"You stole this, or did he give it to you?"

Lyssa knew that tone and could read his concern.

Her face went from a smile to that of business, "A bit of both, really." She leaned forward. "Why?"

He sat back and thought for a second, eyes passing from Lyssa to Chandra. He knew he could trust little cat, but this other one, there was something about her.

"Excuse my…brusqueness. I don't wish to be rude, but my lady, who are you really and what do you want?" He leaned forward to read her better.

Lyssa's eyes widened in surprise. *What are you up to?*

Chandra paused a second.

'…*He is truly an assassin, mistress. He is searching for trust.*'

"As my sister has said, I am her twin. Not that it is of your concern, and not to be brusque, of course, but we have been apart for quite some time. She wished that I meet you, which I have done." She was almost taunting the man.

She leaned back and looked at her fingernails, from which an ever-so-faint swirl of shadow crept.

"Now, um, lord…" she knew this game, "if trust is what you desire, have no fear. You and your…craft are of no concern to me."

The assassin's eye noticed the shadow swirl, and he smirked. *Yesss. She is not a normal woman. And now I know your game.*

Lyssa grinned, annoyed, "Now that the game has been played, shall we all beat our shields and attack?" She shook her head. "Do you really think I would bring someone untrustworthy to meet you?"

There was an uncomfortable silence. He sighed and leaned back again.

"My sincerest apologies, lady. I meant no disrespect. One in my…craft, was it?" he smiled broadly, "cannot be too careful."

The tension in the room eased just a bit as Elda returned with drinks.

"Here's for you, lord. Yer best of course." She went to Chandra.

"Also, for you, lady. My, but that is a lovely necklace." Chandra touched it, flattered.

"And this flagon for our little Cat." She turned to leave.

"You call her a lady? Mead for me? No compliment?" She shook her head in mock disgust as she looked at Chandra.

"I must say, Chandy. When I left, I thought I had them better trained than this. I leave for just a little while and see what happens. I'm appalled by both of you."

They all had a laugh, and the tension was now completely gone.

"Now, tell me about these coins," Lyssa said.

"I've been searching for a certain…special item, shall I say, for quite some time." He sipped his wine. "First, these two coins do not come from this region, as you can plainly see." He looked at them. "The only person I know using these specific coins is the very person who holds the item in question."

"And who might this person be?" Chandra asked with interest.

He glanced at the girls.

"A man by the name of Lord Davin, Davin Elkvahr, a not-so-nice man to say the least."

Looking at each other, both knew they had never heard of him.

He went to a small chart hive and retrieved a large map, pointing to a spot north of Crimson Lake.

"This is where he resides."

"Yes, I know Crimson Lake quite well," Chandra said, looking at Lyssa, who sat quietly absorbing the information.

"Good. There's a small town to the north and west of that called Morowyck, just a farming town, really, but still under his charge." He continued, "His manor falls outside of the king's rule, so this autonomy allows him complete freedom."

"And I know of Morowyck. If I'm not mistaken, the manor is fairly close by?" Lyssa asked.

"Yes, as a matter of fact, just northeast by a league or two." He looked at Lyssa knowingly.

"And what *item* does this man have?" she asked.

"In due course, friends. Right now, I must do more research. Something is amiss, and I must find out why." His brow furrowed in complete concentration.

"You have complete freedom of my home, friends. Little Cat can escort you about." He glanced up. "Lady Chandra, it is an absolute pleasure to meet you."

'...seems you're losing ground, moneychanger.'

Lyssa led her sister to the downstairs study. Again, Chandra marveled at the number of tomes and books contained in the large bookcases.

"Lady Chandra. Ha." Lyssa glared at her, drinking her mead.

"Lady Lyssa? No, that will not do, sister. You aren't refined enough."

She sat behind the small, ornate desk and drank in the ambience of the room, which was comfortably lit by the crackling fire, the dry smell of vellum, tomes and ink. She felt at home here and wished she could spend time studying the secrets of each one.

Lyssa growled, as did Chandra, playing at being better than her.

"That's very lady-like, my dear sister, growling like a wild animal." She smiled. "Mother was right. She had a lady, and she had a warrior."

"Yes, well, father said that ladies were good for crying and cooking, not feeding the family and making coin." She gave her sister a satisfied smile.

"Yes, well, perhaps you should have helped Mother and Father..."

Her face instantly went pale, and she gasped at the words she had just spoken. The line had been crossed. She'd stabbed Lyssa in the heart without even using a weapon.

Lyssa's eyes welled with tears, narrowing. Her fists clenched, her teeth gnashed, her face turned fiery red with fury.

She fought the urge to kill as her anger reached its peak. Chandra started to stand, but Lyssa didn't give her the chance as she slowly, purposefully walked to the nearby door and left the room.

Chandra's heart instantly broke. She knew she could never repair the pain she'd inflicted on her sister. She sat and sobbed, the weight of her own words crushing her. What had she done? She had finally found her sister and then drove her away with hateful words.

A hand touched her shoulder as she cried. Looking up at the assassin, Chandra saw a stone-cold face staring back at her while she wiped her eyes and composed herself.

In a soft voice, he commanded her, "Find Lyssa. We have business to tend to."

His demeanor gave the impression that this man was not to be trifled with, so she stood and opened the door.

There, standing in the faint firelight, was Lyssa, calm, tear-free as if nothing had happened.

Chandra began to speak.

Like a flash of lightning, Lyssa's clenched fist struck her sister on her jaw, spinning her head and sending her to the floor. Chandra's head swam, and her eyesight blurred. As the numbness began to wear from her bleeding jaw, she looked back at her sister through watery eyes.

In the calmest, most terrifying voice she'd ever heard, Lyssa said, "If you ever...ever...speak of that day again, I promise you...sister...you will not utter that last word." The anger in her steel-gray eyes bore into Chandra, sending a chill straight up her spine. "Do not doubt this as the truth." She stared at Chandra for just a second longer to let the message sink in.

Lyssa reached down and gently took Chandra under her arm, carefully helped her to her feet, and brushed the dirt from her dress. Chandra stumbled, still woozy from the painful blow. As the cobwebs cleared from her head, Chandra took Lyssa's face in both hands and begged her forgiveness. The words were never meant to be uttered. She grabbed her sister in a hug, which Lyssa begrudgingly returned and kissed her cheek.

She knew she had weakened their bond with those words and may never be able to repair it.

"Are you finished? We have work." The assassin walked upstairs and into the small study.

Lyssa brushed past her sister and followed her former master. Chandra, heart still hurting, followed her as well, praying the gods' mercy for the pain she'd caused.

'...you were saying?'

The assassin stood behind his desk, poring over maps and pages when the girls entered. Lyssa stood in front of the fire, the warmth mixing with the warmth of her ire.

Chandra sat in a chair close to her.

"Have we resolved our differences, ladies?" he asked without looking up at them.

Lyssa stood, unmoving, but Chandra only nodded her head, glancing at her.

"A runner delivered this request—contract—earlier, to which I cannot deny. Unfortunately, I cannot fulfill it due to a prior commitment. I was hoping you would be so kind as to tend to it for me...if you are capable." The last was meant as a rebuke.

Lyssa turned, saw him holding the contract and snatched it from his hand. She glared at him and proceeded out of the manor.

Chandra looked at the assassin and began to leave when he demanded, "Fix this."

She left hoping she could.

'...whoops.'

Lyssa stood under the large lantern post that cast a yellow-orange glow across the courtyard. Various winged insects dove at the light, causing the flame to jump and sputter black smoke as they died in the small inferno. Holding the pages up, she read the contract and map. She understood now. It was definitely a contract, one where she would have to play the role of justiciar once again. This time, she hoped it wouldn't entail wading through rotting corpses.

Chandra met her there in silence, the tension thick and heavy.

"We have to eliminate a hedge mage to the northwest." Her words were short, terse.

She started for the stables to saddle her mare.

"Wait."

Chandra snapped her fingers. The shadows gathered more quickly now that night had fallen and coalesced into a shining black shadow-mare, its eyes glowing bright yellow flame.

She snapped again, and another mare coalesced, this one with glowing red eyes.

Lyssa, without questioning, walked to the mare, mounted and kicked it hard into a run.

Chandra did the same, meeting here stride for stride in weak silence.

The night was cool, barely a breeze, but the stars in the sky twinkled like fireflies dancing on water. They slowed the horses to a walk while Lyssa tried to decipher the map once again. She tried using starlight to no avail, then used the moon, which was better but still difficult.

Chandra cast a basic candlelight spell to aid with Lyssa's reading, with not the slightest acknowledgment.

She sighed, knowing this was not only going to be a long journey, but repairing their relationship would take a lot of time and trust. She had to have patience and understanding, something she was not used to having. In her mind, she could hear her mother's counsel, *Don't worry, sweet girl. She'll come around.*

The night sky gave way to the coming morning light. They had traveled a great distance thanks to the shadow mares; however, the going would be far more difficult now. The mares would soon dissipate due to the lack of shadow, and the rest of the journey would be on foot.

They came upon a small group of buildings, abandoned and crumbling, where they decided to rest and recheck the map.

"Are you hungry? I'm not the best at conjuring, but I can create food," Chandra asked, hopefully.

Lyssa sat silently and perused the map, looking up and down the road to ensure they were traveling the correct route. She was sure the roofs of the upcoming village marked the turning point at which they would need to leave the road and follow a small goat trail.

She stood and looked off in the distance, shading her eyes with her hand. The map folded easily and was stuffed into her belt pouch, where she removed a piece of dried beef. She left the road and started across the scrub-filled plain ahead with Chandra in tow, searching for a large round tower nestled next to a small copse of trees.

They had trekked until midday before the tower came into view. She adjusted their course slightly so they would stay just out of sight and yet reach the trees by duskfall. They continued silently, much to Chandra's dismay.

When they reached the trees, Lyssa finally spoke.

"Just before the sun sets on the horizon, you will challenge this mage. Apparently, he's been forcing his will on the town, and the townsfolk want him removed."

Lyssa poked her head from behind a tree and searched for a vantage point.

Chandra tried to speak, but she was abruptly cut off when her sister motioned and said, "I'll be over there," pointing to a spot where a tree lay over, snapped mid-trunk and rotting.

"When he comes out fighting, I'll sneak behind him and finish him."

She looked at Chandra. "Do you think you can do that, or do you need help as well?" Her question not only dripped with sarcasm but was meant to hurt.

Again, Chandra tried to speak, but Lyssa started toward her ambush spot.

Oddly enough, Chandra was amazed at how skilled her sister was at traversing the bushes. Barely a leaf or limb stirred. The Cat nickname fit her.

'...pawns divided, delicious.'

She waited. Slowly, the sun dipped to the horizon. As the light waned, songbirds became silent, and the chirping of crickets took their place.

It was time. She moved into plain view before the tower. There was no visible door or portal, only gray stone and weathered mortar. She tried to piece words together to taunt the mage, but none came to mind, and then she realized Lyssa had given her no name. She had no idea what to say.

"PSSST."

Chandra looked to where her sister was hiding. She was motioning angrily for her to begin.

Chandra took a deep breath to compose herself, forgetting about her earlier altercation with Lyssa.

"UMBREN VOKAT THAR!" she announced to the tower. "Charlatan, your end has come."

Then she quickly whispered, *My friend, stay close.*

'...*I am here, mistress.*'

"I say again, charlatan, the shadow calls you." Her heart began to pound. The sun dipped down, and she felt the strength of the shadows growing. She had never challenged another mage, and the feeling unsettled her.

"UMBREN VOKAT THAR!"

There was a flash of light and a puff of gray smoke as he appeared into sight.

"You dare challenge me, wench?"

He was tall, unnaturally tall, broad at his chest, more warrior than mage. His blue, metallic pauldrons, greaves and sabatons glinted sunlight like sunbeams, his black cape barely moving in the breeze. He held a staff made of light in his left hand that she'd never before seen.

"Give cause or die!"

She became nervous. This was not Stidyen nor Tefa anymore. This man held a level of power Chandra had never before sensed, and she truly felt outclassed. She now feared for her life. All concern for Lyssa fled as she tried to mentally prepare for this battle.

She clapped her hands, and her darkwood staff appeared in her left hand, the glowing purple orb vigorously swirling pure shadow.

"The village must be released from your terror at once."

He threw back his head laughing. Chandra felt the heat of anger rise as he mocked her.

He slammed the butt of his staff on the ground, and beams of many colors flashed and surrounded him.

Shite. Elementalist, she said under her breath. Now she knew she was in trouble. The spells were simple but highly effective.

"Word of advice, whore. Leave this place or your ashes will fertilize this soil."

A strange calm came over her. She was already resigned to her death; anything else didn't matter now.

Do what you can, Malhrun—fast.

The shade sped across the field toward the mage, but not fast enough. He seemed to push the air in front of him with his right hand, causing an almost blinding ball of light to appear. He lifted his hand, and the light hung over his head like a bright halo, effectively keeping Malhrun at bay.

At the same time, Chandra began to weave the shadows into a veil of darkness, trying to conceal her location.

He stepped forward, taking the staff with both hands and began to spin it in front of him quickly, forming a bright shield of light. She formed a purple-black ball of darkness and threw it at him. It hit the shield and detonated, sending the mage back two steps, while she tried to quickly summon her shadow demon. Her timing was poor. While using her will and gathering shadows, he threw a fireball, just missing and detonating behind her. The concussion was such that it broke her concentration, but far enough away not to burn her.

She sidestepped to cast another ball of darkness, but uncovered herself from her veil. He saw the opportunity and pointed his staff. A blinding, crackling bolt of lightning surged toward her and found its mark, barely. She reflexively moved her staff to defend, which took the brunt of the bolt yet remained intact, sending it spinning to the ground.

Chandra felt the searing pain of heat and paralyzing numbness of electricity course through her body, throwing her to the ground.

"You should have listened, whore. Perhaps you should return to your books in the city and leave the spells to real mages." He began to move in, sending a torrent of icy cold toward her.

She saw the effect racing in, knowing she would now die, but the torrent miraculously deflected away from her and back toward the mage, which he barely dodged.

'...STAND, MISTRESS.'

She quickly scrambled to her feet and prepared to throw another ball of darkness, but her arm was still numb, hanging limply at her side, refusing to move.

He advanced, the halo of light above him forcing Malhrun to retreat and leaving her completely defenseless.

He knew she was done for, so he clapped his hands over his head, resonating thunder all around and knocking her to the ground once more. He slowly stepped toward her, madness in his eyes and breathing heavily. He held his hands apart, and Chandra saw the blue-white crackling of powerful electricity coursing between his hands. She covered her face with her arm to weakly shield her eyes from the blinding light.

"I told you, bitch, you are no match." He raised his hands to throw the bolt and finish her completely.

Suddenly, the electricity disappeared, and his eyes opened wide as the point of a black dagger protruded from his throat. Then another protruded from his forehead as he slowly crumbled to the ground.

"Don't you dare call my sister a bitch." Lyssa stood behind him, the blood from the mage's skull dotting her pale face.

Chandra let her body fall to the ground, exhausted.

Lyssa stood over her fallen sister, exhaustion and pain in her eyes.

"Only I can call you a bitch." She smiled. "Let's get you up, sister. You've had a rough day."

'...well, at least you tried, coinmonger.'

Talk of the town:

"Those two lasses in the corner last night? Loud as thunder an' twice as fierce. Looked like they hadn't seen each other in years."

"Aye, they laughed, shouted, near scared off anyone thinkin' o' botherin' 'em. Made Belva, here, right jealous with all their carryin' on."

–Garran before he got slapped

"You see them white-haired lasses last night? Gods, they were somethin' fine to look at."

"Aye made half the menfolk forget their mugs. I'd buy either of 'em a drink meself."

— two Merchants Road girls

Of Youth and Fools

"I hate elementalists," Chandra told her sister angrily. "It's the light. It confounds my shadow weaving. Not to mention Malhrun—useless, completely useless." She was annoyed beyond belief.

Chandra shook her head with disgusted grumblings as the shadow mares kept their slow, steady pace.

Lyssa snuck a smug, knowing glance at her sister. She knew if her daggers hadn't found the back of that hedge mage's skull, Chandra wouldn't be sitting with her right now. True, she could tease her as she did when they were younger, but now, understanding the feeling of failure, she let her sister simply stew as they rode on.

"And this isn't the first time this has happened," she continued. "Stidyen tried to do this to me as well."

'...if you will remember, mistress...'

She cut off the little shade mid-sentence. "Yes, yes. I know, Malhrun. I know."

Up until this battle, Chandra had never realized just how important Malhrun had become. It had become more than a mere friend. It was a part of her; her eyes, her wisdom. It was as if it were an extension of her being. What it knew, she knew. What it saw, she saw.

'...no apologies, mistress. We are one. Never fear.'

This time, it spoke loud enough for Lyssa to overhear.

Chandra looked at the glowing red eyes atop her mare's head. "You did that on purpose, you impish puff of smoke," she said, smiling at it.

"Chandra? Apologize?" She threw her head back, laughing. "I never thought I would ever see the day."

Chandra's glare could have withered a rock. If they had still been children, Lyssa would have continued to antagonize her, but as she once heard her father say to her mother, *With age comes wisdom,* and she let it go.

"Sister, you know I would never have let that insufferable, aggravating lout harm you…much," Lyssa said with a knowing grin.

Chandra shook her head at her sister's needling. After their past disagreement, she concluded that she deserved at least that much.

"Alright, sister, I guess I earned that one." She looked at Lyssa and asked, "Can you forgive me? I honestly never meant—"

"I forgive you, Chandra. I know you meant no harm." She smiled sadly. "What happened to us happened. There is no denying it, nor can we ever forget it. Most of all, I don't think either one of us wants to revisit it—ever." She paused, reflecting. "And I hope you can forgive me for striking you, sister. I know you require what little brains you have to cast those spells." She laughed loudly.

Chandra wanted to be angry, but she knew that this was just Lyssa. This was who she was, and this was also why she loved her so damn much.

"Yes, sweet sister, I do forgive you. I must say, though, you should work on your strength. If I hadn't tripped over Malhrun, I wouldn't have fallen down."

'…*but mistress. You didn't…*'

"Not now, Malhrun. The sisters are speaking."

Once again, they had become sisters, the anger and the words now forgotten like smoke in the wind.

The late-night moon had been replaced by thick clouds, bringing with it the sweet smell of impending rain. A mild breeze tossed their cloaks and hair, yet brought a calming inner peace, making both sigh in unison. Realizing what they had done, they both laughed.

They continued to tease and pick at each other as they followed the road south past Kelligan Town, or what remained of it, until they came upon Wortham.

"Sister, you will love this town," Lyssa told her sister. "The tavern is run by the loveliest family. There is a little girl, Tahny, she is the sweetest little thing, and her father, Vergil, how he loves her."

"Why, sister, I don't believe I've ever seen you so excited about seeing other people in my life." She chuckled, but Lyssa paid little attention, eager to see them once more.

With the coming of daylight, their mares dissipated, much to Chandra's disdain. Now she'd have to walk the rest of the way, something she hated above all else. A smiling Lyssa gave her a sideways glance, daring her to complain. Seeing the annoyance on Chandra's face, Lyssa skipped ahead, spinning and laughing while the mage frowned and grumbled the rest of the way.

The clouds began to look angrier and threatened rain, though the two felt it would still be a while off. Just before they reached the tavern, Lyssa stopped, allowing Chandra to catch up. Once she finally arrived, the still laughing Lyssa brushed the dust and dirt from her sister's dress, straightened her circlet and kissed her on the nose.

"There. Beautiful as ever," she said, giggling.

Chandra scowled as she wiped off the kiss and continued on to the tavern.

The tables outside were empty, and there seemed to be very few patrons about, so they took their seats, Lyssa now excited with anticipation. Sure as the sun rises, Tahny came out to ask about her visitor's needs. Lyssa hid her face under her hood and asked that Chandra do the same.

"Greetings, travelers, might I get ye some food or drink taday?"

Lyssa turned to the girl, face still covered, and in a low voice said, "Plum wine, and take this to your father." She handed her a tiny jingling pouch. "If he says to take it back, then you keep it. Our secret."

She looked at the hooded person in complete surprise. "Lyssa?" Tahny asked excitedly, "Is that you?" Lyssa turned and removed her hood.

Tahny squealed with joy, wrapping her arms around her and giving her a big hug. "I missed you so much. I'm so happy you're here."

"Ohh, and I missed you too. I was telling my sister, here, about the cutest girl in the entire kingdom." She motioned to Chandra to show herself.

Chandra pulled back her hood. Tahny's face fell as she looked at Chandra, confused. She didn't know what to say. Both girls looked exactly the same, something Tahny had never seen before.

"Hello, little one. My name is Chandra. What is yours?" she asked, smiling.

Still confused, Tahny did a double-take trying to understand what was going on.

"We're identical twins. Well, not really identical," Lyssa said, laughing warmly. "You see, my sister has a special…gift." She winked at Chandra. "Would you like to see?"

Tahny nodded excitedly. "Show me, Chandra. Show me."

Chandra looked to the sky and tapped her cheek. "Now, what sort of special thing can I show a pretty little girl such as yourself. Hmmm."

Tahny sat almost buzzing.

"Ahhh, I know," she said, pointing a finger to the sky. "Watch carefully."

It started slowly at first. A tiny wisp of smoke crept from her finger, slowly getting thicker. Tahny's eyes went wide with wonder as the spark turned into a tiny flame. The little girl's mouth opened in awe of the spectacle. Then, whoosh, the flame turned to a pillar of fire, shooting high into the sky. She laughed for joy and clapped her hands until Chandra extinguished her creation.

"So, what do you think? Did you like that?"

Tahny ran across to Chandra and wrapped her arms around her. "That was beautiful." She stepped back, fingers interlaced excitedly. "Do some more. Do some more."

Chandra laughed and told her, "I can't right now, sweet girl. People don't really understand magic, and it might scare them away."

Tahny looked around. "Okay, but you have to do that again later, okay?"

Chandra hugged the little girl, "I promise."

She ran back inside, overjoyed.

"Why, sister. I'm surprised at you, hugging her like that. I never knew you liked children." She had a look of amazement, which made Chandra laugh.

"Neither did I. She's so sweet. I can see why you like her."

"Ahhh, my friend, welcome back. I missed you." Vergil left the tavern with a smile on his face, arms wide to hug Lyssa. His wide grin was warm and welcoming, as was his friendly embrace.

"Vergil," she said, hugging the man, "how are you?"

He looked at Chandra while saying to Lyssa, "I'm fine. Fine. And who might this lovely lady be?" he said, curious about the new visitor.

"Vergil, this is my twin sister, Chandra," she said proudly. "We just recently found each other after many years apart."

"It is a pleasure to meet you, Vergil. That is a very cute little girl you have there," she said.

"Thank you. You're too kind," he said, hand over his heart and bowing his thanks. "Please sit, sit. I'll bring drinks. I have my finest for you, young lady," he said to Lyssa, "and for you?"

Chandra said politely, "I will take your finest wine if you please."

He walked off to retrieve their refreshments while the sisters sat down, both smiling at the warm, friendly reception.

"I did not lie, did I, sister?" She beamed a proud smile.

"You most assuredly did not. They are wonderful."

He returned with their drinks and set them down on the table, then excused himself, saying he had other patrons to tend to.

Vergil paused, "Oh, before I leave, Tahny wanted me to tell you she has something special to show you." He winked and then left.

The twins toasted to a successful contract, though not without a sarcastic comment from Lyssa, who "just couldn't help herself."

As they reviewed the duel with the hedge mage, several men, some guards and some commoners, entered the tavern speaking of their travels while laughing.

Tahny came running out just as a guard stepped into the doorway, accidentally knocking the girl over.

"There, there, now. Have a care, little one," he said, helping her up. He gave the girl a pat on the bottom, but Lyssa caught an unsettling smirk from this guard. She almost stood to confront the man, but instead only met Tahny halfway, who was excitedly yelling, "Look, look, look."

With a proud grin, she spun around and around, showing Lyssa the new dress her father had gotten her.

Just then, the rain began to fall. Slowly at first, then gradually harder until it became a full-on downpour, forcing them to all run inside. Shaking the wet from their hands, the sisters selected a table, though not on the far wall where Lyssa preferred. They removed their capes and got comfortable.

Still in her new dress, Tahny continued to serve food and drinks, though there were only four patrons now. The guards in the back had begun to drink more heavily and were now becoming louder. There was a low wall to her back with another just like it across the narrow room. As usual, Lyssa sat, feet upon the table, flagon at her feet, pipe lit and well in hand.

"Oh, sister, must you—a pipe? Mother would make you chew soap and send you to your room," she said, trying to wave away the drifting cloud.

Lyssa chuckled, "Then it's a good thing she's not here now, isn't it?" Chandra just shook her head and took another sip of wine.

More travelers entered and sat close to the door. They were soaked from head to toe and dripping, soaking the floor. Tahny took their orders and left for the kitchen, nearly slipping and falling down.

After several drinks, the sisters grew weary from the excitement of the duel and their long trip. They asked Vergil if there were rooms available, to which he allowed them his finest, free of charge. Lyssa tried to pay him, but he steadfastly refused, citing that they were more like family than friends and he wouldn't hear another word of it.

It wasn't like their home, being bereft of finery, but the bed was comfortable, nonetheless, allowing for a peaceful sleep.

When morning came, they sat at a table where Tahny brought them bread and cheese. She had an eager look on her face, hoping Chandra would do something else special. Chandra told her that she would still do it, but only later, when they were ready to leave. She didn't want to scare her father, to which she informed them that her father wasn't afraid of anything. She left with a huge, proud smile.

Soon, the time had come for them to return home. Lyssa hugged Vergil and Tahny and said goodbye, but unbeknownst to Vergil, she left a small pouch of gold coins under her pillow and a note telling him that he should try harder if he didn't want her to help them out. She didn't sign it, leaving nothing more than a tiny cat's face.

Once outside, Tahny waited patiently next to a tree, still hoping Chandra would do something special.

"Please, please, please, Chandra." She pouted, forcing Chandra to comply or break the little girl's heart.

"Alright. Would you like simple or difficult?" She smiled warmly at her.

"Umm, difficult," she said, grinning and clapping her hands.

"Alright. Stand between us and plug your ears."

Lyssa had no idea what her sister was about to do, so she pulled Tahny close and plugged her own ears as well.

Chandra looked around to make sure no one was nearby, then raised her hands over her head and loudly spoke the incantation, "Astrix Fulminar!"

A huge, bright bolt of blue-white electricity flew from her outstretched hands high into the sky with a deafening boom.

The sound scared both Lyssa and Tahny, making them nearly fall to the ground. Eyes wide with excitement, Tahny leaped into the air, squealing, grabbing Chandra in a huge hug, and not wanting to let go.

Vergil came running out of the tavern, two swords in hand. "By all that's good, what happened?" he yelled, searching for the origin of the noise.

Tahny and Lyssa began to laugh as her father had forgotten to pull on his boots and was trudging through mud and manure barefoot.

"All is fine, Vergil. I was just showing your daughter what lightning was." Chandra said, smiling and sneaking a sideways glance at Tahny.

He looked to the sky only to find that there wasn't a single cloud to be seen, then looked at Chandra, puzzled, waiting for an explanation.

"I'll explain another day, my friend. Until then, let me suggest looking under the pillow in our room. We left you a little surprise." She gave him an impish grin, and they began their trip back home, waving goodbye to the wonderful family.

They followed the road toward Tantyn, agreeing that they would bypass it completely. It brought about far too much pain, and neither wanted to see the tragedy that had shaped their lives.

Once south of Tantyn, it had become dark enough for Chandra to summon her shadow mares, which made traveling much faster. After a few more hours, they began to see the glowing yellow lights of Bakerston, where they would spend the night, then leave out early for home.

The town was not unlike Hazelwood, a small farming village, but with a trader's square and more shops. From what they could see, there were just a few guards wearing the tabards of the King's Talons. Lyssa raised her hood over her head and directed Chandra to do the same. There was danger here, and neither wanted a taste of it tonight.

"Talons? Here? That makes no sense," Lyssa said to her sister, concerned.

"What are Talons, sister? A mercenary guild?" She saw the worry in Lyssa's eyes and became worried herself.

"No, they're the personal guards of the king. But why are they so far south? They should be guards from the First or Second Guards instead." Lyssa's eyes were now squinted, trying to gather information in the darkness.

Knowing that her sister was the like a cat in the night, Chandra followed, spells at the ready.

"Have great care, sister," she warned, "Ashby and I encountered these men in Caer Bryndwyck once. They may seem charming on the outside, but she told me they have far-reaching authority and can basically do whatever they please."

Chandra nodded her head and followed Lyssa's lead. They saw a sign over the door to the Bridge and Barrel tavern and inn and decided this would be as good a place as any for the night.

Once inside, the laughter and bawdy tales hit them like a stone wall. Smoke, stale ale and wine permeated the entire room. It seemed clean enough, at least cleaner than some Lyssa had visited in other towns, but the seating here was unlike the others.

To one side, it was tight and warm, lined with high-backed wooden booths darkened by age, each one scarred by knives and elbows; cramped timber tables filled the rest of the room, far enough apart not to fall over others yet close enough that travelers brushed shoulders whether they meant to or not. To the rear stood a set of large rectangular tables, two men seated at each, laughing and cursing. A half-wall separated the guards from the rest of the rabble, who seemed to only care about their own business.

Lyssa and her sister found seating at a table next to the half-wall; nicks, cuts and symbols deeply carved almost as a warning. The ale maid brought them their drinks, then hurriedly scurried away as if afraid of the guards. As usual, Lyssa's boots crossed on top of the table, her ale next to them, but this time there was no pipe. She needed her concentration tonight. No one seemed to pay any attention to the sisters, who kept to themselves yet maintained a wary eye on their surroundings.

When the girls spoke, they leaned in close and only spoke in low tones.

"Not a good place, it seems, sister." Chandra looked nervous.

Lyssa let out a grunt of amusement. "I've been in worse, dear sister. There was this tavern in…" She was cut off but a mug that had been thrown against the half-wall behind Chandra. It splashed ale, but with none getting on either of them.

Lyssa's eyes narrowed as she glanced at the guards, sizing up future prey. Her blood began to boil; this was her element, and she loved it. Chandra could see the dangerous grin on her face and placed a warning hand on her sister's arm to calm her. Lyssa glanced quickly at Chandra, understood the touch and sat back, trying to force herself to relax.

Then, like words from beyond the grave, Chandra heard it, the voice that had burned itself into her brain from years past.

"Oi, I remember this one time me an' Garth, here, takes down this country hovel near Hazelwood. Didn't know what was what but th' cap'n says we gotta get even fer them killin' Randal."

Her face turned red, and her fists clenched. Lyssa saw her sister's ire, the heat in her eyes, and asked, "Chandy? What is it, sister?"

Chandra stayed silent, listening to his words.

"Well, when we gets done slaughterin' th' farmers we finds these two young things in the room, cowerin'." The other three guards, also listening to the tale, begin to add their ideas on what Garth should have done.

The closer he came to the ending, the angrier Chandra became.

"Sister, by Velkhar's bollocks, what is wrong?" She was desperate to know.

Chandra leaned close and said, "Claw and Fang, keep them close. We're about to get our sweet revenge." Lyssa's hands cautiously reached for her blades, easing them out slowly, ready to act if her sister needed. As they were readied, Lyssa watched as Chandra's face suddenly went blank, no emotion, not even a twitch.

Then came the final words; this time, Lyssa heard them as well.

"We takes 'em an' Renn slams one on the bed, but me an' Garth takes this one. Damn hair, white as snow it was. Anyway, I knocks her head an' Garth kicks her bum." They started laughing.

Chandra stood calmly yet gracefully and turned to the guards who had not yet seen her.

Not a single person in the tavern paid attention to her.

"So we takes 'em inta th' woods an' starts really poundin' on 'em. Well, after 'bout two er three days we gets tired an' leaves th' sack o' meat on th' road ta die." They all laughed as if it were great fun. They had no idea that death had just come to claim its vengeance.

"Sister, sit. You will know when I require help." Her voice was cold, even and dripping with venom.

Chandra stepped into the entrance of the room, waiting to be noticed.

"Oi, lads, now what be this?" He laughed.

"Your story? It seems a touch…off, methinks." Chandra's voice was cold as winter.

"Off! Whatcha know 'bout off? Ya wasn't there. Now run along for we bang on yer head a bit, too." He looked at each man, laughing. The others tipped their mugs and beat the table, cursing this woman.

She looked at the man called Garth.

"You had a cut on your forehead that bled badly." She looked at the storyteller. Oh, she knew this man…all too well. "And you...Kinneth, I believe. Your...bang, was it? Extraordinary. Was more like a child's slap than a punch."

Their eyes widened, puzzled.

"How ya know our names, bitch? We ne'er seen ye afore." There seemed to be just a hint of fear in his words. The laughs and grins became more serious as the others began to glance at each other, trying to understand what was happening.

Chandra slowly removed her hood. Their faces went white, their breath gone. It was her...and they knew it.

"Now, gentlemen, I don't believe you realize just how much trouble you are actually in." Her voice was now as kind as a wildcat's growl.

Two of the other men stood and tried to advance on her. Their eyes went wide with shock as if from nowhere, two shining black daggers cartwheeled silently through the air, striking them in their foreheads and sending both falling back to the wall behind them.

Still, the tavern didn't notice.

"You see, Garth, Kinneth, my sister didn't like how your friends treated me." Lyssa slipped past her sister and removed her hood. There were now two with snow white hair. They had no idea what to do. Confusion, anger and terror encompassed their faces. She slowly advanced and recovered her daggers, wiping the blood on her victims' faces. Looking at Chandra, she smiled and, stepping past, kissed her cheek.

"Don't be long, sister. I'm still thirsty." She grinned, turning to the two terrified guards as she continued past Chandra. Her sister's eyes never left Garth and Kinneth, never blinked.

"Now, boys, I require retribution, but I think I'll leave the method up to you." She remained stone-faced, her voice sweet as cane and looking from man to man.

"Well, I don't hear any ideas." She was becoming impatient.

They glanced at one another, truly terrified.

She raised her finger, and a wisp of shadow began to swirl around her hand to her elbow, eyes never leaving either.

"P-p-punch me gob ifn ya needs to, mum, hard as ye can." He hoped she would take him seriously.

Chandra laughed. "I do love a good jest, but no. I'm afraid that's not nearly good enough. Don't you remember? You beat me for three whole days—both of you—over...and...over. And you laughed." A smile came over her face. Kinneth knew they were done for and soiled his breeches.

"Oh, I nearly forgot." She looked down. "Oh, Malhrun? Would you be a dear and see that Kinneth here doesn't move? I think he would like to see what sort of fun he's in for."

'...yes, mistress.'

Though there was light, it was still dim enough for the little shade to wrap its freezing tendrils of shadow around Kinneth. Tears began to stream down his face, and he silently mouthed; *No, please no.*

"Have no fear. This will be over shortly." She let out a short, amused laugh.

Witnessing the whole exchange and now terrified, Garth said, "I 'pologize, m'lady. Really, I do. If'n ya wants, take me bollocks. Take me arm, take what ya wants. Just don't kill me. Please, don't kill me." She gave him a charming, toothy grin.

"As I recall, I begged for the opposite. I *wanted* you to kill me, to free me from the pain you inflicted. And what did you do?" She paused for an answer. In a growl, she said, "What...did...you...do?"

He began to cry, body spasming with each sob.

The shadows swirled from her arm, drifted and surrounded his neck, squeezing ever so slightly.

"I laughed." More sobs. "I fuckin' laughed." The water ran down his leg and onto the floor.

She released her strands. "Oh, aye, you did. You laughed. But now, since you've begged for your life, I shall do for you as you did for me."

Her hands came together, a roiling ball of thick shadow gathering in between, then she sent it drifting in his direction. It floated slowly, yet gently, surrounding him, then disappeared…into him. His eyes rolled back in his head, mouth opened wide in a silent scream. His death came slowly and painfully. In his mind, he was being beaten… repeatedly… by shadowy demons…over and over. Chandra's wicked laugh was all he heard as his final breath left him. Then she turned to face Kinneth.

After seeing his friends' surreal deaths, his body sagged. He now resigned himself to an equally painful death.

"Now, Kinneth, my dear, whatever should I do with you, I wonder?" she asked coldly.

He shook his head. "Just end it, witch. Have at ye." Tears streamed down his face and dripped onto the table.

"Malhrun, dear, is there anything you can think of that I can do to set things right?" she asked her shadowy friend.

'…Yes, mistress. Receive your stones price.'

"Ah, my dear friend, you know me so well." She smiled warmly, and it blinked in return, seemingly happy.

"You, Kinneth, also beat me. Do you remember?" she said, her face in a snarl.

He nodded. "Aye."

"Do you remember what you said when I begged you to kill me?" She took a step toward him.

"I said, I'll not kill ye, but th' bleedin' ants will," he said, drool now dripping from his mouth. The man looked to be on the cusp of sheer madness.

"Yes, yes, you did. So, my friend, those ants? Well, did you know that they never touched me? Unfortunately, I cannot say the same for you." She gave a sweet, warm smile and batted her eyes at him.

Again, her hands came together, the shadowy cloud, the bodily invasion, but this time the shadows inside him moved, like thousands of tiny ants under his skin…crawling…eating…from the inside out. His body paralyzed in a silent scream of terror, shadowy ants crawling from mouth to nose, from nose to ears. Then, silence. The shadows disappeared. She took a deep sigh and turned to Lyssa, who saw the entire ordeal.

"Shall we, sister?" She knew she needed to get Chandra far from here, and fast.

Then, the raucous laughter ended, the loud jokes and bawdy songs silenced as all eyes turned to the two people facing the dead guards.

No one saw their faces, yet all knew the guards were dead, in what looked to be a most horrific death.

"Do something, sister. Get us out of here." Lyssa whispered, now becoming aware of the crowd beginning to move toward them.

Chandra whispered. "Hold my arm, sister. I'm about to make us famous."

Lyssa held on tightly, not knowing what her plan was, when suddenly, Chandra chanted as she raised her arm, swinging it slowly around in a circle…"Umbra'kal…VEIL'DARUS!"

The tavern suddenly went dark, a shadowy veil covering the entire room.

The girls turned and headed for the door, seeing clearly yet being completely veiled from others' eyes.

Once at the door, Chandra stopped, telling Lyssa, "Now watch, sister. This is my favorite part."

She looked back into the room and spoke in an ominous tone, "Beware the night, for the Cat and Shadow lurk."

They both broke into wicked laughter as they started back down the road toward home. Once past the vendors' stands, still laughing, they came upon the Talons, who had been searching homes on this side of the town.

"Halt. State your business." The man who stood before them was in full plate regalia, his golden armor gleaming in the moonlight. He motioned for two other guards, both also in full regalia but in silver plate, to assist him.

"Again, I say, state your business, ladies." He was gentle and courteous with a hint of danger. This was not a man to be trifled with.

Chandra squeezed Lyssa's arm and spoke. "M'lord, we lost our horses on the road to ruffians near Tantyn. We've been trudging this road all night trying to find the Merchants Road." She wiped her nose as if crying. Lyssa lowered her head and sniffled, faking a sob. "Please, help us. They removed us from the tavern here, very rudely; no one would help." Again, she sobbed.

"Have no fear, m'lady." He touched under her chin, Chandra looking him in the eyes as sweetly as she could.

He turned to one of his men and said, "Spare a horse, a light one, and pass it on to these beautiful ladies, if you will. Give them directions, then let them pass." He bowed low and said, "And have a care, ladies. The roads can be treacherous at night."

Chandra curtsied and said, "You are a fine, fine man, m'lord. I shall tout your kindness in The Crown upon arrival."

A horse was ushered to them and, after the guard helped them mount, they started down the road for home.

After traveling for some time, Lyssa said, "Chandy, that was not a good idea, sister." Lyssa looked back nervously to see if they were being followed. "The Talons are not some band of rogues. If they knew who we were, we'd be finished."

Chandra laughed. "What was it you said yesterday? Oh, yes. It's a good thing they're not here then, isn't it?" Lyssa just shook her head, both laughing and discussing Chandra's vengeance.

Lyssa learned tonight that Chandra had an evil side she would never have expected. She didn't just kill those men; she literally scared them to death. She never knew her sister wielded power of that magnitude, which both impressed her and made her a bit afraid. If she could manipulate the very shadows around her, then she could do anything she wanted. The possibilities were unreal.

"It's over, sister." She gave her sister a squeeze of affection. "You've gotten your vengeance."

"What are our words?" Chandra asked.

They both spoke at the same time, the same words and both with a loving smile.

"No one will ever hurt us again."

If that were only true....

Of Lies and Deceit

The coin clinked as he slid their payment across the table with a smile.

"Well done," the assassin said. "The contract is settled."

He sat back in his chair and glanced at the two.

"I take it your…sisterly…differences are settled now?" It was a sincere question this time with no malice.

"Family matters are seldom simple, my friend." Lyssa gave a wry grin to her former teacher. He looked at Lyssa as if to tell her not to trifle with what she didn't know and received a challenging look in return. It was at that moment they both realized…they'd reached a personal crossroads.

He brushed it off with a sigh, leaned back, eyes distant.

"Now, about that little item we discussed earlier." He smiled. "The coins you brought me pointed directly to the source of my troubles."

Lyssa glanced at Chandra, then back at the assassin waiting patiently for him to continue.

"And now I know where the next piece lies and who holds it."

Lyssa sighed. "Aaannnnd?"

He nodded once. "I have a plan."

That was all he said.

'…will you try again, I wonder?'

'…he is here, mistress.' Malhrun could feel him but couldn't see him.

Chandra knew. *Be still, little one.* She slowly moved forward as if gliding on air.

The night was cool, and a light breeze blew her long black hair against her cheek. But there was an even cooler stillness, and she knew.

She looked to the moon. The glow made her face glow unnaturally, and she slowly closed her eyes as if she were basking in the sun.

Then she felt him. He was not close enough to touch, but she felt the cold life force he emanated.

"Aren't we a pair?" came a sly voice from behind her.

She slowly lowered her head and turned a sideways gaze at him. "Yes." She gave a sultry grin. "We are indeed."

"If I didn't know any better, I'd say you were dreaming."

She turned, facing him. "And how do you know I wasn't dreaming of someone like you?" she asked, looking into his eyes. She noted the barely perceptible, piercing golden glow emanating from them. *Ahh, it IS him*, she thought.

"It honors me to know I am part of such a lovely lady's dream," he said. *Hmm, this one is…very…different,* he thought. He moved closer. She was lovely. Almost as lovely as…

"The moon is wondrous tonight, is it not?" She interrupted his thoughts. "So…bright."

'*…well played, mistress,*' the tiny shadow whispered.

Away with you. But stay close, she scolded.

Malhrun moved imperceptibly to a bush and waited quietly.

"Certainly." He grinned. "But how rude of me." He reached for her hand, which she proffered. "My name is Lord Elkvahr. I am but a humble vassal of our great king." He leaned in to kiss it. It smelled of pine and gardenia and was mind-numbingly intoxicating. "Please, tell me yours."

Chandra pretended to blush. "I am Alyce. Alyce Soryn, lord."

"Oh, please, not, lord." He feigned indignance. "Davin. For you, it is Davin. Chandra is an absolutely lovely name. It uniquely suits you," he said.

She almost believed him. *What is your game, Velkhar? And where are you keeping that damned tome?*

'*…mistress, it is the Cat.*'

Lyssa brushed her hand over the bush, startling Malhrun. He could never understand how a mortal had the ability to sneak up on a shadow, especially a shadow such as he.

"Why, mistress Alyse, I see you've managed to capture another lost soul," Lyssa said in a joking tone.

Davin looked at Lyssa. She was clad in a long, light blue dress that glided along the ground. Her long brown hair was unevenly cut in front, and her twist had begun unraveling. She tried to walk like a lady but was failing quite badly.

Ahh, the hired help. I suppose it's fitting, he thought to himself.

"And who do I have the pleasure of meeting? Your handmaiden?" he asked with an undertone of sarcasm.

Chandra sighed, almost exasperated. "This, Davin," she began, looking disdainfully at Lyssa, "is truly my…handmaiden."

Lyssa caught the hint and tried to curtsy, but stumbled. Trying to regain her composure, she said, "My…sir…lord." She feigned embarrassment.

Chandra almost laughed, remembering all the times she tried to teach her sister a courtly courtesy, only to watch her run away in failure.

"Oh, by the gods, remove yourself," Chandra hissed. "You're embarrassing me, not to mention the fool you're making of yourself. Now, away with you." She waved a dismissive hand while turning back to Davin. "I'm so sorry, Davin. She can be a clumsy oaf sometimes."

Davin grinned warmly at Chandra. "Have no fear, lady. We've all played the fool once in our lives." Chandra took a breath, put a hand to her chest and feigned disbelief. They both laughed.

Lyssa pretended to be mortified. "Lady Alyce, your mother wants you home—NOW." She tried to hide tears of embarrassment as she covered her face and ran away, sobbing. As she passed Malhrun, she winked with a devious smile on her face.

"I am so sorry, Davin. My mother is ailing, and I must tend to her," she lied.

"I completely understand, lady." He was impressed. "Perhaps we can meet again? I can send a carriage to shuttle you to my manor if you'd like."

"Oh my, but we are being a bit forward, are we not, my lord?" She pretended to be taken aback.

"If you prefer not, I'm not opposed to meeting here again at your leisure, of course," he said. *She…is…intriguing*, he thought. *I must see her again. She will work perfectly. Now, how can I arrange this?*

Chandra stood silently for a second, then grinned ever so slightly. "I would love to see your manor…Davin," she said in an almost sultry tone. "I will be here, waiting on the morrow at dusk for my magical ride." It sounded silly to her mind, but by the look of appreciation he gave her, it must have worked.

Davin leaned in and kissed her proffered hand once again. "Until tomorrow then," he said, smiling as he turned and left. *That was easier than I had anticipated.*

Chandra began walking past Malhrun. *Watch him.*

'…yes Mistress.'

'…are you doing what I think, tallyman?'

The Broken Dagger tavern in Morowyck was warm and quiet. Rain tapped gently at the windows. A low fire crackled in the hearth, casting flickers across stone walls and tired travelers. The room was abuzz with laughter and conversation. At a table near the far corner was a group of men drunkenly singing a bawdy song of a serving wench and a cobbler.

The fire to her right warmed her as she sat. She was full of energy tonight, but she had to wait for her sister. There was news, and she had to hear it.

A minstrel started to strum his lute near the bar and sang a tale of a dark woman who had magical powers and who moved like smoke.

The hooded, dark figure sat with a mug of spiced mead by her boot, muddied from the road and propped up on her table. Her eyes were scanning the room like an owl searching for prey, sharp and dangerous. She calmly picked her nails with a sharp dagger of black steel, seemingly unconcerned.

Moved like smoke, Lyssa thought. *I move like smoke, like a smoky cat.* She shook her head and grunted to herself.

A tall woman entered the tavern and, as she slowly let down her hood, the songs stopped, and voices lowered. All eyes turned to her. She had long, black hair that draped below her cloak-clad shoulders, her skin, pale and silky as white velvet, but it was her eyes. Her eyes were gray as a fine steel blade and could cut just as easily. As she began to walk toward the hooded figure in the corner, hushed words began to be spoken, yet all eyes followed her graceful steps.

A man leaned and whispered to his friend, "She don't bloody walk. It's like she's…floatin' on air." The woman next to him must have thought he had been a little too appreciative because she looked at him in disgust and smacked him on the back of his head.

Hearing the comment and seeing the result, Chandra smirked and gracefully made her way to her sister.

"By the gods above, MUST you do that every time you walk into a room?" Lyssa asked, shaking her head.

She pulled off her cloak and carefully laid it over the chair across from her. Slowly, the conversations returned to normal, though many still kept a cautious eye on the lady. She waved for the tavern girl, who came almost running.

"Wine," she said softly, "something red perhaps, my dear."

"As you wish, m'lady," she nervously said, flashing a slight grin of appreciation.

The beautiful mage pulled a chair close, and as she sat, Lyssa said, "Clumsy...oaf, was it?"

She glanced at Chandra questioningly, a smirk across her lips.

"Overplayed?" Chandra asked her sister.

"Normally I'd say yes...but not this time," Lyssa said, resigned. "Just once, I'd like to play the beautiful courtier."

"Oh, my dear sister, you can't possibly believe that you could pass as a courtier," Chandra said, wryly, "especially with that silly brown hair. It makes you look like a boy."

Lyssa sneered at her sister, sticking out her tongue, and they both laughed. She smirked. "You definitely know how to make an entrance, though, I must say." She sipped her mead. "I'm not too fond of the black hair, I have to admit. It makes you look...old."

Chandra's eyes flashed venom at her sister. "How dare you? You churl." Her face softened, and she sighed. "Neither do I, but it was all I could manage in that short of time."

The girl returned with a dusty bottle and a chipped cup. She poured the dark wine and handed it to her, eyes staring as if enthralled. Chandra glanced at the young girl, gave her a slight grin and thanked her. The girl blushed, gave a slight giggle, and took her leave. She tipped her cup, closed her eyes, then leaned back and lightly shook her hair, her gray eyes catching the light like polished steel.

"Are we jealous, dear sister?" she said, winking at her.

Lyssa put her feet down and sighed, exasperated.

"Well...sister?" she began tersely. She leaned closer. "Did you find out anything?"

Chandra's grin was slow, sly...sharp as a knife in the dark.

She lifted the mug, sipped the sour wine and let the silence stretch as she gazed at the fire. A faint grimace curled her lips, more for her sister's benefit than the taste itself. She set the cup down with deliberate slowness, savoring the way Lyssa's patience thinned.

They had played this game before. Her voice became calm, kind... and venomous. "Chandra, dear, I'm annoyed. Do you recall what happened the last time I was annoyed?" Lyssa's eyes narrowed. Her steel irises glinted like bolts of lightning.

Oh, she surely remembered. Chandra and her sister were still children, and she had been continuously repeating every word Lyssa said, even though their mother had told her to stop. Waiting until Chandra wasn't looking, Lyssa scooped up a handful of mud and shoved it in her face, causing a bit to get into her mouth. Of course, Chandra, being the little princess, sat and cried, causing Lyssa to have to sit in a corner for half a day.

Chandra started to laugh. Lyssa sat back and did nothing more than smirk and sip her ale.

"Ohh, as you wish...sister," she said, sarcastically rolling her eyes. "You take all of the fun out of being dramatic."

She leaned closer to Lyssa and, in a muffled voice, said, "My dear sister...have I got news for you."

She glanced left and right. "We are about to do the impossible, my lovely sister. We are about to play the roles of a lifetime." She was smiling so broadly that Lyssa thought her face would split in two.

"Aaaand...." She said, motioning for her to continue. Lyssa was both curious and annoyed...and still waiting.

Chandra sighed and whispered, "Davin is..." she paused for effect, "Velkhar."

Lyssa sat still. Her eyes squinted as if she were trying to absorb the news.

Chandra looked nonplussed. "Um, you know. The deity? Velkhar?"

"Huh?" her sister said, sitting back as if unimpressed.

"That's it?" Chandra was perplexed. "Sister, we are about to face someone beyond mortal measure and 'huh' is all you have to say?"

Chandra was now incredulous. She had given the performance of a lifetime, and Lyssa was showing no emotion at all.

Concern covered her face. Her words came out measured, careful. "Have a care, sister," Lyssa warned hesitantly. "We are in the midst of playing a charade with someone more dangerous than any we've ever encountered," she took another gulp of mead, "not to mention he's a god." She stared at the mug, then glanced up and mumbled, "There's an excellent chance we may not walk away from this at all."

Lyssa's concern hardened into resolve. Her expression turned stone-faced, all business now, and it showed.

Chandra understood. She fell silent, the triumphant grin slowly dissipating.

"I'm sure he has the tome," she said with resignation. "So much so, I am staking my very life on it."

The tone in her voice showed her own resolve, and Lyssa knew at that moment there was no turning back. Her sister had always been headstrong, but only when she had a foolproof plan and only when she knew she had the upper hand.

And the gods knew, her plans NEVER failed, which had always been a sore spot for her.

Lyssa looked at her sister. Her face softened. "My dear sister, we have done many things, but nothing like this." She picked up her flagon, drinking deeply, then wiped her mouth with the back of her hand and leaned in closer.

"I love you, and you know I always will, which is why I would breathe my last breath for you," she assured Chandra. "So what plan do you propose?"

"Exactly," Chandra said cryptically. "Exactly."

Lyssa blinked and sat back.

"Exactly?" It was now her turn to be confused. "By Skippin's arse, what does that mean? *Exactly*."

Chandra grinned, raising her mug to toast.

Lyssa shook her head in confusion, raised her empty flagon and said, "I hope this is a good one. Our lives depend on it."

'*...I call.*'

They dragged Lyssa into the large hall, wrists bound, shoes dragging the stone. The torches hissed and smoked, throwing shadows that danced like watching eyes. They stood her up, her dress torn, exposing bleeding knees.

Lyssa remembered this game. Pure, unadulterated anger welled up in her. *'NEVER AGAIN!'* she thought. She started to struggle.

Calm. Patient. One false move ruins the hunt. Kitikithakis' voice was in her mind. *Sometimes, one must act the prey to lure the predator.*

She willed her muscles to relax. She began to sob, pretending that her legs felt heavy and tried to fall to the floor. The guards, with hands still under her arms, heaved hard and forced her to stand.

She quietly sobbed, "Lady, please. No, I beg of you."

Chandra stood at Davin's side, her hair now cropped short but still black, so like Lyssa's it was uncanny, but she didn't glance at her.

Davin's gaze slid between them, slow and measuring.

"What is the meaning of this, Alyse? Are you...deceiving me?" he asked, kindly but with danger in his voice.

Chandra tilted her head toward him, voice warm, almost intimate.

"Why no, my sweet.... As you can tell, this is my...nosey handmaiden." She shot an angry look at the sobbing woman.

A single brow arched, suspicion sharpening his grin.

"Ahh, your handmaiden," he said, still unsure.

"Stand, stupid girl," Chandra said angrily. "I told you what would happen the next time I caught you spying on me, didn't I?"

Davin chuckled, low yet still dangerously. "Spying?" he raised his brow. "Well, now…you know we can't have that. Stirring the pot is…unacceptable." His grin widened, revealing just a glint of teeth.

Chandra turned to him, ire still on her brow.

"My family has designs on whom my *husband* shall be, and they don't trust my judgment at all." She turned an evil grin toward Lyssa. "More's the pity I fear," she said, sweetly.

His eyes narrowed, the verdict suspended in the air between them. "You know what must be done." *A test….my sweet*, he thought.

"But of course. *One has to be sure.* Isn't that what you always say?" she said almost playfully.

He grinned. *My play, lady*, he thought.

Chandra's lips curled into something softer and more affectionate. She stared sadly at Lyssa, stepping closer until they were almost face-to-face.

"Little one," she said, her tone velvet and venom all at once, "all those years of following wherever I went, spying on me for mother…"

She stood, her hands rose, shadows curling between her fingers like smoke with a mind of its own.

"…Take your last breath, fool. There will be no more tomorrows."

The fog swelled, cold and suffocating, swallowing Lyssa's vision. She began to scream, to choke, her body contorting in sheer agony. The last thing she heard before the darkness took her tortured mind was Chandra's whisper, close enough to feel on her cheek, soft, gentle:

"I gotcha."

Lyssa crumbled to the floor, spasming one last time.

The guards, fighting fear, looked at each other and reached to collect Lyssa's limp and contorted body.

"Oh, leave her," Chandra said. The guards jumped, now fearing the lady's ire. "She's not going anywhere."

Davin regally pulled the sleeves of his tunic down. "The lady has spoken, gentlemen. It behooves you to move," he said, nodding approval.

With a grin of satisfaction, Davin offered his arm. Chandra entwined hers, and they began walking toward the large ornate doors of the dining room. *Now it's your play, lady.*

Without looking at her, he asked, "No more spies?"

She shook her head no.

"No more surprises?"

"My sweet, unless my sickly mother can walk, then we have nothing more to worry about," she said, leaning her head on his shoulder.

Bra...vo, sister. Well done. Now, please, hurry. This beast is turning my stomach, she thought.

'...now, you know that's not allowed.'

'...free play for me, it seems.'

She lay there on the cold floor; her breath so shallow as to be almost imperceptible. *Dammit, Chandra. Did you have to use* that *spell?*

After a few minutes, the effects began to wear off. Lyssa had been listening intently for any movement.

There was nothing.

Slowly, she began to move her body, piece by piece; first her fingertips, then her toes. Her knees were stiff, but they moved. She tried to move her arms, but her left was filled with a sharp pain. *Damn. Forget the pain. It's nothing.*

She slowly moved her head from side to side. No one nearby. The room was completely empty.

Staying low, she crept behind the giant dining table. It was the darkest corner of the room, near a window with large red brocade curtains. She quickly glanced outside to find that the moon had risen to its apex. The only lights that could be seen were the torches that lined the road and led away from the manor. *Ugh, must fix this arm.* There was pain when she tried to flex, but she put it out of her mind.

She hated the dress. It was far too large, too…poofy. *Skippin's bollocks, how does she wear these things?* It definitely wasn't her style. Quietly, she wriggled out of it, rolled it into a ball and hid it behind the curtain. She stretched and unrolled her pant legs to cover the dainty shoes she wore. She hated them, but in this case, they were highly effective. They slipped across the floor, making even less sound than her supple leather boots.

"Okay, now where would the study be?" she mumbled to herself, eyes darting left and right.

The lighting in the hallway was poor, which was a welcome sight. It would make sneaking much easier, especially if there was a sudden encounter. She darted to the hallway entrance near the far end of the table and peered down its dark length. Carefully surveying the hallway, she memorized possible hiding spots and quick exits. Deciding it was possible, yet dangerous, she darted to one dark doorway, clung low to the darkness, then darted to the next. Each door was quietly tested, each open room quietly surveyed. She came to a closed door; glowing orange light peeked from under it. *Could be it*, she thought. She darted behind the curtains across the hall from the large, ornate doors and listened.

"…and then I'll have the guards dump her in the river. No trace." It was Chandra. She sounded…smug. Gods, Lyssa hated that. She'd done it since they were children, especially whenever she'd won a challenge or had gotten her way.

"Of course, my dear. One can't be too careful, now can one?"

She was there with Davin. She began to feel concerned for her sister and anger that she had to be there with this…creature. The longer this took, the more danger she was in.

She tiptoed past the door, almost comically. Just down the hall was another door, candlelight seeping under it like a beacon. She drew nearer, keeping her ears perked just in case it was occupied. Placing her ear gently against the door, she listened. She could hear the crackling of a fire. No steps, no breathing, no speaking. She reached for the door lever when…

Someone sighed and moved the lever to exit. That caught her by surprise. Quickly, Lyssa stood and pressed her body against the door frame, making herself as small as possible. She had become a knot of energy coiled but restrained. Instinctively, her gleaming blade was in her hand, as if it were a claw naturally flexed.

The door creaked open, and a man stepped out, leaving it ajar. Lyssa slipped through the gap and pressed herself against the frame, breath shallow but steady, ready to strike if needed. She watched him move down the hall toward the dining room until he vanished from sight. Only then did she exhale, her pulse easing slightly. Moving swiftly, she slipped into the nearby study, the place she'd hoped to find the tome. Her eyes scanned the room, fingers rifling through scattered pages, open tomes, and scraps of notes.

Nothing—all this energy to find nothing. She gnashed her teeth in anger. *Dammit!*

Her mentor's voice invaded her mind. *To snare the prey, you must be as the prey.*

Exactly. *Now, where would I hide an important tome?*

She glanced around the room at all the possibilities.

There were no real sneaky places to hide it. She went to a desk and chair that was facing the hearth and sat. Becoming annoyed, she leaned on it and began to think. She was becoming increasingly agitated. Time was of the essence, and it was passing quickly.

Your body is the key. Relax. Be one with your surroundings. The ranger's words were soft and reassuring. *Only then will the prey appear.*

She sat back, exhaled slowly, closed her eyes and willed her body to relax. *Start where you are and work your way out.*

It took only seconds.

Her hand reached down under the very chair she was sitting on and found a tiny hook. She slid it from its catch, and a book fell to the floor. *Thank you, my friend. I can always count on you.*

The tome, bound in green cloth adorned with gold filigree, was unusually light for its size. *Light?! Is this even the right one?* Tucking it into the waist pack Chandra had given her, she was amazed because it was easily twice the size of the pack yet slipped inside.

And now comes the hard part, she thought.

Squinting and mumbling, she planned her escape. *"Down the hall past the dining area, through the south door and past the four corners, first left, not right, two doors, two guards and into the courtyard, tree, tree, and fence."* She shook her head. *"I don't like this. Far too many uncertainties."* She tended to mumble while she worked out problems, which made the assassin want to pull out his hair. It was one lesson that never really sank in.

She went to the door and peeked around the corner. Clear. She snuck out, keeping low but moving as quickly as she dared, into the dining area, moving quietly around the table, keeping her ears sharp for sounds. Then she sneaked into the dining entrance and looked past the shadows of the long hallway to the four corners. *Not good*, she thought. *Far too much light now.*

Her eyes darted around the room for any other possible exit. Nothing. *The curtains*, she thought, now moving quickly. Then…

A door opened from where she had come. Crouching low and hugging the darkest of shadows, she watched as Chandra exited the room and went into the dining area. Lyssa, now hiding behind the curtain as before, caught a glimpse of her sister passing, then heading down the corridor. Chandra made an almost imperceptible gesture with her hand, which Lyssa noticed. *Good girl.* A whisp of shadow began to emanate from her fingers and filled the hallway as she continued. Lyssa didn't know if Chandra had planned this or not, but leaped into the swirling shadow to follow her anyway. She easily passed the four corners, but instead of turning left, she turned right, and that was going to leave her uncovered and in plain sight, still with two guards ahead.

Damn!

She bolted to the first door. So little shadow. *No good.*

Then to the second. Not much better. She tried to cling to nearby shadows but realized she was still visible. Her daggers had been reflexively drawn, dark and razor-sharp. If she had to kill them, she would, but that was the last thing she wanted to do right now, as it would completely ruin her plan.

Just then, one guard turned toward her. She held her breath, keeping the daggers hidden, and hoped he didn't see her.

He returned to his watch. Then…

"Oi," he looked at his comrade and said, "Here comes the commander." The other guard looked around and saw nothing.

"Naw, he ain't."

"Sure, right there he is," said the first guard…who lifted his leg and then passed gas.

"What the…ya stinkin' arse-faced rag!" His mate gagged, stepped over and sent a mailed fist to his chest. Trying to wave the malodorous smell from his nostrils, he said, "I should drop ya where ya stands."

The other guard almost doubled over laughing.

Lyssa grinned, fighting desperately to stifle a laugh.

Now, I'm trapped, she thought.

Just behind the smelly guard, she saw what looked like two very small, very faint blinking red eyes. She blinked, trying to understand. What did she see?

Just then, the exit went black as an enormous plume of billowing shadow enveloped the guards. She heard a voice scream in her head, '…*MOVE!*'

She bolted without thinking, swiftly, silently.

The guards, who were terrified by the sudden darkness, quickly retreated into the hallway, leaving the exit clear. She knew if they raised the alarm, she would surely be caught or worse.

Lyssa knew there was no time. *Let them sound the alarm. I'll be long gone by then,* she thought as she bolted for the far wall. Finally reaching her first destination, she looked around at the chaos the alarm had caused. *Perfect. I have time to make my escape.*

Like a shadow in the night, she passed the first and second tree, then leaped to the top of the large stone wall. Glancing back, she hoped, prayed, Chandra was all right and sped toward the edge of the woods.

She stopped behind a thick pine, panting heavily, trying to catch her breath. The entire sequence took less than forty-five seconds, but she felt as if she'd run a league.

Then something cold touched her ankle. It made her feel…uneasy. She looked down and saw a small swirl of what looked like smoke, until it spoke.

'*…mistress knows not that I helped,*' Malhrun said in a whispering breath. '*… say nothing.*'

Lyssa now understood. "Oh, believe me when I say this stays between us. If your master ever found out, I'd never hear the end of it."

The tiny shade blinked once and was gone.

The tension in her body began to ease. In the arms of the forest, she knew she'd be safe. Using the dim moonlight to see, she began to wind her way through the trees toward the road. Suddenly, the sound of barking hounds and the yelling of orders pierced the night. Torches began to fill the courtyards and men, so many men, armed with all forms of weaponry, trooped out of the manor.

Fear now began to take hold. This was no longer an escape. It had regressed to survival. And she was incredibly skilled at survival.

Her eyes darted around quickly, trying to find the best, fastest exit. There. She saw a path that led through a small glade and opened out into a stream. She glanced back toward the manor. A large man emerged from between the two heavy doors, clad in dark brigandine armor. She concluded that he was the leader. She squinted, blinking several times to clear her vision. She felt like she knew this man, his size, his gait, that voice. It boomed when he gave orders. Something wasn't right, and she needed to find out why.

She followed the path to the edge of the stream, then followed it north in an attempt to come full circle back to the wall. Like a hunted fox, she hoped to draw the hounds and guards off her trail, at least long enough to be sure who this commander was. She stopped and cocked her head to one side. They were not too far off in the distance, but she knew there was still time—not much, but enough.

She bolted across the small field that separated the forest from the wall and hunkered low in the shadows. Hearing no movement nearby, she nimbly scaled the wall and peered over. He was gone. *Dammit.*

She decided to take a chance and head back toward the main gate, so she backtracked using the shadows as cover. She stopped just before the gate entrance and glanced back to ensure no one followed. Clear.

She turned back to the entrance and—she stared straight into the eyes of the assassin.

She gasped, stunned. No. This cannot be.

"Well, hello there, little Cat." His wide grin revealed white teeth surrounded by a black goatee. His eyes were piercing and menacing, but he held his hand.

They both stood slowly, eye to eye, each armed and each poised to strike, quickly, lethally.

Her brows furrowed in anger. "Why?!" she demanded.

He shrugged. "I didn't need the strongest or the smartest. I needed the most dangerous, and you fit perfectly." He grinned again. "Do you disagree?"

She paused, thinking. *I fell into his trap. He told me how and when, but not why.* She gulped. *And yet I followed him.*

He stepped back, noticing her look of understanding. "Ahhh. You see now." He looked down the road calmly. "I'll take that tome in your pouch, if you please, little Cat. I believe it's mine."

Her eyes blazed with fiery anger, betrayed.

She told herself to never trust, especially a man. But this time she did and paid for it. Resigned to defeat, she reached into the pouch and handed over the tome.

"Thank you," he said, brushing it off. "There is still time. I will give you until first light to escape." He looked at the sky to see where the moon was. "The hunt will be on afterward. And I think it will be a masterful one, am I wrong?" He grinned and bowed to Lyssa.

She spat on his boot. "Bastard!"

"Now, now. Is that any way to treat your former master?" he said with a pouting lip.

"The next time you see me, you son of a bitch, I will not be the apprentice." She turned and began moving toward the forest and safety. Over her shoulder, she heard him simply reply, "And the next time you see me, little Cat, I will not be the teacher."

She began to trot into the forest and heard him laugh—not a belly laugh but an evil, diabolical laugh.

The hunt was on. She knew it, could feel it. And now, she was ready.

With a sly smirk, she said, "If you think you can catch a Cat on the hunt, then come and get me...if you can."

'...now, let's get serious, shall we?'

She had a vision of Kitikithakis, her mentor. She was younger, and they had been hunting for most of the day. The tracks were from a big cat, and he realized that they had now become the prey.

He told her when to move, when to stop and when to be silent. He would sniff the air and touch the soil. He always seemed to know.

He looked back at her. She was afraid. She'd never been the prey before, not like this.

He calmly whispered, "When being hunted, stay low, stay downwind and stay out of sight."

In her vision, she could see them slinking between shadows and under the brush, just as a cat would.

They came to an old, bent oak. He pointed upward. As quickly and as silently as she could, she climbed up to the first sagging limb. It was low but strong, and she clung tightly to it to look like a natural part of it. He followed closely behind and did the same.

They lay there quietly, listening, looking. It seemed like hours.

He tapped her boot. She glanced back at him as he started to rise, bow string drawn, arrow nocked. He aimed for the far side of the clearing opposite them. She followed suit, her heart pounding like a drum in her chest.

It emerged from the far tree line, a female spotted leopard. She was looking for them. She lowered her head, sniffing the ground for their scent—for them. Gracefully yet dangerously, it stalked, edging closer and closer to their tree. One step, pause, another, slinking low to the ground. She was close, almost a stone's throw away. She stopped and looked directly at them and then froze as if deciding what to do.

None of them moved. After just a few seconds, the cat stood upright, resigning itself to no longer being the hunter but the defeated. She gave a low, almost acknowledging growl, turned and leaped away to make her escape.

They lowered their bows.

Sometimes, the hunter knows when to stop, to admit defeat and to wait another day to continue the hunt.

She never forgot that. The lesson had been burned into her brain.

This was the time. This was the place. And she now understood why.

It was time.

She was the Cat….and she would not be defeated.

'…you should take a hint, corruptor.'

Of Kith and Kin

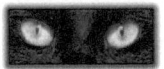

They were still there, she knew; the sour stink of days-old ale, their unwashed bodies and the unerring trails they left. The guards and hunters had been circling like fools all day. Lyssa had been toying with them, intentionally doubling back and crisscrossing paths. Midday, she perched high in a tree, watching them stumble about, trying to figure out how she could walk in circles and vanish. They even looked straight up into the branches where she hid, and still never saw her. More than once, while leading them around, she spotted tracks that didn't belong to her pursuers. These prints were different, more careful, deliberate, sure. She'd noticed them only by chance, and that chance discovery filled her with great unease. Someone else was there, smarter, much more dangerous. She was certain of it…the assassin. The hunt was on.

She came to the Brackenflow Eddies, a wide, violent river that never seemed to rest. The main branch rushed west and south with a current that tore at its banks, curling into endless whorls and black pits where great stones churned beneath the surface. Few dared to cross it without the bridge. The south branch flowed much calmer and crossed into the Whispering Woods, where few dared to challenge the legends in these parts. It was sworn that the Valyn owned this part of the great woods, though no one had actually seen them.

King's Road began here, and the giant stone bridge that crossed it marked the official boundary between the Kingdom of Bryndwyck and the Duchy of Eldorath, a mountainous region filled with scrubland and deep ravines to the west. Bordering King's Road stood the tall, dense trees of the north, and south lay the Whispering Woods.

She thought if she could find Kitikithakis, he could give her some insight or guidance on what she should do next.

The water below looked cool and inviting. Summer had come, the warmest she could remember, making her mouth as dry as sand and turning her exposed skin red. She searched the area for a secluded spot along the calmer south-flowing branch and decided it was safe enough to at least cool off for a few minutes, maybe even scrub the dirt and grime from her clothes.

There was a covered spot near a bend in the river that couldn't be seen from the bridge, so she made her way through the underbrush to investigate. Upon arriving, she observed that it was covered from both the road and upriver, making it an ideal place for her to rest for a while.

Now feeling safe, she stripped off her clothes and carried them into the water, where she began to scrub the dirt and grime from them. It seemed like forever before they finally came clean, reminding her of her mother when she had to clean the girls' clothing after a mud fight. She chuckled, hearing her mother yelling at them in her head. When she was done, they were hung on a bush in the sun to dry while she returned to the deeper water to wash herself. She had almost forgotten what it meant to feel clean, to smell like herself and not a rancid goat, savoring the silence and serenity of being alone. She rolled to her back and allowed herself to gently float on the current, taking in how peaceful it was here. She missed it. She resurfaced close to the bank and shook the water from her face and eyes.

"My little cat returns."

Lyssa's reflexes took over. She crouched, sprang for her blades and stood in a defensive posture.

"Easy, mira'thien. The forests' eyes are alert. You are safe." Kitikithakis stood crouched on a branch. His forest armor looked worn, the quiver that hung from his back was full and his blades were tucked into his boots, just as Lyssa had remembered him. His eyes continuously watched the surrounding area, never once looking at her.

She stood up and casually walked to her clothes and checked to see if they were dry.

"Why is it that you are the only one who can sneak up on me and catch me unaware?"

He looked at her. "I am the forest, mira'thien. Can you sneak up on a tree?"

She shook her head and sighed. "No. The trees speak among themselves." She pulled on her pants.

"I see you have grown to a fine woman." His eyes still kept watch on the area.

She was never embarrassed near him. He had never stared at her nudity as he had no interest in human women. His blood was Valyn, and he was a child of the ancient Whispering Woods. He had forgotten his age hundreds of years ago and, as close as he could say, was about three centuries as human time goes, but didn't know for certain. Time has no real meaning to the wood folk.

"Looking, ranger? I am shocked." She giggled.

He looked at her, almost bored, and said, "I appreciate nice things." He hopped down from the branch and walked to her. "Even the love a sow shows for her brood is beautiful."

She raised an eyebrow in feigned ire. "Kitikithakis! Are you comparing me to a pig?" She turned to him as if she were going to slap him.

He smiled, bent down, and picked up her doublet. "Cover yourself, piggy." Her eyes got wide. She reared back as if to hit him as he tossed it onto her face. "If we weren't friends… "

"I know, little sister. I am glad to call you sister as always. I have missed you."

He reached out his arms and hugged her. She'd missed this. Aside from Chandra, she had no other people in her life that she could call friend, no one she trusted more.

"Come. Ash'Tara wishes to see you. It must be important, she sent me."

"Ash'Tara?" she asked while she finished dressing, picked up a limb and removed what tracks she had made. She quickly looked around to be sure, then followed Kitikithakis. They moved quickly but silently. She had missed the lessons he taught her about the forests. He was always strict but patient.

He would say, "The ways of life are unforgiving, the lessons, painful. Those who survive have earned that right." It was her favorite lesson, albeit one of the most painful as well. There were many times she had erred, and the taskmaster made her understand how serious the mistake was. She loved him for it.

'...tis but the calm before the tempest.'

They had walked for the better part of the morning, and when they neared the village, Kitikithakis held up his hand and stopped.

A voice came from an unseen mouth. "Avara'sen vayura. Nim'ara nama, salen kalyen?"

The syllables were strange to most ears; a song shaped in the throat. But for Lyssa, they sparked something much deeper, a song whispered over her as an infant, held so many years past. Ash brushed across her brow, shadows bending at her fingertips when she was still too young to understand.

She hadn't heard those words since the night her world changed, the night everything burned. Yet, the meaning was clear enough in her bones: name, business, passage.

Kitikithakis raised his bow and replied, "Ithila Kitikithakis en'Avara Valyn. Velara kalyen nim'ara...Lyssa Soryn."

There was silence. A face, small, tanned, fierce, emerged from a copse of bushes. He looked at Kitikithakis. A smile broadened on his narrow face. "Ahai, kara'thien. Valos en'darin. Sevarin thal."

The warrior looked fierce to Lyssa. His armor looked as if it were made of thick tree bark. It was more a heavy jacket than a cuirass but looked sturdy and well able to stop even an arrow. He wore dark green-brown pants with bark leggings and thick, supple boots. Had he stood still, one would have thought him a tree more than a man. His bow looked sturdy and lethal. It was obviously hand-carved, but she couldn't identify the type of wood. It was very dark, almost black, and heavy looking, but he hefted it as if it were made of parchment.

The ranger glanced back at Lyssa, then at the warrior. "Good to see you as well, my brother." They clasped arms. The warrior looked over to Lyssa. There was interest in his eyes. Still looking at her, he said to Kitikithakis, "Tira'shena valen, kara. Sha'ren eshai? Ka veyla en?"

The ranger laughed, "No kara'thien. She has not seen a spirit. Some people think she *is* a spirit." The warrior raised an eyebrow.

He stepped in front of Lyssa, carefully looking at her from head to toe. He spoke with a very thick Valyn accent, "You...be friend... him, you... white hair?"

"Yes. I am Lyssa Socha Soryn."

His face went pale, and he stepped backward. He looked at Kitikithakis, beckoning excitedly, and said, "Vey'ra, vey'ra! Ash'Tara ven lorin. Ven lorin sha'tai." Lyssa began to remember some of the words. Ash'Tara must be the leader Kitikithakis spoke about, a woman by the sound. Vey'ra...come. He was leading them somewhere, maybe to Ash'Tara. The sounds of the language began to bring a rush of memories and feelings back to her.

The ranger looked at Lyssa and motioned for her to follow. Lyssa wasn't sure what was happening and began to feel a little uneasy but fell in behind the two.

They walked quickly through the undergrowth. The deeper into the forest they went, the denser it became. She'd never been this deep before, even though she lived just outside. It had always made her curious, but she never dared to go, even though she was well versed in wood lore.

Before long, Kitikithakis turned to her and said, "We're almost there. Say nothing until I tell you. There's no danger just, how your people say, a courtesy. You are not versed in the ways of our people yet." He looked forward. "It's not wise to offend them."

Finally, they came to an opening, she gazed upon the great wonder of all of the homes in the trees, wood bridges, ropes dangling from treetops….and Valyn. There were more Valyn than there were people in all of Tantyn combined. They looked slight and wiry, their bodies shaped by the forests they called home. Shorter than humans, they moved with a restless grace, as if every step were meant to leave no mark. Their skin color was similar to humans' but more leathery, and their hair ran the colors of autumn, bronze, ash, and deep brown. Their eyes, bright and quick, seemed to mirror the woods themselves; alive, alert, and impossible to read.

"Welcome home, mira'thien." He flourished his arm to present the village to her. She had always loved it when he called her mira'thien. It meant sister in the Valyn tongue. To her, it was a bond that was just as strong as the bond she had with Chandra. There was no other man she had ever called "toh'vah kira'thien" or life brother, except him.

The warrior motioned for them to follow him into a long building made of timber. It was ancient, overgrown with moss and small trees and looked as if it were a living part of the forest.

As they were led into the building, the hall stirred at the sight of their arrival. Armed warriors rose from where they knelt, nocked bows in hand, blades flashing faintly in the firelight. They lined the passage as Lyssa passed, eyes narrowed, every step of hers measured against their distrust. This was no welcome. It was a trial by gaze, by silence, by suspicion.

The walls were lined with small torches, which lit the entire hall and made the shadows dance as if alive. Several rows of people knelt along the walls and watched as they approached a large three-step dais. Off to the left of the dais sat a young Valyn, not much older than Lyssa by his looks, who was intently scribbling in a tablet. There were two seats, one on each side of each step and at the top of the dais sat Ash'Tara. Her seat (a throne?) was clearly made from the stump of an ancient tree, polished to a high sheen with large fern fronds overhanging like a canopy. An advisor stood by her side. He was adorned in a cloak of leaves and held a large, thick staff topped with a skull, possibly human. Lyssa assumed he was a shaman or spiritual elder by the way he presented himself.

Ash'Tara, herself, was not old by any means. Lyssa had envisioned an old crone of a woman with leather skin, wild hair and gnarled hands. Ash'Tara had wheat-colored hair and tan skin. It looked as if she'd spent quite some time in the sun. She looked as old as her mother, as best as she could remember, and her face had a soft, motherly look to it. She was beautiful. Lyssa immediately felt comfortable in her presence.

They stood side by side before Ash'Tara. As Kitikithakis bowed, so did Lyssa, who felt like a mimicking oaf.

"Sevarin, Kara'thien Ithila Kitikathakis. Velora en'darin sha'ta." Her greeting boomed throughout the hall.

The ranger straightened and replied, "Veyrana Ash'Tara, . Veyr'thien en'Valen, kara'thien en'sha'ra."

The language began to click in Lyssa's head. Ash'Tara welcomed the ranger and then said something about honor. She began to get chills at the memory. He mentioned something about being commanded. Her heart was pounding now.

"Ithila, you dare bring this outsider before me? Why should her blood not stain the floor?" Lyssa began to feel the tension. She was an outsider, not to be trusted. If they didn't accept her, she would never leave alive.

"Velara kalyen nim'ara…Lyssa Socha Soryn, Mira'thien en'Ta'Lith Soryn, veyrana en'Kal'La Valyn." Lyssa knew exactly what he had said. She's heard Kalla say it in an offhand way once when she was a young girl. Lyssa, daughter of Talith and granddaughter of Kalla, only this was different. The inflection of the names was more real. He used their Valyn names, and she realized they had meaning. This was the first time she had understood the gravity of her past, of who her mother and grandmother really were. He said he knew of her family before, but why hadn't he spoken about the importance of it?

He tapped her, and she realized she was still bowing.

She straightened up and saw Ash'Tara descending the steps in her direction. The guards closed their circle to protect their mother, blades angled, not raised, but ready. The weight of their suspicion pressed on Lyssa as much as Ash'Tara's stare. Lyssa nervously glanced at Kitikithakis, who closed his eyes and gave a reassuring nod. It was all right.

Ash'Tara stood before and looked to the left and right of her. She leaned closely, studying her face, every line, the color. She pulled down Lyssa's lower eyelid with a practiced hand, staring into the steel-gray iris as if searching for a hidden mark. Her head tilted left, then right, like a craftsman turning a blade to the light. Finally, she drew back, eyes narrowing. She nodded, having come to a decision.

"She is Valyn, there is no denying, except…," she said, looking to the ranger. She looked back at Lyssa and narrowed her eyes. "Ka'ren Valyn eshai?"

Lyssa began to sweat. She must have paused too long because Ash'Tara looked at Kitikithakis questioningly. The ranger nodded at Lyssa. She mustered all the memory she had and said, "Sha'tai…long time. Mira…no, Veyr'thien…mother speak. I…remember…some." She felt foolish. She tried again. "I proud…velora en'darin sha'ta, Ash'Tara."

Ash'Tara's eyes lit up as she pieced her broken Valyn together. Then, like a mother, she smiled, took Lyssa's head in each hand and kissed her forehead. "You are sister." She kissed Lyssa's left cheek.

"You are daughter." She kissed Lyssa's right cheek. "You are Valyn." She wrapped the girl in a motherly hug. Around them, the guards lowered their weapons as one. The tension in the air dissolved like mist in the morning. Ash'Tara had made it known that Lyssa was truly one of them and that she was the daughter and granddaughter of one of the ancient family lines. She would never be rejected and would always have a home among her people.

"We will meet at sar'eth, mira'thien." The ranger bowed as Ash'Tara stepped forward to lead Lyssa away. It had been a long day so far, and Lyssa knew she would be of a clearer mind in the morning.

Kitikithakis stood aside as Ash'Tara took Lyssa's hand and began to walk with her toward the door. She nodded at the young Valyn, who began writing madly on vellum pages.

His eyes narrowed. He could read the signs. The tracks had been wiped away. There was a sign. No creature did this. He gazed into the trees. No shadows moved, the birds still sang. His target was not here. He searched for tracks and continued his hunt.

Ash'Tara showed Lyssa around the village, where her grandmother had once lived and where her mother had been born. She had always assumed that Talith had been born at home like everyone else. She had never known about the Valyn except in the tales that Kalla and her mother told. Even her father liked them and never questioned the reality. It was all so new and wonderful.

The children ran to her while pointing and speaking in the Valyn tongue. She would squat down and let them touch her so they could ensure that the *silver-haired* one, or eid'harra, was real. The children pressed in, brushing her hair, whispering in awe.

"Ooh...eid'harra," they breathed. The others repeating it, their voices like the twittering of sparrows.

An older girl leaned closely, fingertips lingering in the silver strands, feeling the soft hair dance across her fingers. She tilted her head in wonder. Her gaze darted to Lyssa's eyes, those pale, unearthly pools that seemed to look through rather than upon. A glint of light reflected from them as if they emitted a strange power.

She pulled her hand away quickly as if burned. She cupped her hand to another's ear and whispered, almost trembling, "Ip shyr'aeth…"

The words clung to the air like frost. The other child's eyes widened, and she drew back, clutching her wrist as though afraid they had spoken something forbidden. The circle fell quiet for just a heartbeat; their awe suddenly sharpened with unease.

Ash'Tara did not correct them. She only smiled and folded her hands before her, watching the children give Lyssa back the names of legend. Waving her hands toward the children, dismissing them, Ash'Tara continued to show Lyssa around. As the two walked away, the children stared and whispered excitedly as if they had just met a hero.

"They like you," she said. "The one born during *Vayl'tharyn a'veshra*. You call it…" she paused, thinking, "ah, the Long Night Moon."

She smiled and looked at Lyssa as if she were her own daughter. Lyssa had no words. Every word that Ash'Tara spoke was like a song gently ringing in Lyssa's ears. The smooth tone, the way the words slipped from her tongue, it was a beautiful language, and it made Lyssa sad that she couldn't speak it. She was never given the chance.

Without realizing they had stopped, Lyssa heard Ash'Tara ask, "Are you alright, mira'thien?"

Lyssa smiled. She realized that this moment was perfect. This place was perfect, and this new world had become…perfect.

She struggled to find the right words. "Alla wondrae. Nevr'ae somni, et'a tru'en." She began to chide herself. She knew it wasn't right by the motherly look on Ash'Tara's face, like a mother trying to teach her child to speak for the first time.

Slowly, Ash'Tara corrected her. "No, no, mira'thien." She spoke slowly. "Alla wondrae or it is all wonder. Now, you say."

Lyssa repeated it slowly.

"Ah, good, child. Now, Nevr'ae somni or I never dreamed. Now you." She motioned for her to repeat it.

"Never'ay somni," she said.

"No, no. Nevr…ae somni. Like nevray."

"Nevr'ae somni." She looked questioningly at her teacher.

"Good, Good. And now et'a tru'en" again she motioned for Lyssa to repeat it.

"Et'a tru'en."

"Good, now you say. Alla wondrae. Nevr'ae somni, et'a tru'en."

She took a deep breath, hoping she would get it right this time. She closed her eyes, and her mother's face came to mind. "Alla wondrae. Nevr'ae somni, et'a tru'en." This time she added, "Is'ma domae, et domae ancestrae."

Ash'Tara was amazed. Then she squinted deep in thought. "You closed your eyes, mira'thien. What did you see?"

Lyssa thought for a second. "I saw my mother. She was sitting by the hearth. She turned and told me it was all alright, and to feel the words in your heart then sing them."

"Do you know the words?"

"This is my home and the home of my ancestors," She blinked in disbelief. It was as if her mother were right beside her.

"Ta'Lith was a good girl, a good mother," she said as she lowered her head with sorrow. "What happened?" She shook her head. "She fought like a *Val'ethra*, a Queen of Power or strength."

Lyssa saw the anger begin to grow inside her.

"What you did…" She jabbed a finger at Lyssa's chest, "was Val'ETHRA!" She said it with pride, almost reverence.

"Never forget. NEVER forget." She held up a finger to the sky and exclaimed, "You are Valyn. The blood of the ancients, of Kal'La and of Ta'Lith, courses through your spirit. And it is strong." Her eyes narrowed, and Lyssa could feel both anger and sheer pride emanating from Ash'Tara's entire body.

Several people stopped what they had been doing to listen to Ash'Tara speak.

"You hold the strength. You hold the power. You ARE Valyn." She exhaled and calmed visibly. "On the day of your birth, you were named Lyssa. Lys'Sa. The name means *dark cat* or *shadow cat* in your tongue. You are the dark cat. Never forget this. It is in your very being. You are meant for something. We know not what, but always follow your heart, for it knows. It always knows."

She drew a breath. "Chan'Dra. A mira'thien. You love your sister, eh?"

Lyssa nodded. "She's my world, Ash'Tara. I can't live without her," she admitted.

Ash'Tara nodded in agreement. "You are correct. You *cannot* live without her. You are separate but as one." They began to walk again.

"Chan'Dra or *One Who is Shadow* is the night itself. She is beautiful....and dangerous."

Lyssa nodded. "I know. She always teased me as a child." A remembering smile crossed her lips.

She pointed a finger at Lyssa's chest. "You must always trust in each other. You are both kith and kin. That is a powerful bond that no one can break. Blood is blood. Blood must keep blood. Blood must avenge blood." She looked sternly at Lyssa, waiting for her reaction.

She looked at Ash'Tara. "They killed our family. They took my sister. They..." She looked down. Tears of pure rage welled in her eyes.

"Good mira'thien. Good. You are truly Val'ethra." Turning toward Lyssa, she placed both hands on her shoulders. "There is a life debt that needs to be collected, for you and your people. Gather that debt. Make them pay their debt." She hugged Lyssa tightly. She kissed her forehead, turned and as silently as a breeze, walked away.

Lyssa stared silently as Ash'Tara walked out of sight. She knew what she must do. Her running as prey had ended. *She* would become the hunter. There was a debt to be paid.

And *how* she would make them pay.

'*...do you smell rain?*'

She'd slept well that night. The night was darker, and the stars seemed brighter from inside the forest. Lyssa was still concerned, knowing she was still being hunted, but also knew her skills would help sway the hunt in her favor.

The sun released its first rays of morning as she stretched and stood to greet it.

Much to her surprise, she was served her morning meal, something that had never happened to her before. Smiling, she graciously accepted and ate it hurriedly. She needed to meet Kitikithakis at the edge of the village so they could begin to plan a trap for the wandering guards and bounty hunters. They had been searching far too close to the village, and that was not to be tolerated.

In the past, entire regiments of outsiders had been completely vanquished without a trace. The Valyn were never to be trifled with, even under the best of circumstances.

She reached the outskirts but didn't see the ranger there, which was very odd. She sat on a fallen tree and began to hone the tips of her arrows with a sharpening stone as she waited for his arrival. It was almost midday, yet he'd not arrived, and she became concerned. He would never do this unless something untoward happened, so she stood and began her search.

The woods were less dense here, and the underbrush was much thinner than she liked. She felt uncovered, so she crouched low and moved slowly, watching, listening.

She'd searched in wide arcs around the village similar to a clover, but to no avail. She widened her arc as the sun had fallen almost to the horizon. Coming to a small stream, she bent to cup water to her mouth.

There, footprints. No Valyn made these, nor did Kitikithakis. It was a man, and a fairly large one by the depth of the prints. She looked around carefully. The hunt was on. She was now the Cat, and she was searching for her mouse.

The tracks were clumsy, as if it were someone lost. They wound from tree to tree as they had been searching for some invisible trail. She tracked them past another stream and into a glade…where she found him.

Kitikithakis had been pinned to two trees, a dagger in each hand and an arrow in each foot. He'd been posed so he could easily be found. His tunic had been stripped down to his waist, and a bloody message had been carved into his chest… *I see you.*

She stood staring at her friend, tortured, defiled, posed as a message…to her.

At first, her rage slowly boiled until she could hold it in no more. Her scream of fury had been so loud that it reverberated from tree to tree and was heard in the village.

"I WILL FIND YOU!"

A grin of satisfaction crossed his lips. *Come to me, my prey. My blade hungers.*

'…ha ha ha ha!'

Her return to the village was met with fear. Her visage had become one of hate, of rage, of murder.

She moved with a purpose. No one got in her way, not even Ash'Tara.

Lyssa gathered what things she had and turned to begin the hunt. Her face never changed, her breath, heavy, and her pace, with measured strides.

Ash'Tara saw her return and stood her ground. As Lyssa approached Ash'Tara said, "Mira'thien. Hold. I wish to speak." Lyssa continued toward her. "LYSSA SOCHA SORYN, I SAID STOP, NOW!"

Lyssa halted directly in front of Ash'Tara, breath heavy, pure venom painting her face.

"Tell me." Her eyes flicked to the gathered crowd. Her people. The people she must protect. "What has happened? What have you seen?"

Lyssa spoke through tightly clenched teeth. "Kitikithakis....is...dead." Her expression and her breathing never changed.

Ash'Tara's eyes went wide. "How?"

"A human...a hunter...or assassin. He...was...desecrated." She never blinked, tears of anger welling up.

There was no sound from the village folk. Everyone watched and listened to the exchange.

Ash'Tara was silent for some time. Lyssa started to move when the woman began to speak in a quiet tone, almost a whisper.

"He was kara'thien, not in name but in blood. Syl'vear...Kitikithakis Syl'vaer, my kara'thien."

She looked at Lyssa with a single tear that slowly fell from her face. She suddenly looked older, her heart broken.

Lyssa was still breathing heavily. She was like a mother bear protecting its young, every muscle flexing for release.

"Avenge him, Val'ethra. Avenge my kara'thien. Bring me his head." Ash'Tara stepped aside. Lyssa glared, and a diabolical grin crossed her lips.

"Ena, amma. Voren su."

Lyssa's mother knew she would not fail.

It turned dark by the time she returned to Kitikithakis. Her rage had abated, but it had now turned to that of the Cat, the hunter. She would become the most dangerous animal in the forest.

She removed his bow, *Lor'Vaelyn*, his daggers and arrows, and gently laid him on the ground. She examined each wound and each cut. *A person who knows what he's doing. This is an assassin. Him?* She removed the trinkets and baubles and placed them in the small belt pouch at her side to give to his sister. She looked at his now pale face. The memories of the past rushed to the forefront of her mind. She brushed a lock of hair from his face and gently kissed his forehead.

It took her the night to clear an area to prepare his pyre. She didn't concern herself with the forest. It had always been his friend, and she knew it must mourn as she did. She lit a makeshift torch with her flint and set the pyre alight. She watched silently as the flames engulfed him and made him one with his home. She wiped a tear away, turned and drew his bow. *Tonight, Lor'Vaelyn will have its vengeance as well.*

A light breeze passed through the trees as if it, too, wanted revenge. She would make it right or die trying.

'...your time is at hand.'

He was sure she would come now. He heard the scream of anger and had begun preparations. His false tracks, double-backs and harassing traps should lead her exactly where he needed her to be. He would wait. He had time.

She traveled light, only his bow, Lor'Vaelyn, quiver and her daggers were needed here. She kissed the bow and nocked an arrow. *Valyn's justice, may your arrows sing true. Avenge our friend.* Her eyes saw every movement. Her ears heard every twitter and snap. Her steps made almost no sound. Everything that was unnecessary for this hunt was left behind, hidden near the pyre for later retrieval. She had become nothing more than a shadow in the forest, sleek and silent.

She carried her bow in hand, held close to her body to avoid hooking a limb or bush. Each step was purposeful and well-planted. She could stalk for hours on end. Fatigue was ignored, and pain was but a memory. Only one thing mattered.

She stopped near a stream and heightened her senses, as this was a perfect spot for an ambush. Waiting, looking and listening for a few minutes assured her there was no one lying in wait, so she began to cup water to her mouth. The water was cool, sweet, and helped to refresh her.

She began across slowly but stopped just before reaching the opposite bank. There was something odd here. In the early morning sunlight, she noticed that the twigs and leaves seemed to be misplaced, lying in unnatural positions. She looked closely with her fingers, making sure not to disrupt them.

A trap. Whoever was after her was well seasoned and ready for her arrival. This played into Lyssa's hand and gave her a slight edge. She now knew how to think like this assassin. This had to be her mentor himself. The tables had finally turned. *Not today, I will not be the apprentice.*

She backed up a step and proceeded downstream for several minutes. She then climbed the bank and continued on. There would be no trace of him here. He was far more cunning than that. She made her way through bushes and ravines, stopping every so often to listen. She had no idea where he could be because the forest here was so vast and wild. Every so often, a rabbit or stoat would pass by, staring nervously. As long as she didn't startle them into a full run, she would be alright.

Lyssa decided to move to her left to regain his trail. She knew that was unlikely, but everyone made errors now and then, and she hoped he would as well. She stopped for a second to catch her breath and slowly yet carefully stretch her limbs. Hours of stalking had begun to take their toll. She lay flat, quietly drawing leaves and brush to cover her and help her blend into her surroundings.

It felt good to take a break, but she kept vigilant, still listening and looking. Her stomach grumbled. She froze and searched the area in fear. Nothing. She'd brought no dried meat or kibble. She had to eat something, or her hunger would reveal her, and she'd lose the upper hand. Quickly, she looked around.

Then she realized she was lying under an old beech. She found some young green leaves and slowly began chewing. They were slightly bitter but sweet and nutty. She'd been told by Gran that some leaves were safe to eat as long as you knew the tree they fell from. After she'd eaten several leaves, she slowly regained her feet and began stalking once more.

After a few minutes, she located some tracks. Kneeling and touching them, Lyssa concluded that she was getting closer. Good, the quarry was near. She followed the tracks with her eyes and noticed something very odd. They seemed to be heavier in one direction than in the other. She moved closer to further examine and realized this was a trick to get her to circle back if she followed them.

She understood now. He was no longer close. He was here.

She carefully inched backward. Her eyes were as focused as an owl's. She couldn't make a single sound, a single mistake. It could cost her life.

She hunched behind a tree and nocked an arrow, keeping the bow low. Staring at every tree individually, she examined each one for several seconds in an attempt to recognize any differences: a stone too round, a lump at the base of a tree, a limb that narrowed too quickly.

Carefully, she surveyed, desperately trying to find him before he found her. She saw nothing. She noticed a shallow draw behind her. She decided it would be a better vantage point there as she could stand better prepared for an attack.

She inched her way backward and quietly eased into the draw, making sure not to slide, causing clumps of dirt to roll. Any sound now could give her away. It was as she thought, deep enough to stand, which she gratefully did. She wiggled her toes to allow blood to flow into them again.

The sun was low in the sky. She'd been tracking him all day now. Yes, this had to be him. She felt it in her bones. She knew there wasn't much more time before nightfall. She could still hunt, but it would be far more perilous. She really didn't want to tempt fate, but she knew there wasn't much choice now and picked up a small loose stone. Looking down the draw, she saw a large puddle of water and gently tossed it, splashing like she'd hoped. Glancing back over the edge to see if there was anyone moving, if they'd taken the bait, she tensed her muscles and got ready to pounce.

No movement at all. She began to think she may have to sleep here tonight, but really didn't want to. It was far too dangerous.

Some movement, almost imperceptible, but there it was. She hoped it was him. Lyssa set her bow in her palm and got into a comfortable stance. The shape was moving toward the puddle, slowly and carefully. This was no animal, as it stopped behind a tree and searched the area. She knew she was in such a position that she couldn't be seen. Again, it moved forward…but this time in her direction.

Shite. She didn't want this. She'd have to set down the bow and arm her daggers, which wasn't a problem, but if she did this and the target moved the other way, she would have to rearm the bow, and that would waste too much time and possibly the kill.

She gently armed only one and stood poised to leap. Still, he backed in her direction. She could tell he was interested in looking back up the draw and away from her. He looked down and carefully slid into the ravine. He was now no more than two body lengths from her. Her heart started to pound hard. *Calm, little cat. Relax your body. Prepare to spring.*

She relaxed. She was ready.

He was unaware of her presence and continued to move.

Like a bolt of lightning, she sprang into action, left arm ready to grasp him and the other ready to pierce.

He heard her move and dropped a shoulder in hopes she would overestimate her angle. She did just that and started to sail over his back, but managed to grab his face, fingers reaching into his mouth and spinning his head all the way over. He was thrown off balance and rolled to his back, face up. She rolled to her feet and launched another attack. Then, he made a dreadful error. Instead of rolling to his opposite side, he tried to stand. Lyssa landed on his chest, hand around his throat, and brought her dagger down hard. He moved his head just in time as it missed and bit deeply into his shoulder. He let out a scream and tried to roll her off, but she was far too nimble for that. Lyssa hung on tightly, removed the dagger and went for another lunge. The searing pain in his shoulder prevented him from fully raising it as she sliced him again on the side of the head. His ear flipped in the air and landed not far away. His strength began to wane as he tried to roll in the other direction, but that left him vulnerable from behind. She rolled off him, crouched and let him continue to roll. He turned his head, but again, it was far too late. This time, her dagger found its mark. It embedded deep into his chest. His eyes went wide as he realized his time had come. She released the dagger, rearmed with her other and leaped back, waiting for his retaliation. It never came. He lay there gasping for breath, dagger still protruding from his reddening chest. He then realized this was a woman. She had moved so fast, so quietly, that he could never get a clear look until now.

Her eyes narrowed as she realized…it wasn't the assassin.

He slowly, painfully pulled himself backward with his back against the side of the draw. She stood and watched.

He kept his eyes on her as she stepped forward, her eyes locked on his, fury searing her face. She could taste the kill.

"Why?" she asked through clenched teeth. He smiled and then laughed. She reached toward his chest and removed the dagger while twisting. He screamed in agony.

She stood. "Why?!"

Once more, he laughed. In one quick motion, she flipped the dagger in the air, grabbed the blade with thumb and forefinger, and flung it at him, blade sinking deep into his calf.

He screamed again.

"I have all night," she said, voice full of fury. "Why?"

"He sent me." She could tell his strength was waning as his life seeped from his body.

"Where is he?"

"I don't know."

She reached and removed the dagger, once again twisting it as she removed it.

"Where?" She raised the dagger again, threatening to throw it at him again.

"At the manor, he's at the manor waiting for me to return."

She raised her head and looked down her nose at him. He wasn't lying this time.

She leaned closely, almost nose to nose. "He was my brother, my family."

"I had a job…"

His words ended with a gurgling attempt to speak and a cough of blood. Her blade cut his throat to the spine, nearly severing it from his body, before he could finish. She wiped the blood from both daggers using his face and sheathed them.

Ash'Tara, you are avenged.

She slowly walked into the village and headed for Ash'Tara's hall. People began to gather behind her, murmuring and pointing. She was still covered in his blood.

Ash'Tara watched aghast as Lyssa entered and walked toward her. Each step was labored from fatigue. She waited for the news. Lyssa looked into her eyes, "Var su, mira'thien." She tossed the assassin's head at her feet. "Var en'dral." She heard an audible gasp as she turned and silently left the hall.

Ash'Tara stood and watched her mira'thien walk away. *For you, my life-sister. For our people.*

She knew he was avenged. She knew he was now one with the forest. And she knew the forest had a Val'ethra...forever.

'*...the hammer of wrath rings loudly.*'

Talk of the Valyn Village:

"Did you see her? The silver-haired girl? Mama, she smiled at me! She's real—Val'ethra is real!"

–little Valyn daughter

"I wish to be like her when I grow!"

"You can't. She's magic."

"So? Maybe the forest will like me too."

–Sel'yra to her mira'thien

Of Facades and Bonds

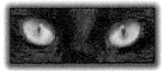

There was a commotion outside. *What are you up to now, sister?*

She left her room and started down the corridor where she'd helped Lyssa. She was worried. What if she were injured, or worse, dead? Chandra knew she couldn't lift a finger to help her lest she give away her motive.

She got to the large double doors and watched as a guard in dark armor began to bark out orders to the other guards. She'd never seen this man before, which was odd because she'd been here long enough to see them all.

The big guard glanced back and yelled, "Go back, lady. There's an assassin on the grounds."

She knew it was Lyssa, and now she knew her sister lived. She feigned fear and darted back into the manor and down the hall toward Davin's study.

As she reached the kitchen, Davin, trotting down the far hall, met her mid-step.

"What is it?" He looked angry.

"I don't know. The guards are searching the grounds for an assassin." She pointed down the hall. "The guard captain in black shooed me in here for my safety."

Davin looked at her, squinting as if puzzled. "What guard captain in black? I have no guards in black." Chandra looked puzzled as well.

He quickly turned toward the doors and ran with Chandra in tow. When they reached the yard, the guards were busy searching every corner with hounds. Davin grabbed a guard by the shoulder, spun him around and demanded, "Where is this guard captain in black?" The guard pointed to the front gate, then rejoined the search.

He reached the gate but saw no guards, no captain and no hounds.

Well played, Lady. Blocking my vision was a brilliant move.

Davin shook his head in disgust. Chandra reached him and asked, "Was he there?" She had an angry look on her face.

"No. Something is not right." He sneered. "But I will find out what."

They returned to the main receiving room, just off the dining area. A guard reported in, panting heavily.

"Lord, we searched the entire grounds and outside the wall but found nothing."

"Bring me the two hall sentries—now!"

He snapped to attention as he realized things were about to get extremely dangerous and ran to find them.

Silently, he paced, scowling and mumbling to himself. Chandra had seen him like this before and, though she enjoyed it, also knew that this was the time to tread very carefully. He was a deity, after all, and for now, an unsuspecting one.

Soon, the guards returned with the sentries. He dismissed them, much to their elation, but kept the sentries, who were about to incur his wrath.

Davin glared at the two, who stood at attention but were visibly nervous. He slowly paced calmly behind them and whispered in a courteous tone, "What happened after the lady and I left?"

"Lord, we left and took up post at the front gate." His mouth had turned to desert.

"And what of the young handmaiden my lady…left behind?"

"We don't know, lord. Her ladyship demanded we leave her. We never saw her again."

Davin glanced at Chandra and gave a curt nod. Chandra knew she had to play the part, now. It wasn't her way, but she knew she couldn't deny him and had to maintain the ruse.

Chandra moved like silk toward the guards. "Are you sure about that?"

They nervously glanced at each other, then back at her. "Y-y-yes, my lady."

She stood next to the taller one and ran her finger under his chin menacingly. "I hope you're right. I would hate to think you were…lying."

"N-n-no, my lady. I would never."

The shorter guard began to sweat. He had the feeling he knew where this was headed, and he wanted no part of it.

She moved to the next. She looked into his eyes and smiled. "N-n-no, lady. He speaks the truth."

She glanced back at Davin, who turned his back to her.

Dammit.

She had to do it now. She knew they knew nothing, but Davin apparently didn't believe them…and he wanted to know. The lives of these two guards meant nothing to him.

She looked at the men sadly and pouted. She raised her left hand, palm up, fingers stiffened as if they were talons. In her palm, a darkness began to rise. She stared at them now with an evil grin. It turned into a dark, black-purple flame that grew larger.

The guards were visibly terrified now. She raised her other hand, which quickly produced another flame. Bringing them closer, they joined, creating a single large flame. "Our lord wants to know…if you are LYING!"

The last word echoed down the hallway, and the shorter guard fell to his knees, begging for his life and still denying knowledge.

The taller guard stood shaking, accepting his fate but saying nothing.

Chandra stepped closer. They could feel the flame…but it was ice cold. Their very breath froze as it touched the flame and fell to the floor as ice crystals.

"Now, Chandra, my love. These gentlemen seem to be honest sorts, do they not?" Davin turned back to the men.

Chandra allowed the flames to slowly die down as she stared into their eyes, her smile turning to a snarl.

"Please, gentlemen, be at ease." He went to the taller man and put his arm around his shoulder and, in a gentle, friendly tone, said, "What is your name, friend?"

"Allyster, lord."

"Ah, now Allyster, as the new captain of my guard, will you do me the service of collecting the other guards in the yard so I might address them?"

"At once, m'lord." He snapped to attention, spun around and quickly marched out.

He turned to the other guard. "Tsk, tsk, tsk." He shook his head in disgust. "Now, young man, stand up."

The guard quickly stood to attention. He was visibly shaking now.

"And your name is?"

"Bartholemew, lord"

Davin turned to look at Chandra with a grin, fighting the urge to laugh. "This one is Bartholemew, lady."

She put her hand over her mouth to stifle a grin.

"Well…Bartholemew. Have no fear. As I said, I believe you and do not hold you to blame. Rest easy."

The guard was having no part of it. He remained at attention. "What I'd like you to do is post a sentry in the middle of the yard. The men will form up on you, and we'll begin to sort this out. Understood?"

"Yes, lord. As you command." His knees almost buckled as he spun and ran for the yard.

He moved and stood next to Chandra.

"So, your handmaiden is missing. She must be undead because I see no other way for her to leave." His voice was even and friendly.

Chandra knew this game. She didn't fear him, and he knew it.

"Are you suggesting I had something to do with this? I would truly hate to think that." Chandra turned an annoyed glare at him.

He closed his eyes and raised his eyebrows, then turned away. "Huh," he said matter-of-factly.

He started for the yard. "Join me?"

She gave a sarcastic nod of her head, lips curled with anger, and took his arm as they left.

The guards were formed in four ranks of five, with Bartholemew posted as commanded. The newly appointed captain stood in front of them, arrow straight.

Davin and Chandra looked almost regal as they stood in the stone archway, surveying the formation. "Quite impressive, are they not?"

Chandra gave a shrug of indifference, to which Davin began, "We have a problem, gentlemen." He again sounded friendly and warm. "We've had an…intrusion." He stepped forward. "Apparently, someone has gained entry in order to cause chaos in my home, whether it be for theft or murder." He began to pace. "IN MY HOME." The sheer volume made the men flinch.

Now, more calmly, "I've interrogated two men, who are, at least to my knowledge, of no suspicion. One I have promoted to guard captain, Captain Alyster, and the other is… " he cleared his throat to maintain his composure…Bartholemew." He motioned to the guard. "Would you please step forward, my good man?" The guard marched as militarily as he could, posting himself in front of Davin. "Please face the formation if you would."

He nodded to Chandra, who also stepped forward and to the right of Bartholemew. "This man was so brave and truthful that he fell to his knees crying and begging for his life."

Chandra's hands began to rise and swirl as black shadow began to billow from them.

"Now, is this the sort of guard you would be proud to call brother?"

All of the guards could now see the horror that the mage was about to unleash. Fear began to take hold among the ranks.

Bartholemew began to shake.

Chandra took another step forward and was now in full view of the terrified guard.

The black mist thickened, twisting into the shape of a human figure.

"Artaha lesh rthiem." The words were whispered and mysterious.

The wraith floated toward him and drew him into its arms. For a heartbeat, it looked like an embrace. Then, they saw his skin begin to shrivel, his eyes roll white, his mouth frozen in a silent scream of terror. The corpse collapsed in a brittle heap. Chandra's hands dropped, and she slowly, purposefully, returned to Davin's side, leaning her head on his shoulder.

Every guard stood paralyzed in stark terror.

Davin let the lesson burn into their very core before he spoke. "There now, gentlemen. Now you understand your service requirements…and the price for failure. Serve me well, and your lives are your own. Fail me, and hers is the last face you will ever see."

He turned to the captain. "Captain, if you will, please dismiss the guards."

He snapped to attention. "Yes, m'lord." Spinning on heel and toe, he gave his order. "Detail…dismissed."

Every guard ran as fast as they could to their posts.

"Captain, to my chamber, if you please." Davin led Chandra into the manor, her head still on his shoulder.

'...the winds of change are blowing.'

When the captain entered the chamber and stood at attention, Davin was sitting in front of the hearth with a golden goblet in hand, Chandra standing beside him, and facing the guard.

"Ah, Captain," she began in an almost sultry tone. "Our good lord here wishes to go into town with a detachment…and question them." She took a sip of wine from her silver goblet. "Do be a good boy and see to it, will you? We'll follow along soon."

"Yes, m'lady." He nodded and turned to leave.

"Oh, Captain?"

He turned back to her. "Yes, m'lady."

"Silly me, but if I'm not mistaken, the term is… yes, *my* lady, is it not?"

The captain's face went pale. "Yes, my lady. My apologies, lady. It will not happen again."

She waved her hand to dismiss him.

He bowed again, turned and marched away to carry out his orders.

"Do you really think it could be her? How could it be possible for her to withstand *my* magic?" She stood behind the other chair and faced Davin. "Impossible. There had to be another."

"Perhaps you used…the wrong spell?"

"Another test, my dear?" A hint of anger shone in her eyes. "You do know how I love to weave. Sometimes, when I'm not even thinking." Her shadowy eyes began to shift and swirl as she glared at him. "Oh, yes, I know. It does impress me so. But I don't recall you ever weaving…a storm's wrath. It truly is impressive when witnessed, to be sure." He flashed her a menacing smile.

She stood up and took one dainty step back, gently smiling at him lovingly, a spell already in hand and just as quickly cast.

"Come, my dear," Davin said, offering his hand toward the door. Chandra inclined her head not to him, but to the darkness beyond his shoulder. From the shadowed corner, two red eyes blinked.

Locate that tome.

'...As you command, mistress.'

She took his proffered arm, and they proceeded to the courtyard. Once there, they stopped where he leaned close and kissed her cheek. "It is this fire we have that I love most," he whispered into her ear.

Chandra did all she could not to retch. His very presence sickened her, but she knew she had to endure and keep up the charade, at least until she could return to Lyssa.

Dammit, sister, where are you?

The short carriage ride to Morowyck was tense and quiet. Infinite scenarios filled her mind. What was his plan? How brutal were these interrogations going to be? Was she going to be forced to murder? She was no murderer, and the thought of it angered her. She would have to find a way to either fool him or bypass the violence altogether. He was not much of a fool. Arrogant? Yes. Diabolical? Absolutely. Brutal? To be sure. But not a fool. She would have to wait and see. She was good at improvising. Lyssa taught her that.

Morowyck was similar to Tantyn. The center of town was where most of the selling and bartering was held, while the outer parts were shops, smithies and homes intermingled with taverns and places of a more personal nature.

It was nestled just inland from the Sea of Tears to the north, Whispering Woods to the east and Straggler's Bog to the west.

The farmland soil was rich and always produced the most bountiful of harvests. They even harvested peat from the bog for heating, though the peat cutters who worked nearby would always spin eerie tales of their encounters there.

On the shore, the fishing shanties dotted the coast with nets and dinghies that filled the makeshift docks. The variety of seafood caught was amazing, so good that it commonly attracted the king's minister, who would come to personally purchase shellfish for special occasions. Their arrival was always a very special event, sometimes calling for the finest of festivals.

The carriage came to a halt in the center of the town. Townsfolk instantly made way for the procession, who, upon seeing the lord, immediately fell to bent knees.

Davin assisted Chandra from the carriage. He climbed back in to get a better view of the people and waited as his guards took station behind him.

He began in a courteous, respectful tone. "Rise." There was hushed murmuring. "A person was seen on the manor grounds. He or she was last seen fleeing toward Morowyck. Any information leading to their capture will be richly rewarded."

He looked around, expectantly, but the crowd remained silent.

"Please, step forth and have no fear. It is just the information that is required." He waited patiently, but still there was silence.

"No one here has any information?" Again, he looked around.

"Withholding information will incur the heaviest of penalties, I can assure you."

People looked around, trying to see if anyone at all would come forward.

He glanced at a blood-covered, overweight butcher. Haron, he recalled. He stood proudly and shook his head, no. Davin knew him to be a good man and discounted him immediately.

He glanced at an old woman, Chala Riddle, if memory served. She was half blind, so he discounted her as well. The brown-haired boy next to her, holding her arm, looked down and shook his head, no. He was dirty and wore rags, probably a fisherman. No one went near the docks due to the smell. No, he wouldn't know.

He turned to his captain and said, annoyed, "Captain, dismount and begin the search. Bring anyone suspected to Lady Chandra and myself for further…interrogation."

"Aye, my lord." He made sure to pronounce his title to avoid incurring any wrath from the dark lady. "Detail…dismount." He jumped to the ground and began yelling orders to his men, who immediately headed to the far reaches of the town in search of the escapee.

Davin sat and looked down on Chandra. "I've no doubt we will find this person." He sat back and smiled.

She searched the crowd and tried to look menacing. This was not what she wanted, nor was it something that she and Lyssa had even planned. Lyssa had always said, *Plans are nothing more than a list of things that could go wrong.* She knew what she was talking about, though Chandra would never admit to it.

They watched as guards milled about, entering homes and shops, manhandling others as a means to get information. Most didn't want to be heavy-handed, but it was either the townsfolk or them, and they had all seen what the dark lady could do.

Many people had stayed close to witness what transpired, including the butcher and the young fisherman.

A young man was brought to Davin, scraped and bleeding. "This one here spat on Ferin, lord."

Ferin kicked the man's arse, knocking him down.

"Ahh, insolence. I so love a strong-willed person. Don't you, my dear?" he said with a grin.

She glanced down at him. "Why, yes. I do." She bent down to look him over. The guard backed away, fearing Chandra was going to incinerate the man.

The man looked up and spat in Chandra's face. "Endless dark take ya, witch," he hissed through clenched teeth. There was shock and fear all around.

Chandra stood up without wiping it off. She grinned and stepped back.

Raising her hands over her head with an insane look on her face, she gently said, "Arvan petrus falvala."

A bolt of darkness enveloped the man, lifting him to his feet. Then came the horrible, terrifying scream. It started loudly and slowly quieted to a whisper. He only breathed once. It had only taken seconds, but it felt like a lifetime.

She lowered her hands and walked to the man who was still standing, paralyzed and dead. The look of sheer terror on his face even chilled Davin. *Interesting. Absolute power.*

People who had been watching fled in terror. They now knew who this mage was and fled for their lives. The two guards present knew they could not move for fear of bringing on the same fate.

Chandra's anger abated, and she turned to Davin, who produced a kerchief and dabbed the spit from her beautiful face. "My apologies, lady." The gleam in her eyes was like that of an inferno. Davin knew that toying with her at this moment could lead to dangerous things, so he sat back and waited for the next suspect. Chandra's knees buckled, and she nearly fell, using the carriage to steady herself. "Are you alright?" He quickly leaned forward as if to help. "It weakened me a bit. That spell is so immensely powerful." She forced herself up, trying not to look weak.

Very soon, another person was brought forth. This was a young girl. She had blonde hair and a sweet, cherubic face. There were tears streaming down her dirty face, and she was crying uncontrollably. Her clothing was torn as if she'd been attacked, but was otherwise all right. Chandra stood before her, glaring down. The girl looked up at Chandra and began to beg for her life. She swore she knew nothing and saw nothing. She glanced at the guard. He looked at her and showed no fear. His face was greasy and damp as if he'd been running but tried to hide the faintest smirk.

"The truth, girl. Your death will be painful."

"I swear, lady, I swear. I don't know nothin'."

Chandra looked at Davin and said, "I have a way to pry it out of her if you wish. It is tiring for me, painful to her, but it will yield the truth."

Davin nodded. Chandra turned and looked at the girl, placing her hands on either side of her face. She closed her eyes and began to concentrate. Her hands started turning black, and wisps of pure shadow floated from them to the girl's head, causing her to shriek.

The brown-haired boy and the butcher looked on as the dark lady plied her trade, seemingly without feeling. The butcher turned and went back to his shop, shaking his head in disgust, but the brown-haired boy stayed and looked on. He showed no emotion but remained steady and watched.

CHANDRA! What are you doing?

The brown-haired boy doubled over as if she were gut-punched. Her sister, how could she? Anger welled up in her as she clenched her fists.

This is not who you are, sister.

'...like a whirlwind...'

When the mage's spell was complete, the girl collapsed to the ground, living and unhurt, but she felt pain like never before.

Chandra stood and looked at the guard. "My sweet, this girl knows nothing." She kept staring into the guards' eyes. He could almost feel them burn.

"You made the attempt, didn't you?" she said to the guard. This piqued Davin's attention, and he stood.

"Attempt?" he asked with a raised eyebrow.

"Yes, dearest. He made an attempt to take this child. In front of her family, even," Chandra replied, still looking into the guards' eyes.

Davin turned his gaze to the guard who was no longer smirking.

"My dear, you look drained. Perhaps some rest would benefit you." He called over two more guards, leaning down, and in a gentle, friendly tone commanded, "Please chain this animal and drag him to the dungeon until I return." He looked at the guard. "Remember, drag him."

"As you command, lord." Both men smiled at the other guard as he struggled to resist. Chandra moved her hand, and a stream of thin shadow wrapped around the guard's wrists, causing him to stop wrestling.

She slowly walked to him and ran her fingernail under the guard's chin. With the wickedest of grins, she said, "Oh, we're going to have such fun." His face paled, and his mouth went dry. He knew his life was now forfeit, and had become too stunned to speak. *How did she know?*

She stepped into the carriage as the guards tied the animal to the carriage and escorted them almost half a league back.

Lyssa was furious. Her sister had not only joined Davin but was now doing his bidding. She felt betrayed, yet again. This time it would not stand. Sister or no, betrayal was intolerable and would be met with the harshest of punishments.

'...stronger and stronger...'

"To the dungeon." Chandra stood and allowed a guard to help her from the carriage. She looked at the bloody, half-dead guard, smiling, then turned and went into the manor. The two sentries standing in front quickly opened both doors and stood at attention. As she passed, they closed the doors and glanced at each other, thankful she didn't stop.

'...I've found it, mistress. It sits on the desk in his chamber.'

She walked slowly down the long hallway and through the kitchen. This time, there was no ruse. Her weaving did take a toll, making her feel weak and tired.

The smell of the evening's meal permeated the entire manor, making her stomach growl. She walked down the hall and into the chamber Malhrun had spoken about, where she easily found a tome sitting on the desk. This time, she opened it to ensure this was it. It wasn't, much to her chagrin.

Malhrunnnn...?

Two red eyes blinked in the corner near her.

'... the real one can be found under his chair, mistress.'

Reaching down alongside the seat cushion, she found the hook release, slid it over and felt the tome fall to the floor. She opened it to ensure that this was actually the correct one. It was. She compared them side by side and saw that the fake was almost an exact replica, but the wording changed slightly. The calligraphy and illumination were of improper color and looked too fresh.

She replaced the fake tome under the chair and left with the true tome.

Inform me of his arrival, she thought to Malhrun.

She stood and walked to the hearth where a comfortable fire burned, sparks gently floating up the flue and out of sight. The heat that radiated from it felt comforting and warmed her skin.

Sitting in the padded chair, she opened the tome and began to read. She could understand most of the writing, but some was unknown to her. Some glyphs and runes made no sense, and some of the wording had been cryptically constructed so that she couldn't decipher them.

...until...

'...MISTRESS!'

A hand clasped her mouth tightly and yanked her head back, exposing her throat. A thin edge of searing cold touched her, making it impossible for her to weave.

An almost undecipherable, yet familiar, ominous voice whispered in her ear, *"Gotcha...sister."*

Chandra didn't move. "What?" Chandra mumbled through Lyssa's tightly bound fingers.

"So, you went for power after all."

She could feel Lyssa's warm breath against her skin.

"Mother would be very disappointed, sister." She pressed the edge just slightly closer.

Chandra was beginning to get nervous now. For the very first time in her life, she felt completely helpless. Why was Lyssa doing this? What was wrong?

"Why have you turned against me, dear sister?" The edge was almost too close. Any more would surely cut her.

Chandra tried to speak, but Lyssa's hold was too tight. Lyssa relaxed two fingers enough to let Chandra speak.

"...found the tome." It was enough.

"And what were you doing in town, eh? It wasn't playing a pan flute." She squeezed her hand tightly over her mouth, contemplating breaking her soft neck. She loosened her grip enough for her to speak again.

"He made me," she said. She saw Malhrun in the corner of her eye. *You stay out of this.*

Lyssa moved the dagger away and shoved her sister to the wall, rage painted on her face, eyes flashing venom.

Chandra returned Lyssa's glare, angry beyond belief, a roiling strand of shadow at the ready.

In a calm, terrifying voice, "If you release that spell, sister, all bets are off, and you will know the taste of fine steel." A mad grin crossed her lips. "Mark my words, *sweet* sister."

"Put the blade down, Lyssa," Chandra said, never breaking eye contact.

She knew Lyssa was far more deadly, faster and, for the time being, held the upper hand.

"Why did you betray me, Chandra, dear? Why did you murder and torture those townsfolk?"

The spell in Chandra's hands was now complete. All that was left to do was release it, and Lyssa was hers. She truly was afraid of hurting her sister, but between killing Lyssa and dying herself, Lyssa would lose. Lyssa had an inkling of what was running through the mage's mind and cut her off.

"Sister, you may be Queen of Shadows, but I *am* the shadows."

Lyssa knew she had to put an end to this madness. Never in her wildest dreams did she ever think it would come to this, sister against sister. She could almost hear her mother's sobs echoing in her head.

Then, as if Talith herself had screamed at them both, a deadly dagger fell, and a spell dissipated. Each sister shook their head, confused, regaining their composure.

That voice, was it real? Lyssa thought.

Mother, was that really you? Chandra asked.

Chandra blinked, knowing this was not over, and took a step back with her hands in front of her as if to ward Lyssa off. She turned and sat in the chair behind her.

Each narrowed their eyes at the other, now distrusting what they had heard or what was happening.

But Lyssa had to know…

"Did you…?" she asked, suspiciously.

Chandra cut her off, "No." She knew it couldn't have been her sister.

They sat, staring at the floor silently for several minutes, trying to make sense of it all.

Chandra slowly looked at her sister, hurt in her eyes, "Why do you think I betrayed you?" Sadness covered her face.

She replied in a whisper, "You killed for him. You tortured for him." She was restraining her fury. Chandra saw it and tried to avert another confrontation.

She calmed her tone. "Lyssa, please, understand. I had to kill, or he would have seen through the ruse. We had to keep up the charade so you could escape with the tome." She took a breath.

"When I turned down that hallway, I thought you wanted to go and talk in my chamber. I didn't know you already had the tome." She could see Lyssa was calming but just barely.

"As for him, I had no idea he was even here until I saw him return with it." She looked at the book lying on the desk. "He was working for Davin. He is the one who betrayed. He betrayed both of us. I think he meant for us to do...this." Tears began to well up in her eyes.

Lyssa thought for a second. It made some sense. She retrieved her dagger and eased it back into place, eyes never leaving her sister. "Why did you use that spell. It almost killed me."

"It was the only one I had that would look real enough to fool him and not kill you."

There was a pause of silence in the room. Lyssa began to realize that her sister not only made sense but proved herself right.

Chandra thought about her sister's words and began to get angry. When their eyes next met, Lyssa could see the building ire on Chandra's face.

"What makes you think I would EVER take his side? He is an arrogant, pompous ass. He makes me ill every time I get near him. He thinks of only himself. He is cruel, conniving and he smells like a goat's arse." She stood and took a step toward Lyssa. "Why would I EVER betray you, you ignorant ragamuffin? Have I ever lied to you, senseless dolt? Don't I always take your side when we get into trouble?" Her face had turned a bright red. She stepped to her sister and gave a hearty shove, knocking her over, pointing a stern finger. "I promised you that I would always care for you, I would always be by your side. And NOW you think I BETRAYED you?" Lyssa rolled to escape her, but Chandra shoved her down again. "WE ARE ALL WE HAVE, YOU IGNORANT FOOL!" She turned and walked to the door with her back to Lyssa.

Then, for the first time in her life, Lyssa heard it…

You and Chandra are one. The bond cannot be broken. Heed Ash'Tara's words.

She was stunned. What was that voice? It whispered in her head. She looked around. Just to the left of Chandra, against the wall in the corner, two red eyes blinked at her. It wasn't the shade.

Kitikithakis!

Just then, Ash'Tara's words came rushing in like an untamed river.

You are correct. You cannot live without her. You are separate but as one.

She could almost feel Ash'Tara's hands, strong yet motherly.

You must always trust in each other. You are both kith and kin. It was as if Ash'Tara stood before her once again. *That is a powerful bond that no one can break. Blood is blood. Blood must keep blood. Blood must avenge blood.*

She remembered her eyes. The sincerity in them. The faith and trust she put in her to carry on their ways.

Lyssa stared at her sister for just a second, her anger quickly washing away. Chandra stood and walked to her, taking those dangerous hands in hers, giving them a light shake and said, "We cannot waver, Lyssa." She sighed.

Lyssa lowered her eyes, the voices in her head quieting. She paused, gathering her thoughts.

"I found our people, sister," she said, looking into Chandra's eyes. "There was a wise woman who looked into me, into my spirit. She told me that we are one and would always be one. She told me that blood must keep blood. I forgot that. I let my anger and mistrust rule me, and I was wrong for it."

Lyssa looked in her eyes. "I'm sorry. I should have trusted you." She pulled Chandra close. They stood there in each other's arms.

Chandra pulled back just a bit. "I told you, I will never let anything happen to you. I would die first."

Lyssa smiled, fighting back a tear. "You almost did." She winked, leaned in and kissed her sister's nose and whispered, "I gotcha."

Chandra pulled back, still holding her sister's hands and said, "Sister, you got me, this time." She reached for the tome and said, "But please, don't do it again. Shadows can hurt," and winked at her.

"We are one, sister," Lyssa said. "No one can ever change that."

Together they left as one....

There was business to tend to, and someone was about to pay—dearly.

'...until what, pray tell?'

'...I grow weary of this, my arrogant friend.'

Chandra concluded that she hated the forest. She *really* hated the forest. Insects crawled up her dress, venturing into places not meant for them to go. Leaves and limbs slapped her beautiful face and tangled in her hair. Dirt and mud sullied her dainty shoes, and all this soured her mood. Through it all, Lyssa maintained a bright, warm smile and a lightness that only made Chandra's temper burn hotter.

Lyssa moved as if the woods themselves parted for her, stepping over roots and ducking under branches with the ease of a fox on familiar ground.
"Almost there," she called softly over her shoulder.

Chandra muttered something unholy and tried to free her hem from another thornbush. "If *almost there* means another mile of misery, I'm setting this whole accursed forest on fire."

Lyssa only laughed. "The Valyn wouldn't appreciate that much, sister."

"The Valyn," Chandra grumbled, "had better have a bath waiting—and wine—preferably both at once."

After a short while, the trees thinned, and the sisters stepped into a clearing washed in pale green light. Smoke curled from hidden chimneys, and faint voices drifted through the leaves in the Valyn village.

Lyssa turned to her, now completely miserable sister, her smile softening. "Try to look less like you plan to kill someone. They're wary of strangers."

Chandra brushed a leaf from her hair and sighed. "Sister, I *am* a stranger. And after this march, they should be wary."

Lyssa only shook her head, still smiling as they started toward the campfires.

The faces turned, all remembering their Val'ethra, the children running to greet her, laughing and smiling.

Chandra marveled at the grandeur of this small village in the woods. She was so used to seeing *modern* housing and conveniences that she had no idea beauty could present itself like this. Lyssa smiled warmly at her.

"So, what do you think?"

"Sister… this is marvelous." She looked from house to house and from person to person.

"You remember the tales Gran used to tell us? Well, they were all true." She spread her arms wide, presenting their new home.

Children of all sizes hugged and spoke to Lyssa all at the same time, each trying to gain her attention. She laughed and touched each hand while walking toward the long house where she hoped Ash'Tara was. Some children looked at Chandra, wary but smiling, wondering who this lovely person was.

Warriors appeared, as if from nowhere, spears and blades drawn, acknowledging Lyssa but partially encircling Chandra.

The leader of these warriors, Ket'balan, greeted Lyssa but had to find out about her sister.

Lyssa stopped. "Alright, sister, listen closely now," she said, looking at Chandra. "Don't make any sudden moves and only speak when I say." Chandra rolled her eyes.

"Sister, this is no jest. They don't know you and will kill immediately you if they think you are a threat."

Chandra nodded, understanding the gravity of her situation.

Lyssa raised her hands over her head; her black daggers displayed for all to see.

"Veyrana en'darin, kira'thien. Sha'len kalyen en'var. Ka Valyn velora en'shai."

Ket'balan's broad smile warmed Lyssa. "You Syl'va...good. Learn...you."

Chandra was completely lost. "What did he say, sister?"

Lyssa quickly glanced at her sister. "Shh." Then, to Ket'balan, "Velara kalyen nim'ara...Chan'Dra Soryn. Mira'thien en'sha'ra, veyrana en'Kal'La Valyn. Ithila en'Veyrana Ash'Tara sha'thien."

He smiled and motioned for them to follow, the other warriors still hesitant to lower their weapons. As they started off, Chandra whispered, "What were you saying? They sound angry."

"First, I gave the formal greeting, more honoring him than anything. 'Honor to you, brother of life. The path brings many shadows. May the Valyn guide your steps.'" Chandra blinked at the explanation. "How long did you live here. It sounded like you've been speaking like this all your life."

Ket'balan looked back at them, puzzled.

"Next, I told him who you were and that I wanted to ask Ash'Tara to accept you." She looked somewhat concerned.

"Ash'Tara? Who's that, now?"

"She's the...leader, if you will. You'll see. Now hush."

As they were being led to Ash'Tara, wood folk from all across the village came out to greet Lys'Sa and to see who the new outsider was. They spoke and whispered in hushed tones, pointing and smiling. Chandra tried to keep her eyes forward, but the sheer wonder of the village wouldn't let her. She found herself looking at all of the people, the trees and the houses. It was a jolt to her senses, one she was falling in love with.

Finally, the long house loomed before them. "Now, sister. Say nothing...nothing." She gave a stern look. Chandra nodded, trusting her sister's advice as she put her life in her sister's hands.

Chandra saw the simple grandeur of the hall. No extravagance, no finery, yet beautiful in its own way. She noted the various ranks of people attending as they moved closer to the dais. Some were armed, the warriors. Some had staves, the mages or shamans. And a lone figure sat just to the left of the dais, who seemed to be a scribe of sorts.

They were led to the dais where Ash'Tara sat. Lyssa bowed, and Chandra curtsied. "Bow, dammit," Lyssa whispered loudly. Chandra, now confused, bowed low, embarrassed.

As they both recovered, Lyssa spoke, "Veyrana Ash'Tara, Veyr'thien en'Valen, Mara'thien en'sha'ra. Velora en'darin sha'ta."

Ash'Tara stood and slowly stepped toward, her eyes on Chandra as if evil had walked into her home. She kissed both Lyssa's cheeks, then her forehead.

"This is Chan'Dra," Ash'Tara said. There was distrust in her eyes.

"Yes, Veyr'thien. She is mara'thien." Lyssa looked at Chandra and took hold of her hand, which she held tightly.

Ash'Tara stepped in front of Chandra, inspecting her from left to right. She walked behind her and touched her long platinum locks, then returned. She then gently pulled down her eyelid, inspecting, but Lyssa noticed concern. Was this going all right?

Ash'Tara showed her teeth to Chandra, who followed suit, feeling foolish as well.

"Hmm, mara'thien you say." Ash'Tara glanced at Lyssa.

Chandra quickly looked at Lyssa, begging for help. Seeing this, Lyssa shook her head, no, and Chandra faced forward once more, fear now creeping into her bones.

Ash'Tara looked at Lyssa and nodded for her to stand near the dais. She was now bewildered, not understanding what was happening.

Ash'Tara stepped back two steps and raised her hands as if to cast a spell. "Can you defend yourself, Chan'Dra?" The woman's hands began to brighten with flame as she began to cast a spell. Lyssa's eyes went wide with fear.

Chandra frowned and stepped back, beginning to cast a spell of her own.

Ash'Tara's hand lowered, her spell fading.

Chandra followed suit, though she still frowned, anger now taking the place of wonder.

"It is you, Chan'Dra, the One Who is Shadow." She looked back at Lyssa, who moved back to Chandra's side and grabbed her hand.

"You were both born during Vayl'tharyn a'veshra. You call it the Long Night Moon." She looked around the room sternly and raised her arms, "Mira'sha'en valra, the sisters of darkness, have come to the Valyn, my people. Ka'Lohane has spoken; we listen."

All at once, everyone fell to their knees. Then, as she did to Lyssa so long ago, she smiled, took her head in her hands and kissed Chandra's forehead. "You are sister." She kissed her left cheek. "You are daughter." She kissed her right cheek. "You are Valyn." She then wrapped the girl in a motherly hug.

She motioned for everyone to stand, then took them both by the hand and led them up to the top of the dais, placing them on either side of her.

She looked at Lyssa. "Lys'Sa Socha, Dark Cat," She closed her eyes tightly. "Born feet-first; walker, and not watcher. Her silence speaks louder than words. She befriends shadow. She is moon-bound, wood-tied, always listening, always waiting. This one speaks with the forest. And when she walks, even the shadows tremble. She is Valyn."

The throng of onlookers each repeated as one, "Sa en'Valyn."

She turned to Chandra. "Born headfirst, mind first. The odd one, the listener of things no one else hears. She will know what others fear to know. She, too, will befriend shadow. This one will be moon-bound. This one speaks to shadow. And she will never fear the darkness. She is Valyn."

Again, they each repeated as one, "Sa en'Valyn."

She motioned for them to stand before her and kneel. She placed her hand on each one's head. "I am the one who spoke these words. I am the one who pulled you into this world…and I am the one who burned your names into the world itself." She raised her hands high and spoke the binding words of the Valyn.

"Ka'Lohane, Valyn en'ka'mira, the One Who Breathes Life. Mark the names Lys'Sa, the Dark Cat, and Chan'Dra, the One Who is Shadow, into the eternal forest of life if they are worthy. Your will is our will. We are one; we are Valyn."

She went to each sister and, once again, kissed their forehead and bade them to rise. As they faced the people, they were met with cheers then led outside. Once outside, Ash'Tara announced, "Ka'Lohane has spoken. The forest glows with thanks and love." To the sisters' amazement, each tree and bush shimmered with a vibrant greenish glow, bathing the entire village and all of its people.

After a short while, it dissipated, leaving torches as the only source of light. Ash'Tara led them to a small wooden house across from the hall that they could stay in as long as they liked with her blessing, then left.

Inside was a large bed with a hearth nearby, a small table piled with fruit and nuts and a child's small black cat doll made of darkwood and twigs.

"What just happened, sister?" Chandra stood motionless and confused.

"I thought the same thing when Kitikithakis brought me here." She smiled. "We are Valyn, sister. The tales that Mother and Gran told us about, they're all true." She took Chandra's hands. "Mother spoke about the midwife who helped us into the world, remember?" Chandra nodded. "Ash'Tara was the midwife. Mother called her Elma. Only Gran knew."

Chandra was still confused. Lyssa explained, "We have a family now, sister. These people have been all along. Gran and Mother kept everything a secret; us being born on the night of the Long Night Moon, being Valyn, everything. We could have been killed at birth if anyone knew."

Chandra's eyes lit up, "So that's how we found each other? That's why we're so close?" She blinked, then looked at her sister. "And that's why we can never part."

Lyssa nodded. "Yes."

They remained in the village for several weeks. Ash'Tara answered their many questions, learning more and more about who their gran and mother really were. Their fascination led them into many areas: the ancients, their history, the language. Chandra learned that her specific line of magic was more a blessing than she'd known. Several of their ancestors had worked shadow magic, but she was the first in several generations, begging the question: Were they here for some special purpose? Ash'Tara had no answer for that except to say that the gods or goddesses put them here at this time for some reason and that it would be revealed when the time came.

They were sent to the village sha'len mirae, the keeper of words, where they were taught the proper way to speak in the Valyn tongue. Here, once more, they encountered the scribe who was writing madly in what now looked like a tome. Much to Chandra's disdain, Lyssa already knew how to speak Valyn thanks to Kitikithakis and from spending so much time with Gran. Now it had become her turn to tease Chandra about how dimwitted she was. She would correct her sister mid-sentence and shake her head like Chandra did back when they were children. Oddly enough, Chandra took it all in stride, now understanding how Lyssa felt those many years ago. It was all in fun, and they both realized that it only made them stronger, together.

The people of the village became more comfortable with the girls. They were seldom seen apart, and they both fell in love with the children. Sometimes, before the sun fell, they would sit in a secluded area of the village and just tell stories or play little games.

When time permitted, Ash'Tara would confer with Chandra on the various forms of magic, as both a teacher and an apprentice. Together with the val'kara, nature wardens, who could weave magic to help defend the forest, and the ka'thalen, the spiritualists, who weaved "listening" magic to commune with Ka'Lohane, they spent many hours deep into the night learning and understanding each other's disciplines and how they fit together. Nothing pleased Ash'Tara more than to see Chandra intently listening and learning from her newfound people.

Lyssa, on the other hand, trained with the Ka'shiraen valra, Hidden Thorns. Called such because, not unlike Lyssa, they hunted from stealth and knew the forest from their birth. Lyssa was an icon to these warriors, learning every aspect of fighting from the shadows. The village knew her as Lys'Sa the Cat, but to her warrior clan she was *Sha'kar valra*...the Shadow that Kills.

At night, the girls would lie in bed as they did as children and discuss the day, how they felt and sometimes teased each other. Each came to love these folk in their own way, considering each of them their family. Unfortunately, neither liked being considered "special" to them. They feared it could bring danger and bad fortune, which they couldn't bear the thought of.

Their thoughts returned to their main reason for being there in the first place...the assassin. The very word brought ire and hatred.

"It's time, sister. He has to pay his debt." Chandra was the first to become serious. There was a short pause of silence.

"You can't fight him, Chandy. He's far too skilled." She glanced at her sister. "I'm not teasing this time, sister. I don't think I can beat him either. You saw how easily I was able to get to you, and that was in a fortified manor. Imagine his skill; he taught me." That was meant as a slight tweak to her sister.

"Together then, sister. We can't lose if we stay together." She smiled back.

Lyssa sighed. "The second he caught wind of us together, he would either leave and never to be seen again or he would kill us both."

"Sister," she faced Lyssa, "*NO ONE* can kill us both."

Lyssa pulled Chandra close and put her head on her shoulder. The warmth of her sister's body and her rhythmic breathing started to make her sleepy. "I trained with him for a long time, sister. I've seen what he can do, and I know he has contacts in nearly every town this side of the Argent River."

Silence. Chandra had no words. She snuggled closer to Lyssa and fell fast asleep.

The sound of children laughing outside their door woke them. Slowly, they stretched and dressed, shaking away the cobwebs of sleep and preparing for another beautiful day. When they opened the door, the children ran off, laughing and taunting Chandra to chase them. They both smiled and walked across to the hall, hoping they didn't miss the community meal.

When they got there, the aroma of roasted nuts, meats and spices filled their senses. Several warriors were sitting at a far table and signaling Lyssa to join them.

"Oh, go. Who am I to keep you from your playmates, sister?" That earned Chandra a playful glare as she joined them.

Chandra spotted several of the val'kara and went to join them, each smiling at her and making room.

Lyssa sat and talked to the warriors about some of her adventures and how she was trained by an extraordinarily talented man, but didn't give his name. She mentioned his manor on the King's River and it being close to the Black Hollow Mill. One of the younger ka'shiraen valra, a girl named Sel'yra, spoke up. "I know of...place this."

Lyssa was taken by surprise at this comment. She didn't know that any of the Valyn roamed that side of the river.

"We...every woods." She smiled.

Lyssa looked at her, pausing to gather her thoughts. She explained that her training took her there and back many times and how she never liked it. I made her feel...uneasy.

"You...not see. I there...see you."

That raised her eyebrows. She was seen there by Sel'yra? What else has she seen?

"See...big," she raised her hand high over her head, indicating the man was very tall, "Him...teach you...yes?" This was getting interesting. Lyssa nodded yes and asked her to continue.

"Me...know him leave. See...him with horse...go."

She found out that the assassin had left the manor several days past and was loaded heavily on horseback, heading toward the Duchy of Eldorath. Interesting.

She asked if Sel'yra knew where he might have gone, but she just said into the duchy. Lyssa grabbed her hand and squeezed it gently, thanking her for that information. Sel'yra blushed and smiled happily as the other warriors began to tease her.

Lyssa stood, quickly going to Chandra and excusing her intrusion to the others. She whispered into her ear about the latest information. Chandra's eyes lit up.

They excused themselves from the table and headed to their home to discuss a possible plan.

They talked all day, coming up with many ideas, then discarding them for one reason or another. The frustration was beginning to show when they started to snap at each other. Lyssa's face lit up as a foolproof plan came to mind. Chandra rolled her eyes but let her speak anyway.

"He has eyes all over every town. That works in our favor, my sweet sister." She laughed. "We go into one of the towns on the duchy side." She thought for a second. "No. We let people see us having words on the king's bridge. There are always a lot of people going back and forth there." She began to pace, deep in thought. "He's already seen us fight." She started to giggle at the thought.

"What, pray tell, is so funny, sister?"

She looked at Chandra. "I remember that fight; the look on your face when I knocked you to the ground, eyes as black as the doll Gran gave you at our seventh season fest." Her eyes looked to the ceiling in remembrance, "Gods that felt good."

Chandra stood. "Ooohhh." Her teeth gnashed, and she started toward Lyssa. "I still owe you for that one." She tried to grab Lyssa, but she was just too fast for her until something grabbed her foot, making her fall to the floor. Chandra saw her chance, pounced, and they began to wrestle and laugh, breaking their tension from their earlier frustration.

Tired and breathing heavily, Chandra went and sat down.

Looking at her sister, Lyssa smiled and called out, "Oh, Maallrruunn. Come out, sweet shade. I have something I want to do to you."

Two red eyes blinked close to her, but made a dash to the far corner. "You tripped me, little shade. That's cheating." She leaped toward the corner, but the shade danced to the opposite side. Chandra began to laugh. "You'll never get him, sister. He's a shade."

And there was her advantage. She darted toward the corner, knowing it could only move in the shadows. Malhrun started for another corner, but Lyssa rolled and cut him off, causing him to return. She saw the red eyes blink and an ever so slight glance at its next move. He started off, and she dove...and captured the little shade, holding him fast, deep in the shadow.

Chandra was shocked. She'd never seen Lyssa move like that, nor did she know it was even possible to capture a shade.

"Little shade," Lyssa smiled, "it's not nice to play dirty with people, especially with one who knows what you are." It seemed as if the little shade was actually afraid.

Chandra was speechless. Lyssa placed her hand on the shade's head and petted it. "Now, you go play with the dust in the corner and let the big people talk, hmmm?" She released it, but it only stood there staring at her. "Go on now; go play." Her voice dripped with sarcasm, and she returned to her sister.

"How...but...how by Velkhar's hairs did you do that?" She was both impressed and confused.

"A shade is actually a corporeal entity. If you catch it before it melts into the shadows, you can hold it. I mean, at the point where shadow becomes light." She smiled and winked at Chandra. "See, sister, dear, you're not the only one who reads." She sat on the bed and laughed heartily as she removed her shoes. Chandra never knew that. In all of the books and tomes she'd ever read, she'd never seen that information.

"Now, where was I? Oh, yes, the...fight." She grinned broadly and gave a sideways glance to Chandra.

Her sister sighed, "Alright, alright, get on with it."

"We let everyone see us fight, maybe threaten fists or magic." Now it was Chandra's turn to smile. She tapped her cheek with a finger, eyes looking to the ceiling and mock thinking, "Do you remember that time at Davin's manor when I...what was it? Oh, yes. Killed you?" She leaned back in the chair, Lyssa's face contorting into mock anger. Chandra was laughing so hard and leaning back so far that her chair fell backward, causing them both to laugh uncontrollably.

When they finally regained their composure, they both sat on the edge of the bed.

"Alright, we stick to the subject now." Chandra looked sideways with a grin. "Chandy, we need to be serious now."

"Okay. Go on. We fight on the bridge."

"Right, we end up going our separate ways. Here, you have to make it look real. If they get any idea that we're not serious, then the spy follows me, and we lose him." She thought a second, continuing to piece the plan together. "I know someone on the road will be his eyes. He's been following me since he betrayed us." Chandra's eyes widened.

"Not in here. The ka'shiraen valra would have eaten him for morning meal." She smiled, knowing that those warriors very well might have eaten him.

"Once he sees you leave, the spy will stay with you. He knows me, but you are the question. You are the one he can't account for. He'll want to keep a close eye on you."

Chandra thought about the plan. There was no flaw that she could see, and it was very basic. Fewer things could go wrong.

"It sounds good to me, sister." She looked outside, and night had fallen. She got undressed and rolled under the covers. Lyssa was still pacing and thinking.

"Sister, stop. It's a good plan. It'll work." She smiled and pulled aside the covers. "Come to bed and sleep. We can start tomorrow with fresh minds."

Lyssa begrudgingly relented. She stripped off her clothes and climbed into bed. Chandra blew out the lantern, and they slept.

At the foot of the bed, two glowing eyes blinked.

Of Reckonings and Debts Paid

They awoke in the morning feeling refreshed. They had a purpose now, a reason. They dressed and went outside. The early morning sun cast an orange glow that beamed through the trees. There was no mist this morning, but the birds still chirped their joyous songs, much to the delight of the scampering children.

The hall had been prepared for the community meal. The val'kara and ka'shiraen valra warriors ate on the right side, the ka'thalen, mages and seers, the left, and at the head sat Ash'Tara and her mirae advisors.

It was not yet full when they entered, but some of the ka'shiraen valra were present and asked the girls over. They were especially impressed with Chandra, though they couldn't understand how her magic worked and why she had no weapons.

Making their way to the thorns, they were met by the young scribe who bowed and continued to write.

Lyssa continued to the table, but Chandra stopped, a curious look on her face.

"I'm curious, but you don't seem to be a…" she thought hard, looking for the word,"…kashi'ren valra."

The scribe smiled and stopped writing for just a second. He bowed and looked at Chandra.

"I am Kae'Len, Kaelen in your tongue. And no, I am not a…" he thought a second, "thorn as you call them."

She paused a second in thought. "You are a scribe of sorts. Um, kath'alaen. No, ka'thalen, yes ka'thalen. Am I correct? Are you a mage or shaman?" Her interest was now piqued.

"Ka'en val Ash'Tara, dra'len var." He smiled. "Oh, excuse me, Chan'Dra. I am the writer," he thought a second, "chronicler for Ash'Tara. I write the…history…for our people. I am one of many."

"Dra'len var—chronicler—very interesting. And your name. Kae'Len, is that right?" She smiled.

"Yes, Chan'Dra. I am Kae'Len."

"Well, it is a pleasure to meet you. I've a feeling we'll be speaking again." She turned and joined Lyssa at the table.

Kae'Len returned to his place near the dais and continued to write, looking her way every so often.

The food was strange to the girls, though Lyssa had tasted it before; pine nuts, berries and a sweet, thick liquid mixed together with a hardened egg, which Chandra found tasty and delightful. Lyssa, on the other hand, found it less than appetizing but ate anyway rather than offend her people.

Chandra found the ka'shiraen valra remarkably interesting and discussed how their battle prowess and her magic would form a very formidable defense for the village when a small but robust young ka'shiraen valra girl sat next to Lyssa, proffering spiced and seasoned chicken.

She was short for a warrior but muscled and very lithe for her young age. Lyssa could tell she wasn't very battle-worn because of her youth, but noted a fire in her eyes. As she grew, Lyssa knew this one would be a force to contend with.

Lyssa smiled at her and set the plate between them, offering to share it.

"Veyr'nai, mira'thien valra. Please share this with me." The girl's eyes widened excitedly. The Val'ethra thanked her for bringing food and wanted to share it with her. She blushed at the honor.

"Val'ethra…proud m-m-ake…you me." She was almost in tears. The rest of the ka'shiraen valra became silent, watching the exchange. Lyssa placed her hand on the girl's shoulder, and she almost fainted. Her warrior brothers laughed.

Lyssa turned a warning glare at the men, who immediately fell silent. Chandra smiled at the men. "Sha'kar valra...is that right?" she asked a warrior.

"She, yes," he said almost reverently.

"Sha'kar valra loves all of you. She's strong and dangerous, but do not fear her. She will never hurt her people." She turned to Lyssa and whispered.

"Careful, sister. Too much of a good thing can turn bad quickly." She winked at Lyssa so she would understand.

Lyssa nodded, then looked at the girl. "What do they call you, mira'thien?"

The girl bowed her head, "Sel'yra, Val'ethra." She smiled.

Lyssa raised her chin to look into her eyes. "Mira'thien, bow your head to none other than Ash'Tara and Ka'Lohane. You are ka'shiraen valra, as are you all," she said, looking into each warrior's eyes. "You are proud, and you are strong. Never forget that." She nodded to drive home the message.

"You are the one who gave me information on the tall man, aren't you?"

Sel'yra grinned and nodded.

With a warm smile, Lyssa tore off a bit of meat and ate it. Then she tore off another and held it out for Sel'yra to take. Sel'yra looked at the other warriors, then took the meat and ate it. Lyssa took another piece and held it out for another warrior, who smiled, taking it as well. She did the same for each and every warrior at the table until she shared with the last one.

"We are ka'shiraen valra," she said in an even tone, looking at each. "We fight as one, we live as one, and we protect as one. Never forget." Each one nodded their head, giving her their full attention. She stood to leave, as did her sister. As she turned to go, every thorn stood and gave their salute to her.

"Lys'Sa, Val'ethra, Sha'kar valra." They touched a closed fist to their chest.

Lyssa returned their salute. The sisters turned to leave and were met by Ash'Tara in the center walk of the hall. She looked at them both and did something no one had ever seen her do. She hugged them both and bowed her head to them.

"Thank you both. You have made this mother very happy today." She turned from them and returned to her seat on the dais as the girls left the hall.

Neither spoke to the other until they reached the edge of the village, where they looked back.

"So now you're a hero, sister? Or is it a goddess? One never can tell." Chandra laughed at Lyssa, who blushed for the first time since they were children.

"Stop, sister. I'm no hero, and you know it."

Just then, Sel'yra came running from behind them. "Lys'Sa, I come. Help."

"You were saying, sister?" Chandra laughed, and Lyssa gnashed her teeth in mock anger.

"Mira'thien, where we go is great danger. Stay with the ka'shiraen valra."

"No," she stomped her foot. "Me lead…bridge to. Come go." She started leading the way, stepping over branches and under limbs. Her smile couldn't be denied, so the girls realized that they now had a scout.

It would take some time to get there since Chandra wasn't used to moving in the forest. Lyssa would have to slow her pace to keep her sister in sight.

Once again, Chandra came to hate this part of the journey. All of the trees, bushes and *damned thistles* drove her half mad.

Her slow pace annoyed Sel'yra, but Lyssa made her understand that Chandra wasn't good at walking in the woods. Mages are smart but clumsy, which brought a nod and a huge grin to her face.

They walked for most of the morning and just past midday, when they finally came to the edge of the forest. The King's Road and bridge lay just ahead, several groups of people already crossing on foot and in wagons and carts. Lyssa thanked Sel'yra for escorting them and tried to send her back to her village.

"Me follow Chan'Dra. You…hunt man."

"Ka'ren sha'len velora?" Lyssa asked. Neither Lyssa nor her sister had spoken of the plan to anyone, so this took her by surprise.

"Me…hear. Night…last." She smiled. "Me follow Chan'Dra. You hunt. Chan'Dra…little like one." She looked at Chandra.

"Did she just call me a child, sister?" she asked. Lyssa smiled.

"Ask her yourself." She laughed.

Sel'yra moved along the wood line, staying out of sight yet remaining in the woods. She was so quiet that Lyssa barely heard her leave.

They checked the road and, seeing it clear, began to make their way to the bridge.

"I hope for your sake she didn't call me a child, sweet sister. It wouldn't end well for you." She mocked Kalla's angry face.

Lyssa looked at Chandra for a second and took the hint.

"Bah, what are you going to do, cry? It would be typical."

Chandra stopped and glared at her while Lyssa just kept walking. Several people were walking the opposite way, catching a quick glance at the sisters about to fight.

Lyssa made it to the bridge, turned and waited for Chandra. A man with a pull cart and three older women walked toward them, heading into the duchy.

"By Velkhar's arse, Chandra, hurry your fat bum up. I haven't got all day."

One woman mouthed to her friend, "Ooohhh," and covered her mouth.

Chandra picked up her pace angrily and stopped in front of Lyssa.

"I've had enough of you…sister." The words dripped with sarcasm. Three men, who had been behind Chandra, now walked over the bridge and were almost upon them.

"I'll tell you when you've had enough, hag."

"You half-witted, bugger-faced rag." She drew back her fist to punch Lyssa, who feigned fear and tried to cover her head. One of the men rushed to stop Chandra.

"Ladies, ladies. Please. Not here in public." It was an older gentleman, not very well kept, but not poor either. "What is going on here?"

Lyssa looked the man up and down. "Make your exit or my boot'll find yer arse."

The man's eyes went wide at the challenge, but he stood his ground.

"Please calm yourselves, ladies."

Chandra looked at Lyssa. "Don't speak to me. Don't look for me. I never want to see you again. And damn you if you try." She stormed off down King's Road toward the city in a huff.

The man let her go and looked at Lyssa. "Well, that wasn't very nice."

Lyssa reached back and hit the man in the face, felling him in one punch. "I warned ya, ya rag." She rubbed her knuckles and headed back toward the duchy, never looking back.

Sel'yra watched as the man stood, brushed himself off, looked down the road at Lyssa and spit. He looked the other direction and started to follow Chandra, staying just far enough back so he didn't look suspicious.

The rain was incessant, but she didn't mind it. She was used to it. She used it as a coat and slippers. It helped her stay warm…and silent.

She'd been following him from town to town for a week. Sel'yra's information had been dead on. She had been silently following him and passing information to Lyssa as it came. The girl was fast and very observant. Lyssa thought she would make a good assassin, justiciar he would call it, if not for the fact that she became lost outside of the forest far too easily.

Lyssa thanked her, kissed her cheek, telling her that her information was invaluable, and she'd definitely proven herself ka'shiraen valra. Sel'yra blushed, smiled, and headed back to the village prouder than ever.

Malhrun had informed Chandra that she was being followed. *The plan worked. Now just a bit farther.*

She continued to follow the road, muttering in mock anger. Every once in a while, she would stop and angrily turn back from where she'd come to curse Lyssa, stomping her foot and even ranting once. She did this to ensure the spy was still there, each time confirming it.

She stomped on cursing for almost an hour while keeping an eye on the half sun. Finally, she stopped and turned, still seeing the spy. They were both alone on the road now, nothing but a field to the left and forest to the right. He bent over pretending to drop a coin, but standing, he found himself face-to-face with a shadowy apparition. It was Chandra's shadow demon who she had silently summoned. The shadow demon wrapped him in its freezing grasp and began dragging him toward the forest. She followed the beast and, once inside the woods, calmly insisted on his release.

The spy was terrified, paralyzed by the sight of the demon and its sheer cold.

"You should really learn to be more careful," she said. He began to move, but only slightly.

Chandra looked to the demon and kindly said, "I thank you for your service, my friend. You may return." It bowed and dissipated.

As she turned back to the spy, his hand reached out, trying to grab Chandra by the throat. She smiled as he stopped short, realizing several spear tips were now poking him about his torso.

"As I was saying, you really should learn to be more careful. This area is home to many, many dangerous creatures, me being the least of them."

She leaned toward Sel'yra, "Thank you, my friend. You have been most helpful." She bowed to the young thorn. "You may do as you like with him. He is of no more concern to me."

Sel'yra glared at the spy. "Varen su'tel Ash'Tara. Sae'len vor dra'sal." The warriors roughly grabbed him and began to drag him to Ash'Tara.

"Ash'Tara will decide." She grinned at Chandra, bowed, and left. One warrior remained.

"Kae'Len? Why are you here?"

The scribe smiled and bowed to Chandra. "Ash'Tara insisted I come write you."

She smiled back. "Write *about* me." Kae'Len looked down and began to write.

"Yes, about." He stopped and looked at her, saying, "Ash'Tara wants for to follow and write *about* you. I go you with."

Chandra almost laughed but managed to stifle it.

"You can't follow me, Kae'Len." She pointed toward Caer Bryndwyck. "I have business in the city. It could be dangerous for you."

He looked down, dejected.

"I have an idea. Follow me."

Chandra created a small portal and told Kae'Len to enter it. He vehemently shook his head, obviously afraid of it.

"I promise it will not hurt you. Do you think I would anger Ash'Tara by hurting my," she paused thinking of the correct word, "kir'atein?"

He looked confused, wondering if it was a good idea to try to correct her Valyn.

"Kira'thien, kira'thien. Brother, as you say."

Chandra smiled warmly, and he understood that she had done it on purpose. She stood next to it and said, "It's a doorway, if you will, to my home."

He looked at her, still afraid, yet stepped into it and disappeared.

Once inside, his eyes became full of wonder at such finery. In all his life, he had never seen anything even close to this. She took his hand and led him around the library and alchemy table, where to eat, and told him that he could do all of his scribe work here, free from harm. He was completely amazed. He knew of magic, but none that could create this sort of grandeur. She delved into some tomes searching for a certain unique spell she'd seen years ago, while he continued to adventure through the room.

Once she located it, she called him over and let him try to read it, with no success. She laughed at the faces he made while attempting to sort it out, then showed him what the words meant by actually casting the spell.

In the center of the large, darkwood table formed a magical mirror of sorts. It showed Chandra in the library with Kae'Len, which amazed him. He had never experienced this before and became completely mesmerized by the entire event.

"This is called a *scry* spell. In it, you can see everything that is happening to either Lyssa or me, depending on to whom you are concentrating. Here, watch." She looked into the image and began to concentrate hard.

The scry shimmered, and she was able to see Lyssa sneaking into a town, the assassin not far off.

"From this, you will be able to chronicle anything you see. Unfortunately, you can't speak through it, but at least you see what's happening. You try. Just concentrate on someone, and they'll be seen."

His eyes widened, and he moved in front of the scry. He closed his eyes and concentrated. The scry swirled and then shimmered. The image that showed was that of Sel'yra. He looked at Chandra with fear in his eyes and desperately tried to alter the image, finally settling on Ash'Tara. His body visibly relaxed, but Chandra already knew.

"Ahn, I see now." She had a grin from ear to ear.

"I am sorry, Chan'Dra. I did not mean..."

"You love her, don't you."

He looked down shyly.

"Don't be afraid, Kae'Len. We all have loves, there's no shame in it." She put her hand on his shoulder. "Does she know?"

He shook his head. Chandra was sad for him. They were both outcasts of sorts, the warrior and the scribe, and neither could tell the other how they felt because of true apprehension.

"Have no fear, Kae'Len. The Mother knows, she has a plan, and everything has a reason, you'll see."

"I can keep watching for you and Lys'Sa?" He opened his book and began to write again.

"As much as you'd like, my friend." She showed him where he could find more ink and journals and bid him farewell.

She walked through the portal and then portalled to Ash'Tara where she asked if he could be in her employ. Ash'Tara was overjoyed and agreed. Chandra also relayed the heartfelt incident to her. She, of course, smiled and taught her that it was Ka'Lohane, the Valyn's Father-God of the First Breath, who had a plan, not the Mother. Chandra made her apologies and deferred to her.

She always stayed just far enough behind him to avoid being seen, for this was no common prey. This animal was cunning, fast and lethal, unlike any beast and far more dangerous.

Lyssa didn't like the duchy in the least. The ground was dry and cracked, only allowing scrub to grow; there were few tall trees and those that were looked sickly and barren.

The town she was in, called Briarfield, she thought, was a sad place. The buildings were poorly constructed, and the town layout was confusing and poorly thought out.

She sniffed the air. Nothing new: meat cooking on a fire, manure, stale ale, and mead.

It was nearly dark. He'd been there for hours, but it felt like days, and she knew he wasn't there to drink. *Leave dammit.*

She was never impatient, but this was no ordinary prize. He owed her, and she was going to get paid, with coin or with blood; it made no difference to her.

The Cat slowly moved to a better vantage point, very slowly, like a cat when hunting a mouse. Then…like lightning, she darted to a wall, leaped and grabbed onto a rafter under the overhang of a building across from the tavern. She stopped, hugging the beam as if it were a lover. Her eyes darted left and right for movement. Nothing.

Quietly, carefully, she righted herself for balance on a narrow perch and waited still as a statue. She could now see the front and back of the tavern he was in. *And now I wait…again.*

The barkeep sneered at the drunkard at the end of the bar. His leather jerkin was covered in spilled mead and ale. He smelled—bad.

"Oi, ya stinking slob."

The drunkard slowly raised his head, eyes blurry from drink.

"It's time for ya ta be goin,' mate. Leave out," he said belligerently, waving his thumb toward the door.

"Baaah" was all he said, then he put his head back onto the bar.

The tavern owner just shook his head in disgust. He turned his head and barked at the large man near the door, "Gint, get this yub outta here, will ya? I need the seat for real customers."

The strongarm, named Gint, was a real tough. He'd been a soldier in his earlier days, a sellsword later on and was looking to live a…quieter life.

As he stood and stretched, the noise around him dulled. Everyone had seen this dance before, and all were glad it wasn't theirs. The man was a bear among men. He had to bend down to clear the door, and the floor groaned beneath his weight. People cleared a wide path so the big man didn't walk right over them. He'd done it before.

"C'mon ya skunk. Time ta go," he bellowed in a deep bass voice.

His big hand grabbed the drunk man by the back of the neck and pulled. He came out of his seat with ease, and Gint dragged him to the back door. When the door opened, the noise level rose again as everyone went back to their merriment.

Gint tossed the drunkard out the door and into the alley, where he followed to make sure his coin was in the correct pocket—his, of course. The man was lying on the ground face down, so he reached for his shoulder and pulled. *Let's see what ya got, mate.*

The last thing Gint saw before the man rolled over was the flash of steel that severed the artery in his neck, quickly, silently.

His eyes flashed terror at the suddenness of the act, but it was too late to yell. He never realized that he was already dead as he fell to the ground.

Draemon stood. There were times when he actually felt something for his marks. This wasn't one of them, of course. He reflected on the wording of the contract. "When complete, leave in the open to be seen." He didn't like leaving traces; they caused too many problems, but *a contract once taken…*

He checked the big man's pockets quickly and smirked as he found a pouch. Giving it a quick shake, he heard the jingle of a coin and shoved it quickly into his pocket. Looking around, he calmly walked down an alley, over a low wall and into the cellar of an abandoned house. He quickly washed some of the stink and blood off with the water barrel he had placed there two days prior and donned fresh clothing.

The stairs ahead were broken, so he stepped carefully to the top floor. Deep breath, quickly looking for passersby and out into the street he stepped once more.

He loved it when jobs went right. No surprises, no mess. He smoothed his hair back and began to walk at a normal pace.

Lyssa saw the act. Clean, fast, precise, just as he had taught her.

She watched as he looked around alertly, then ducked down an alleyway. She thought it strange that he left the mark bleeding in the middle of the alley, something he trained her to never do.

Now.

She made a calculated fall. The light thud of her leather boots helped keep her balance. She landed on the balls of her feet and rolled. Crouched with one hand down for balance, she searched for the best route to keep him in sight. She quickly concluded that the only way to keep track of him was on foot and down the alley. Any other route would entail climbing. *Too much wasted time,* she thought. *Must stay close.*

She hugged the wall and did her best to keep hidden, feeling the shadows caress her as she moved quickly yet silently.

So, into the cellar you go. She smiled. She could try it here, but the chances of survival were slim. This was his territory, and she knew it.

She'd seen him do this before. He was truly the master. She never doubted that for a minute.

But this time the master was the prey, and the Cat *NEVER* lost.

'...you've done your best...'

Well, that was easy enough, he thought. The night was cool but dusty. A breeze blew from the north. *Fall is coming.* He nodded at some farmers walking the other way. *Time to head home and wait for the next contract.* He smiled contently.

He made his way to the stables. As he passed the tavern, he could see that the atmosphere had not changed. No one knew; no one cared.

He opened the door to the stableman's office. "Hello, Rodger," he said to the old man who was almost nodding off. "I hope my friend wasn't too much trouble for you."

"No, sire. He was a right good boy, he was," the man said happily as he yawned.

Draemon looked his big, dappled mare over and, satisfied, paid the man his due. "And this is for you." He tossed the stableman a solid gold coin.

The old man looked at it wide-eyed and in awe. He was so taken that words eluded him. This was more coin than he could make in months.

Draemon mounted the horse, gave an approving nod to the stablemaster and rode off. "Safe travels to ya, sire. Gods keep ya."

She watched. He wasn't running the steed. That was good.

Walking a horse at night, though? In this location? That was bold. Then again, the master feared nothing and no one.

She quickly looked around and saw only empty road. *Time to go.*

She ran toward the stables, around the side and out back where she kept her mare. She was black as pitch and fast as the wind.

She mounted, gave her a kick, and as if she knew where Lyssa wanted to go, the horse bolted. Lyssa loved running her; the feeling of the wind in her hair, hearing the thunder of hooves beating the ground, feeling the muscles work—exhilarating.

The route she plotted was more direct to the next main road than his. She was certain he was heading home, like he always did after he claimed his due from a contract.

It was now full dark when he arrived at the crossroads. There was a nice tavern down the road to the west that had decent food and drink, and an occasional bard or minstrel. It would be a good diversion even if for just a little while.

A sigh. He thought better of it. The realization that he was far too road-weary for any of that made him slump in his saddle. He took a deep breath and straightened. After all, a man does have limits, and he had almost reached his. He urged his mount forward to his home instead, taking his time and fully unaware of the plot against him.

He mulled over the recently completed contract. He'd been tracking Gint down for a week; day after day, town after town, place after place. Apparently, he was looking for sellsword work and was having sparse luck. The assassin never bothered with the particulars; it wasn't a part of the job. Finally, he settled on the tavern and made Lyssa's work so much easier.

She saw him pass. *Not too close. Stay downwind. Be patient.*

She quickly and quietly rode ahead, anticipating his arrival. She had already set the scene of his demise. It was a plan she and her sister had set into action months ago for just this moment. She was almost giddy. *Dammit. Patience. Do the job and then feel good about it. Business first,* she reminded herself.

He arrived at his home, where he could see the light near the stable and slowly followed the rocky road to it. Hearing his master's arrival, the stable hand met him. "Welcome home, m'lord. I hope your journey was good." He held the big horse's reins as his master dismounted. "Here ya go, lad. Take care of him. It was a long ride."

He stopped under the lamp post and looked up at the night sky. The stars twinkled brightly that night. He took a deep breath of the fresh, clean air, opened the front door and walked down to his study to review the now completed contract. He leaned over the small desk, sighing with fatigue. Almost asleep on his feet, he rolled the contract, heated and dripped sealing wax on the parchment and sealed it. Then, to mark its completion, he burned one end, just slightly, as a personal symbol and set it against a stack of four others and chuckled. He'd been busy of late, and he felt it.

Elda came in and said, "Beg pardon, m'lord. Would ya care for some food or drink tonight?"

"Not tonight, Elda. It's been a long night, and I just want to rest."

She curtsied and began to turn away when he added, "Elda, I'm feeling generous tonight. Take tomorrow for yourself. You've earned it."

"Why, thank ye, m'lord. Thank ye," she said with an ear-to-ear grin as she happily walked off.

He pulled off his road-worn boots and sat in his chair by the freshly lit, flickering hearth fire, sharpening his blade with steady, unhurried strokes. The day had been long, his fatigue a testament to his long hours. He began to get lost in thought, the hunt, the mark, the ride.

The room was silent but for the rasp of steel on stone…until it wasn't.

A sound? Elda moving in the far rooms, perhaps?

His blade stopped mid-scrape as he paused to listen…and then, as cold steel kissed his throat, he knew it was already too late.

"It's been a long time…master."

He knew the voice. He knew her smell.

He froze. Slowly, a breath escaped him like wind through old leaves—calmly, calculated. "Ahh. The little cat returns, and as she once said, 'not as an apprentice,'" he said, almost in a whisper. "I suspected the day would come, eventually."

He swallowed hard. "If nothing else, you were always true to your word." He gave a nervous grin. He'd never felt like this before. This was the first time he'd ever danced this closely to death.

"I've waited a long, long time for this day." He could feel her breath on his neck. This was no game, and he knew he was caught.

"If you would grant your former master a second, stay your hand…before you take your prize, you should read this." He put up his empty hands down to show his compliance.

"If I may…" He reached onto the table by his side…deliberate, no sudden moves…and placed his hand on a large, weathered scroll, encased in dark, cracked leather, and mounted on an ebony spindle. Underneath, a tome, no title, just a seal burned into the cover. He raised the scroll with one hand and gently held it in front of himself so she could see the writing…a royal seal emblazoned at the top, a pedigree. His name in bold, then the words…

She paused, her eyes darting quickly to the words, then back.

"A trick?"

"No. A truth. One you need to see before you take your prize."

Lyssa's hand didn't move, didn't waver. Blade steady at his neck, her eyes locked on the tome still resting on the table. The very tome he'd taken from her those many months ago.

"What is it?"

"The scroll, a history, a record, the truth of what happened before the throne fell to liars."

It was officially written with a practiced hand, the final words of the king to his old court advisor.

Names, places, the mark.

She glanced down. "Why should I trust this…or you?"

The assassin slowly tilted his head, exposing a faded, half-burned royal sigil, scarred into the skin behind his right ear, a brand decades old.

"If you don't believe me, then take your prize. I won't resist."

She wanted to fight the temptation. She dreamed of this day for a long time. She tightened her grip on her razor-sharp weapon, but it wavered. Her breathing slowed. If he moved, she had to be ready to react quickly. He could feel her tension begin to relax.

She hesitated, thought, then realized the truth. *He's never lied to me, even when he had me dead to rights.*

She lowered the blade.

"Read," he said softly. He felt he could trust her now.

She did, both the scroll and the tome.

The shadows watched as the little cat's world took another turn.

'...but one must know their place...'

The Merchants Road was busy today. It normally was this time of year. Summer was just giving way to fall, and the crops were all being driven into the city for one last sale. The carts and wagons came from all over with the hopes of going home loaded with coin.

Lyssa was sitting, feet propped up on the table as usual. She had a large flagon of mead by her feet and a dagger in hand, picking her nails. The Wayfarer's Respite was packed on this day, with all sorts of folk. There was raucous laughter and a minstrel playing upstairs and noisy conversation downstairs. The tavern maids were busy walking back and forth serving food and drink, and the tavern owner went table to table, meeting and greeting his patrons. He tried to visit with the dark figure in the corner, but a nerve-shaking glance told him to move on to another.

Midday was always the most active. Several times a day, whole caravans would pass by loaded with goods and vegetables. Some would come in to eat and drink, some would try to hawk wares, and all would avoid the hooded woman in the far corner. She didn't mind. They were mostly an inconvenience, to be tolerated at best.

Earlier in the day, a flamboyant fop tried to make sweet words to her. When she drew her shiny black dagger and kissed it, he quickly departed, laughter following close behind. The patrons had seen her before, or at least her type, but this one had a special air of danger about her. They all knew it would be better, safer to just leave lying cats be.

Chandra entered the tavern and, as usual, things quieted down. People pointed and murmured, men would get slapped or punched by their women and young men, and sometimes women's eyes would wander lustily.

She never tired of the attention, but it made Lyssa so weary, sometimes jealous but mostly just tired. She walked up, removed her cape and draped it over the chair near her. She shook out her long platinum hair, grinning as usual, and sat. It had been just over a month since they'd seen each other last, and she missed Lyssa terribly.

"Doesn't it ever tire you being stared at, sister?"

"Why, sister? Are we—"

"Jealous? Are we jealous? And I'd say, 'Why no, sister. I'm not.... Tee hee hee hee.'" She shook her head and laughed. "You are truly amazing, dear sister."

Chandra motioned for the nearest tavern girl, who came over quickly. "Yes, m'lady?"

"Your best wine, in the bottle. And if it's not the best, I will be angry." She winked at the girl who sped off.

"So, what is so important that you needed a drink to tell me? You know how busy I am this time of day." She laughed.

"I've come across some information you may find very...interesting and useful."

"Huh, you say that as if it's extraordinary."

The tavern keeper approached with a flourish, setting down a silver goblet and a peculiar vessel, a flagon of dark green glass, heavy and bulbous, worked in the crude likeness of a stag's head. A pewter collar ringed its neck, etched with lantern motifs that caught the firelight. The tavern girl who escorted him stood close by his side and tried not to get in his way.

"Greetings, m'lady." He bowed deeply. "I bring you the finest wine I have, just brought by caravan from Braelon, far to the south. The flavor is so rich, so subtle, that the four kings of Gadotra once quarreled over the last cask at their table. Some claimed the dispute sparked a war that burned three provinces to ash and all for a taste of this crimson vintage."

Lyssa and Chandra sat silently and stared, unamused. The man stood and waited for one or both to say something, anything. Yet, they continued to stare. He had now become fully uncomfortable.

"Would you care for a sample?" he nervously asked.

Lyssa shook her head, grunted and returned to picking her nails. The man began to sweat.

"Perhaps a challenge would be in order, my good man," Chandra began sweetly. "You see, I am from Braelon." She put on a half grin that Lyssa noticed and rolled her eyes at. "Here we go again," she whispered.

The tavern girl saw her whisper and put a hand to her mouth to stifle a laugh, which in turn made Lyssa smile.

"Ahh, then you know how fine—"

"And I know the tale as do you." She gave a sly grin. "I also know that wine of that supposed refine is also so terribly expensive."

He swallowed hard, looking from her to Lyssa and back.

She raised a finger, and a wisp of shadow emerged and wrapped around it like a tiny snake. "So, my challenge is this: I taste your sample. If it is to my liking…and it is truly the wine in question, then I will purchase the entire bottle no matter the cost and no further questions."

He grinned broadly.

"However, if it is not to my liking and it turns out this is not the correct wine, wellll…."

The wisp of shadow grew darker and larger. It now wrapped around her entire forearm and writhed like a smoky snake.

The man gasped, now realizing the predicament he was in. He was silent for a second, weighing his options. His brain screamed danger, and he knew he needed to separate himself quickly before this got out of hand.

Finally, "Lady, because it is you...a-a-and you are s-s-so beautiful, it would be my honor t-t-to give this wine t-t-to you as a gift." He gingerly handed the bottle to her.

"Why, thank you, kind man. And such a charming gift as well." She flashed her kindest grin. He stepped back and quickly made his way back to the ale board and wiped the sweat from his balding head.

Lyssa flashed a bored glance at her.

The tavern girl motioned to Chandra that she would like to open the bottle so the beautiful woman might sample it. She opened the bottle, allowing Chandra to give it a cursory sniff and poured a small amount into the goblet. Chandra smiled at the girl who blushed. Swirling it around, she took another sniff, letting the aroma sink into her senses, then took a sip, trying to savor the essence of the wine and find each note.

"And?" Lyssa continued to pick, not looking up from her work.

Chandra motioned her head side to side. "Eh, I've had better."

Lyssa snorted. "I thought as much."

The tavern girl looked disappointed, set the bottle down and turned to leave. "Tut, tut. One second, dear." Chandra produced a gold coin and placed it in the cleft of the girl's bodice. "Thank you for trying." She leaned closer to her and said, "Women know the dance; men just stumble through it." She winked. "By the way, I think my sister is fond of you," she said and dismissed the girl, who quickly glanced at Lyssa. Lyssa glanced up and flashed a wink and a smile at her, eyes gleaming. The tavern girl blushed bright red and left them, nonplussed.

"Sister, you are terrible," Lyssa said, smiling.

"It's a small town. We have to give them something to talk about."

Chandra tipped the bottle and took a closer look at its craftsmanship. "So, what is this news, sister? You've got my attention."

"I need to take you somewhere. You cannot ask where, and you must be blindfolded once there."

She raised her eyes. "You jest."

"No, not at all. Believe me when I say the surprise will be extraordinary. Have faith."

The mage took another sip and thought. "Alright, sister." She set the goblet down. "I'll play your little game."

Lyssa swung her boots from the table and stood up. "Good. Meet me at the south crossroads at sun fall, and I'll take you the rest of the way."

She headed for the door and passed the tavern girl filling a flagon at the ale board. Lyssa swatted the girl's bum in passing. The girl startled, then smiled when Lyssa winked at her again on the way out.

Chandra finished her wine and stood to leave. In passing, she said to the owner, "The wine was not too poor, though not the quality I had hoped for. Thank you again, dear man, for the gift." She placed a silver coin on the board. "Please enjoy your evening." She flashed another sweet smile and departed, much to his relief.

She hired a carriage south to the crossroads like Lyssa had asked and, sure enough, there she was, sitting on her mare, waiting. Her sister placed a blindfold over her eyes. "Please, try not to mess my hair, dear sister." Lyssa intentionally tied some strands into a knot just to tweak her sister's nose and then followed the road to a good-sized manor in the woods that backed up to the King's River.

Lyssa rapped on the heavy door, and an older woman let them in. "Lyssa, so good to see you again, dear."

She'd heard that voice before. "Where are we? Take this thing off of me, sister." Lyssa chuckled.

"Oh, be still. We're almost there." She winked at Elda and stepped in while leading Chandra inside carefully. "Thank you. Is he here?"

"Lord Draemon is in the study, lady."

"I've told you before, I'm no lady."

"That is no lie. Trust me, she is truly no lady," Chandra said, laughing. Elda chuckled and pointed the way.

Lyssa led Chandra along and walked her directly into a wall. "Oops, sorry, sister."

"I'll get you, Lyssa, by the gods I will."

She took a few more steps and then was stopped.

"Are we here?"

A male voice spoke up. "Oh, yes indeed, lady, you're here."

Chandra froze and went silent. She knew that voice. Her hands began to entwine, black shadows roiling from the fingers.

"Calm, yourself, sister. You must trust me."

Lyssa removed the blindfold.

Chandra took a deep breath.

"You!"

'...one must know their limitations.'

The explanation of their meeting and its results made Chandra's head hurt. It somehow went from trying to kill this man to not only being friendly but helping him in his endeavor…yet again.

They all sat in Draemon's study. Elda brought some biscuits and rose tea for Chandra and Draemon, but, as normal, Lyssa needed her mead.

Chandra still couldn't believe what she was reading. It was apparently all true, yet unbelievable. The telltale was the scar. No one else knew it was there, and even if they did, no one knew what it meant.

Chandra perused the pedigree. She read it three times and still could not believe her eyes. Lyssa sat in a chair facing the fire in a rather unladylike fashion while Draemon and Chandra discussed the information.

Chandra finally sat back to absorb everything. There was much to think about, especially since he threw them to the wolves for his own gain.

Lyssa, on the other hand, believed his story as well as the proof she had already read. What she didn't like was the fact that she finally found someone she could trust, and he destroyed that by using her as a pawn in his personal game.

Draemon stood and faced the twins.

"Ladies, I have been searching for this information for over thirty winters, since my father was killed, murdered. I was but a babe when they hid me away, but the story had never been kept from me." He lowered his head, trying to quell the pain. He straightened himself and continued.

"Yes, I've used and killed to get what I've been searching for, but rest assured, not one single innocent was harmed. On my honor, I swear it."

Both girls looked at each other. Both sensed that what he said was true.

"I am truly sorry about all of this misdirection, but I needed the guards to do my searching while I looked for the pedigree." He turned to Lyssa. "I'm most apologetic to you, Lyssa…little cat. Please believe me when I say that night outside the gate…I sent all the hounds and guards in the opposite direction." He stood, hands outstretched. "I had to use the persona of *the assassin* to send you to the correct places, and I must admit, your accomplishments were nothing short of amazing."

He took a deep breath as if he were about to impart some revelation, and said, "And you may not believe this right now, especially after what happened between us, but I have always looked upon you not only as my ward…but as a daughter."

She looked at him for just a moment, trying to decide if this was another apology or if this was actually truth.

Instead, she simply snorted with indifference.

493

Lyssa took a gulp of mead and asked, "So, who was the other damned assassin, the one who killed my friend, the one I tortured for information to get to you?"

"I honestly don't know. Perhaps Davin sent him. He's been known to keep several *friends* under thumb." She looked at him with full distrust. Could she ever trust him again?

"Typical answer from a *royal* mouth." She sneered. "Used again." She shook her head in disgust while stepping in front of his desk, where he stood and closed the tome.

"Well, according to these notes, some of those *friends* are about to find out why you don't kick a cat." She drank a mouthful of mead and put the mug down.

"When the time comes, be sure your claws are sharp. You'll need them," he said.

It got quiet while the two read, and Lyssa sat staring at the fire, carefully planning the many ways she was going to execute the killers in question. They were all very tired and had not slept for quite some time.

Lyssa looked at Draemon with a wry grin. "Oi, I forgot to ask earlier, do we call you Draemon, sire, lord or just late for supper?"

Chandra's eyes went wide and then narrowed. She looked at the assassin questioningly as well.

"I don't know, really."

"Okay then," Lyssa laughed, "bollocks it is." She raised her mug in a mock toast and filled her mouth with the savory mead. Draemon made an odd, disbelieving face. Being so fatigued, she laughed hard, and the mead was sent rushing through her nose, which made Chandra laugh harder than Lyssa. Those two laughing made Draemon laugh so hard he snorted onto his arm, which made everyone laugh even harder. Finally, after several minutes and much drooling, they were able to compose themselves enough to continue.

"For now, just Draemon will do. We've proven nothing yet, and I've an inkling that I'll be getting ill from hearing sire every other word."

Chandra took up the tome, turned a page and continued reading. "Your great-grandfather was King Alenoy of Behtany?" Chandra asked, impressed.

"Yes. My father spoke of him a lot when I was young. He always bragged about how good a man he was. It's a shame he was so careless."

Chandra said, "Good man? Good king: one of the more beloved, I should say."

"What happened to him?" Lyssa asked, still staring at the dancing flames.

"He was out hunting with his steward and some squires one day, and he managed to take down a bear cub with his crossbow. But...what he didn't see was its mother, who was none too pleased. He was looking the wrong way when she attacked. According to my father, there wasn't much left to bury." Draemon shook his head at the story.

Ignoring the tale, Chandra continued to read. "Have you read all of this?" she held up the tome.

"No. I've been studying the pedigree mainly. I believe that's what will prove my case."

"No, it seems that's not true. I've read here there are six men, hopefully still breathing, that will pose an obstacle. Any one of them can refute your claim, and you're done for."

He leaned over the desk and read where Chandra pointed.

"Arton Versy? I know him. He's still alive. He's the captain of the Second King's Guards."

Lyssa's face went pale. She slowly turned to Chandra.

"Sister! What is wrong?" She was instantly nervous.

"He's a tall one, black hair, scar across his forehead to his ear?"

"Aye, the very one. Why?" Draemon said, watching Lyssa's growing ire.

Lyssa squinted her eyes in sheer rage. Through gnashed teeth, she said, "He's one of them." She was so angry, tears began to flow. Draemon became nervous. He'd never seen Lyssa do this before.

Chandra went to her and put her arms around her. "You mean…them?"

Lyssa looked up at her sister.

Chandra said to Draemon without looking, "This one must be caught at all costs." She glared at him. "*ALL* costs."

She looked back at her sister. "Sister, we are going to have such fun with him." They both stared into the abyss, plotting their *fun*.

After Lyssa had calmed somewhat, Chandra returned to her reading. She found another name.

"What about Gerald Haverton?"

Draemon looked at the ceiling in thought. "Gerald Haverton, Gerald Haverton, I know the name, but I can't remember from where."

"Ahhh," Chandra said, looking up, "this one I know—Allyster Baine." The assassin looked up, as did Lyssa. "He's Davin's new guard captain."

"Yes, I remember him. Too big and too smart for his own good. He challenged me that night our little cat made all that trouble."

"The man's an oaf. No need to worry about him. He can't lift a blade, let alone use it properly," Lyssa said.

Chandra knew when her sister summed up an opponent, she wasn't wrong.

The other three, Draemon identified as lesser guards, easily dispatched and more easily forgotten.

They plotted deep into the night. Each time Lyssa discarded the plans, saying they were all lists of things that would go wrong. Draemon was becoming annoyed at her, and they began to get edgy.

Chandra decided they should all get sleep, and they would revisit it all in the morning, to which the others agreed.

Sleep came slowly for Draemon. He knew that, if the gods willed it, his life could be altered forever, and justice would at last be served.

Chandra's mind wouldn't stop long enough for her to sleep. She kept searching for a plan, the best way, a happy medium, yet finding none. No matter what the thought, it always ended badly.

Lyssa's head touched her pillow, and it was morning.

'...and one must know their capabilities.'

Morning had come. Each had little sleep, except the Cat, who slept very well indeed.

Chandra and Lyssa were sitting at the small dining table, eating a wonderful dish of seasoned pigeon eggs, pork and small, boiled potatoes that Elda happily served them.

The girls liked Elda. She was kind and sweet, reminding them of better days with their mother. Chandra had even called her mother accidentally and was embarrassed. Elda didn't mind, though. She considered it a compliment.

The girls had been talking for quite some time while Elda had been cooking. It really was like their younger days, with them eating and Talith cooking and tending the kitchen. She would ask about their childhood. They would remember and laugh.

"Are we a nice, happy family, now?" Draemon came in and smiled.

"Just reliving a past life is all," Lyssa said, sighing.

"Elda, if you please, some rose tea and biscuits."

She already had it prepared. "Here you are, lord. Just as ya like 'em." He smiled. "Elda, have I ever told you how wonderful you've been since—"

"Yes, you have, nearly every day. Now, shut it an' eat. Yer getting thin." She rushed down to the larder.

He looked at the girls. "And that, dear ladies, is why I never remarried." He began laughing.

He took a sip of the hot rose tea and said, "Are we ready to get to business?"

"We've already got a plan," Lyssa said, jabbing a potato with her dagger and stuffing it in her mouth. Chandra gave a disdainful look. Lyssa looked back, food still half chewed in her mouth and said, "What?!"

The mage just shook her head and continued, "The only thing you must do is go to Davin's manor and retrieve Allyster Baine." She looked at Lyssa, who was now eating a slab of pork she had stabbed with her dagger, juice dripping down her mouth.

"Oh, dear sister, must you? Mother did not raise you to be an animal."

Lyssa swallowed. "What?!"

Chandra's eyes shot to the ceiling. "Mother Hearthmae, please help me."

Lyssa took another bite and continued to chew.

Draemon watched with amused eyes. "Are you two always like this?"

"Nooo. She's usually worse," Chandra said, disgusted.

Draemon chuckled and got back to business. "I must go to Davin's and bring back Allyster Baine? Why alone?"

"Lyssa and I are going to Caer Bryndwyck. It will take us both, and the final piece will be him." She grinned at Draemon. "You are better suited to the task than my sister, who I need for the start of the plan."

He nodded his acceptance. He finished his meal, went to Elda and kissed her hand as always, thanking her, and set out for Davin's.

The girls grinned at each other just as Elda returned.

She looked at the two and said, "What are you two plannin'? You up ta no good?"

"No, my dear Elda. Not at all. We are setting up an enormous surprise for him," Chandra replied with a warm smile.

Elda gave them each a wary look before she returned to the kitchen.

"Shall we, sister? I believe the time has come."

Lyssa wiped her mouth with the back of her hand and left with Chandra.

The road to Morowyck was wet and muddy. The rain began to fall lightly, and the mist became thick as soup. It was cold to him, but not cold enough to wrap in a cloak. He enjoyed days like this. Raw, quiet, the birds and crickets were silent, and the only sounds were those of his mare's hooves and her breathing. An occasional crow would fly by and caw as if greeting him, but continued on its own journey to places unknown.

He breathed in the cold, heavy air and smiled as he let it out. He was almost there and had already devised his plan. Not far from the gate, he led his mount into the woods, removed a satchel and donned the clothing he'd packed within. He now looked like a traveling merchant who might have lost his way. He topped the disguise with a large furry hat that hid his hair, and he headed toward the gate.

At the gate, he greeted the two guards who, of course, tried to ward him off. He told them he'd known Allyster for some time and wished to speak to him if he could. They tried to threaten him away, but a few gold coins changed their minds, and soon the captain arrived in his now signature black brigandine armor. He'd become more refined, Draemon noticed. His armor was cleaner, and the metals that adorned him were now polished like new.

"Oi, what are ya wantin'?" Allyster asked gruffly.

"Um, my good Captain, you are a captain, correct?" he asked. "I seem to have run into a spot of trouble."

"Out with it. I 'avent got all day."

"Ah, yes. Well, I was accosted along the road to the city, you see."

The captain was becoming very impatient now.

"What I was hoping…" Draemon produced a small pouch that clinked, "You might be persuaded to escort me?"

Allyster looked left and right to see if the guards might have overheard. "I can help ya. That won't be any trouble at all." *This one is going to be easy*, he thought.

"Wonderful. Shall we then?" Draemon motioned for the captain to lead.

"Oi, lads, I'll be back afore dark. Some banditry in the woods ahead. Tell Frealin he's in charge fer now."

He motioned for Draemon to follow.

Unknowingly, he began to lead Draemon back toward his horse.

"What wares ya sell?" the captain asked, matter-of-factly.

"Oh, all sorts of items, my good man: clothing, boots…weapons."

Allyster turned to look at the merchant…

He awoke to the feeling of being bounced. His head had been covered with a hood, which made it impossible to see through, and his hands and feet had been bound. As he bounced, pain radiated across his head like fire. He tried to speak several times, but the bouncing made it almost impossible. He resigned himself to the fact that he was powerless to escape and he'd have to wait until he arrived at his destination.

Gerald Haverton was the turnkey in the dungeons of Caer Bryndwyck. He'd been appointed to the task after King Maelor Rudric took the throne. He was, by all accounts, not a nice man. He was used to *extract* information for the crown, and, apparently, he was very good at his job. Lyssa knew this would be no easy task. She'd have to sneak into the dungeon, devise a plan to get this man under her control and get him to Draemon's manor all without being seen or heard.

Draemon never prepared me for this.

She thought about the layout of the city as best as she could while riding. She knew most of the roads, shops and alleyways from the filthy cobbles of The Fringe to the pavers of The Crown. None came close to the entryway of the dungeon. For that, she'd need to go through either the king's great hall or the main guard barracks in the courtyard. She thought of the sewer grating near The Crown, but they only led out of the city and into the river. No good there. There was always the sewer aqueducts that ran under the city. She hated the thought, but would use it as a last resort.

Nothing was coming to mind until she remembered...the sewers from The Crown ran out of the back of Caer Bryndwyck and directly to the river. She could check the grate and see if she could gain entry. From there, it would be almost a straight path to the dungeon, which ran right beneath the keep and courtyard.

She smiled and kicked her mount into a run.

The riverbank was muddy, and the shadows grew longer as the sun went down. She managed to remove one of the restraining bars from the sewer that had been there for nearly a century and had grown rusted, weak. Her assumption of the sewers was correct, thank the gods, and her trek to the dungeon, though twisted as a maze, had been fairly uneventful. She could have done without the rats, which were as large as cats, but she finally found the grate for the dungeon.

Every so often, Gerald would leave his table near the dungeon door and walk the corridors, which were filled with many cells. He rarely had trouble with prisoners. He once had a prisoner give him

501

advice on what he could do with his mother, which earned him injuries so devastating that he died the next day. There was silence from thereafter. The long corridors were dark, dank and foreboding. Moss covered the walls, and rivulets of water dripped from them and the ceiling. A few of the oubliettes had filled, drowning the men inside, but it never bothered Gearald, who had seen far worse in battle. The water would then flow down the gutter in the center of the hallway and down into the sewers.

He returned from walking the hallways, broke wind loudly and sat, returning to the card game of angles he had started.

"Oi, Gerald, open up, mate. I got yer supper."

The big man stood and fumbled for the key that unlocked the door. After a few seconds, he found it and pulled the heavy door open.

"'Ere ya go, mate. Need anythin'?"

"Did I ask fer anythin' ya buggerin' churl?"

"No, lad, ya didn't." He turned and left without another word.

Gerald slammed the heavy door, threw the bolt and locked it tightly.

"Bugger yerself, ya doxy dog-whore," he heard the guard yell.

Gerald began to laugh so hard he almost fell from his seat. "That'd be me, mate."

He felt a slight prick on his neck. He slapped it, turned and just as he went unconscious, saw a girl with platinum hair. "Gotcha," she said as he fell.

Lyssa sighed. "Now comes the hard part. I have to drag this one's big arse through the damnable sewer."

She remembered that Chandra had set the plan, and now she understood why. "Shite. It was for the wall." She grinned at Chandra's play. "Okay, Chandy, my turn." She spat on the big man and began to drag him back to the now-open sewer grate. "All right, big man, down ya go." She pulled him and sent him feet-first into the sewer. She wrinkled her face at the odor, then jumped down.

Chandra donned her least favorite dress. She thought it was horrible the day Lyssa gave it to her. Initially, she thought her sister had given it to her as a prank, but the look on her face proved that it wasn't, so she pretended to like it to make her happy.

'...*in the gatehouse, mistress. Three.*'

The sun was half below the horizon when she arrived. She climbed down from the wagon and ran toward the main gatehouse at Caer Bryndwyck. She hated running. She had always thought it beneath her to hurry, but she had to put on airs for this lot.

As she arrived, the gate guard stopped her and asked her business. She glared at him and insisted on seeing the captain at once. To tarry would cost time, which they did not have.

"Alright, lass, wait here."

He returned with the captain, who had a stern look on his face. "This better be important, lass."

"Captain Arton?"

"Yer wastin' my time. What is it?"

"Father sent me here to get you." She put on her best fear face. "He captured three men from Eldorath. Da said they could be spies. They burned one house so far and killed the family." She pretended to be out of breath.

The captain's eyes grew wide. "Eldorath? We've no quarrel with Eldorath."

"My father was a soldier in the king's vanguard. That's what he said—Eldorath." She started to move back toward the wagon as if she were leading the captain there.

He could tell she wasn't lying. "Rhen, Milard, on me."

"I got 'em," the captain said as they all climbed into the wagon. "Where?"

"Down Merchants Road just past the hawkers' stands." She tried to get them to hurry.

He flapped the reins, and the horses bolted. He never realized these were palfreys and not draft horses.

They passed the stands quickly and reached the crossroads, where she pointed them down the road that led to Draemon's manor. The sun was nearly gone now, and shadows swallowed the courtyard, trees looming tall with only slivers of light breaking through. They jumped down, swords drawn, and looked around. Chandra stepped away and turned to face them as they searched in vain.

"Where are they, lass? Where's yer da?"

Chandra just smiled.

Arton turned to her just in time to see two red eyes blink.

"Malhrun, if you please."

The three men were pulled together by some unknown force. They tried to struggle free, but the more they tried, the more entangled they became.

"Ye scullery rag." The captain kept fighting his restraints. "Yer arse'll be dead when I gets free."

Rhen and Milard were now red in the face from their struggle. Tighter the shadows squeezed.

It didn't take long for the fatigue to set in, and they finally gave up their struggle.

"To the cellar, if you please." She motioned to Malhrun, who easily lifted them from the ground and floated them to the open cellar door and down inside. The men began to yell, but Malhrun covered their heads with bands of wispy shadow, and they became silent.

Once inside, Chandra flicked her fingers and a gentle fire bloomed in the hearth, filling the cellar with a warm orange-red glow. She traced a slow circle in the air, and one by one the candles and lanterns flared to life. The guards' eyes widened, only now understanding the peril they were in.

"See that they're comfortable, my pet," she said, ascending the stairs.

Elda was in the kitchen as usual, preparing the evening meal. It smelled wonderful. She stepped toward the cauldron and swung it closer to get a better view of what was cooking. A small hand gently slapped her away. "Uh, uh, uh, young lady. Ya get back till it's done. Go now, shoo." Chandra smiled and sat on a chair in the nook and watched the woman work. She reminded her of her mother so much that she began to pine.

She heard a thump coming from the cellar and stood. One of them had returned, and she needed to meet them.

"What's that. Rats again?" She started for the cellar.

"Please, Elda, never you mind. I'll look after it." She opened the cellar door and went down. When she got to the bottom, she saw a giant beast of a man who was lying face down in the middle of the room, hands bound to his feet. Lyssa was bent over trying to catch her breath.

"Well, look what the cat brought." She smiled at Lyssa.

Still bent over, she looked at Chandra and just shook her head. She stumbled her way over to the desk near the fire, laid her arms on the table and put her head down.

"Why, dear sister, you seem a bit out of breath. Are you quite alright?"

"I'll get you," she said without looking.

"Now, now." She grinned widely. "Oh, what is it you say?"

Lyssa looked up.

"Oh, yes. Gotcha, I think it was." She flashed her sister a sarcastic smirk.

Lyssa leaned back in the chair and threw her feet up, crossing them. She shook her head muttering, drew her dagger and began picking her fingernails.

A few minutes passed, and Lyssa finally caught her breath. The room was fairly large and well-lit. To the right of the hearth sat Lyssa behind a small desk. Against the back wall sat the traitors still in Malhrun's tight grasp. Two chairs sat a comfortable distance from the hearth with a small table in between. At the far end stood a cupboard and the stairway up.

"Oh, dear sister, I had almost forgotten," Chandra said.

Lyssa looked at her sister, who was standing next to the men on the floor. The hair on her neck began to stand on end.

"Look who I found."

As the words passed her mouth, Malhrun removed the shadows over the men's faces. For a second, she wanted to slash every inch of their bodies. The memory of the physical assault on her young body enraged her.

She stood and stepped toward them, barely containing the urge to rend their flesh from their bones. Arton immediately remembered who this girl was. He began to struggle in earnest, now knowing his life would surely be forfeit. Rhen and Milard felt Arton struggle and looked over. They, too, realized who this was. Milard, who was in the center, began to shake uncontrollably. He lost control of his bladder, and the liquid spread across the floor. Rhen began to sob, the large tears streaming down his cheeks.

"Lyssa, my dear sister, would you like me to leave you with your new toys?"

She stood before them, her face now calm, cold, calculating.

"If you would, Chandy dear, please dismiss Lady Elda for the evening. Her services won't be needed tonight." Her eyes never left the terrified men.

Chandra went upstairs. She could hear Elda talking to her sister and was trying to understand why she should leave. After a few minutes, she relented, trusting that Draemon had given her leave. Chandra came walking down the stairs, one dramatic step at a time. She walked to Lyssa and stood next to her, leaning her head on Lyssa's shoulder.

"Sister dear, make your revenge sweet."

Lyssa's eyes twinkled as she started with Rhen. His face was unmistakable. The scar that crossed his right eye, she would never forget.

She bent down so he had a clearer view. "You held my arms," she said in an almost sultry tone.

She drew her dagger and slowly dipped the tip into a small jar, making sure the men witnessed her actions. The clear liquid dripped from the black blade. She moved close to him, cocked her head to the right and, in one lightning motion, nicked his neck. Within a minute, the poison had coursed through his entire body, causing him to lose all muscle control, leaving him paralyzed yet fully awake.

Malhrun released Lyssa's prisoner. Taking the man by the hair, she dragged him in front of the others. The Cat stared at Arton, grinning.

When she spoke to Chandra, her words were like ice. "He must not bleed, sister," she said, never breaking eye contact.

"Gladly."

Arton's eyes stared in absolute horror as Lyssa slowly, carefully and methodically removed Milard's arms with her dagger. Tears streamed from the man's eyes, yet he could not move or scream.

Deep inside, Lyssa felt the pain of him pinning her arms washing away. *Could this be what healing feels like?*

Chandra quickly pointed her finger, and a small, white-hot flame cauterized the wounds.

She tossed each arm into the fire, where they began to sizzle from the searing flames.

She dragged her dagger across Rhen's face from one corner of his mouth to the other, creating a large, bloody smile.

"This is how I felt." Her face turned to stone. "Do you like it?"

Then she stood and moved before Milard.

"You stood and watched." She quickly nicked his neck with her blade, and he lost control as well. Malhrun released him, and Lyssa dragged him over to Rhen by the ears. She placed him nose to nose with his accomplice. She leaned down and sliced off his ears.

"This is because I wished I couldn't hear my own screams."

For the first time, the echoes of those screams in her mind began to fade.

When she was finished, she stood and locked eyes with Arton. His twisted nose, scarred lip and broken teeth had also been etched into her memory.

Witnessing the sheer brutality that her sister was performing on these men made Chandra almost shudder. *Let it out, sister. No one has earned this more than you.*

"Dear sister, whatever will you do with this one?" Chandra asked sarcastically.

Still staring at her nemesis, she said, "This one," she began, fury in her eyes, "why, this one is yours, Chandra."

Chandra looked at Lyssa with questioning eyes. "Really? But why?"

As Lyssa stared, Arton visibly relaxed, but just a bit...until.

Her eyes narrowed to slits, and a diabolical smirk emerged on her face. "Because I want to watch this one suffer." She stepped back. "Please use Screaming Shadow. He should understand what it feels like to be... abused. Over—and over—and over."

Chandra chuckled. "Ooohhh, now that *IS* special."

She stood and slowly, seductively, walked to Arton. She ran her finger across his chin. Lyssa pulled a chair across and sat directly in front of him.

The beautiful mage stood behind Lyssa and raised her hands to her chest, palms facing each other. She closed her eyes and concentrated. She slowly raised them over her head and whispered... "Arvan petrus falvala."

Billowing shadow crept from her hands. Malhrun waited until her spell was almost over him when he released Arton and melted into Chandra's shadow.

Arton watched the shadow drift directly in front of him. He screamed, Lyssa grinned as the shadow entered his body. Visions began to pour into his mind. He was being held. He began to feel the abuse: the pain, the horror, the utter helplessness. He saw it repeatedly, one shadow after another. The faces blurred, the pain became unbearable.

His screams of terror started as a high-pitched wail, his body beginning to wither and draw in, then silenced as the last breath left his body.

The visage of her assailant was frozen in an eternal scream. Lyssa stared, and a teardrop slowly fell from her eye. Still, she stared.

Lyssa sat motionless, the last of her energy drained with his final breath. Chandra lowered her hands, gently picked her up and wrapped her arms around her sister.

"It's over, Lys." She hugged her, kissing her head. "I know the pain will never leave, but for now, this chase is ended. You are avenged, dear sister. No one will ever hurt you again."

She held Lyssa for some time, letting the sobs and tears heal her. She would never be the same, but, for now, the healing could begin.

Lyssa sat behind the desk, as always, feet up and crossed, cleaning her nails. Chandra was in front of the fire, the last of Rhen's arms poking up like kindling.

The door to the cellar opened, and Draemon walked in carrying Allyster on his shoulder. He turned to drop the guard and saw both sisters already there. He walked over to Gerald and dropped the unconscious guard on his lap.

Allyster let out a yelp. "Shut up," Draemon said, kicking him.

He turned and looked at the bodies and the blood.

"You've been busy." He glanced from corpse to corpse.

"We had some unfinished business of our own to take care of," Lyssa said in an even tone.

"I see. Did you get information?"

"That wasn't the sort of business we needed to tend to," she said, not looking up.

"I see." He looked at the giant. "Is Gerald at least alive?"

"Have no fear. The beast is asleep, but he'll wake shortly." She was still somber.

He removed the hood from Allyster's head. He blinked his eyes hard several times and looked around, trying to get a look at the room.

"Welcome to your trial, Allyster." Draemon dragged the other chair closer to him.

"What damned trial ya talkin' about. I ain't done nothin'."

Lyssa piped in, "Neither did those three."

The captain glanced at the corpses and swallowed hard. He knew he was in trouble.

"Now, I'd like to know about the assassination."

"I don't know 'bout no damned assassination."

He looked down at the guard with a pouting face.

"Malhrun, if you please." Chandra was smiling.

Draemon's eyes widened as the dark shade moved across the room and stood next to Allyster.

He glanced at the mage but didn't ask.

The guard began to feel cold.

"I'll say it again, my friend. I'd like to know about the assassination." His voice was even and calm.

"Bugger yerself, ya rag-eatin' shite."

It felt as if an ice-cold hand wrapped around his neck, tightening slowly.

"One last time."

The captain only shook his head, still withholding the information.

Gerald began to wake, mumbling incoherently.

"Ahh, the giant stirs."

They waited silently until the big man regained his senses.

"Where am I? What sack o' shite tied me up an' sealed his fate?" He was fully awake and trying to fight his bindings.

"Such poor language. And in front of ladies, no less. Tsk, tsk, tsk."

"Untie me, and I'll be showin' these *ladies* a thing 'r two." He licked his lips in appreciation.

Chandra quickly pointed at the big man, and a small bolt of shadow left her finger and hit the man on his cheek. The cold ball burned a hole in his it, and he bellowed like a man falling from a cliff.

"Manners, my good man, if you please," the mage said in her most prim and proper voice.

Gerald's eyes grew wide with fear. He'd never encountered a mage before, but he'd heard tales. Understanding the predicament he'd found himself in, he went silent.

"I am about to ask you some questions, and I truly would like to hear your most honest answers. If you help us, we will gladly send you on your way. We will not even try to stop you," Draemon said sincerely.

Gearald nodded, and Draemon began.

"Who killed King Torvain?"

"Keep yer gob closed, Gerald. They ain't gonna do nothin'."

Draemon looked at Allyster, crossing his lips with a finger. "Shhhh."

"Oi, shush me arse, ya rag."

Before he could blink, Draemon grabbed his dagger and nicked off the bottom of Allyster's ear. He barely saw the assassin move.

Returning the blade, he once again motioned "Shhhhh." Gerald's eyes widened. "I don't know nothin', mate." He wasn't as gruff as before.

"You don't know anything, you say?" He shook his head and looked at the floor. He turned toward Lyssa, who had finished cleaning her nails and was leaning crossed armed on the desk. He gave a slight nod to her, and she understood.

"Would you come with me, sister?"

Chandra followed her upstairs, where Lyssa drew a mug of mead and leaned against the closed cellar door.

"Why are we here, sister? We should be down there with him."

There was a loud roar of pain from behind the door.

Chandra's eyes widened, realizing what was going on.

"That would be his nails, I believe," she said, calmly taking a drink.

"Well now," her sister said, looking down and admiring her own well-manicured fingertips.

"Perhaps I should pour some wine and get comfortable, then, yes?" She looked at Lyssa, who shrugged.

"I would. This could take a bit."

Another roar, louder than the first.

"I believe that would be an ear." She was nodding her head, confirming her guess.

Chandra sat. "Was this part of your training, dear Lyssa?"

"Not completely. I started in a different place."

Chandra nodded, took a sip, then swirled the goblet and savored its texture.

It stayed quiet for some time. Chandra looked to Lyssa. "Is he done?"

There was a muffled scream. "I would say, no, not yet."

Another quieter roar followed by sobbing.

"And that would be… Well, I won't say in front of a lady, dear sister."

Chandra toasted her candor.

"I think that should just about do it." Lyssa drained her mug and motioned for Chandra to follow. Once in the cellar, she saw Gerald dead and Allyster sitting in a puddle of his own making.

"And just like that, we have our information," Draemon said, wiping his hands on a bloody rag. Turning to Allyster, "Thank you, sir, for your cooperation. Now, we will send you on your way."

He nodded at Lyssa, who walked to the terrified Allyster. She smiled, drew her black dagger and slowly moved it side to side before him, letting him see the blade that would kill him.

Then she set the tip against his chest.

He looked at Draemon. "B-but...ya said ya were gonna send me on my way."

"I am, my friend. And we will not stop you...on your way to the Endless Dark." He smiled, "Oh," he looked over his shoulder as he started for the stairs, "save me a place, will you? I'd hate to be lonely."

She very slowly pushed the dagger into his chest up to the hilt. "This is for my family," she said softly, "you son of a bitch."

His eyes sprang open; his mouth went wide. There was no scream. He gasped, and they watched as the last breath of his life left him.

"So, now we have the truth," he said, starting up the stairs. The girls stood to follow him up.

"And that truth is... ?" Lyssa asked.

"It was Maelor all along."

They sat at the large table as he explained the entire plan, as Allyster had confessed to him. According to him, the plan was begun by Maelor as vengeance, but then convoluted to include several people, who were later killed to keep their circle tighter. They went to the tome and retraced the events, putting them in chronological order, and finally understood the coup. Chandra wrote the notes on parchment as quickly as she could; her letters were almost artwork unto themselves. Lyssa was always impressed by how beautiful her sister's writing was compared to hers. Together, they devised a plan that would not only prove his pedigree but also discount and destroy the king in the process.

The time was right.

The place was selected.

The proof was in hand.

Let the end come on swift wings.

'...and you have been found woefully wanting.'

Talk around Caer Bryndwyck:

"Three gate boys gone, just...gone. Vanished off the front post like ghosts hauled 'em."

"Aye, and the jailor too. Found his keys in the muck near the sewer grate. That ain't bandits' work."

"Add the three others missin' round town, and that's five men wiped clean. Five in a single night."

"An' not a single word spoke of it. Keep yer eyes open, mate. No tellin' what's happenin' next."

–King's Talons guards

"Guards going missing, you hear? Quite the disruption for those of us who prefer order."

"Disruption? Feels more like someone's rattlin' the throne."

"Please...half of the crown's been muttering the king wears his crown like a borrowed coat."

"Borrowed? Hmph. Stolen, if you ask the right folk."

–A crown fop and a wealthy merchant

Of Truths and Kings

The midday sunlight, like rays from the hands of the gods themselves, shone through the high upper windows, casting a pale yet bright hue across the throngs of nobles and commoners alike. They crowded the galleries, their murmured talk a restless tide beneath the vaulted ceiling. At the far end, raised high upon a broad dais, the king sat flanked by his queen and their son, crowns catching the glow of firelight, resplendently clothed in the usual royal garb. The first order of business was about to be announced when the echoing sound of metal on wood interrupted the chamberlain's words.

All eyes turned as the great double doors groaned open on ancient hinges, and in the widening spill of daylight stood Lord Draemon Torvain, poised at the threshold, the moment of his ascension heavy on his shoulders.

For this auspicious occasion, he chose his finest black studded leather jerkin, the silver studs glinting in the light. He wore his ceremonial rapier instead of his usual daggers, adding to his controlled menace. His polished black knee boots were pulled over supple leather trousers, completing a look meant to show his more regal side.

The chamberlain, who stood next to the queen, stepped forward, taking a deep breath to speak, but Draemon, only then, began his slow, measured journey to the dais, thus silencing him. The chamberlain cleared his throat at the minor insult and awaited this man's audacious arrival.

Draemon's eyes fixed on the king, hands behind his back, putting emphasis on each step to enhance the echoing throughout the silent gallery like thudding heartbeats. He took his time, intentionally prolonging the tension and intensity until he stopped two paces from the dais, silent, glaring.

The chamberlain stood between him and the king, looking down on the trespasser, pausing to ensure his dramatic entrance had ended.

He took a deep breath and spoke, "You stand before King Maelor Rudric, Father of the Kingdom, Protector of the People. If you have business with this court, state it truly and quickly."

Draemon stood silently.

The chamberlain glanced back at the king, then at Draemon, who continued to glare.

He spoke no words but held out a scroll in his left hand, patiently waiting.

The chamberlain sighed in exasperation. He looked back at the king, who nodded for him to investigate.

Carefully descending the steps, he came to a stop in front of Draemon, glaring intensely. "You play a dangerous game, my friend," he said softly, but received no reply.

He took the scroll, the pedigree and, unrolling it, silently read each word, lips moving as he read. He raised a sheet, glanced at Draemon and continued to read, eyes fixed in concentration.

Draemon continued to glare at the king, eyes never blinking or wavering.

Another sheet was read, and the chamberlain's brows furrowed. "How can this be true? What proof have you?" he asked just quietly enough to not be heard by the royals.

Draemon handed him the tome, which he opened to a bookmarked page. The royal seal highlighted an illuminated page with handwritten words penned as if forced and hurried.

He looked at Draemon questioningly, then returned to the next page, where his eyes widened in disbelief.

"Proof."

Draemon leaned his head to the right and pulled the helix of his ear forward. The chamberlain's eyes grew somber with resignation as he saw the scar, described as written in both the pedigree and the tome, which confirmed the truth.

Draemon turned to another bookmarked page, and the man began to read again, page after page.

When done, he closed the tome, staring at Draemon, then back at the king. As he returned to face Draemon, his face softened, and he stepped back. He bowed and allowed Draemon to pass.

The king's face grew angry, seeing Draemon daring to climb the steps toward him.

He stood and bellowed, "HOLD!" Turning to his chamberlain, he demanded, "What is the meaning of this?"

Draemon stopped two steps from the king, staring, beginning to burn holes in the king's confidence. His queen and son began to squirm in their seats nervously.

Draemon calmly turned to the queen, his face softening and speaking in a soft, respectful tone. "Lady, I beg you return to your chambers."

She looked at Maelor, who stared defiantly at Draemon.

"Once again, lady, I beg you. Please return to your chambers at once." His eyes conveyed his sincerity. He didn't want her to witness a fight if it came to that.

She quickly stood and made haste to her chambers without uttering a word.

Maelor watched her leave and returned to Draemon, fire in his eyes at the insolence.

"I would beg you to leave as well, young man." He looked at the prince, who stood clearly prepared to defend his father if necessary.

Draemon glared at the boy and, in a more forceful and menacing tone, stated, "I know your thoughts— boy. You *will* die; of this I can assure you. Now, please…be a good lad. Retire to your chambers and save face."

He looked at his father, who nodded for him to comply. He stood, side-stepping his seat and slowly, reluctantly, backed out of the room.

"Now," he demanded, hand resting on the pommel of his sword, "what is the meaning of this? Speak now or die by my hand."

The gallery remained silent, bearing witness to the confusion before them.

"You, *king*," the phrase dripping with sarcasm, "perpetrated the plan and subsequent assassination of King Elaryc Torvain—my father."

The gallery gasped.

"I have proof in hand that you conspired with and used members of the guard, the Second Kings Guard to be exact, to carry out your plan, five of whom have already been executed." Fire in his eyes, Maelor looked around the gallery. Looks of mistrust, disbelief and anger began to paint the faces staring back at him.

"Lies, all lies. Your proof is made up and therefore invalid."

He attempted to draw his sword, but the tip of Draemon's rapier halted that motion. His movement had been so fluid and direct that the king hadn't time to counter. Draemon slowly shook his head no to Maelor, whose shoulders began to sag.

From behind the throne stepped Lyssa and Chandra, who had, unbeknownst to Draemon, posted themselves behind it.

Lyssa's leather looked well-worn but clean, and Chandra's black and purple dress radiated a glowing aura. Both were armed with daggers and spells in preparation to assist Draemon, whose stare dared Maelor to resist.

The chamberlain stayed well clear of the confrontation, letting it play out. Seeing the action's finality and still holding the tome and pedigree, the chamberlain now held them above his head.

"I have read this notation of pedigree. It is exact and true. I have read this history. It, too, is exact and true."

He turned to Draemon. "This man has the scar of the Torvain line, to which there is no mistaking."

He turned to the king. "The annal I hold is an accounting of the final days of our good King Elaryc. It describes the events and names of those involved as well as the king's seal, still unbroken."

All eyes were now on Maelor, sweat now beading on his brow.

Draemon lowered and sheathed his rapier. He smiled warmly at the now defamed king, reached across and disarmed him.

"Lord, I am Chamberlain Jareth Adley," he said to Draemon. "If you would allow me the honor," he asked, bowing. Draemon nodded ascent, eyes still locked on Maelor.

"GUARDS!" The words echoed through the gallery. There was now whispering and debate among the onlookers, slowly growing louder as it played out. Jeers began to be voiced toward the king:

"USURPER!"

"MURDERER!"

"LIAR!"

Twelve men from the First Kings Guard marched out in full polished black plate with halberds and surrounded the throne.

"Take this usurper to the dungeons. Please ensure it is the lowest level and chain him. We wouldn't want him to…hurt himself," he said with a smile.

Two guards roughly grabbed him under his arms and began to haul him off.

"Um, one second." He reached atop the usurper's head and removed the crown, then dismissed the guards. Maelor could be heard yelling curses and threats until the large doors slammed shut behind, silencing the entire hall.

Draemon turned to the gallery, who was now pointing and whispering. "I am Draemon Torvain, son of King Elaryc Torvain." He looked around the court.

"I came upon this information more than a fortnight past, thanks to these two very special ladies."

The girls stood behind him on either side, fidgeting uncomfortably in front of the crowd.

"Once the record of my claim has been confirmed, and I insist they be confirmed, I can assure you it will be posted city-wide for all to see."

Jareth cleared his throat to gain Draemon's attention.

"My liege," he said, stepping in front of him and raising the crown. "It is my honor to return this crown to your family in the name of the people." He placed it on his head. Then, in a quieter tone, "At least until there can be a proper coronation, of course." He smiled.

A chorus of nervous cheering and applause erupted from the court. Draemon did not expect his acceptance this easily and was taken completely by surprise. He turned to speak to Lyssa, but both she and her sister had vanished, leaving him alone with Jareth.

As the gallery began to noisily empty, Jareth bowed to Draemon and said, "Sire, if you will now accompany me, there is the business of the realm to attend to."

Draemon looked about the court, smiling. He drew a deep breath. He'd finally done it. All the years of hard work, his distasteful yet necessary doings, and desperation had culminated in this one fateful moment.

He turned and left for the antechamber with Jareth.

'History is written by the victors.'

"How do you think he'll do, sister?" Lyssa asked.

"I don't really know, but I can tell you one thing," she said, looking at her sister.

"And what might that be?" Lyssa replied with a sideways glance.

"He won't do it with us," she said. She squeezed Lyssa's arm.

As the last piece fell into place, Lady Destiny smiled. She turned to see Velkhar's ire, her gaze calm as a still sea. Then, with the smallest shrug, as though the fate of kings and kingdoms were no heavier than a tossed coin, she said,

'After all... I always win.'

Epilogue

I am Kae'Len, the chronicler. Advisor to Lyssa the Cat. She, whose name is never invoked, always whispered. Associate to Chandra, Mistress of Shadows, she whose name men dare not speak beneath the moon. Their story is written in blood and shadow, in the silence of assassins and the roar of the gods. It falls to me, not to wield the blade, not to weave the shadows, but only to bear the memory. So, listen well, for the tale of my blood is the tale of your world.... Yes, I *AM* the chronicler. And, yes, this tale *IS* true. So, heed my words.... Learn. Understand.

And, above all else....

BEWARE!

"Oi, Nigel. Draw me an ale."

"Be mindin' yerself taday, boy. Don't want no trouble in here, got it?"

"Bah. Leave off. I got other louts ta be dealin' with, eh? 'Side's I'll be off shortly. Just gotta wash the dry outta me gullet."
Gods, that's bitter like gnawin' bark. Waste o' coin, that is.

"Oi, Gailna! You're a fair sight today, lass. Come warm me lap, eh?"
Pfft. Off ta th' old men with ya then. Don't know what you're losin'.

Gah. Ye can strip rust from steel with this ale. Won't be drinking that piss ag'in. Right then. Kae'Len's due a knock, callin' his self a chronicler. By Skippin's prick, what even is that? Chronicler. Been needin' a knock fer a long while. Aye. Let's go pay the lad a visit.

"Ya gonna pay fer that? Yer father'll be hearin' about it!"

"Yeah, yeah. Take it, ya rag."
Payin' fer that dog piss. Bloody tragedy it is.
"Oof. Mind yer step, woman!"

"Oooh, by the goddess, pardon m'lord. I'm so sorry, so sorry."

Huh. Fine form on that one…an a right fair face. Huh, eyes grey as me steel blade. Witch's eyes, them. Bah. No matter. Best see to Kae'Len before the sun's down…
"YAHH….kkhhkkh…"

"Meow."